Deep Water

All My Seas, Volume 1

L. Rambit

Published by L. Rambit, 2020.

DEEP WATER

First edition. January 17, 2020.

Copyright © 2020 L. Rambit.

ISBN: 978-0578559063

Written by L. Rambit.

Don't care if he's guilty; don't care if he's not.
He's good and he's bad and he's all that I've got.
O Lord, O Lord, I'm begging you, please,
don't take that sinner from me.
— The Civil Wars, *Devil's Backbone*

...

Got my knife, got my gun,
let's see how fast you can run.
You might think that you can hurt me,
but the damage has been done.
It's pathetic, I know.
A jealous fool who won't let go.
If I was sorry for my actions,
would I ever stoop so low?
— Air Traffic Controller, *This is Love*

...

Warning

Deep Water contains heavy topics that some readers may find triggering. While these topics have been meticulously and respectfully researched, and are presented in a light that is sympathetic towards survivors, there is no shame in wishing to avoid them.

These topics include: past rape, past child sexual abuse, past child prostitution, torture, human trafficking (all non-graphic); enmeshment, suicidal thoughts, substance abuse/addiction, disordered eating, domestic abuse, and murder (mildly to extremely graphic).

The safety of my readers is my top priority. If these topics cause you any mental distress, please put this book down. You have my complete understanding.

Deep Water is a story of recovery and triumph. The purpose is not to titillate, nor to wallow in, despair. I have a deep and personal hatred of narratives that imply a victim is forever tainted by their experiences. Life after trauma **is** possible and worthwhile. You are **not** dirtied by, at fault for, or doomed from your sufferings.

Stay safe. Be well.

L. Rambit

Chapter One – Magpie

stomach wounds: the ultimate ice-breaker.

...

I don't realize they've shot me until I see Ricket's eyes bug behind his wire-frames. The stoic professor seldom emotes, so I can only assume the world is ending.

Looking down at myself, my upper body protruding from his sunroof, a trench knife in each fist, I see a dime-sized splotch of red growing on my side.

Darn it all; this was one of my favorite shirts!

"Ow?" I ask the universe, incredulous. Offended. I've never been *shot* before. I hate guns! Call me naïve for bringing knives to a gunfight, but at least I have standards!

The gunshot doesn't hurt as much as it should. It feels like a punch, rather than a projectile. Am I numb from adrenaline, or is it not as bad as it looks?

Ricket swears. At least, I think he's swearing. I keep meaning to learn Navajo, but there never seems to be the time. It doesn't help that I can scarcely hear him over the roar of the engine.

He wrenches the steering wheel so hard that I seize the frame of his Jeep to avoid becoming a Pollock painting in the barrel cacti we crush beneath meaty tires. I lose my grip on one of my knives, which tumbles, glinting, from sight.

Double damn — those are expensive military blades, and aren't exactly street legal. I can't just pop into the local Kmart to buy a new set whenever the whim strikes. I swear I always lose *something* valuable each time my gang plays hunt-the-trafficker.

You always were careless, I hear my deceased wife, Cero, chastise from the back of my brain. She's been oddly chatty lately. Where once I only heard her voice on occasions of great exhaustion, now we talk almost every day. *Mind your head.*

I duck. From the tinted rear window of the armored truck we're chasing, I see the double-barrel of a sawn-off shotgun protrude before hearing the resultant, deafening BOOM!

This attack isn't going to be a success. My fault — we typically plot these things for weeks in advance, and have a whole team working on our side to ensure every little detail goes according to plan. Off-roading it like this, just me and Ricket against Isaac Müller's lizard-tattooed goons, was an impulsive gamble I'm starting to regret.

Ricket snags me by the spike-studded belt, hauls me into the footwell, and shuts his sunroof before I can pop back out like the obnoxious whack-a-mole I am. I whine a protest when he pins me there and steers one-handed into the skid, great rooster-tails of dust pluming on either side of us.

"What are you doing?!" I hiss, struggling to claw his hand off my belly. It's no use; he's bigger than me, and the angle is all wrong. "We're gaining on them! Speed *up!*"

Injured or not, given half the chance I *would* chase Müller's dogs through the Sonoran Desert and out the other side until I found that elusive love-nest I *know* they're storing hundreds of kids in, being prepped for sale into slavery. I guess I have a one-track-mind like that.

Ricket doesn't listen. He winds us in numerous shrinking circles until we shudder to a halt in the desert's bowl with the sun beating upon us, dozens of miles from any known civilization.

Only then can the Jeep sigh, its overheated engine ticking louder than a cartoon bomb. The abused tires reek of melting rubber. All the world is dust. It's in our lungs, our hair, our eyes. We'll be sneezing gray gunk for days.

The truck that'd once been close enough to touch is now nothing but a speck on the horizon. Damn it all...

My second-in-command wastes no time hauling the hem of my bloody T over my belly, flipping me onto my side to survey the damage. He's a real rip-the-band aid-off kinda guy.

"How bad is it?" I ask, hardly daring to look. I prefer to keep some band aids on.

In response, he takes the surviving knife from my hand to slice my ruined top from hem to bust, forming a tourniquet of thick strips like he must've learned in the Navy. I allow him to bind my ribs so tightly I can scarcely breathe, resisting the urge to make an off-color joke about breast binding.

Ricket is a trans dude over a decade older than me, born before the internet made proper, safe binders easily accessible. He knows more about that dangerous type of pain than I ever will.

When I catch sight of blood staining my best friend's palms, I look instead towards Camelback Mountain until my queasiness subsides. From this distance, it's just a sandy curve against the cloudless, too-blue sky.

Usually blood doesn't get to me — kinda hard to have knifed as many people as I have and still be squeamish — but my *own* blood? Forget about it!

Ricket's probably glad he bought a Jeep with black leather upholstery, although his terrier sheds short white hairs all over the place. If the seats had been pale to start with, they'd've long since stained brown from our gang's oxidized fluids. More impromptu medical procedures have been performed on these seats than is sane or healthy.

This man has saved my life once before. Last time, with the two of us curled like rabbits on the floor of my apartment, he'd used a drinking straw and a dissected ballpoint pen to MacGyver the two of us at the elbows, gifting me a blood transfusion directly from his veins. He and I are blood brothers in every way but biological.

"Sorry I keep screwing up," I mutter, heart heavy with regret, as he uses my torn shirt to apply pressure to my midsection. "Someday I'll rescue *your* ass."

He smiles, all even white teeth, and digs around in his glove box. I think we've still got most of a first aid kit in there. "I look forward to it."

Chapter Two – Magpie

...

When people talk of vigilantes, they're usually imagining rebels in masks, subverting the system and defying The Man. And sure, we do all that stuff. But every couple weeks, on days like today when a breeze rolls off the ocean's waves to spray the sky with sweetest salt, we gorge on waffles and annoy the shit out of each other like any normal family.

We congregate at the beachfront home Jane Clay shares with her wife, Rhys. As a red-carpet fashion designer, Clay's the only one of us with the green for opulent SoCal living.

Unfortunately, as a semi-famous trans lesbian activist, she also has the most to lose should we ever get caught.

"Good morning, beautiful." Tall and thin as a palm tree, she bends to hug me after I climb the seashell-studded steps to her unlocked front door, my helmet tucked under one arm. She smells like lilies. The pleated chiffon skirt she wears whispers with every step. "How are your ribs healing?"

"Good," I say with a smile, and once we're inside her spacious, modern living room — all wide windows and reflective glass, watercolor paintings, and trickling water features — I show her by unzipping my leather jacket and lifting the hem of my shirt.

Her ice-blue eyes rove my brown skin. She touches a cool hand to my undamaged side, rotating me as she studies the curved line of stitches there, marching above the arch of my fifth rib. They show no sign of oozing; no swelling; no stink of infection. Just a four-inch dash of tidy black X's.

"Ricket did well stitching you up," she approves as I retreat and straighten my clothes. "But you were very lucky, young lady. You could have been killed. I don't much fancy running our show without its leader!"

I duck my head. "Yes, ma'am," I say, pretending she's chastised me into good behavior. She sighs, too familiar with my shenanigans to buy my humble act for a moment.

We part ways in the hallway. I step into her half-bathroom, setting my helmet, backpack, and gloves on a shelf left empty just for me. I gather my black hair into a high ponytail, exposing the puckered, crescent-shaped scar that carves me from hairline to jaw, making a gargoyle's grimace of my face.

I adjust the many piercings in my ears, twisting gold studs and hoops so the orbital rings face forward, then wash my hands before walking to the spacious dining room, comprised entirely of floor-to-ceiling windows that overlook a private beach.

"Magpie!" a chorus of voices greet as I join the party. It seems that I am, as always, the last to arrive.

"Hey, guys." I smile and take my seat beside Ricket, hooking my foot around his good ankle. He bumps my shoulder with his own. Judging by his serious demeanor, you wouldn't think he'd be such an affectionate guy. I know I found him intimidating when Cero first recruited me into her gang, but he warms up fast.

"Well!" Navier, the loudest and chattiest of us all, pounds a beefy fist on the oak table. "Now that Fearless Leader has deigned to grace us with her presence—" he flashes a toothy grin to show he's only teasing " — can we *please* eat?"

He grabs for the waffle platter; one of many that Clay's private chef Candi assembled for us. Clay frowns at him, smacking his scarred welder's hand with a spoon. "Navier. Be polite."

"I *said* 'please,'" he whines, but doesn't cross Clay again as heaping trays of food make the rounds.

I help myself to a mountain of crispy golden waffles loaded down with cream and jam and servings of fruit: berries and kiwi and grilled — yes, *grilled* — banana. It smells like being nose-fucked by an angel.

My friends, accustomed to my voracious appetite, ignore me as I pile on the eggs and thick-cut bacon, shiny and marbled with artery-clogging heaven. I toast them all with a wink and a frosty mimosa, then spend the next few bites listening to the hallelujah chorus.

As a cashier for a gas station, I can't afford to eat this way when left to my own devices. I save what money I can, but my fixed-income apartment is on tenuous grounds already, and food stamps aren't always reliable, what with joyless government employees invading my finances every month to debate whether my cousin and I "deserve" to eat. Ain't poverty a trip?

Nobody reputable would hire a fired cop; them's just the facts. What right have I to complain, right? I have my health and my gang, and though my career path went down and sideways, I wouldn't trade our "extracurricular activities" for all the world. Life is better than fine, and that's the lie I'm sticking to.

Across the table, my cousin Crown waves to signal my attention. He's a young Māori man built as though Navier's blueprints were set to 'enlarge,' 'darken,' and 'soften.' Pretty sure he could bench-press ten of me without breaking a sweat, but he prefers the sedentary lifestyle of a computer geek to the Cajun's Jersey Shore-inspired fitness routine.

'How is Tip?' Crown signs, finger-spelling the name with practiced ease.

Ah, Dylan Tippling. The junkie turned international surfing star turned burn victim turned jailbird. The boy who'd cared for Crown and I as a trio of foster children with enough collective behavioral issues to fill a season of 'Scared Straight.' The teen forced into sex work throughout high school to ensure we all got enough to eat. The one who now haunts my apartment like the world's grumpiest vampire.

That Tip.

"He's good," I reply cautiously. "He's clean. Goes to work. Goes to school. Eats, presumably."

Celebrity and wealth mean only that many of society's rules no longer apply. It's this fact, among others, that led to my growing disillusionment with the American justice system. Too many baddies get off with a slap on the wrist because they have enough money and clout to buy the world's silence. It's true what they say: life is a shit sandwich. The more bread you have, the less shit you eat.

Tip had been famous. Tip had been rich. Tip is a pretty white boy with dreamy, color-changing eyes, floppy blond hair, and pouty pink lips. Ergo, Tip spends his nights on my sofa instead of in a jail cell.

Is it fair? Hell no. Am I a hypocrite for loving and defending him anyway? You know it.

Crown nods his tattooed head, picking at the frayed sleeves of his Captain America hoodie. This is the best news about our troublesome cousin he could hope for.

Ricket is very carefully *not* looking at me throughout this exchange. We'd agreed not to tell the gang that Tip is in Ricket's UCLA graduate program. It's not a big deal or anything, but Ricket hates a fuss, and it could prompt a lecture from Clay about taking care to avoid crossing streams.

Navier changes the subject to his most recent conquest. His salacious rambling gives me reprieve to take stock of my people.

To Ricket's left is Rhys. Slender and elfin with skin the color of deepest night, she nods along with the conversation, a smile in place as her milky eyes drift a few inches north of Navier's animated face.

Beside her sits Navier, his hands miming the act of weighing melons on a scale, unaware of the whipped cream moustache standing in stark contrast against his olive skin. His rambunctious, ginger-brown curls threaten to snap the elastic he'd imprisoned them with.

Clay is next, and then Crown, using his fork to break strawberries into even pieces. He spears them on the tines, dips them into blueberry syrup, and eats them one at a time. Despite how large his hands are, they are impeccably precise and delicate; well-trained from a lifetime of comic book artistry. It's hard to tell how much attention he's giving the conversation, but he's smart and competent and marches to his own drum. If it matters to him, he'll hear it.

There aren't as many of us as there used to be. There weren't enough of us to begin with. We're six average Joes doing our best to bring about my late wife's vision of a world where children aren't chattel. We do what the cops won't: we get the dirty work done.

Ricket nudges me. I realize everyone is looking my way, awaiting an answer. I stammer a guilty laugh. "Sorry; I zoned out around the fourth time Navier said 'massive tits.' What's up?"

It's Rhys's sweet voice that asks, "When are we making our move on the Jacobis?"

I risk pouring myself a second mimosa — three, I've found, is the limit before Clay makes pointed comments about drunk driving, though my tolerance has far exceeded this for *years* — and smile grimly. There's a "no talking about work during meals" policy in place to keep us all sane, but none of us adhere to it. Sanity is for pussies.

Cash and Cotton Jacobi are our current targets; a pair of brothers we'd stalked for weeks before confirming our suspicions. They're working as coyotes for Müller, using their moving business as a cover to transport children into his desert hideout.

"Soon," I promise, hearing the impending storm in my voice. "Rhys, you're keeping track of their business, aren't you? The next time they're scheduled for Nogales, you know what to do. Crown?"

He looks at me without making eye-contact, which he hates.

"You've hacked into their financial records, right? Gave Rhys the access she needs?"

'Yes,' he signs, a fist held at collarbone-level. Clay is quick to translate this for her blind wife. 'It was very easy. They use the same passwords for everything.'

"That's my superstar."

He smiles.

Navier, the muscle of our gang, cracks his knuckles. The veins in his arms strain. "When I get ahold of those no-good kiddie fuckers..."

He trails off, and my grim smile widens. I wasn't always this cynical, but life lays waste to us all. I've seen what Navier does to "no-good kiddie fuckers." It's not pretty.

He turns to meet my eyes. "Think we could, ah, skim a little off the top, cher? Since Crown's found all their secret bank accounts, and all? Hell; give that big brain of his a McFish and some diet Coke, and he'll chase the paper trail all the way to Müller's pocket! We'd be millionaires by Tuesday."

I shoot Navier a frown. "We're not in it for the money," I remind him, disliking the way he uses my cousin like a clever pet, to be bribed with treats for tricks. "That's dirty money. That's 'Kids We Didn't Save' money."

"Which we will then use to save *more* kids!" he wheedles, dark eyes glinting. He fixes me with the sort of smile used to coax supermodels from their G-strings. "Don't you think them bébés would be *happy* to know they'd helped someone?"

Unfortunately for Navier, it's been a long, *long* time since any man has been able to charm me. I'm beyond disillusioned with their species. "I *think* they'd've preferred not to be sold at all, you peabrain!"

Clay clears her throat, glaring at the both of us. I relent, scowling down at my plate. Navier does the same. Rhys manages to coax the gang towards more emotionally neutral waters, and the tension eases.

By the time Clay's housekeeper starts making pointed glances into the dining room, no doubt willing us out so she can get her job done, almost two hours have passed. If I want time to go home and shower before my shift, I'd better get moving.

I say as much, stand, and stretch. My belly feels hard and tight from too much food. That little motion is enough to make my stitches complain.

Clay stands, too. "Let me make you a to-go box."

I murmur my gratitude and offer parting wishes. Crown doesn't return my hug, but touches the top of my head with his palm when I wrap both arms around him as far as they'll go. Rhys takes my chin to kiss both cheeks. I'm still feeling huffy with Navier when he scoops me off my feet, gentler than usual due to my injury.

"Don't be mad," he croons, nuzzling my neck with his stubble-raspy face. "Come *on;* you know you love me."

I sigh, then wrap my arms around his neck. I don't want to fight him. And I'm a slut for physical affection in any form. I'll take what I can get.

Clay stuffs my backpack with goodies and hands me my helmet. Ricket follows me out the door. I wait for him to catch up, listening to the soft clink of his C-brace hitting the cement walkway with every other step.

Years before I met him, a torpedo off the coast of Chicago splintered Ricket's left femur, annihilating his crew and leaving him with an honorable discharge certificate to accompany his PTSD. Multiple surgeries and countless hours of PT later, and he still requires a brace to prevent his misshapen patella from performing acrobatics beneath his flesh.

When he reaches me, he offers his arm like a true gentleman. We walk together to the garage where his Jeep and my Kz1000 — a neon green monstrosity serving as the only holdover from my highway patrol days — patiently wait between Navier's Tacoma and a small selection of Clay's luxury vehicles.

"How are you, dear?" Ricket asks as I lose my ponytail and jam my helmet on, protecting my three pounds of wibbly gray matter from streaking the asphalt with nothing but scratched fiberglass and some polystyrene foam. Helmets are pretty damn awesome. Having peeled my fair share of congealed human remains off the streets of Los Angeles, I can attest to that.

"Fine as always," I reply, which is half truth and all baloney. "Yourself?"

He waits me out, dark eyes disbelieving.

"I'm serious!" I protest. "You took good care of me, Professor Nerd. My stitches are holding up just fine. Work is going okay." If the soul-crushing confines of minimum-wage capitalism can ever be construed as '*okay,*' that is.

Using Ricket's nickname earns me a smile. I revel in the victory. He seems to have no further questions, so I mount my bike.

"Cero would be proud of you," he says, and it's so unexpected I nearly trip over my kickstand.

My wife, Ricket's friend, *our* leader, died of cancer just two years ago. The gang tiptoes around this fact like they're afraid just mentioning her name will send me down yet another depressive spiral; the kind that always ends in booze and blood.

"You're a good man," I tell Ricket, because someone needs to. I kiss two fingers and salute him, rev my throttle twice just to be annoying, and peel onto the street before my emotions can catch up to me.

Chapter Three – Tip

...

For someone so damn short, my cousin Magpie is ludicrously noisy. Her lung to body ratio must be off the charts.

When I'm woken by the nearby patter of shower water and my cousin wailing her way through Sonic Youth's entire discography, I heave a deep sigh and reach for my pillow, bunching it over my face. Maybe I'll suffocate down here. Wouldn't that be a mercy? *"Please shut up..."*

She doesn't hear me. Our apartment is tiny, but thankfully not *so* tiny that a whisper could pass through two doors. The singing doesn't stop until the shower does, and is quickly replaced by the soft tread of her little feet on the worn gray carpet.

The door between her bedroom and the rest of the apartment swings open, releasing a cloud of shampoo-scented steam. Mags flops onto my bed to a chorus of complaining old springs, no doubt drowning my sheets with her wet hair as she does so.

"Tip, Tip, Tip!" she trills, a hand on my shoulder and the other on my hip to wiggle me back and forth like a loose tooth. "Tippers, Tippy-Canoe, Rudyard Tippling!"

"If I ask 'what,' will you *leave?*"

She pouts. Silently, but I still know she's sticking that lower lip out. When we were little, I used to tell her that doing so would incite a bird to fly by and poop on it.

When I say nothing, she sighs and lays on her side behind me, the terrycloth of her bathrobe tickly against my bare back. She snuggles close, a damp arm around my waist, her forehead to my neck.

Though she fits herself against me like a second skin, I notice that she's careful to avoid the many burn scars that disfigure my left arm and upper chest. Guess I can't blame her. They — *I* — am pretty fucking disgusting.

"Crown asked about you today," she says, her breath a coffee-scented inferno on my spine. Her words are the carrot to drive a mule. It's not playing fair, and she knows it. Crown is one of the few people left in this world I still give half a shit about.

I bite the carrot. It's the first time I've spoken today, and my raspy voice is proof of it. "What did you tell him?"

"The truth! That you're doing well in school and work, and you're clean..." She sounds so upbeat and hopeful; a first grade teacher encouraging her slowest student.

Every week she tests my piss for drugs, and I know for a fact she regularly digs through my stuff, hunting for nonexistent stashes. Unless you, too, have handed cups full of hot yellow piss to the kid you practically raised, you've never really known shame.

"Did he ask to see me?" I ask, because my court-mandated therapist, Tessa, says I'm self-destructive to a fault and can't resist an opportunity to salt a wound.

Magpie's silence is answer enough.

I'm a head shorter and about a hundred pounds lighter than our youngest cousin Crown, but that same adrenaline rush that gives mothers the strength to lift cars off their trapped children allowed me to drag his hemorrhaging body from the trunk of Cero's blazing Jaguar. The following gas tank explosion almost killed me. I wake every morning heavy with regret that it hadn't.

Crown and I were rushed to La Jolla Hospital, where surgeons treated his stab wounds and my first-degree burns. The anesthesia hadn't fully worn off before I was arrested for attempted murder. The cops had to handcuff me to the bed by my ankles, as the skin grafts were too fresh for anything on my wrists.

Correctly guessing that I'm sinking into one of my funks, Magpie is quick to change the subject. "Are you excited for school?" She gives me a nudge with her chin, her fingers nesting in the gaps between my ribs.

I feel the familiar 'don't-touch-me' itch begin to pool between our every point of contact. In a second I'll have to shove her off, despite having more tolerance for her than I do most people.

My professor, James Ricket, is taking me and his two classroom aides out on a dragger tonight. Trawling squid with cranky fishermen isn't most people's idea of fun, but the research will be useful for our group thesis about how climate change affects the mating cycle of *Loligo opalescens,* and whether endangerment is on the horizon for them; whether we should petition to restrict their sale as a food source.

It's a tiny step towards what I want to do with my life. Huge, when you consider I'd never planned to live this long. Astronomical when you realize that my boyfriend is going to murder me.

"Yes," I confess, and feel my cousin smile against my shoulder. I think Mags believes that if I shake off my depression, she'll be able to do the same with her own. She's a glass-half-full kinda gal.

Muffled in her bathrobe pocket, her phone suddenly blares the chorus from Dorothy's 'Raise Hell.' Magpie rolls onto her back to retrieve said phone, then groans when she sees who's calling. "Oh, God. It's *Nina.*"

I grimace. Magpie's mother-in-law is a neurotic nutjob with an accent thicker than week-old stroganoff. Ruth and Naomi, they ain't.

Magpie answers. If she hadn't, Antonina would've just called back again and again, leaving increasingly distressed messages each time. "Hey, Nina!" she chirps. "I was just getting ready for work."

"Oh, Alexis!" I hear the harried woman gasp on her end of the line. "Alexis, my darling..."

Nobody else calls Mags by her first name. Even her coworkers call her "Lex." Nina is just *that* kind of person.

"Do not go just yet. I have terrible feeling... Sonya visited me again in a... A dream. A vision. She says, you *must* seek medical—"

Sonya?

It takes a second to connect that name to the stocky, ill-tempered woman Magpie married. Cero was pushing thirty before she learned her birth name. I guess being kidnapped and sold to some American perv as a toddler really screws up your self awareness, or something.

I roll over and look at my cousin, watching as she sits up to talk. She's finger-combing her wet black hair with one hand, propping the phone between her jaw and shoulder with the other.

At this angle, I have a clear view of the scar my boyfriend carved into her face. I feel a vicious stab of envy before I can tamp it down and quickly avert my eyes, sick with shame.

Vince tried to kill both Mags and Crown before skipping town, and he nearly succeeded in both attempts. I know he did it to hurt me; to punish me for neglecting him while I was on tour. I'm pretty sure that's why he and Mags were fucking, too; a fact that she doesn't know I'm aware of.

Vince never carved his mark on *me,* and we'd been together since high school. Yet just a few tumbles with my baby cousin was all he required to claim *her* as his own? Typical.

As always when it comes to Vince, my feelings are a stomped-on bag of Chex Mix. I'm furious for his attempt on my kids' lives. I'm guilty I wasn't there to protect them; that I brought him into their world in the first place.

I long for the day he'll return to end my life at last.

Mags falls back with her head pillowed on my hip. Into the phone she huffs, "Nina, we've talked about this. These bad dreams about Cero — about *Sonya* — are just that: dreams. Sonya is in heaven. Let her rest in peace."

Cero? In heaven? Hilarious. Surely even her widow can't be-lieve *that*.

"I am telling you, that is not true. Sonya talks to me still. She says you do not heed her warnings, that you keep... Keep burying her. Pushing her down! Do you at least still wear your rings, Alex-is?"

Glancing at the digital clock on our kitchen microwave, Mag-pie stands and shuffles back to the only bedroom of our apartment. It's so close to my sofa-bed that I could touch the doorknob from where I lay without really stretching, if ever I felt so inclined.

Mags is far from body-shy, so she doesn't close the door when she drops the bathrobe and picks through her mountains of laun-dry for an outfit that's not too stained or smelly. Around her neck dangles the jewelry in question: her and Cero's wedding bands, bound together by Nina's own hand.

"Nina, I know you're going through hell right now. You didn't get very much time with your daughter before losing her again — no mother should ever have to experience that. But you need to keep your therapy appointments, okay? Promise me you're still tak-ing all your meds?"

She steps into her khakis and reaches for a belt. I'm assaulted by a view of her hairy pits when she wriggles into a polo shirt, on which she clips her badge. Her ever-present leather jacket zips over her chest, despite the late spring heat.

I'm too far away to hear what Antonina says next, but it dis-pleases Magpie something fierce. Her mouth pinches into a tight line, and she yanks on the elastic of her ponytail so sharply that it snaps. She grabs a fresh one and tries again.

"I need you to *stop* calling me like this, okay Nina?!" she de-mands, teeth bared. She's luckier than Crown and me in that, de-spite the poverty the three of us were raised in, her teeth are naturally decent. I don't know how she manages to drink as much coffee as she does without staining them. "This feels like harassment."

As far as I'm aware, Mags has never talked back to her mother-in-law before. It takes a lot these days to rile her into her old spitfire self. She usually prefers to play Bollywood Barbie and pretend all is peachy-keen.

With an irritated huff, she shoves her ancient iPhone into her pocket and kicks junk around on the floor until she unearths her keys.

I lay back down and tug the blanket to my chin, once more closing my eyes. Since I work in the mornings and attend school at night, I grab naps whenever I can.

She stomps past my bed to the front door, then turns back. Her hand settles in my hair. "There are waffles in the fridge," she prompts, giving me a gentle shake. "Maybe eat some? They're tasty."

Why she still bothers, I have no clue. "I'll think about it," I lie, and a disappointed sigh seems to rise from her toes. She kisses my temple. I don't react. She completes her journey to the door.

"I love you," she informs me, just before stepping out. She doesn't stick around long enough to hear a reply, knowing none will ever come.

•••

I close my eyes when I shower the garbage stink from my hair, then keep them closed as I brush my teeth, counting each stroke until I reach an acceptable number. Otherwise, I wouldn't be able to stop at all.

Obsessive-compulsive disorder is a bitch. Neurotypicals assume we only have issues with germs and tidiness, but that's not how it manifests in me. I don't have to check that my shoes are still in the closet four times a night, or run home every two hours to ensure I turned the stove off, though I've met people like that back when I attended a support group.

No; *my* biggest compulsion is the act of starvation, which makes catching accidental glimpses of myself in the mirror a singularly unpleasant experience.

I don't starve myself because I want to be thin. I starve myself to feel like I've got a sliver of control in this world of chaos. So long as I dictate what gets put inside my stomach, nothing bad can happen. Or so my disorder tells me, anyway.

I can't control how my limbs shrivel and my belly bloats. I can't control my hair falling out in clumps, or my kidneys shutting down, or the alien fuzz that grows along my skin when I'm no longer able to produce sufficient body heat. I can't control being too weak to make a comeback in my surfing career. But I *am* in control of what and how I eat.

I try not to look at the containers of waffles and fruit Mags shoved into our refrigerator. There is no control to be found in that madness. My brain goes crazy trying to add up the calories, which is impossible, seeing as there's no way to know the exact ingredients and measurements within.

I know precisely how many kilocalories fill my bowls of plain white rice, zucchini, and Roma tomato slices. It's easier to eat while food is cold. It seems less dirty that way. I swallow water icy enough to make my throat burn between each bite. In my mind, this prevents my intestines from getting dirty.

My careful efforts are almost ruined when the compulsion to glance into our refrigerator, to *look* at those distressing waffles again, takes hold of me. I succumb for just a moment, then slam the door for good.

The urge to throw everything away just to kill the leaden feeling of *wrongness* in my chest shadows my every move throughout the rest of my routine until I'm out the door and halfway to the bus stop. I am in control. Not the food. Not the disorder. *Me.*

The sea is so close to the coffee shop where we agreed to meet that I can hear waves shushing in time with my pulse. The ocean in all her wildness makes my heart break in ways love and drugs and sex never could. It feels like there's a second ocean forever raging in me, desperate to flood free.

The pavement is damp and glossy under the streetlights as I cross the street to the café; secluded and surreal with its big windows and butter-yellow fairy lights combatting the fog of night. Most of the tables inside are empty.

I spot my professor immediately. He sits in the corner, his back wedged between two walls, with a clear view of the door and windows like the ex-SEAL he is. Rather than take advantage of his watchful position, though, he instead hunches low over his coffee and crossword, oblivious to the world.

Framed by a lion's mane of unruly black hair going gray at the temples, James's features are striking: dark, heavily lidded eyes; a large nose with a prominent bump on the bridge; thin lips ever falling in a thoughtful frown. He's mixed-race — white and Navajo — with skin forever a gorgeous olive regardless of season.

He dresses like a theatrical approximation of a professor; all sweater-vests and turtlenecks and Chinos. Tonight he's got his quad-point cane beside his chair. I wonder if he's in pain, or just worried about slipping on the dragger.

"Hey," I greet, approaching his table, and he looks up from his drink. Man; he and Mags should hang out sometime. They'd have a blast snorting lines of instant coffee together for all they rely on it.

"Tip! You're early." He flashes me a distracted smile, eyes vacant under the glasses he wears. He hasn't shaved, and I feel a tug of envy at the roguish comfort of his dark stubble. Contrary to popular belief, I *do* grow facial hair, but it's patchy and blond and ruins the "twink for sale" aesthetic I've curated since high school, though I'm far too old and damaged to convincingly pull it off anymore.

"I live by the fickle whims of SoCal's public transport." I take the seat across from my professor, beating down the habitual urge to be enticing. James is not a client. I am not a product.

"Can I buy you a drink?" he asks.

"I'm good, thanks. Keep doing your puzzle. Ten across is 'burgeoning.'"

He blinks, silver eyelashes long enough to brush the lenses of his glasses, and looks at the crossword. His pencil scratches. A look of pleased surprise crosses his face. "It fits."

He works quietly, and I close my eyes to savor a truly mellow soul. He's a walking Xanax. There's just something about his presence that promises all is under control and it's okay to relax a little. In my veins, the ocean is soothed.

My peace is short-lived. Announced by the bell above the café door, the obligatory Cute Heterosexual Couple of our year saunters in like a four-legged creature, matching sweaters and all. Like most of the class, they're embarrassingly younger than me; something I try my damndest not to think about.

Bambi and Tariq's scores are just above mine in our graduate program. They're smart as hell, and they work their asses off. That gives us three the privilege to attend trips like this, while the other aspiring marine biologists have to hear our accounts secondhand .

They greet us and cluster at the counter, purchasing drinks with enough addendums and clauses to impress my lawyer. *Non-dairy creamer, substitute for peppermint flavor, dark roast, hold the whip...*

I can tell James wants to get up. I noticed the first day I met him that he doesn't like to do so while people watch his struggle, so I stand and wander towards the pair, allowing our professor his privacy.

"Hey, Tip," Bambi giggles, looking plump and adorable in a cranberry hijab that flatters her sweater. I muster a smile, though it's getting harder and harder to force those nowadays.

Tariq's hand — tonight, his fingernails are painted mint green — rests on his girlfriend's back. The sight makes a pained lump form in my throat. *Vince never touched me like that...*

Sometimes my brain just does this: sails off with no anchor to ground me, until I'm sunk into re-feeling and re-thinking, questioning, doubting. Even with the coping skills my therapist and I are developing, it still threatens to drown me every time.

Hey, Surfer-Boy. Give us a smile. Show off those pretty teeth I paid the big bucks to fix. This sack of shit thinks he doesn't have to pay what he owes me, but you'll show him, won't *you?*

I taste hot blood spraying the back of my throat; feel the weight of severed fingers hit my tongue. I hear screams in my ears, screams caused by me; monster, monster, I always *was* a monster...

I jolt when James' palm presses, of all places, to my spine; a gentle pressure that keelhauls my thoughts to kinder waters. "Is everyone ready to go?"

Chapter Four – Magpie

at the ol' stop-and-rob.

...

The gas station's security cameras don't work and, as far as I'm aware, never have. They're just glorified plastic boxes to scare away would-be shoplifters. Occasionally, they even succeed.

Confident in my privacy, I waste no time helping myself to a hot dog from the grill and a cup of coffee from the carafe by the pastry cabinet.

Old Magpie would never steal, the voice in my head gloats, more amused than scolding. *Remember how straightedge you used to be?*

"Yeah, well, New Magpie is hungry," I snap, taking a vicious bite of the rubbery, overcooked dog. I realize my mistake too late and cringe. First sign of insanity? Hearing voices. Second? *Answering* them.

You're not crazy, the voice reassures me, a dead ringer for the unsettling whisper-wheeze my wife developed during her final stages of A.L.L. Too many tubes shoved down her throat; not enough drive to drink any water. All her fluids were introduced intravenously by that point. I can still see the needles, the bruises, whenever I close my eyes.

There's a reason I drink myself to sleep most nights.

Is this what I've sunk to? Inventing conversations with a corpse two years cold? I had imaginary friends as a child, but this is too much. I didn't do *that* many drugs during my Vince-fueled bender...

Okay, fine. I did. But why has this been happening so *much* lately?

You've been shutting me out, Miss Cop, Cero explains patiently. *I still have to shout for you to hear me at all. You are so, so stubborn.*

No. Not Cero. This breakdown is *not* my Cero, no matter how much it sounds like her. I have to believe that, or I'll lose my marbles harder than Antonina Vasiliev could ever dream of.

I envision myself grabbing hold of that reinforced iron door I built in my brain way back when I was still an unwanted, smelly foster kid; ideal for keeping bad memories and worse coping skills tightly contained. I slam it shut with all my strength; banishing every negative emotion and irrational thought with the sheer force of my will.

The voice of my deceased wife falls utterly, eerily silent, with nothing but a distant ringing to fill the void.

Swallowing the last of my dinner, I wander the empty station looking for messes to tidy. I restock the napkins, check the condiments, and pull stale pastries from the back of the cabinet to throw away, save for a strawberry-frosted doughnut I tuck into my backpack.

In the daytime, there are two employees at this station: one to man the counter, and their supervisor working in the back office. For the slow overnights, however, it's just me and my thoughts.

I pass the liquor aisle with my eyes shut tight, whistling through the graveyard. I can get away with stealing fountain beverages and dogs and the occasional pastry — we toss that unsold stuff anyway — but if I help myself to itemized goods, I'll definitely get fired. Besides: I have a secret flask handy in my back pocket should the night run too dry, as most do nowadays.

The rusty cowbell strung above the door clangs, drawing my attention to the front. A voice calls over the fuzz of the radio, "Magpie?"

I know *that* voice. I glance at my reflection in the glass door that covers the refrigerated soda cans, hurriedly licking both of my palms to smooth my hair flat. "I'll be right with you, Rosa!"

Rosa Santiago, owner of a Fourth Avenue biker bar called Buenas Ruedas, is tall and thick as a noble oak. She could *easily* crush my head like a watermelon between those thighs. As far as I'm concerned, she's welcome to do so any damn day of the week.

If homosexuality is vanilla ice cream, and heterosexuality is chocolate, then we bisexuals are strawberry: not a mix of the two, but our own flavor entirely. I personally have a strong preference for women and nonbinary folk. Men aren't that exciting to me for more than the occasional roll in the sheets. But there are plenty of bis who feel the opposite, or those who don't care about gender at all.

There are as many variants to gender and sexuality as there are flavors of ice cream, and it only becomes complicated when one listens to societal norms, rather than to people as individuals.

I wish I'd done more than the bare minimum with my appearance before leaving home tonight. I've never worn makeup, unless you count that flesh-colored goop Cero taught me to hide bruises with, but I could've at least worn a shirt without a brown stain on the sleeve — barbeque sauce or blood, probably.

I hurry to my counter, and there she stands waiting for me: six feet of lace and leather and shiny red lips. A tattoo of a jewel-bright scorpion adorns her clavicle. A drop of sheer venom gleams threateningly at the tip of its arched stinger. Kudos to her tattoo artist; that thing looks real enough to breathe.

As one who appreciates a good beer (or two, or three...), I'm a regular customer of Rosa's. In my frequent visits to Buenas Ruedas, I've seen her throw down with the best of them. Once, we both noticed a shady guy trying to slip something into a youngster's drink. Rosa had the bastard by the throat before I could so much as draw my knives — and trust me; that's *high* praise.

She shook him like a dog attacking a shoe, lifting him high off his barstool. Then, with the grace and strength of an Olympian, she flung his ass out the door and roared like a lioness, fierce enough to send him scrambling for dear life. My heart — and other parts of me, too — have been throbbing ever since.

"What can I do for you?" I ask, flashing my dimples and the Big Brown Eyes. I might be a disaster 75 to 100% of the time, but I'm a pretty damn cute one, if I do say so myself.

She blinks, as though she's just now noticing this fact for herself. I feel hope bloom like sunflowers in my chest. The two of us talk sometimes, but it's not like she's ever noticed me as anything more than a customer.

"Three packs of Luckies and twenty bucks on pump nine." Her smile is perfunctory; strained at the tips. Maybe she's tired from a long night of work. Or maybe she secretly hates me and wishes I'd drop dead. "Please."

Feeling deflated, I turn and collect the cigarettes. I have to stand on a stool to reach them. Navier calls me "fun-sized." I never quite hit the five foot mark, and stand only one inch above the legal cutoff for dwarfism. Being vertically challenged means that I do a lot more climbing than most people, and being muscular means I'm too heavy to stand on the shelves directly. The stool and I are well acquainted.

Seeing as I had to watch my wife suffer and die from cancer over the span of many torturous months, selling cigarettes has got to be the shittiest part of my job; worse even than scrubbing the bathroom. But it's not my place to judge what customers buy, even when they're customers I care about.

"I'll slip you my employee discount," I say with a wink as I scan the packs. "Don't tell anyone."

She blesses me with a much warmer smile than before, and suddenly I understand how cartoon characters sometimes float on trails of hearts.

After she pays and leaves to fuel her hog, I turn and watch from the little frosted window behind my counter. I try to do so for every customer, as this isn't the safest part of town. In the absence of security cameras, it's the best I can offer.

Once fueled, she startles a dopey grin onto my face by waving goodbye in the direction of the window, as though she'd known all along that I was watching.

My Kawasaki is a vocal beast, even with the muffler, but it's got nothing on this full-sized Harley's roar (and the ensuing, subsonic thunder that rattles my chest-bones) as she leaves the station behind. It's an untamed, barbaric yawp that never fails to gladden my soul.

You really like her, huh? Not-Cero asks, tone neutral.

"Does that bother you?" I question, forgetting for a second that I'm supposed to ignore her impossible voice.

I haven't hit the sack with anybody since my wife died, unless she counts what Vince did to me all those times I was too high (or too unconscious) to fight him off.

It doesn't bother me. And everyone knows that guy's a rapist piece of shit. Has been since y'all were kids.

For a figment of my lonely subconscious, this pseudo Cero isn't half bad.

I work the next few hours in silence. The sky is just beginning to lighten outside, misty with ocean fog, as I put away my supplies.

The clang of the door opening has me straightening to return to my counter, but before I can stand, I feel the unmistakable kiss of a pistol's unforgiving muzzle against the nape of my neck.

"Alexis Magpie?" a quiet male voice asks.

"That's me," I reply, working hard to keep my voice steady, my mind clear. Is this a consequence from tailing Isaac Müller's goons with Ricket? Did his entourage finally track me down?

To my great surprise, the gun falls away, and the stranger takes a step back.

I lurch to my feet and spin, shoving my tall attacker's arm until his gun threatens only the ceiling; not my body, not the shelves of merchandise that could so easily cause ricochet.

I sweep my leg to catch his before barreling into his hips, just below his center of balance. He goes down like a sack of bones. Still holding his wrist, I'm on him before he can make a noise of protest.

Fights, *real* fights, are nothing like you see in movies. They're fast and dirty and almost silent. Straddling his waist, I pin his hands under one of my thighs, where I carry most of my strength. Then I bring my elbow to his Adam's apple, threatening to crunch down if he makes a move.

When he shows no sign of fighting back, I use my free hand to pat his oversized hoodie down for more weapons, of which there are none. However, my palm comes away ruby-red and sticky.

Confused, I peel his hood back from his face. I'm shocked to discover that my attacker is only a boy; a dark-skinned teenager perhaps sixteen or seventeen years old with proud Ethiopian features: a high forehead, sharp cheeks, and wide brown eyes.

His face is shiny and wet with blood. Fresh blood. *His* blood.

"Help me," he pleads, grunting under the strain of my weight, and promptly loses consciousness.

"Oh, hell's *bells*," I hiss, checking for a pulse with two fingers under his jaw. It's present; steady and strong, but I'm not about to relax just yet.

Facial injury, Not-Cero assesses. In my distracted panic, I must've let that iron door between us creak back open. *Left side. Too much blood for a good look, but faces always bleed like a mother.*

"I have eyes too, thanks," I snap sarcastically. She wasn't there when Vince used a butterfly knife to carve his calling card on me, then later drove it six times into Crown's gut, but I'm not about to forget saturating my own mattress with blood anytime soon.

You need to stop the bleeding if you want him to live long enough to provide answers.

I stand and fetch a stack of paper towels from the bathroom before kneeling again, taking the kid's head into my lap to apply pressure. Pressure leads to faster clotting, but it doesn't exactly feel good. He groans, lips twitching.

Working quickly, I hunt down the Smith & Wesson from where I'd kicked it, flick the safety on, and jam it into the waistband of my khakis, just at the small of my back. I don't like guns, but I like leaving them for just anybody to find even less.

I squat and lift the boy in a soldier's carry, hauling his gangly butt to the bathroom before dropping him on the closed lid of the single toilet. He's a far cry from heavy, and I do plenty of weightlifting in my spare time, but he's so tall and limp that carrying him is kind of like carrying an unfurled sleeping bag packed full of sand.

We have a first aid kit in the postage stamp-sized back office, so I use my utility key to collect it from under the ancient desktop computer. It contains nothing more substantial than gauze, surgical tape, Pepto-Bismol, and Aspirin, but it's better than nothing.

On taking the kit to the kid, I wet more paper towels to clean his face as best I can… And stop once I see what's underneath the river of blood.

The fresh, jagged cut down the boy's temple forms, when viewed from an angle, an almost perfect letter V — nigh identical to the scar bisecting my *own* face.

Well fuck me gently with a chainsaw, Not-Cero whispers, aghast.

"My thoughts exactly."

The urge to slam the bathroom door shut, to hunker down and wait in darkness for Vince's inevitable approach, makes my heart spasm. *He's nearby. Right now!* He put his hands on this boy, cut him, and sent him straight to me like some sick telegram. He's going to find us, and when he does, he's gonna—!

The teen stirs. I see strips of white beneath his fluttering lashes. He slumps. I catch his shoulder, steadying him before he can hit the floor.

Damn, damn, and damn again; what do I do now?! I suppose I could leave this place; this helpless, bleeding kid. I could grab Tip, skip town, and tell Crown to do the same. But...

But you won't, so stop your bitching and get to work.

Not-Cero is right. "Are we men or are we mice?" I mutter, and wrap the kid's head with gauze, wracking my brains for who to call for help. There's no way in hell I'm leaving this building without a vehicle. The kid can't even keep his eyes open, let alone sit up and hold on tight, so my Ninja ain't gonna cut the mustard.

I won't call the police; that's for sure. You know something's rotten in the state of Denmark when you wouldn't trust the local authorities, not even your old academy buddies, with an injured kid. *Especially* a kid containing any more melanin than your average slice of Wonder Bread. They've been murdered for less, even when they're *not* armed.

I wet yet another paper towel and press it to the back of the kid's clammy neck before leaving to find my bag and phone. His hand catches a loop on my belt as I pass. He's got all the strength of a sick kitten, but his plaintive voice stops me anyway. "Don't go! He might come back..."

Whether he's begging for protection or warning me from harm, my heart melts, and alongside it, my fear. Screw Vince for always turning my world upside down. *Screw* him for hurting a kid.

"I'll kill him if he tries," I promise, my voice silky calm, and the boy's hand falls back to his side. Maybe he trusts me. Maybe he's plum out of strength.

I draw my knives as I walk from the relative safety of the bath-room, checking every aisle, every corner, until I'm back at my counter.

I'm quick to lock the doors and register before flipping the "OPEN" sign over to "SORRY, WE'RE CLOSED" — something I'm not meant to do, ever, but I can hardly keep the place running at a time like this.

I could call Ricket. He'd come for me — of this, there is no doubt. I almost do just that before I remember he's out on a dragger with Tip and the rest of his nerd-crew. They won't dock for hours. Even if there *is* cell service at sea, he still couldn't reach me in time...

And what if Tip overheard? No doubt my cousin would be furious to learn his beloved professor and I are partners in crime. More importantly, I'd sooner die than alert him to Vince's proximity. Ricket is not an option for me right now.

Rosa, suggests Not-Cero, after a considering pause.

"You think I should call her?" It makes sense. She's nearby. I trust her. And after a quick Google search, I have the number to her bar pulled up nice and handy on my screen. Still, I hesitate to dial.

I'm reluctant to endanger Rosa. People who get tangled with Vince always regret it. I could be condemning her to some serious hell.

You already know you're gonna to do it. Get it over with.

That's such a Cero thing to say. And she's right: Rhys and Clay *would* see this as yet another instance of me dragging my baggage to their doorstep. Crown and Navier live too far away. Cero didn't like for me to have any relationships outside of her control, and forced me to drop them when I moved in with her. Who else does that leave?

I push the little green button on my phone. It rings five times before I hear the world's sleepiest "Hola," and despite all the insan-ity going on, my heart trips at Rosa's voice.

"It's Magpie. Listen, I need to ask you for a *huge* favor..."

Chapter Five – Magpie

...

By the time I've cleaned my bloody boot prints off the floor, fished the gun from under the shelf to tuck beneath my waistband, and written Brittanie an excuse note (it's hard to argue with explosive diarrhea), the kid seems to be doing better. He's already Very Hungry Caterpillar'd his way through some Aspirin, three doughnuts, and several gulps of water.

"Hurts," he mutters, reaching to touch the gauze on his cheek.

It's gonna get worse before it gets better, I'm afraid. I still need to wash and stitch that bad boy up, and I'm no Ricket when it comes to first aid. He's good at finicky precision. I'm better at making things go *boom, bang, crash!*

"What's your name?" I ask, sitting on the floor before the cashier counter, my knee touching his. I'm wearing my backpack and holding my phone, prepared to leave at a moment's notice.

He looks at me, all round doe-eyes with curled lashes a supermodel would fiddle the devil for. "Omar."

"Where can we take you, Omar?" I try, fishing for information. "You live with your parents?"

I don't want to take him anywhere before hearing what he knows about Vince, but I'm no kidnapper. If he wants to go home, I'll take him home.

My words have the opposite of the calming effect I'd been going for. He pulls away from me and struggles to stand. *"No,"* he insists with sudden vehemence.

"Whoa!" I catch his wrist. "Hold your horses. Forget I even said that. Please sit. Drink more water."

He does, but he doesn't look too happy about it. Lucky for me, that's the exact moment Rosa checks in; this time calling from her cell phone instead of the landline in her bar.

"I'm out back, like you said," she announces, meaning she's outside the doors from the tiny office where truckers deliver stock. "In the blue truck."

"Sweet." I don't hang up, instead keeping the phone trapped between my jaw and shoulder as I stand and offer Omar my hand. He tries to make it on his own, but ends up leaning against me as we walk.

I don't draw my knives again — unlike my octo-limbed comic book counterpart, designed and illustrated by Crown, I only have two hands — but I'm wary to be stepping out while Vince is afoot.

To my immense relief, Rosa is idling precisely where she said she'd be. What's more, she's already loaded my Kawasaki into her truck's bed. Omar looks surprised to find a Hispanic woman in a turquoise '63 Dodge awaiting us.

"I sorta thought you'd called the cops," he admits as I help him into the back. The interior smells overwhelmingly of pickle juice and cheap cologne. "You promise you're not taking me to the police?"

Rosa looks at me in the rearview mirror, awaiting my answer. "No," I insist. "We're not doing that."

Rosa shrugs, jerking her chin towards the passenger seat in a clear demand. I close Omar's door and walk around, climbing in beside her. "Hi, Rosa. Thank you for doing this. I owe you big time."

"Yes," she agrees, jaw tight. Her knuckles are ten white crescents strangling the steering wheel. "You *do*. Does somebody want to tell me what's going on?"

"Drive first," I advise. "I don't know if we're being tailed. A roundabout route would be best."

Again, she fixes me with that hard look. Rosa is not a woman to mess with. If she kicks us both out, I'll understand. But when she glances over her shoulder, I know she sees exactly what I see: an injured kid in some serious hot water. If we don't do something, what might happen to him?

Her harsh expression softens, and I know in my heart she'll follow through. "Seatbelts on!" she barks.

My feelings for her only grow as she eases through the narrow alley between buildings and makes a beeline for the freeway, semi-congested with morning commuters. The traffic only extends so far before it's devoured by the morning's fog, which hugs each of the truck's windows. We are so alone in here.

"I didn't know you had a pickup," I remark as she swerves across four lanes of traffic, straight into the HOV lane, before flooring the engine. We're driving in the exact opposite direction from her bar, but at least we're moving.

"It's not mine. Patches had a few too many last night, so I swiped his keys and got him an Uber home."

Ah, Patches. Though technically retired from the biker lifestyle, he's rowdy well into his seventies. I hope I'm still kicking at that age.

You know you'll be partying it up til they put you in the ground, Not-Cero laughs, and I have a sudden mental image of myself, gray and wrinkly and toothless, saggy breasts flapping unhindered as I twerk on tabletops.

"Thanks, baby," I reply sarcastically, and Rosa shoots me a startled glance. I realize I've never seen her without makeup on before. Her freckles make me weak.

"Did you just call me *baby*?"

I can't quite quell my grin. "Only if you want me to."

She rolls her eyes so hard I'm surprised they don't plop right out of socket. "Enough screwing around. Tell me what's going on. Right now." The *"or else"* is unsaid, but heavily implied.

I begin the tale with the gun pointed to my head as Rosa takes an unexpected exit and a few random side streets. We get back on the freeway; this time approaching the correct direction. "Where is it?"

"Hidden." In my pants, which is the polar opposite of proper gun safety. Gran must be rolling in her grave. *'I told you to always be careful with firearms, Alexis, but did you listen?!'*

Rosa glances in the rearview at Omar, who is listening lethargically, his good cheek pressed to the window. Despite how punk I fancied myself at his age, the thought of driving God-knows-where with two strangers would've spooked me silly, but he seems unfazed.

"What's your story?" Rosa asks him. He looks like he wants to keep mum, but one glance at her stony expression unlocks his tongue.

"I was looking for work last night." I get the impression he's trying to make his voice sound deeper; older; like if he's careful, we might mistake him for an adult. "Outside the Motel 6 on Belmont. Panhandling, I guess. This guy comes up to me and says he's got a job in room twelve that I don't want to miss."

"What kind of job?" Rosa asks. At the same time I inquire, "What did he look like?"

He answers my question first. "White guy. Dark hair. About my height. He was all tatted up; lots of piercings... Oh, and his eyes were freaky. Had to be colored contacts."

They aren't contact lenses, but I know precisely what Omar means. Vince's eyes, green as poison, have been disturbing as hell since I first met him, back when I was in middle school.

Just remembering the way those eyes glow in the dark, I feel the phantom ooze of unwanted fingers under the waistband of my jeans. I shudder, changing position as though to throw his hands off.

"What kind of job?" Rosa repeats. There's an edge to her voice, like she already kinda knows. I want to tell her to drop it. With Vince, it's *always* drugs or sex. Is this something she really wants to hear?

Omar heaves a deep sigh, at last resigning himself to the fact that Rosa never lets sleeping dogs lie. "He didn't say, but I got the meaning. Look, lady, a guy has to eat."

My already troubled stomach churns sickly. This is Tip all over again, but worse. At least Tip and Vince are close to the same age. Does Vince now get his jollies from perving on kids too young to vote? The guy is pushing forty!

Maybe Omar is relieved that we're not judging him, or maybe our silence only encourages him to fill it. He continues: "He tells me to shower first. Points me to the bathroom in his little motel room."

Rosa snarls ferally. Her eyes blaze with hellfire. I focus on keeping the acidic contents of my stomach where they belong.

"While I'm showering..." Omar swallows thickly, as though also suffering some digestive troubles. On instinct, I reach behind my seat to offer my hand, which he takes with a refreshing lack of hesitation. "He gets in behind me. I think, oh, maybe that's how he wants it. I'm just thinking it's kinda weird he's still dressed, but then... *Then* he holds a knife to my throat."

I picture the scene exactly as Omar describes it. The shush of falling water. The humid lick of steam. A tall man shadowing my naked back. Cold metal pricking my frozen, breathless neck...

I know what Vince looks like when he holds a knife. I know the way his pupils expand; his breathing intensifies; an erotic flush plumping his lips and coloring his fair skin. His legs frame my torso; his fist grips my hair; how did he even manage to crawl through my bedroom window? He...

Omar's hand clenches in mine, snatching me away from the precipice of a flashback that could easily have become a panic attack. He's shaking like a beaten dog.

I want to give him the opportunity to collect himself. I doubt he wants to cry in front of two strangers. I close my eyes and let my truth spill out.

"That man is named Vincent Rasmussen. He and my cousin used to deal drugs together."

Vince always had a plethora of the highest quality to sell. He was the savior and damnation of addicts along SoCal's coastline. Prescription? Party? Coke? Meth? Smack? Dab? Salts? Blot? Pick your poison, and he'll name the price! Make very sure you can pay your bill when he comes to collect, though, lest he sic his loyal, lovesick dog on you.

"Two years ago, he left our other cousin, Crown, for dead in a burning car. Took him a while, but it looks like he's finally back for more."

•••

Rosa's cozy little apartment is brightly lit and filled with round windows, baskets of hanging spider plants, and cushions to sit on. A friendly little cat with snow-white fur greets us at the door. I drop to a knee on the creaky wooden floor, offering it my hand to sniff.

"That's Hugo," Rosa says. "He was born Deaf. That's how he stands the racket from the bar every night."

Hugo punctuates this by meowing far too loudly, unable to meter his own volume.

Oh! Not-Cero gasps, delighted. I scratch Hugo's ears and chin. In life, Cero had two exceptionally large male ragdolls named

Rorschach and Schrödinger (Roar and Ding). They live with Navier and Crown now. If I think too much about that, I start to feel sad. And guilty.

Not your fault, Miss Cop. You don't have the money or space to take care of anything nowadays. They're doing just fine with that old chatterbox.

How kind of my hallucination to absolve me of my failures.

Rosa, bless her saintly soul, brews a pot of coffee in her kitchen. She uses the sink-hose to fill a suitcase-sized washing machine with water, then unearths a well-stocked first aid kit to produce a bar of medical-grade antibacterial soap. She peels the wrapper off, then passes it to Omar.

"If you think you can avoid fainting, go shower now," she orders; totally calm, totally in control. "Bathroom's down the hall on the right; towels are in the cupboards. It's gonna sting like a bitch, but you wash that cut out good, *mijo.*"

He shuffles off to do just that. I stand on tiptoe to sneak a curious peek into that kit; at the impressive collection of bottles, bandages, syringes, and wraps it contains. Looks like Rosa is prepping for doomsday.

"Bar fights," Rosa explains. "Have you ever treated a biker who's been glassed? Not pretty."

She slides me a mug of coffee and frowns at my blood-streaked polo. "Cold water," she points to the sink, then sits in a chair at the kitchen table, stroking Hugo's back when he hops into her lap.

I peel my shirt off and twist the taps, rinsing the fabric as best I can. I feel her eyes on my back, sweeping up and down my wings, which start at the shoulders and extend to my hips. Some primary feathers wrap around my arms and ribcage like a permanent hug from the one I miss the most.

"My wife designed the tattoo," I explain. "It's modeled after an Australian magpie."

"It's beautiful," Rosa compliments. I keep my face down so she can't see my goofy grin. "I always wondered if you were married. I see you wearing that ring-necklace sometimes."

"Cero passed away two years ago," I use my thumbnail to scrape at Omar's dried blood until it rinses down the drain. "She fought the cancer, and the cancer won. I've been on my own ever since."

Rosa processes this as I wring my shirt out and rest it on the edge of the counter. "I'm sorry for your loss," she says, and sounds sincere.

I turn to look at her, grateful I bothered to wear bra today. I'm a lifetime member of the itty bitty titty committee, so I don't always.

When she stares at me, I vainly assume she's checking me out before realizing her eyes are glued only to the handle of the Smith & Wesson, not to my stomach or biceps.

Her expression tightens. I belatedly recall the strict policy about guns inside her bar — that policy being *Do Not, Ever*. I don't think I've ever met anyone who dislikes them as much as she does.

As slowly as I can, I remove the weapon and set it on the counter, then step away. This is Rosa's home; her safe place. I never intended to violate her boundaries like this, and feel terrible for doing so.

"I'd feel more comfortable with that in my safe," she says in forced calm. I nod, staying back as she approaches. She pops the cylinder to count each bullet, then takes the dismantled firearm into what I can only assume is her bedroom, leaving me with my coffee.

Omar emerges from the bathroom, damp and towel-clad, and sits in Rosa's vacated chair. I admire his bravery. Considering what happened to him the last time he took a shower around a stranger, he's showing us a remarkable amount of trust. I hope we deserve it.

"How are you doing?" I ask.

He grimaces. The gnarly gash on his face opens ever further, yawning like a slicked mouth. A stringy blister is clearly trying to form, but the constant, tiny movements of his face repeatedly tear it. Fresh blood seeps from the cracks. "I've been better."

Out of her bedroom steps Rosa, arms laden with fabric. She doles out clothing. A striped tank top and pajama bottoms for Omar; a Smashing Pumpkins concert tee for me.

I blink, admiring it in all its faded glory, before slipping it over my head. It falls well past my knees, the sleeves gaping huge. I love a gal with good taste in music!

My polo and Omar's previous outfit are both dropped into the tiny washing machine, which chugs industrially away in a fragrant foam of softener. I move to stand beside the teenager's chair.

Academy training teaches many rules for handling victims of abuse, so to ease any stress of the unknown, I explain my next actions aloud. With a syringe and a bottle of Lidocaine in my latex-gloved hands, I regard Omar's cleaned wound, then pierce the needle into the fattiest portion of his cheek. He doesn't flinch. Tough kid.

The effects quickly take hold. Injecting drugs is useful like that; even more so than snorting, which absorbs particles through the nasal membrane, or swallowing, which requires an hour or more for the liver to process. When Omar can no longer feel the left half of his face, I set to work.

The thread is nylon. Acceptable, but I would've preferred self-dissolving. This will have to be manually removed once Omar's face has healed. I line the ragged edges of his wound as best I can and use a quick whipstitch to seal it, then slap a bandage on top. It only takes a minute.

"Thank you," Omar mutters as I finish and clean my mess.

I pat his arm. How to explain that I feel responsible for what happened to him? Vince targeted him because he was vulnerable, and he did it because he knew an endangered kid would catch my attention like nothing else could. Were it not for me, this would never have happened.

Rosa watches everything I do, Hugo held tightly in her arms so he won't get fur into the cut. When she sees that I'm finished, she speaks up. "Omar, what happened to you after Vince held you at knifepoint?"

As though he'd been rehearsing what to say since we arrived, Omar tiredly recounts, "He pulled me from the shower. Sat me on the toilet. I promised if he let me go, I'd keep my mouth shut. He said he didn't care who I told, and then... Then he cut me." He blinks hard, lips thinning as he presses them, fighting to keep his tone even. "I thought for sure he'd kill me."

"He does that," I console. "Plays cat and mouse. If you'd thought there was no way he'd kill you, then he'd probably have done it just to prove you wrong, regardless of what his initial plans had been. You survived, Omar. You're *here*."

I shut up for the rest of Omar's recounting: How Vince had him get dressed again, stealing his backpack as he did. He'd driven him to my gas station, handed him the gun, and told him what to say and do. That he'd kill Omar if he didn't comply.

"Was there anything else?" Rosa asks.

"Nope. That's all." Omar prods at his still-numb jaw, then groans. "Man, that backpack had all my clothes, my school shit, my money... I'm *fucked!*"

It's the most emoting I've seen from him since he told me not to leave him. To some, it may seem strange that he cares more about his stuff than his face, but I was a foster kid. I know well how a black garbage bag containing a child's every earthly possession is far more precious than gold, providing an anchor as we're dumped in home after home with no way to know if we'll be hurt or helped this time.

The cop in me wants Omar's guardian's address so I can bully them into treating him right, but life experience has taught me that it's rarely so simple as all that.

You're learning! Not-Cero praises. The black-and-white way I'd once viewed the world had frustrated her to no end when she was first training me.

"I was once a homeless teen," Rosa confesses, apparently coming to the same conclusion I'd reached. "I've got a perfectly good sofa and some spare bedding for you."

Omar's brow creases. "I don't take charity," he protests, but Rosa cuts him off with a sharp shake of her head.

"I'm not offering any. I have work. You'll help. You said you're in school? You'll keep going to that, too."

When Omar hesitates further, Rosa bulldozes on: "Just until your face heals, *mijo*. You'll need someone around to remove those stitches before they get infected."

This, at least, gets through to him. He slumps in his chair and huffs a sigh that borders on an incredulous laugh. "Well... What can I say but thank you?"

Chapter Six – Tip

...

"Gray whales, James," I babble, grasping my professor's elbow with my good hand to shake it enthusiastically. *"Gray whales!"*

He's smiling, eyes crinkled and warm behind his glasses, both hands steady on his Jeep's steering wheel. He doesn't once take his gaze off the salty road, though traffic is light this close to the docks. "I saw them too, Tip."

I emit a shrill noise I'll surely feel embarrassed for later, my hands flying to my face before I remember all the squid I've handled. Even that isn't enough to ruin my mood. I'd swallow one whole if it meant I could stand so close to *Eschrichtius robustus* again.

James stalls at a red light. He may have been born and raised in Navajo Nation, but he's a true Californian. Stopping completely is for snowbirds and tourists. Only then does he turn to regard his other students, who are piled like puppies in the back.

Tariq is snoring, head pillowed on his girlfriend's ample chest, long legs cramped against the back of my seat. Bambi is struggling just to keep her eyes open. It's distressingly cute, even though the Jeep's heater intensifies our brine-stink to sickening levels.

"Do you want breakfast?" our professor asks.

Bambi shakes her head no. "Can you take us to my mom's place? We need sleep before we can get our reports done."

He glances at me. "Is it okay if I drop them off first? I know you have work after this."

"Go for it. You only need to take me to a bus stop. I've got to get home and change clothes."

I'd put in for a late-start at work, but it looks like I'll be pushing even that. I try to keep my work record spotless so my parole officer

46

has nothing to bitch about. I forgot we'd have to stop for Bambi and Tariq to say the Fajr prayer, and it pushed me further behind schedule. My fault.

Bambi's mom lives in a pale pink single-story, shaped kind of like a muffin and situated within biking distance of UCLA. Bambi nudges Tariq awake when we pull to the curb after forty-five minutes of sunrise and silence, and together they say goodbye and zombie-shuffle to the idyllic picket fence that protects the butterfly garden.

James waits until they're inside the house itself before using a neighbor's driveway to reverse. I like that about him; how he notices people, and protects them in his quiet little ways.

"I don't suppose *you* want breakfast?" he asks hopefully when we're on the road again.

I laugh, my spirits higher than they've been in weeks. (*Three* gray whales! A pod! One was a calf! It should be easy-peasy to find them on any whaler's database, and then I can track their migration.) "James, you're allowed to just say *you* want food. It doesn't have to be for someone else."

His cheeks redden, twin ripe apples blooming just below his grizzle. I resist the urge to tease him further; to see if I can make that blush spread. I shouldn't find it as appealing as I do, and I know it. If I was a better person, I would feel ashamed.

I never claimed to be a saint.

"Hey, now," he mumbles, sheepish. "I had a hankering for coffee."

Typical. "Bet you a dollar my cousin has a brew on. You can have some; she won't care."

"I wouldn't take that bet." I glance at him, wondering at the nonsensical remark, but he's too busy watching the road to notice. "That sounds lovely. Thank you, Tip."

I direct him to our apartment, hoping he won't judge our financial state too harshly.

At the height of my career, Crown and I lived together in gorgeous apartments hugging the coastlines of the world, paid for by sponsorships, commercials, and prize winnings.

We traveled too often for me to appreciate what we had — I guess I grew accustomed to living well too quickly, after a childhood spent well below the poverty line — but hospital bills and lawyers and parole will pick a savings account dry like crabs on a carcass.

Companies pull your adverts *fast* when you're incriminated in a scandal, but the internet never forgets. Bye-bye, royalties. All my social media accounts are under a fake name; I wouldn't Google "Dylan Tippling" if someone held a gun to my head.

There is no code at the gate leading into our parking lot. The spaces line up directly with the numbered doors of the first floor.

Magpie's motorcycle is too small to require a parking space of its own, so she shares one with our neighbor's moped. That leaves *our* designated spot empty for James's Jeep.

He takes it, unbuckles his seatbelt, and follows me to our front door, leaving his cane behind. He's taller than me (as I stand at just five-six, many men are), and his proportions are different. I'm all legs, while he has a lengthy torso. He might be a few pounds overweight, but I get the impression he's like Magpie; just naturally, comfortably thick.

I can only pray that he's too nearsighted to spot the discarded syringes and tied-off condoms that litter every cracked-concrete corner of the dingy complex. They're not mine, no, but not so long ago, they very well could have been. I have more in common with our neighbors, who tinfoil their windows and try to mask the telltale reek of crack with Febreze, than I ever will to anybody in James's classroom.

I feel better once we're inside the apartment. The bitter odor of strong coffee overpowers us when I close and lock the door behind him, grateful that for once Mags *hasn't* marked her path from the door to her bed with a snail-trail of discarded clothing.

"I think there's some creamer in the fridge," I say, as James looks around our kitchenette. It, like the rest of the apartment, is bare-bones. Twin-burner stove beneath a greasy hood. A sink piled sky-high with moldering dishes. A refrigerator that looks like it was built when bell-bottom pants were all the rage. "Help yourself to whatever."

From the drying rack, I bypass Magpie's chipped selection of mugs featuring girl bands and Disney characters for my own drinkware, handing a plain white mug to James.

The coffeepot looks full to the brim. I see why when I pass through our kitchenette to the main room of the apartment, where Magpie is passed out, fully dressed, on my sofa-bed. Must've been too tired to even pour the first cup.

"Oh, for *fuck's* sake..." I reach to jab her puffy cheek (Vince used to call her 'Squirrel-Face' for a reason) with my finger. "Mags. *Move.* You're on my shit!"

She's out cold, drooling on the uniform I'd laid out for myself the night before.

The idiot pushes herself to stay awake for as long as possible, massacring her adenosine with caffeine until she's keyed to the max. Whenever she finally succumbs to sleep, she crashes *hard*. The building could catch fire and she probably wouldn't notice.

After a quick sniff of her lips to ensure she's truly asleep, rather than passed out drunk, I waste no more time trying to wake her. Over the past few months, I've tried every trick in the book to drag her from her screaming night terrors, up to and including slapping her and pouring cold water on her face. Nothing works.

Instead, I struggle to lift her, then to pull the uniform out from beneath her body. I fail at both. She's heavy, and I don't have the strength I used to.

James, watching from the half-wall of our kitchenette, sets down his mug to approach. "Let me," he offers.

"Um..." I may not be a beacon of morality, but I'm still hesitant to let an outsider touch my comatose little cousin. If he were anyone else, this would be the part where I politely suggested they leave; perhaps while holding a kitchen knife to their genitals for incentive. "What about your leg?"

His expression hardens, and I wonder if I've said something insensitive. The guy wears a brace from ankle to crotch, and was leaning heavily on his cane all night long. What good will pretending I didn't notice do for either of us?

"I can *do* this," he insists, and the stubbornness I hear in his voice is iron-strong. I must've hit a nerve.

"Fine, then. Knock yourself out."

I lead the way as he carries Mags, apparently without difficulty, to her messy bedroom. Her marriage bed is buried under battered paperbacks, bars of half-eaten chocolate and, when I stack the pillows, two clanking, empty Svedka bottles.

I hastily stuff those last items into a bedside drawer, uncomfortable with the way they make James's expression pinch. What business is it of his if my cousin is a closet lush? Our problems aren't his to touch.

I peel back her comforter, a gaudy tricolor of bi-pride stripes, and he sets her on the bare mattress underneath. There isn't much left to do but smooth her hair and pull the covers up to her chin.

"Let's go." I beckon him towards the door, but a framed photograph on the wall catches his attention.

It's of Magpie and Cero on their honeymoon, standing shoulder-to-shoulder before Sleeping Beauty's castle at Disneyland. Dole

Whips in hand, rainbow mouse ears set at jaunty angles, the whole shebang. Mags is cheesing like a hyperactive five-year-old, and even Cero has a rare half-smile softening the harsh lines of her angular face.

This was taken back when Cero still looked like a person instead of a Halloween prop: square features; button nose; stocky body; a bob of white-blonde hair. She's not especially attractive, but she exudes an aura of refinement and control that I think Mags liked.

"That's her dead wife," I say bluntly, propelling James out the door. "Mags keeps this room like a shrine to her. S'creepy, I know."

James frowns at me when I firmly shut the door behind us. "Maybe she misses her."

I shrug. What can I say to that? Everyone misses *somebody*. I don't know what to make of his sudden interest, so instead I snag my jumpsuit from the couch.

"I need to get dressed," I say, leaving him to sip his coffee in the kitchen as I slip back into Mags's room to change.

...

I never asked James to drive me to work, but when we walk outside together, he opens his Jeep's passenger-side door and looks at me pointedly.

I consider refusing. The coffee may have paid for the ride home, but I don't have cash for gas, and there's no such thing as free kindness.

But I really am running late, and this is my professor; not some random John. I'm not naïve enough to think that'd stop him from taking advantage, should he feel so inclined — any vulnerable moment spent with a person gives them more weapons to inevitably hurt you with — but I'll admit he's won a tiny modicum of trust from me over our semesters together.

James peeks at the logo on my uniform as I retake my seat wondering already if I'm making a huge mistake, or just a medium-sized one. "How did you land a job at that aquarium?" he asks. "I hear they're exclusive."

He circles the parking lot and comes out the other side, waiting for the right of way to turn onto a busy street.

He's right; they *are* somewhat exclusive. Due to proximity with UCLA, a lot of research and training takes place in the basement, as oceanic fauna is treated and rehabilitated. Some high-dollar essays and memoirs have been written because of our property.

Nevertheless, the question tenses my muscles and clenches my jaw. Is he poking into my history with drugs? The arson charges, maybe? Or is he simply implying I don't deserve my position?

"It has nothing to do with being a surfer," I snap, earning a startled frown from the man beside me.

"I never said it—"

"I'm just a janitor, okay? Nobody even recognizes me." Sure, the woman who'd hired me was a fan, but aside from her...

James drops his hand on my knee. I know it's meant to be calming, like patting a horse's flank, but it's exactly the wrong thing to do to me, especially when I'm already defensive. Touching just makes everything worse; makes my insides tie into knots. All of my focus is latched fearfully on that five-pointed star of flesh searing like a brand through the canvas of my uniform.

Please no. Not you, too... I wanted so badly for you to be special!

A dim part of my brain knows I'm being crazy. That I'm being, as Vince would say, 'a real PMS-ing bitch.' Being aware that you're mentally ill doesn't magically take your symptoms away. So it's all in my head? So *what!* My brain lives in there!

"Tip?" James asks, concerned. "Is everything okay?"

I open my mouth to smile and reassure him. Maybe to flirt him into a forgiving mood. It's a survival tactic that's kept me alive in far too many situations just like this one.

Instead, what ekes out is a quiet, "Please stop touching me."

Oh, that was a Grand Canyon-sized mistake. Men *hate* it when you question their entitlement to anything; especially if that entitlement is to your body. I wait for James to blow up; to hit me; to prove beyond a doubt that he can do whatever what he wants to me...

"I'm so sorry." He withdraws his hand. "I'm the middle child of a large family. I'm accustomed to casual affection, but I understand not everybody is comfortable with that. Please excuse me, Tip; I meant no harm."

I'm speechless. He sounds sincere. He *looks* sincere, when I dare peek at his face. Maybe he's just covering his ass? Planning something worse for later? Whatever it is, I still feel the ghost of his hand like a venomous spider on my thigh, even though it's now back on the wheel where it belongs.

My heart performs a complicated series of acrobatics, and I think all the moisture in my mouth has relocated to my palms. I should say something. I *have* to say something. The silence stretches like taffy, broken only by the maddening tick-tick-tick of his turn signal.

I am beyond incompetent at being a functional human being, and in that moment, I feel my alien otherness like a second skin beneath my own.

"Big family?" I manage at long, long last. The olive branch sounds stupid even to my ears.

He smiles cautiously. I watch him do it from the corner of my eye. "Two sisters and a brother."

"You must've had to wait forever to use the bathroom in the mornings," I say, relieved when James laughs. Gradually the knots in my intestines loosen.

"If you'll believe it, the bathroom of our family home isn't even inside our house. There was an outhouse nearby that we had to walk to. It was a pain waking up in the middle of the night needing to pee, and first having to hunt down your shoes and a flashlight."

I think about that, frowning. I know life on reservations isn't ideal, but damn...

When we arrive at the massive, glass-walled aquarium, I direct him around the back to employee parking and entry. I groan aloud when I see a distinctive truck and trailer idling at the delivery curb. "Didn't anyone tell Jacobi I'd be late today?!"

I don't know why or how Cash Jacobi became my problem. We *have* a security team. If they ever stopped taking hour-long smoke breaks and did their fucking jobs, us janitors might stop getting blamed for every little thing under the sun. Maybe.

James looks sharply my way. His dark eyes, normally soft and docile as a deer's, are narrowed with the deadly precision of a sniper. "What did you say?"

I point to the truck, wishing to avert that hawk's gaze. "Cash Jacobi. He stocks our vending machines twice a week. I usually sign him in, but I filed for a late-start. Someone else should have handled him."

Upon noticing us, Cash emerges from his truck. The man is balding and stocky with thick, muscled arms and a potbelly. He scowls and brandishes his clipboard at me, swearing loud enough to hear through the windshield.

I fumble for my seatbelt, but James's hand unexpectedly clamps on my shoulder so tight it aches. He hauls me back against his chest. "Don't," he hisses in my ear. "Stay here."

He's strong. It scares me. I *hate* that it scares me. Before my body can lock up, I force myself to move; to shove him away. "I said no!" I bark, snapping my teeth in his face.

It's worlds better to be angry than afraid.

James flinches, grip loosening, and I retrieve my arm. The ocean inside me rages: a maelstrom, a tempest. Maybe he sees it in my eyes. Maybe he senses that I've hurt people before, and I'll do it again if I have to. Good. I was an idiot to think he was special. This pure disappointment is a bitter pill to swallow.

"Thanks for the ride, *professor*," I sneer, letting myself out and slamming the door as hard as I physically can before stomping towards Cash.

"Asshole!" he barks at me, heavy Chicago accent in full flux. His expressive hands flutter with the words, drawing my attention to the weird lizard tattoo that winds his thumb. "Do you know how long I've—"

"Stuff it, fucknuts." I interrupt, swiping my badge to unlock the backdoor with violently shaking hands. "It's not my fault nobody around here can read a fucking email."

"What, so you have all the time in the world to blow your boyfriend over there and make me late for a moving job?"

Oh, right; he and his brother run a moving business on the side. I forgot because I don't care.

I pointedly hold the door open for him to wheel his dolly of boxed snacks and drinks inside. His parting shot of *"fag"* makes me smirk, cold as ice. Those who'd call near-strangers slurs are too pathetic to explain the nuances of multi-gender attraction to.

I bite back a dozen retorts, each brutal enough to get me fired, and we go our separate ways. He can let himself out, or not. It makes no difference to me.

There are two customer accessible floors of the aquarium, as well a third floor for offices and conference rooms; a basement for non-display animals; and a kitchen for exhibit meal prep. (Yes, 'animal chef' is totally a job and yes, I'm kind of jealous).

That, plus the café and gift shop, equal six pairs of bathrooms, total. Thankfully, I'm rarely scheduled to clean outside the main two floors.

I locate my cart of supplies and shoo customers out of bathrooms, scrubbing toilets and emptying trash cans, mopping floors a section at a time. The heavy keys on my belt jingle as I move, announcing my presence wherever I go. I keep track of my tasks on the Blackberry my manager gave me.

I snap at some kids for being too rough with the manta rays in the petting tank, and smile in secret at my favorite exhibits: Annie the Harbor seal, who'd been injured in a speedboat accident, and Joffrey the rockhopper on loan from U of NE. The tanks of tropical fish, bright as jewels, make my heart ache for snorkeling in Sydney. The spotted jellyfish, serenely drifting, reminds me of competing in Maui.

My favorite part of the day comes at lunchtime, when I dock my cart and slip to the basement, making a beeline for Agwe's tank. I have to swipe my badge at every door I encounter. If anyone cares enough to ask why there's a record of me coming down here every day, I haven't heard it yet.

Great security for such an "exclusive" aquarium, huh?

"Hi, pretty girl," I whisper, gazing adoringly at my chunky, gray-skinned love, and feel all the tension seep from my bones as I watch 900 pounds of manatee happily munch turtle grass with blunt, yellowed teeth.

I pull my own lunch from of my bag and sit cross-legged before her, glad for the company, the sloshing of water all around, the cool temperature they keep things down here.

"Salad for both of us, huh?"

For once, I don't count each slice of cold zucchini as I eat them. Agwe's gentle presence, her musky odor, is enough to soothe the storm in my veins. I love her *so* much; her wrinkly, whiskery face; her flippers; the sedate way she moves. I could weep.

"Someday," I tell her, watching her do a barrel-roll for the pure joy of movement, her nostrils squinched into slits, her whiskers streamlined, "I'll become a scientist, and then *I* can take care of you."

It's an unrealistic dream that I'll even finish school, let alone get hired anywhere — be it for research, practical veterinary skill, or anything else for that matter. But the thought still keeps me going when nothing else can.

I grin as she shoots twin streams of bubbles from her nose, her remaining eye in its raised nest of scar tissue — poachers are the reason she'll never be on display. Strangers give her too much anxiety after what the bastards did to her — rolling to see me.

Glancing around to ensure nobody is in the room to witness my foolishness, I press my forehead to the cool glass of her enclosure and tell her all about the good parts of my night; the squid, the whales. She might not understand me, but I know she's listening. For these all-too-few minutes of my day, I feel whole.

Chapter Seven – Magpie

what's a couple bruised testicles between friends?

...

I wake just past noon with a dry mouth and a throbbing headache. *Hey, Miss Cop,* Not-Cero greets.

"Morning, baby," I reply, too groggy to know better. I sit up in bed and grind my knuckles into my eyes, swiping the grit away.

I feel cold hands touch the back of my neck, thumbs massaging where spine meets skull. I lean contentedly into the touch, only to realize there's nothing solid to lean *against.* There's nothing there at all.

Unsettled, I stand and yank open my side-table drawer, fumbling for a bottle of aspirin. There's no water within grabbing distance, so I wash the pills down with a swig of vodka, hiccupping tearfully at the welcome burn.

You didn't always drink so much.

"You didn't always nag so much."

As I walk through the empty apartment, I notice I'm still wearing Rosa's concert tee; a souvenir from Smashing Pumpkins' 94 tour. Seeing it gives me the first smile of my day.

After popping leftover waffles into the microwave, I stand by the table pushing Tip's textbooks aside (he takes most of his classes online) to reach our laptop. I scroll through my many saved playlists until I find the one I'm looking for, then sway my way around the kitchenette to Pisces Iscariot, imagining a young Rosa with stars in her eyes and music in her heart.

"How come you never danced with me?" I ask, eyes closed, arms high above my head.

Not-Cero doesn't answer for so long that I start to feel stupid for trying to engage my hallucination in conversation, but then—

I did. Don't you remember?

My smile grows at the recollection. When Cero led the gang, she focused on earning enough money to *buy* individual trafficked children; re-homing them in safety. As a notorious thief, she topped my personal most wanted list: the one who always got away. Sure, her primary goal was to help children, but she enjoyed living well. Fast cars, nice clothes... The kids were only one of her priorities.

"I hate high society," I say, remembering our dance. "I'll never forgive you for making me wear a dress."

I feel her laughter like a cool breeze ruffling my hair. *You shouldn't have bothered with the disguises. Your posture always gave you away. That, and your height.*

"Did not!"

Hands take my waist. They feel so solid I almost open my eyes, puzzled as to why Tip is here when he should be studying at the library. But it's not Tip. I know, because I feel the slippery material of Cero's violet Armani scarf draping my neck, weighty and tangible.

A chilly night for a dress so sheer, Miss Cop, Cero murmurs. With the echo of those old words, I feel past and present streaming fluid and stretchy. A confident gloved hand takes mine. It's not Billy Corgan's psychedelic shredding we're swaying to anymore, but the strings of a live quartet weaving through the conversations of socialites.

I gasp, lurching away from a Cero that is young and whole and alive with mischief in her mismatched eyes — one blue, one brown — and find myself once again alone in my apartment. There is no scarf. There are no socialites; no party; no gallery of art to steal. There is no Cero.

I've gone from unsettled to rattled. I shut off the laptop and poke at my waffles, but my stomach is too twisty to eat. Maybe exercise and company is the answer.

I change into a casual outfit and am out the door in minutes, crossing the parking lot and bounding up the metal staircase to my neighbor's apartment.

Besides sharing a parking space with me, David O'Callaghan lets me use his free weights and treadmill. In return, I pretend not to notice the way he ogles my ass.

I've almost reached his door when I feel something drip onto my upper lip. I wipe it away and am startled to find my wrist streaked with red. "What the..."

On the other side of the door, Zelda the pitbull barks.

"It's me," I reassure thickly. He won't answer the door if he doesn't know who's knocking; a weird quirk, considering he's a white guy and the worst he could get busted for is weed, but that's just how it is.

I hear chains rattle when David unlocks his door. We face each other; he, a pale, long-faced kid with blond dreadlocks piled atop his head and me, the bottom-heavy Indian chick with attitude in every line of my posture.

"Hey," he greets, pulling his screen door open. "That's some nosebleed."

I smile sheepishly and gag a little when a trickle of blood sluices into my mouth. "It just started," I explain, leaning over the rail to spit into the dirt.

He steps back. "Come in. I'll get you some tissues."

"I've never had a nosebleed before." I enter and sit on his plastic-covered sofa, trying not to drip as he steps into his bathroom and emerges with a roll of toilet paper. David is unusually tidy for a stoner; he keeps the place clean and organized. He seldom visits my apartment, as the mess gives him hives. "Unless you count when Gracie Thompson decked me Freshman year."

Zelda worries her face between my knees, blinking up at me with mournful golden eyes. I scratch the oily fur of her ears —

scarred and cropped from her years as a bait dog — until her stump-tailed butt waggles in easy doggy joy.

"Do this," David says, sitting beside me and leaning forward to demonstrate. "Drain it through your nose, not down your throat. You don't wanna be puking Dracula's breakfast."

I laugh, then mutter my thanks as he gathers up a wad of paper to pinch the bridge of my nose for me.

"Why'd that Gracie kid hit you?" he asks curiously as the minutes pass and the bleeding slows.

"'Cuz I threw her purse down a storm drain."

This time, David is the one who laughs, his clear blue eyes bright. He has an untreated acne problem, and the racial appropriation of his hairstyle is off-putting, but if he put himself out there more I think plenty of girls would find him cute. "You wild child! What for?"

"She called my Autistic cousin a retard." It still makes me mad just remembering it.

"Ahhhh." David trails the word out long and slow. I wonder if he's hit the grass early today. I can't judge him, seeing as my own breakfast consisted of aspirin and booze. "I feel that. My big sis has Down syndrome. I whooped ass whenever anyone talked shit."

Sometimes David can be pretty okay. He looks too scrawny to whoop *anyone's* ass, but what do I know? Maybe he has hidden reserves.

I use his bathroom to freshen up. Like mine and Tip's apartment, the only bathroom is located inside his bedroom. An inconvenient design for guests, but there's nothing we can do about it.

When I emerge, he offers me a cup of water, but frowns when I take it. His long-fingered hand is gentle when he grasps my wrist, twisting my arm back and forth under the light of his lava lamp. A large bruise mottles the outside of my forearm.

"Did somebody grab you?" he asks, eyes narrowing.

I'm just as surprised as he is. "Not that I remember." It doesn't hurt; it's just ugly, spreading like spilled wine under my dark skin.

His frown lingers as I take my arm back. "If someone's hurting you, you can tell me," he promises, puffing out his chest like he's more than a malnourished vegan in Batman pajamas. "Friends watch out for friends."

"Thank you, but I swear it's nothing," I insist. "You know me. Tough as nails."

This seems to reassure him. "Maybe your blood's just thin. You eat like crap. Get some iron in your system, okay?"

I promise I will, and then we work out together for about an hour, though I take things easier than usual. We cool down by taking Zelda on a sunset stroll around the block, enjoying the light burn of our pleasurably achy muscles.

He walks me home just as Tip approaches from the bus stop, free from work; a few hours to spare before class begins. The two men nod stiffly at each other before David waves goodbye.

According to Tip, David is a burnout loser draining his mom's retirement fund like a lamprey does a trout. According to *David,* Tip is a chaotic entity who projects terrible negative vibes; a true Scorpio through and through. According to me, they're both weirdos.

Once inside our home, I wrap my arms around Tip's waist and squeeze him breathless, just because I have excess energy to burn and I miss his smile. "How was last night? Did you have fun poking seafood with sticks?"

"Ow," he grumbles. "Stoppit. You smell."

"You should work out with us," I wheedle, though I can feel the painfully sharp blades of his hips stabbing my tummy. If he wants to exercise, he's *got* to eat. "It's so fun. We listen to music and act all goofy..."

Tip goes limp and glassy-eyed in my hold, waiting me out until I feel bad for forcing affection on him.

When I let go, he shuffles to the couch, tosses the cushions aside, and unearths the bed within. I wince at the screeching of the metal as he drags the bed out and throws himself onto the thin, bare mattress, closing his eyes like half the weight of the world rests on each lid.

"Don't you at least want the sheets?" I try, already knowing it's futile. "I brought them back from the laundromat yesterday."

He doesn't respond, not even when I grab his newly washed comforter from the top of the basket and fluff it out over him.

"Bad day at work?" I ask.

No answer.

"When do you next see Tessa?" I ask. I don't know how to deal with him when he shuts me out like this. Reminding him of his therapist, and the coping skills she teaches him, is all I can think of right now.

He points at the desktop calendar propped on the back of the couch. I look over all the days with "work" and "class" etched in his chicken scratch until I find "mandatory bitching, 2 PM" written four days from now.

Sometimes living with Tip is like living with a corpse. It reminds me too much of those last few weeks of Cero's hospice stay. Sure, he's there, but not *really*.

For one terrible moment, I feel the words I *know* Tip can't ignore start to form in my mouth: *Vince is back.* At least that would make him *look* at me!

But I can't tell him that. Because then Tip will go searching for his boyfriend, and I truly don't believe my cousin can survive a second round with that monster of a man.

...

I justify my actions to myself by pretending I'll only have two beers tonight. I don't have the money for more. I don't really have the money for this much, either, but that's future-Magpie's problem.

At her counter, Rosa is swamped with patrons. Some flirt outrageously with her. Those, she smirks at and waves away. She pours them all tall, frosty glasses of beer with invitingly dripping sides, or pops bottles and stuffs limes inside each with well-practiced hands that never fall still.

I want to ask her how Omar is doing, but she's so busy it looks like I'm not gonna get the chance to. I hope the kid is upstairs playing with Hugo and getting some homework done.

In the dim overhead lighting of Buenas Ruedas, I'm surrounded by leather and sweat and muscles and epically long beards; raucous laughter and deafening music that I feel more than I hear. It throbs through my veins in place of blood, rattling my bones deliciously.

Just outside, the revving of engines and the sexy stench of gasoline makes me feel more alive than a thousand volts of electricity directly to the urethra.

"Hey," a dude built like a brick shithouse slurs, knocking into my side. I push back. It's like a mosh pit in here, and I'm starving for touch; *any* touch. His hand slides low on my back and I nearly moan from the much-needed contact. *Touch me more. Please touch me!*

Rosa points a stern finger at him when she catches sight of us. "Hands off, Riley. Mags is *my* friend."

My mood brightens considerably. I grin at her. She's looking especially lovely tonight — the woman pulls off leather and lace like nobody's business. Her dark brown hair frames her face in enormous corkscrew curls, and her lips look like they've been stung by bees and painted with the blood of demons.

Mollified, Riley ducks his head. "Sorry, ma'am." His hand falls obediently away from my ass.

Rosa's got all these hound-dogs acting like puppies. This is a good place, made even better when she sends a frosted bottle sailing my way across the polished countertop.

I catch it with satisfaction and toast her before drinking deeply. We each of us have our vices, no? Bottoms up.

I find a place at a booth in the back, which isn't hard to do. I'm not the prettiest flower in the bouquet, but I'm okay, and beer makes the eye of the beholder ever so kind. I join a table of older guys egging their pals on in a disastrous game of darts, enjoying myself immensely as I boo and heckle and cheer with the best of them.

"Want a warmer seat, honey?" a blond with a gingery beard offers, patting his lap. I consider it (*touch me, please!!!*), then smile and shake my head no. I'm only on my second beer. It'd take a few more to get past the small coil of fear in my gut.

"You old horndog," Patches huffs, his face brown and wrinkled as a walnut. Vitiligo mottles his neck, his mouth, one of his ears, and a few of his fingers white as snow. "Little Maggie-girl is far too sweet for our scaly hides."

I'm really, *really* not. But I appreciate the sentiment enough to clink my bottle against his.

The doors open, and in saunter a coed gang of seven, all wearing BACA cuts — red on black, showcasing a white fist with their acronym tattooed upon its knuckles. On seeing them, everyone seated immediately stands. Bikers remove durags and helmets in respect and admiration. The BACA members wave in acknowledgement before placing their orders with Rosa.

Bikers Against Child Abuse are *amazing*. They travel the states to attend court cases where children have been mistreated. They sit squarely between the victims and their abusers, ensuring no minor is ever left alone with a threat. For kids who've been through hell, there's something so empowering about having a gang of beefy guardian angels on their side.

Patches, who is in the early stages of Parkinson's, can't stay standing for long. I offer him my hand as he carefully sits, watching in dismay as he wraps shaky arms around himself in a tight hug. Catching my worried look, he offers a reassuring smile.

"Getting old ain't for sissies, Maggie-girl," he informs me, voice the gravelly rasp of a lifelong smoker.

"Nope," I agree, sitting, letting him keep my hand. "That's why only tough nuts like you can hack it."

He laughs, swiping a thumb across my knuckles. "Amen. Hey — have *you* considered joining BACA?"

This startles me. I look again towards the bar where people have given up their best seats so the honored gang can stick together. A few wander off to the pool and foosball tables in the back. *"Me?"*

"Why not? It's a cause you believe in, *sí?* You've been flying solo too long. You needs a flock."

I *have* a flock, though I can't talk about my vigilante work with anyone, not even Patches. Who knows who might be listening? I change the subject, and grin when Riley brings me a third beer.

•••

I've used the unlit alley behind the bar to catch my breath at *least* a thousand times in the past. Occasionally you'll catch someone pissing or puking back here, or a couple making out as they wait for an Uber, but mostly it's just me and the garbage and the feral cats.

Going anywhere so secluded by myself while Vince is on the warpath is damn stupid, but I'm bordering on drunk — the guys kept supplying me with drinks — and sated from so much socializing and physical contact. I'm not thinking straight.

When I feel an arm loop around my waist, my blood freezes solid. My mind overflows with images of glowing green eyes; tongue piercings clicking against Cheshire-cat smiles; kisses full of poison and thick long tongues spiraling down suffocated throats.

I feel a man's weight crushing my chest; his hot breath bathing my mouth; the phantom touch of a knife to my cheek, tickling, teasing, waiting for me to wake...

"No!" I roar; a warrior's shout so raw it feels like it'll shred my throat. I stomp as hard as I can on his foot while driving my elbow into his gut, my brain too panicked to register that this man holding me is far too bulky to be lean, catlike Vince.

When he doubles over, I jam my fist between his legs and squeeze for all I'm worth, with every intent to burst and rip and destroy. The man sings a high C, crumpling in on himself.

I turn, intending to drop that motherfucker and kick him in the head with my combat boots until he stops moving forever, then halt in my tracks upon recognizing the brown eyes staring fearfully up at me.

"Mags..." Navier pleads, looking only a heartbeat away from vomiting all over himself. Tears bubble from his eyes, dripping between his white, wobbling lips. "*Merci...* Stop!"

...

It takes an ice pack and twenty minutes of curling in a ball, gagging, before Navier will even speak.

I chug water — gifted by a steely-eyed Rosa, who'd sprinted outside with half a dozen bikers when they heard my scream — like it's going out of style, attempting to sober up. I must have apologized a dozen times. When I say it again, he holds his palm up for silence.

"Enough." He doesn't sound like his usual self, but at least he's not crying and dry-heaving anymore.

"You know, Italians used to castrate little boys to halt larynx development for 18th century choirs," I babble, only slurring a little. I read that in some book or other. I'm always reading weird shit when I can't sleep. "Talk about sacrifice for art."

Navier doesn't laugh. If he doesn't want to hear my jokes, then I'm stuck asking questions. "What are you doing here?"

"Getting you."

"How'd you know where to find me?"

At this, he raises both eyebrows. "I *called* you and you told me. Your exact words were 'Come and get it, sexy Cajun.'"

I dimly recall answering my phone some time ago, but that entire conversation is a void in my memory. How far gone was I?

Navier seems to garner this from my expression. An uncomfortable look flits his face, and his mouth bunches to one side. "Cher..."

Oh, I know *that* tone. That's the 'Mags, you have a problem' tone. I don't want to hear it, especially from the self-titled king of Mardi Gras. "What did you want me for?" I interrupt.

"Ricket wants us. There's somethin' going down with the Jacobis."

That sobers me faster than the water. "Are they on the move?"

"Your guess is good as mine. C'mon. We've wasted enough time."

He climbs gingerly to his feet. He limps and I stumble through the alley and around the corner to the bar's parking lot.

Crown is waiting for us in the back of the shiny Tacoma Navier purchased shortly after Cero's death. It's his baby. He waxes it every weekend and vacuums the seats, considering every speck of dust his personal enemy. It's so tall and I'm so tipsy that Navier has to lift me in, though the effort makes him whimper from a fresh bout of testicular agony.

I catch him when he straightens, locking my arms around his neck and my legs around his waist, smashing my face into his shoulder. "Sorry, sorry, *so* sorry," I whisper.

He grunts, and I know I'm forgiven. "I know, sha. Do *not* puke in my truck or I will kill you. Slowly."

I snap him a sloppy salute and push my head out the window for most of the drive until I feel normal enough to sit back and pop breath mints.

Through all of this, Crown remains quiet, reading the comic in his lap with a clip-on booklight.

"Hey, superstar. How's Spidey doing?"

Crown cups his hands like he's begging for bread, then brings the flat of his left to his lips. 'Good.'

I hook my chin on his arm, looking at the colorful pages of web-slinging action. He turns them more slowly so I can read the speech bubbles alongside him, like we did as kids.

Crown doesn't make enough money in graphic design and freelance inking to live alone. He blatantly refuses to put out a roommate ad, and Ricket's episodes are a lot to handle. Clay and Rhys, though generous, are reluctant to extend their paradise to anyone long-term.

Navier was the only person left whom Crown could ask to live with. It seems to work out for them.

In the dark, I can barely make out the tattoos on my cousin's face. After he and Tip returned from their first competition in Australia (back when I was still training in the police academy), I'd hardly believed my eyes when I first saw the dramatic inks drawn on his skin.

Crown had, on his own, gone to New Zealand to reconnect with his Māori roots. With the help of the Ngāpuhi elder, he'd tracked down his birth mother's kin. I never got the full story, but apparently some Christian missionaries thought they were "rescuing" babies by kidnapping them and sending them to white American families, though the only place their "help" landed Crown was the foster system.

A deeply selfish part of me fears the day Crown will inevitably return to his family for good. I want to keep him for myself, even though he was wrongfully stolen. The ink he wears now, depicting fish scales for health and spirals for new beginnings, hooks for posterity and dog skins for courage... They remind me that someone else has a claim on my little cousin; more legitimate by far than the one I have.

Not so long ago, Vince tried to take him away forever. Though two of the six stab wounds had been superficial, the other four did some serious damage. One punctured Crown's left lung. He'd lost his entire gallbladder and a segment of large intestine. He'd barely survived. If he wants to leave us after all that, how can I blame him?

When Navier parks in Ricket's long driveway beside Clay's shiny, pocket-sized Lexus, I climb out and walk on my own without swaying or tripping even once. Navier is still limping.

Ricket's two-bedroom home is an older single-story with a low roofline. Like a slice of pie, it's wider at the base than the tip. It snuggles into the curve of the cul-de-sac, giving it a larger backyard than is typically seen in SoCal. In it, he's built a brick fire pit, a grill, and a play area for his service dog.

The tall, gray stone wall and strategically planted hazelnut trees that crown the yard lend an aura of privacy, making this one of our best meeting spots.

Hero the Jack Russell nyooms through the tall grass when I push open the back gate. I hold my arms open, and she bounds straight into them. I cringe and hold her at arm's length when her tongue attempts to invade my facial orifices. "Jeez, dog! At least buy a girl dinner before Frenching her nostrils."

I carry Hero to my gang seated 'round a crackling bonfire, fixing a smile on my face. Hopefully the fire's strong, distinctive scent will mask any bar-smells on me, but if they take note of my skimpy, leather-based outfit, there's nothing I can do. I'm an adult; I should be able to go barhopping whenever I feel like; but try telling *them* that! They've become such teetotalers lately...

"What happened to him?" Clay frowns at the tender way Navier eases himself into a lawn chair beside hers and Rhys's.

"I've met my match," he replies, trying to sound mysterious.

"Planned Parenthood offers inexpensive testing for venereal disease," Clay remarks innocently.

"Jane!" Rhys scolds, and Clay leans into her shoulder, badly hiding a giggle. Clay and Navier always bicker like siblings.

When I approach, Navier tugs on my belt until Hero and I stumble into his lap. He drags my head forcefully under his chin, somehow making the act of cuddling an aggressive one.

I huff in mock-irritation, then make myself comfortable against his chest, relaxing for real once Navier begins to stroke my hair with work-callused hands. Some people might object to their friends throwing them around, but according to a hokey online quiz we took for fun, "physical touch" is both mine and Navier's love language.

We share the lawn chair so Crown can have his own, distanced from both the group and the pit. Nobody is surprised when he spreads his Spiderman comic over his knees and resumes reading in the fire's warm, flickering light.

Look at Ricket, Not-Cero whispers.

I do, taking in the way my best friend is seated, his back hunched and his legs outstretched. If our circle of chairs were a dinner table, his place would be at the head, electric knife in hand to carve the Thanksgiving turkey. This is his party, but he doesn't look ready for celebration. His face has gone eerily blank as he gazes into the fire without actually seeing it.

As though also noticing this, Hero hops from my lap and hurries to her master, lapping at his hands, whining and squiggling until life returns to his bones, aborting his dissociative state before it can take root. All this excitement has distracted her from doing her job properly. She's a little behind schedule.

"Ricket, honey?" I venture, and the rest of the gang glances his way, too. "You doing okay?"

He lifts his dog. She squirms in his arms until she can press her head to his chest. He takes a deep breath and, using Hero's strength, pieces himself back together. When he meets my eyes, he is once more Calm Ricket; Calculating Ricket; Take-Over-the-World Ricket.

"No, dear, I'm not," he responds, tone almost as blank as his eyes had been. "I've looked deeper into the Jacobi situation, and found that they're moving faster than we're prepared for. If we don't do something, they're going to transport a haul of children far larger than anything we've ever dealt with before."

Chapter Eight – Tip
*the word 'platonic' derives from plato's belief that teachers
shouldn't bang their students. philosophers are boring like that.*

...

I'm just emailing in my calculus assignment when there comes
a knock at the front door. Assuming Magpie's forgotten her keys
again, I shuffle to unlock it before resuming my work.

The knock sounds again, more hesitant this time. Puzzled, I
stand once more to ease the door open properly, and am greeted by
a pudgy Japanese teenager dressed in a pink-striped uniform, her
smile a mess of wires and bands.

"Tip?" she asks, whistling around her braces.

Her smile falters when she takes in my shirtless state. Tessa insists that "mirrors are mere errors," but she never adds that the reflection in a stranger's eyes is the most brutal honesty you'll ever receive. I once graced magazine covers. Interviewers jokingly called
me Heath Ledger's long-lost twin.

Nowadays, I'm a half-emaciated burn victim. The way this little
candy cane takes a hasty step back fills my guts with ice.

"Did you want something?" I ask with more vitriol than necessary. "If you're a singing telegram or whatever, just don't and say
you did. I'll tell anyone who asks that you sang like a perfect little
canary; I promise."

I make to shut the door in her face, but she's already recovered
from the shock and is quick to catch it with her patent leather shoe.
"No!" she protests. "I'm here from Yakamoto Flowers." She produces a potted bouquet from behind her back. When I don't take
it right away she insists, "These are for you!"

It's a heavy terra-cotta pot full of dirt and weird blue and purple
bunches like big lollipops. Their scent, while pleasant, is dizzyingly
strong. Considering my sense of smell isn't what it should be after
decades of inhaling gritty substances, that's saying something.

"The hell are these?" I ask, dumbfounded.

"Hyacinths!" Candy Cane's lisp catches so hard on that one I'm lucky she doesn't drown me in spit. "We don't get a lot of orders for those, but he insisted!"

"Who?"

In response, she fishes an envelope from her apron pocket. "I can't stay," she apologizes when I take it. "Lotsa flowers to deliver. Bye, mister Tip."

She scampers into the parking lot, looking like a zebra sponsored by Pepto Bismol. I watch her hop into the back of an equally pink van, shake my head in bewilderment, and shut the door.

Carrying the flowers to the sink, I pluck the information sticker off the pot and follow all the instructions, dampening the soil with tap water and setting the whole thing on the windowsill. They look kind of nice up there, brightening our dingy apartment and masking the smell of dirty dishes.

Only then do I run my thumbnail under the seal of the square envelope. The card inside is plain, marked with only a crimson letter "J." The back reads, in near-calligraphic lettering:

Tip:

> I cannot apologize enough for my behavior yesterday. I caused you to feel unsafe in my company, and in so doing, broke your trust.

> If you ask not to be touched, it is vital that your wishes be respected. I was a terrible professor and a worse friend.

> I hope you can find it in your heart to forgive me.
> Yours humbly,
> J. Ricket

This day just keeps getting more bizarre. Is he doing this so I won't report him to the schoolboard? He needn't have bothered. And does he really think that we're friends? Sure, we've spent many a night emailing (arguing) back and forth about the latest news in nautical science, but...

I hide the card in one of my textbooks to prevent Magpie from finding it and getting nosy. If she asks, I'll tell her I bought the hyacinths. Let her assume it was a compulsion, if she wants.

What really gets me is this: nobody's ever sent me flowers before. Nobody has ever apologized to me for anything, either. I'm clearly not worth the effort. So what does this *mean?*

I try to distract myself with homework, which devolves into an idle browse of Facebook. Some people I used to surf with, back when surfing was just a hobby for me, are attending a beach party at dusk. I'm invited, presumably out of obligation.

When I can no longer bear the curiosity, I snatch up my phone and dial my professor.

James picks on the second ring, oddly out of breath. "Tip?"

For some stupid reason, I can't get the words out. I drown stupidly.

"Tip, are you alright? What's wrong?"

"James," I croak, my heart beating harder than necessary. The fuck is the matter with me?! I haven't felt this manic since my days of snorting lines off Vince's dashboard.

He says something to someone on his end before returning. "Is this an emergency, or is it acceptable if I call you back in ten minutes? I need to wrap something up."

For a wild moment, I wonder if he's in bed with someone. The thought is so out of left field I want to laugh, or maybe die. "It's not an emergency. I'll be here."

I hang up and return to my browsing. My leg bounces with repressed energy. When my phone rings — an alien sound, as I seldom get calls — I have to force myself not to snatch it up right away. No need to seem overeager.

"Excuse the wait," is what James says when I finally answer. "I was in PT."

Crown and I also had to do physical therapy after The Incident. Anti-contracture positioning and pressure therapy; massaging and moisturizing; all that which accompanies being Frankensteined into skin grown inside a vat.

"I didn't mean to interrupt."

"Not at all! I'm always happy to hear your voice. How has your day been?"

My day? I went to work; came home to find Magpie asleep, screaming loud enough to rattle the walls; held her down so she'd stop clawing at her own chest and face (she won't remember punching me repeatedly, which is fine); then passed out until about an hour ago. Such is the glamorous life I lead.

Instead of boring him by answering, I say, "I got your flowers."

"How do you feel about them?"

Are he and Tessa both alumni from the school of asking irrelevant questions?!

"I *feel* like you worry too much. I went overboard bitching you out because that's what I do. Don't take me so seriously."

He stays quiet for so long I feel an irritated urge to hang up on him.

"I care about you, Tip," he says, so softly that I feel it like a harpoon to the chest. I can't deal with that. I can barely process it. My throat threatens to close up, and my right palm sweats almost as badly as it did that day in his Jeep. I'm sure if the eccrine glands in my left hand hadn't been seared shut in the fire, they'd be doing the same.

"Meet me at the beach at seven," I say, voice creeping high. "There's a party."

I describe the exact location, then disconnect before he or I can say anything else.

•••

After Tessa helped me gain some control over my eating, my hair grew back darker, coarser, and wavier than it once was; closer to bronze than gold. I comb it out carefully, counting every stroke.

Clothes are more difficult. I wear very little at home, and at work I rely on my uniform. Most of what I used to dress in no longer fits. I tell myself I don't care, but I'm about to see people who know what I used to be. If someone says even one pitying word about my wasteland of a body, I'll snap and start throwing punches.

I end up stealing Magpie's turquoise t-shirt and some shorts I have to belt tight. I choose a white hiking sleeve, thin and cool and breathable, to protect my burned arm from the salty air. Then I don a pair of enormous, mirrored sunglasses. Forcing people to look at themselves instead of at me is one of my favorite forms of defense.

When the bus finally stops for me, I find it full. I stand holding the handrail and pretend I don't notice an elderly woman frowning at my stick-legs all the way to the beach.

By the time I find the party, roughly a hundred people have gathered at the shoreline by some rented cabins. Bikini-clad girls are deep in a game of sand volleyball. Further out to sea, I glimpse a handful of people on boards attempting to ride the waves.

They won't have any luck tonight; I feel it in my blood. The ocean can't settle. She's restless; in no mood to play with pesky humans. If she grows any more agitated, I'll know she's thirsty for blood.

I ache to be out with them anyway. Better drowning than dry.

Driftwood burns lilac from the potassium chloride it absorbs from the ocean. Burning it at all is illegal due to the toxicity, but I'll be damned if it isn't pretty. I don't know most of the people circled 'round said lilac bonfire. Some are dancing to the music. Most are seated on towels or lawn chairs, talking and drinking tepid, canned beer, or passing spliffs.

Pot was never my drug of choice. It makes people slow and heavy, when all I ever wanted was to soar. Besides; even an accidental contact high might show in my next test. I give the whole scene a wide berth, stopping only to kick my shoes off into the pile under the snack table.

"Is that who I think it is?" a boisterous voice booms, and I turn to see Haleigha, looking strong and bronze and larger than life. "Hey, Shark; what's going on?!"

I don't resist as he gathers me into a solid embrace, though he's far gentler now than I remember him being. Is he going easy on me? Last I saw him, we were wearing opposing sponsorship labels for the Quicksilver Pro Gold Course. It was an honor to come second to such a legend.

Haleigha doesn't comment on my radically changed appearance. He simply holds me, so I allow myself to be held. Something about the smooth, sun-warmed expanse of his bare chest reminds me of Crown.

"What brings you to the mainland?" I ask when he sets me down, speaking loudly to be heard over the "ironic" surfer rock vibrating the nearby wall of speakers. It's possible the racket and the stink of pot will lure a few bored cops, especially if they notice the tipsy minors; the abundance of non-white people; but I doubt it. This is California. Beach culture is just different that way.

"Haven't you heard?" he replies, voice carrying with little effort on his part. "I'm getting married!"

My jaw drops. "No! Who's the lucky lady?"

He grins, a white crescent moon rising in his dark face, and beckons a woman over from the snack table. She's a full head taller than I, and still he dwarfs her.

I shake Leilani's hand as her fiancé makes the introductions. She no doubt puzzles over how a washed-up husk like me could ever be referred to as a "true bastard of a shark," while I only wonder why the hell anyone would leave Maui to marry here.

They tell me the details of their wedding, then ask if I'll attend. I promise I'll try. I'm about to accompany them on a walk to the shoreline when two deeply tanned arms twine my neck from behind.

"Long time no see, lovvie," Kyle purrs in my ear, his tongue darting out to tap my lobe. I recognize his voice immediately, and feel a twinge of discomfort in my chest. He takes me by the shoulders and turns me around, plucking the sunglasses from my face to wear on his own. "I missed you. Missed those knockout eyes."

Kyle Aristarkhov is a wiry, slippery weasel of a man gracefully entering his seventies. A decade or so before I was born, he made quite a name for himself by selling top-tier boards; a hobby he continues to this day. Surfers fly in from all over the world to admire his wares. There's even a Netflix documentary he features heavily in.

He's got big hands and intensely blue eyes, and happens to possess the first circumcised penis I'd ever encountered, back when it was forced down my throat at the tender age of fifteen. I was pretty high at the time, but I still can't look at him without remembering the way he hooked his thumb in my mouth, stretching my jaw wide. *Watch the teeth, lovvie.*

I don't have to tell him I'm no longer open for business. He knows. He just doesn't give a fuck.

"Hey, you," I greet dryly, and allow myself to be dragged towards the bonfire and into a mini-reunion of familiar faces.

It's easier to do what Kyle wants than attempt to resist him. It's easier being around people who have no problem using me. At least I know what to expect from them.

I decline all offers of spliffs and pills and drinks; even water. No drink is safe when Kyle is around — and yes, I *do* speak from experience. When I catch him eyeing some teenager, a blazed little blonde who wandered out from the flock to sway by herself, I waste no time in heading her way. Kyle likes them towheaded and young.

Upon reaching her, I hook an arm around the kid's damp waist and fumble for her hand, tugging until she twirls with me. Her surprise very quickly melts into a childlike laugh as we dance, our bare feet spraying sand with every step.

"Your eyes match the ocean," she tells me earnestly, leaning so close that I smell the Corona on her breath. She hooks skinny arms around my neck and dips herself to gaze at the stars while I struggle not to drop her.

When I herd her closer to the fire and manage to shake her off, I leave her with a giggling pile of girls cuddled in someone's pool chair. There's safety in numbers.

Watching my efforts, Kyle laughs and toasts his drink my way, eyebrows arched. He silently mouths the words *"well played"* with an amused smirk twisting his thin lips. I turn away from him; from the party altogether.

The sun has set, bruising the sky a deep violet that the sea reflects as black. When I walk close enough for my heels to leave wet impressions in the sand, she wraps cool fingers around my ankles and tugs playfully. *Come here. Come home. Dylan...*

I want to. I want to enter her embrace until I'm neck-deep; until I can't keep my feet under me and have no choice but to swim out to her heart.

Her lover, the moon, glows pearlescent above, coaxing her into wildness. The sea is never more dangerous than at night. I know in my bones that if I gave into temptation, my body would never be found. Tonight, the two of them would devour me whole.

Magpie would never know what happened to me. She would never stop looking. I picture her, old and gray, walking the shorelines and calling my name.

It's this thought that has me pulling away, freeing myself from the sea's deadly whispers. Someday, she will have me, but that night is not tonight.

I glance over my shoulder at the party, startled to see just how far I'd walked from the glow of firelight. It feels like a pinprick in the distance; nothing but a purple firefly's spark.

I read once that humanity evolved into our current success *because* of domesticated fire; that the combination of extended REM sleep (uninterrupted by pyrophobic predators) and the meditative effect of gazing into flames changed the very workings of our brains.

We grew smarter, and then we took over the world. It's only natural that we're still mesmerized by flames today.

It's borderline inhuman, then, that my heart yearns only for the dark solitude of deep water, rather than the safety of fire; the company of others. Over a billion years ago, the first tetrapods left the sea, creating life on land as we know it. So what is this thing inside me longing only to return?

I've got to snap out of this strange mood. Where the hell is James, anyway? It has to be close to nine now. Did he ditch me? If so, I guess I can't *blame* him, but...

I pull my phone from my pocket to call him, and my professor answers on the first ring, like he'd been waiting for me. The dead cadence of his tone stops me cold. "Evening, Tip."

Like hell I'm dicking around with pleasantries when he sounds like *that!* "What's wrong?"

As though discussing the weather in Canada, he explains, "I have a difficult time walking on sand."

Oh, hell. "I am *such* an ass," I realize in great wonder. "James, I'm—"

"I'd prefer you not apologize, actually." His voice is still off, causing the hairs on my neck to prickle. Is he mad at me? What sorts of things does James do when he's mad?

The silence on the line grows, and still we don't hang up. "Where are you?" I ask at last, finding it easier to leave the sea when I have a clear destination in mind. "Gimme a sec to get my shoes. I'll find you."

...

I follow James's voice to a covered parking area. He spots me first, flashing his Jeep's brights twice to ensure he has my attention, then disconnects the call.

My feet crush gritty sand with every step. Sand that could so easily incapacitate the delicate joints and clasps of a brace until they ceased to function, trapping the wearer where they stood like the Tin Woodsman awaiting Dorothy Gale and her oil can.

James pops the locks on his Jeep for me, but otherwise doesn't react to my approach, staring only at his steering wheel. When I open the door and lever myself into the passenger seat, I see in the back a pair of crutches and two different canes, as though he'd hoped at least one tool would be the one to get him to the bonfire.

"Hey," I greet, guilt chewing my insides.

He nods. Says nothing.

Fuck.

"I'm glad you're here. I haven't seen most of those people since my accident, and it's... Things feel different now. The memories aren't all good ones." Not to mention I'd been contemplating sui-cide-by-ocean again; something I'd promised Vince I would never do.

This earns me a slight reaction. Life returns to James's eyes, and he glances at me. I've never seen him dressed so casually before; a loose white t-shirt that showcases his strong shoulders and excellent collarbones; the graceful column of his throat.

His black slacks are equally loose and light. Not beach appropriate, no, but I know why he wears them. It's the same reason I never leave the house without a hiking sleeve.

As always, his very presence is a balm to the ocean's madness in my soul. Despite the fight we'd had in this Jeep not two days prior, he makes me feel *safe*.

"Did you like the flowers?" James asks unexpectedly, and I look guiltily away from his throat, back up to his golden-brown eyes.

"Yes," I reply sincerely, a tad embarrassed to hear my voice crack. "I love them."

He nods, like my answer was what he'd hoped for; like that settles that.

Silence resumes; not uncomfortable, but oddly anticipatory all the same. I play with the threading in his Jeep's dark upholstery.

"Do you want to go somewhere else?" I ask, when the tension becomes too much to take. "I can buy you a coffee, or...?"

"I want to go home," he replies in full honesty.

"You could take me there, too," I say, and only when he looks sharply my way do I realize how that sounds; what it implies.

I swallow, but do not rescind my thoughtless offer. Instead I return his steady gaze and feel a fork of lightning streak inside me. My blood springs to life as it hasn't in years; buzzing and electric.

"Tip," he breathes, and in that moment it's clear as day: James Ricket likes me. Perhaps a lot. Perhaps for a long time now.

Closing the door, I turn to rest my good hand on his softly stubbled cheek; not much worse than when he'd touched my knee. Just another baby step towards a cliff, is all.

Where we connect, I feel the buzzing inside my awakened blood transfer to him, until we both hum beneath the skin. He does not move away; does not drop his eyes.

"Can I?" I ask, because nobody *ever* asks for my permission. Maybe because I wish someone would.

"This isn't wise," he murmurs; a warning, but not a dissuasion. I barely refrain from snorting. I could have told him *that* much.

I slide closer and nuzzle his soft, warm throat. Here, I can just hear the hitch in his breathing, the beating of his heart. I mouth my way across his salty skin and feel his gulp beneath my lips. "That doesn't answer my question, professor."

He exhales, long and slow. "Yes," he agrees, voice rich as the sea is dark.

I take my time trailing lips across his jaw, curling fingers in his coarse hair.

He reaches for me, then hesitates, no doubt recalling our fight. I take his hand and rest it on my thigh, granting permission. Though the location of the touch is the same, everything else has changed. Here, I am charged; alive. Here, I am in control.

He's got his eyes closed, allowing me to do as I like. I take a moment to appreciate this. To slide his glasses off and set them aside before climbing into his lap, my knees framing his hips in the cramped space of his seat. The steering wheel is a ring of ice against my spine.

I kiss the corner of his mouth and run my thumbs along his cheekbones, feeling the shape of his face; the structure of his skull. His long eyelashes flutter against my knuckles like the wings of moths.

When he groans, I kiss him properly, sampling the taste of his lips; trying his expression on for my own.

"Can we go to your house, James?" I ask again.

He blinks, fuzzy without his glasses, and nods.

Chapter Nine - Tip

...

"Surely I needn't tell you that a sexual relationship with your professor is ill-advised."

My therapist Tessa has the buggiest eyes I've ever seen. With her flat face and strong widow's peak, she reminds me of a barn owl. That, coupled with how young she is, makes it hard to take her seriously.

"I thought you'd be happy for me," I remark glibly, though I kind of knew she wouldn't be. "We use protection. It's consensual. Kind of a step up for me, isn't it?"

She crosses her skinny legs, an elbow on the lap-desk where she occasionally scribbles notes. Her windowless office is small; just one of many on this floor. It features a desk, her rolley-chair, my loveseat, and a potted, six-foot palm that may or may not be fake. (I'm interested in oceanography, not phytology.)

Tessa tries to make the space feel less industrial with watercolor paintings, sofa cushions, homeopathic crystals, and an electric kettle for tea, but nothing masks the gray flooring, stark white walls, and ominously thick door. For reasons unknown, management likes to keep the building in arctic conditions. I've never seen Tessa without her layers of scarves, sweaters, and gloves.

None of what James and I do is illegal, or even strictly against school policy (I checked to be sure), but if Tessa tells me not to see him and I disobey, that *might* qualify as violating parole. Though she's yet to fuck me over by tattling to my parole officer, there's nothing stopping her from doing so if ever the mood strikes. It's in my best interest to convince her that I'm harmless, even if I doubt it myself.

"How does James make you feel?"

I can't say, "He provides a good distraction" without triggering a lecture. But I can distill the sentiment. "James is... Refreshingly normal. He likes his family. He likes his job." And, apparently, he likes me. No accounting for taste, I guess. "He has a dog."

"Do you like dogs?"

"Normally, no. Land mammals aren't all that exciting. But this one is smart."

She makes a note. I'm sure my parole officer will be thrilled to hear my apathetic opinion on *Canis lupus familiaris*. It's probably a result of my bloodtype, or the position of the moon above the crackhouse I was born in.

God, I hate psychology.

When she's done writing, Tessa focuses her owl-eyed stare back on my face. I wonder whether complimenting the dark purple lipstick she's wearing is a normal thing to do, or if it'll make her send me back to the psychiatrist for new medication. I decide to keep my mouth shut.

"What do you and James do together?"

Despite my resolve, I can't contain the smirk that inches across my face. That's too good of an opening not to bring out my asshole tendencies. "Do you want a full account, or just the highlights?"

My therapist doesn't blush, but still rubs at her nose and mouth. I suspect she's embarrassed. "I wasn't referring to any bedroom activity, but if you care to share, I'm here to listen."

I'm sure she'd be more than interested to hear how a disabled trans man and a selectively touch-averse former prostitute bump uglies. She'd probably get an entire session from the fact that I've never before had sex while sober, or how a horrible part of me feels unsatisfied without a few grams to snort from James's truly excellent collarbones.

"Today we're going grocery shopping together. Don't get too excited; it's not a date. He's just going out of town for the weekend and wanted to see me first."

"You wouldn't say you're dating?"

My answer to this is immediate: "Hell no."

I see in Tessa's eyes how much she wants to poke and prod. Despite what she may think, it's not that I'm resistant to relationships. It's that Vince never gave two shits who I fucked. What do dogmen care if their pitties rut with the other hounds, so long as they still fight, still *win,* in the ring?

I can't tell Tessa any of that. She believes wholeheartedly in my lawyer's fine web of lies: that *I* started the Jaguar fire. That *I* stabbed Crown. Sometimes, even I wonder if I did it; if Vince's involvement, Vince's very *existence,* is only a figment of my disturbed imagination.

These doubts always lead me, a step at a time, towards complete mental devastation. I try and curb them when I can. I don't think Gran would like it much if *two* thirds of the kids she raised became screaming lunatics.

After all, I have no photos of the man. No records from the various schools the four of us — he, Crown, Magpie, and I — attended together. He's never made any social media accounts. Short of requesting a statement from his mother, which she would never provide, I've got no legal case in favor of my innocence.

Unrealistic as it sounds, Vince has a way of bending people to his will. If he asks for his files, the police hand them right over. If he demands "no photography," all cameras are pocketed. When he suggested the authority figures in our life should forget his face, well... I can see why so many believe him to be a lie I cooked up.

"I'm just worried the emotional toll of a relationship might trigger you into relapse," Tessa presses. "Your relationship with sex is very complicated, and far from healthy."

I snort. "I couldn't afford smack if I wanted to."

That's a lie. I could ransack the apartment for scrap. Rob Mags or James blind. Commit any number of crimes; auto theft, armed robbery... Heroin is remarkably cheap if one isn't picky whether it's cut with baby powder; whether or not it's "safe" to use. If I wanted it, I could get it.

My veins throb at the muscle memory of needles slipping beneath the surface. Vince was good to me. He always provided new, sharp ones for me to use. I never had to worry about bad product from him, either. In all his years as a dealer, there were no accidental deaths from his wares. Nothing to taint his reputation as best of the best.

In most cases, syringes can't be acquired without a prescription. Junkies share the ones they do manage to scrounge up, wearing the points down to dullness through repeated use and then hacking themselves open just to get that blunt tip inside a vein, any vein...

Not me. I was coddled. Kept. Protected.

Enabled, because an addict boyfriend is so much easier to control than a sober one.

"You look colorful." Tessa interrupts my rabbit-chasing by changing the subject, inclining her chin towards my high-tops; leggings; hoodie; all in various pastel prints.

"Mags calls me an arsenic cupcake," I reply without thinking. "I look sweet until someone takes a bite."

It worked better *before* I resembled those plastic skeletons people hang on their doors for Halloween, but I'm too set in my ways to change styles now.

To my surprise, Tessa laughs. She has a nice laugh; chesty and warm. "She sounds like a hoot."

"Yeah, she's a real laugh riot." My tone is sarcastic, but I feel a small grin forming on my face all the same. Tessa spots it, too.

"You soften when you talk about her; did you know that?"

I'm almost charmed, until I remember something Tessa suggested once: that I stabbed Crown out of some weird attempt to keep Magpie's affection for myself. My cousin had to testify in court that she was confident I would never harm her. I could see in my lawyer's face he didn't believe her. In his opinion, she was signing her death warrant by agreeing to live with me.

Outsiders never understand us. They don't know what it's like to grow up a trio of unwanted souls; worlds apart from traditional sibling relationships. There's a reason I never felt comfortable calling Mags my sister. People think we're so close it must be sexual; borderline incestuous, though we were never officially adopted. That I'm such a junkie piece of shit I probably groom my younger "cousins" for my own selfish use.

My smile falls, and I elect to switch off my emotions for the remainder of our session, passing the time on autopilot. What is my opinion on using anti-anxiety medication to treat my OCD? (Neutral.) Have my compulsions changed or worsened since our last session? (No.) Am I eating enough? (I'm not dead yet, am I?)

Then comes the part where she goes over what we've discussed (her summary of events is always leagues apart from my own, but I never correct her), and sometimes she assigns homework. Articles to read. Exercises to try.

Lastly, we set to scheduling our next appointment between her other patients and my work and school hours.

Today, though, Tessa shakes things up a little. With an apologetic grimace, she rolls her chair to her cluttered desk and digs around in a drawer. "Before you leave, your cousin hasn't emailed me your weekly report yet. I'm obligated to ask you for a test."

I'm not surprised. Magpie's been weirder than usual lately; more stuck in her head. She's not looking too great, either, with her eyes all puffy and her complexion gone to ashes. She slept solidly through the afternoon twice in a row without even one scream. Must be getting sick.

I take the plastic cup from Tessa's hand, leave her office, and make for the bathroom. Like any good dog, I always piss on command.

...

James and I drive to the open-air Fish & Farmer's Market for our not-a-date, deep in debate on the endangerment of basking sharks. In the cupholder between us, his thermos of coffee steams fragrantly while my iced water condensates.

I suggest, offhandedly, that perhaps Scotland's new conservation laws will help reverse the damage. James audibly snarls through his teeth. He launches into a rant about blocked coastlines and lip-servicing politicians until he catches my smirk.

"You're baiting me on purpose." His expression dries like a river in a drought. I have to turn away fast before I crack up, faking a cough when a laugh or two escapes. He's so goddamn cute it's not even fair.

He parks in the dirt lot behind the market, grumbling under his breath all the while. Grabbing our drinks, we depart. It occurs to me that it's good both James's bed and his vehicle are so high off the ground, making it easier for him to stand.

After fetching his cane, James comes 'round to my left side and offers his hand, like he knows me well enough to guess I'd never hold him with my burned hand.

(Don't get too mushy-gushy, genius. He probably just thinks the other one is gross.)

I switch the hand I'm carrying my water cup with in order to take his hand, realizing too late that at some point, my damaged fingers locked up without my noticing. I can't open my hand in time to wrap around the slippery cup, and end up dumping wet ice all over my high-tops.

Mortified by my own incompetence, my face flames.

"Oh..." James breathes, making to bend and grab the lid and straw from the dirt, but I move faster. I snatch them and the cup, tossing it all through the open Jeep window to land in my vacated seat.

"Pretend that didn't happen and I'll blow you later," I say, all in one quick breath. It's the first offer that comes to mind.

James's eyebrows raise. "That won't be necessary, Tip."

I whirl on him with teeth bared and fists clenched, my feet squishing ridiculously inside my sodden shoes. "If you don't want me, then why the *fuck* do you hang out with me?!"

Grand. Five minutes into this not-a-date and I've slipped into full-blown Douchebag Mode. My shouting earns curious glances from rich Californians parking their Teslas and grabbing their reusable bags from the back. As Magpie would say, "this is why you don't have any friends, Tip Van Winkle."

What would Tessa tell me to do here; take a deep breath? Count to ten? Remind myself that not everything is meant as an attack? I close my eyes and breathe until my heart is a little better padded from stings. When I open them again, James is watching me calmly.

I wonder if I'm meant to apologize. Sooner or later, he'll come to the realization that I'm a waste of time, but I'd sort of hoped this would last a little longer.

All he says is, "Tariq left some shoes in the trunk a while back. You can try them on and see if they fit."

I open my mouth, think better of it, and shut up to nod. Squelching my way to the trunk, I pop it and poke through empty boxes — presumably for groceries — a spare cane, a small dog carrier, and finally unearth a pair of worn old sneakers.

Tariq is a tall boy with appropriately sized feet, so these aren't a great fit, but anything is better than wet socks.

I think back to being a kid at the start of a school semester. Gran would drive us to an affluent neighborhood. The Goodwills there had a higher quality selection of wares than the ones in our neck of the woods. She'd held my ankle in one gnarled old hand, measuring my heel against her palm and then finding some shoes to fit.

I don't think about her often. We fought daily after I started turning tricks and shooting up, and hadn't spoken in years when she unexpectedly kicked the bucket... Though I still sent checks home every month after I made it big. *Someone* had to pay for Mags's academy training.

Unlike Mags, I never kept my sexuality a secret. I don't know if Gran hated it because of her strong religious convictions, or out of some sense of failure. She'd needed my money just as much as the kids, especially after the price of insulin multiplied outrageously, costing hundreds per vial; something not seen in any country but America. (Land of the free in-fucking-deed.)

In the time it takes me to tie up Tariq's laces (yet another process my burned fingers fights against), I feel blooming chagrin and regret for my outburst. I'm accustomed to partners who fight back; who up and hit me for lipping off. James doesn't react in any of the ways I'm used to, leaving me unbalanced and overheated.

I care about you, Tip.

I emerge, shame-faced, from the trunk, and find James waiting where I left him, playing with a lighter. His expression is neutral. I guess I did warn him that I bitch people out for no reason. He can't be *too* surprised.

"Can we start over?" I ask. I force a smile. He does not. But he does nod, and he once more extends his hand.

I take it, lacing our fingers together, and into the market we walk. It's less Renaissance-style and more Whole-Foods-Forgot-To-Construct-Any-Walls style. Twenty-somethings with colorful hair and bushy beards sample homebrewed hops, while faux-Bohemian grandmas in filmy, layered skirts sniff kale and scoop Mesquite flour. James might be the only non-white person in the entire damn crowd.

Whole fish lurk in troughs of ice, or hang dry on hooks. Vegetables I don't recognize are piled in barrels, attached at the tangled roots.

The prices have me raising my eyebrows. Trust California to make people bone their own fugu and shell their own cashews, then charge through the nose for the authentic chemical-burn experience. "Must be nice to be rich," I sigh in mock wistfulness.

"Oh, it is. I do so enjoy bathing in piles of gold, by dint of Scrooge McDuck. We teachers are just dripping in wealth, you see." His dry sarcasm is as much an olive branch as my snarking had been.

We approach the closest stand, which boasts jars of fair-trade honey, arranged just so to catch the sunlight in gooey amber waves. I bat my eyelashes and simper, "Are humble gutter-rats like myself invited to watch you dripping in your money-baths, highness?"

He sputters, cheeks flaming in that cute blush I love so much. "Aren't *you* fresh," he grumps, and that's all she wrote. I bury my face in his shoulder while I snicker. The honey vendor blinks in bemusement.

My professor takes my chin, prying me off his arm, and tries to look stern, which only makes my smile grow. Feeling puckish, I stand on tiptoe to steal a quick kiss; then a second, softer one. I taste the coffee on his lips; appreciate the rasp of his stubble.

His glasses knock into my face, which only sets off more giggles. I remember the last time we kissed heavily; the way his lenses fogged up the same way they do when he opens his dishwasher. My chest shakes with repressed wheezes.

"You are pure trouble," James murmurs, taking control of our third kiss by holding tight to my jaw, using it as punctuation for his statement. Something about the way he says the words sends warm, happy little bats swarming through my bloodstream.

He steps back when he notices people watching us; not gawking or mocking, but certainly interested. We're probably safe in this crowd of rainbow pins, patch-covered denim jackets, and combat boots, but he experienced more of the eighties than I did. He knows how quickly a mood can turn. We resume walking; shopping.

"So," I say, watching him peruse the cucumbers and daikon radishes. "Is this your thing? Food?"

"Food is a source of pleasure for me, yes." James puts his cucumbers in a canvas shopping bag he'd brought, paying with a swipe of his Debit card through the chip reader in the vendor's smartphone. "I use cooking to manage my depression. If I can make one nice thing for Hero and myself, I see it as a day not entirely lost to my disorder."

It's refreshing how he talks about these things without an ounce of shame. I know I'm far from the only sad person in the world, but it sure feels like it sometimes, what with people like Magpie hiding everything bad behind happy masks.

I watch him examine a pink, marbled selection of tuna belly, choosing a slab that, to my amateur eye, looks no different from the rest. The gloved vendor weighs it and wraps it in brown paper. James asks me, "Do you do the shopping for you and your cousin?"

Maybe it's because I'm in a better mood than usual that I answer truthfully. "I have to. She'd spend all the money on booze if I let her. I shop for her, and then try to find stuff I can eat with the rest of our EBT."

"Special diet?" he asks lightly, because he's had his hands up my shirt, and he's not stupid.

I have no allergies or food intolerances. I only have my own disorder to control. "I'm... picky," I say uncomfortably. "I don't want to talk about it." *Ever*.

He purchases amaebi and boiled octopus and fresh salmon. There's something pleasing about how tidy all the little brown packages are, stacked like Lego in his bags.

As I hold open a tiny bag for James to pour roasted sesame seeds into, I notice two middle-aged women approaching from the west. Even on the busy market path, they part the crowd with serenity, undisturbed.

One is alarmingly tall and blue-eyed, her hair a gray pixie-cut. The younger, a dainty black woman using a white cane, has long locs accessorized with golden beads.

They're striking in this crowd, and not only because of their gender nonconformity. Something about them just *glows* with power and confidence. When they notice us, the taller woman's eyes light up in a smile.

"Well, if it isn't Ricket!" she exclaims, guiding her partner our way and resting her hands on my professor's shoulders. She bends to press her lips to James's cheek.

"Oh! Hello, Jane," James blinks rapidly: a tic I've seen crop up whenever he's especially uncomfortable. Immediately on the defensive, I square my posture.

The other woman's cane sideswipes my borrowed sneakers. "Pardon me," she says, flashing perfect teeth in an apologetic smile. I notice that her sunglasses are delicate things, their gold stems made fashionable with textured butterfly etchings. She extends a manicured hand my way. "Rhys Gurira-Clay."

I'm in no mood for touching strangers. Normally I'd ignore the hand, but I'm reluctant to shame James in front of his friends. I give it the briefest shake possible. "Call me Tip."

Jane looks sharply at James. "You didn't tell us you had a *friend*." The way she says the word 'friend' carries volumes of implication.

"My *student* and I," James corrects, "are working on a project."

Oh, are we, now? How funny. Minutes earlier, I was "trouble" purred in a voice of silk, and now I'm just a student? And is it my imagination, or did James just take a step away from me?

Jane regards me without blinking, not at all abashed to scrutinize a stranger. I stare challengingly into those striking, ice-blue eyes until realization dawns. "Jane *Clay*?" I ask, incredulous. "As in, the *designer*?"

Her name is flashed with aplomb on catwalks. It came up a few times during last year's Met Gala. I recently saw the former model on an episode of the Ellen DeGeneres show.

Damn; I knew this place was fancy, but I didn't know it catered to the Beverly Hills crowd. Do they get a lot of celebs here, or are these two slumming it?

"So you've heard of me. How flattering." Jane shifts her shopping bags to plant a hand on one narrow hip. "One wonders, Ricket, who all knows of this relationship?"

"There *is* no relationship," James objects flatly. "And I'd love to chat, but I need to get this fish home."

Jane arches a dramatically painted eyebrow. "I see," she says with obvious disapproval. "Then I'll let you go. But come over early tonight, won't you? I'd love to catch up."

She touches James's chin as she leaves; the lightest brush of fingertips that looks almost maternal, though she can't be more than a few years his senior. Rhys gives me another million-dollar smile as she exits in a rustle of skirts. "Bye, boys."

I turn to glare at them over my shoulder, seeing how Rhys leans against her wife's side to whisper into her ear.

James is regarding me nervously, no doubt expecting an avalanche of questions. Perhaps he's worried I'm offended over his denial of a relationship. I consider it, consider fanning my earlier indignation over his 'student' comment, then let it go.

I was a teenager who sucked dick to cover the electricity bills when Gran's reduced SSI no longer cut the mustard. People are often ashamed to be seen in my company. So I'm just a casual fuck to him? So what. I knew that all along. It wasn't like I expected anything else.

His life ain't my fucking business, I remind myself. "You have interesting friends," I say, and leave it at that.

...

James is the only dog-owner I know who feeds his pet carrots and apples instead of biscuits — though, thankfully, her meals are still meat-centric. He'd never abuse an omnivore with a vegan diet.

For something to do, I sit on the living room floor and lead Hero through her repertoire of tricks: sit, stay, speak, roll over, beg. She munches the green beans straight from my palm and lets me stroke her cinnamon-colored ears with my fingertips. The pink, fur-free area on her lower tummy is freckled, so I count the spots while she licks my hair.

In his kitchen, James chops tofu and beats miso in a tiny pan with a tinier whisk. I should leave soon. If I stay too long, he'll feel obligated to offer me dinner, and then I'll have to think of an excuse to decline, which he won't believe, and then he'll smile in that blank way of his, and...

When he releases a sharp, coyote-like yip, I lurch to my feet and approach, watching him fold over the steel-topped island with a pained grimace. He lands on his elbows.

"What happened?" I ask, sounding far calmer than I feel as I stare at his back. My heart is giving fluttering, bruising little rabbit kicks beneath my breastbone.

"*Oh*," my professor grunts, pained. "Oh, my leg locked up again. My kneecap just flipped over... Can you bring me a chair?"

He'd gone into his bedroom to remove his brace when we first returned from shopping. He doesn't often wear it at home, insisting it's more of a hinderance than a boon. I didn't think *this* would be the consequence!

His kitchen and dining room are one big area, sharing the same tile floor. I have to step around him to reach the cherrywood table, snatching one of the four sturdy chairs that encircles it. The rungs make a cringe-inducing noise as I drag it towards the man.

Hearing his coyote-yip at close range when he tries to turn around makes the hair stand up on my arms; worse even than the scraping had been. "Stop!" I snap. "Just stop."

Taking his hips, I guide him back into his chair and help him sit. He uses his hands to haul his leg out before him, massaging the drum-tight strings of tendon surrounding his knee in quick, circular palpitations through the loose fabric of his slacks.

When the misshapen kneecap returns to its rightful place with an audible pop, he collapses in on himself, arms folded, face buried. I think there are tears in his eyes. Anything that can make the impassive James Ricket shake that way must hurt pretty damn bad.

I reach to turn the stove off before his soup can scald. "Is there anything you're supposed to do when this happens?" I ask. Sometimes when I'm anxious, I sound angry without meaning to. This is one of those times.

"I'd be most grateful if you'd bring me the Hydromorphone from my bathroom cabinet," he replies, voice muffled in his arms. "I didn't take my dose before we went out because I... I wanted to be in full possession of my faculties. I need it now."

This stops me in my tracks. Hydromorphone, the generic name for Dilaudid, is an insanely strong and highly addictive opiate. Baby junkies try and pretend they're not hooked on heroin by crushing and snorting those pills instead, but truth be told it's not all that much safer.

"You aren't supposed to dick around with doses like that," I accuse, actual anger replacing the anxiety in my voice. If anyone knows the long-term effects of opiate abuse, it's me. I didn't suffer through in-patient rehab *twice* just to stand by and watch someone else spiral. Living with Magpie's alcoholism is bad enough.

"Don't lecture me," James whispers. "Not right now. I... Later, alright?"

I struggle with my tongue for a moment, then snort my frustration and stalk into the hallway, stepping over Hero as she goes to her charge. We addicts sure have a way of finding one another.

There's only one bathroom in the house; a tidy little thing with grab bars drilled into the walls. There's also a plastic seat poked full of draining holes secured in the back of the shower, and multiple non-slip surfaces to make hygiene as safe as possible for a disabled man living alone.

There are a *lot* of little orange bottles lined up like soldiers in the cabinet. A dealer like Vince could turn an astounding profit from such a haul.

I'm proud of myself for being so unaffected by what I see, until my eyes land on a twenty-pack of fresh, new syringes, and then my knees go weak. Oh... *God...*

I understand immediately. The syringes are on the same little plastic shelf as his vials of testosterone, which James must self-administer daily by injecting his own thigh. I've never seen him do it, but I don't need to; it's not a difficult concept to grasp.

It's perfectly innocent, reasonable, and logical that James should have these things in his possession.

And it doesn't matter in the slightest, because I blink, and the pack is in my ruined hand while my good thumb pops the cap off the Hydromorphone. This is not a choice I am making. This stopped being a choice I could make or not make almost two decades prior.

At twenty-two, I was mainlining China White every three hours. It didn't matter that I was constantly vomiting until I threatened to rot the new teeth Vince bought me, or all the times I fucked up and nearly killed myself on accident — when I injected an artery and my arm puffed like the Michelin Man for a week straight, or the solid month my body was speckled scalp to soles with red Dalmatian-spots; the result of an all-over fungal infection carried by the drug.

It doesn't matter that whenever Vince felt mildly annoyed with me, all he had to do was deny me my drug, and suddenly I was begging his forgiveness and sobbing at his feet, willing to do anything for my fix. That I crawled around his blood-spattered bathroom for wads of discarded cotton to suck the dregs off of. I would've sold my cousins to the devil himself for an ounce of dope; for the sweet bite of a needle in my veins.

("Veins" being a relative term. After I collapsed all the tracks in my neck and armpits and between my toes, I had to inject directly into my wasted muscles.)

None of that matters, because I've got two pills on the counter, and a syringe right beside them. There's a blue candle ("Fresh Laundry," it's called) sitting on the back of the toilet, and a book of matches in a drawer. There's a bag of cotton balls under the sink.

I just need to grab a belt from James's closet, and a spoon from the kitchen. If James wants to stop me, he'll have to fight me. He'd better be prepared to win, because I'm not going down easy. My body quakes, vibrating with the all-consuming *need...*

I catch my crazed reflection in the bathroom mirror, my face flushed red; my eyes a turbulent storm-gray; my lips swollen and parted as I pant in a near-sexual frenzy.

Hanging on the wall behind my head, I notice a series of framed 5 x 7 photographs, all maritime in theme. In the first, a playful, pink Amazon river dolphin breaches the waves; the shape of its narrow, upturned beak distinctive in length.

The one beneath it features a submerged humpback whale, lumpy and serene as it drifts amidst slivers of ice.

But it's the third photograph that grabs me by the lungs and *twists.* The manatee so resembles Agwe that I'm not entirely convinced it *isn't* her; young and whole, with both chocolate-drop eyes boring accusingly into mine.

I promised I'd take care of her someday. I promised I'd finish school, and graduate, and take my degree to higher levels. I could become an expert; a specialist. A man to change the world for creatures like her.

Before there were drugs, there was a boy in love with the sea. I'm still that boy, even if I forget it sometimes. I don't have *time* for another relapse; I have work to do!

It sounds stupid. Shallow. The syringe, half out of its packaging, screams at me; a whistling shriek like a stovetop teakettle about to catch fire.

"Fuck," I whisper in pure, sick horror, realizing what I almost did. I stare at the mess I made on the counter. If there was any food in my stomach, I'd surely puke it up now.

I grab the open bottle I'd been sent to collect and leave the bathroom behind, shutting the door on my ghosts and screams, and all but sprinting to the light of the kitchen.

"Here," I say, and thrust the pills at James like the poison they are. "Never make me do that again."

James stares at me, confused, before horrified understanding dawns. "Oh, Tip..."

I look away from him, scowling at the far wall. My eyes sting. Despite my best efforts, a salty tear escapes to lick my jaw, followed by another, and another. I scrub my wet cheeks with my knuckles and pinch my lips tight to stop them from shaking.

James takes the glass of water I offer and swallows his pills. When I sink to the floor with my back to the island, Hero slinks into my lap and rests her little head on my chest. Under her warmth, my heart calms until I can breathe again. The tears take a little longer to stop.

James looks at me, and I look right back at him, runny nose and all. "What a pair we make," he laughs bitterly.

When I gently shift Hero off of me, she trots back to James. Apparently, even the trained service animal can't decide who needs her help the most.

I stand and remove my protective sleeve, setting it aside, then scrub my hands under too-hot water at the sink. "Do you have any latex gloves?" I ask.

He does. Right under the kitchen counter, in fact.

I make myself at home in James's kitchen, digging around all the cabinets and drawers. I unearth a cutting board, a large glass platter, and a knife block. From the refrigerator I pull out all the fish he purchased. "How do I do this?"

He blinks.

"How do I make nigiri?" I clarify, voice thick with congestion, and I can't tell if I'm snarling or pleading. I need something to do with my hands, or something bad *will* happen. "It's a big deal that you have a nice meal, right? And you're going off to your weirdo celebrity orgy all weekend, so you should eat first."

At his instruction, I fill two cups: one with rice vinegar, and one with ice water. I dip gloved fingers into each as I pat cool rice from the cooker into twenty-gram cakes. I slice the meat (against the grain, for texture) into perfect rectangles, smear one side with wasabi paste, and set them atop their base of rice.

"Do I *have* to add wasabi?" I ask as I work.

"No," James reassures.

The platter fills fast. Purple octopus and pink tuna and red salmon and striped shrimp, all wrapped in deep green nori and garnished with cucumber. I can't deny that the tidy packages are exceptionally pretty.

I re-heat the miso. I pour the saké. I set the table with two plates, cloth napkins, and matching chopsticks on little wooden blocks. When James sits, I sit, too.

I use the chopsticks in my undamaged hand to transfer four pieces of nigirizushi onto my plate; the ones I made *without* wasabi for glue.

They taste clean.

Chapter Ten – Magpie

...

I'd told Clay to keep a low profile for this run but, like her deceased boss, she has a taste for the finer things in life.

"Damn," I whisper, stalking around the upscale hotel room she booked for me. The carpet is so plush I feel myself sinking an inch with every step. "No wonder you and Clay got along so well."

A woman with class, Not-Cero agrees.

I suspect I'm being snubbed.

"Look, you," I snap, and pull open the closet doors, revealing a space larger than my entire bedroom at home. "Just because I run things different than you doesn't mean I'm doing it badly." We've doubled the yearly children rescued since I took over. More, if you factor in how we eliminate traffickers *entirely,* rather than encouraging them by meeting their demands.

Sure, we're only inconveniencing the wolves by picking off their coyotes one by one, but it's a legitimate strategy! Müller is continuously having to outsource for more traffickers every time his best and brightest wind up dead. The more we inconvenience him, the less time he has to harm actual children.

So what if I live in constant fear of his inevitable retaliation? At least I'm doing *something.*

Sounds a lot like suicide with extra steps. I never said you were doing a bad job; only that you're living in squalor. There's no reward for poverty, Miss Cop; only a hungry belly and a cold bed.

"There's more to life than money."

It sounds like a good argument, but in truth I'm psyching myself up to ask Clay for a loan. I might've been able to cover the upcoming month's rent on my own, but then the Jacobis made their move, and I had to take two consecutive nights off of work.

Just ask Tip to pay more this time, Not-Cero suggests.

The slash of panic I feel is a decades-old trauma I try hard to keep buried.

"He pays all that he can," I argue. If I told him we didn't have enough money, he might try and find *another* way to earn some. A way that will violates parole and may ends with him dead in a ditch, the bruises of some John's fingerprints wrapped around his throat.

An unrealistic fear? Perhaps. Still not a risk I'm willing to take. Tip has long since proven that he's willing to do any stupid thing to keep us afloat, no matter how much it kills him. He's such a god-damn martyr.

He'd kept me as sheltered as possible regarding how he put food on the table and gas in Gran's car, but I still remember the bruises on his face; the emptiness in his eyes. One recurring client had a penchant for extinguishing cigarettes on his arms. I can still see the scars in the right light.

You think you owe him, Not-Cero observes. *You think that if you love him enough, you can make up for what happened to him.*

I want to argue; to say that family should *always* help family, no matter what. But perhaps there's a grain of truth to my wife's words. My brain knows one person can't fix another. My heart hasn't quite received that memo.

Ricket enters our room then, bearing a bucket of ice from the cooler down the hall, and I end my conversation there. Arguing with the voices inside my head probably won't inspire confidence in my sanity or leadership prowess.

"Hey, Professor Nerd," I greet, noticing that he's limping quite heavily tonight. Did he strain his knee again?

He returns my smile. "Did you find the safe?"

His pupils are pinpricks in an expanse of brown; an effect that never fails to remind me of Tip, and I know he's been dipping into the heavy-duty meds again. Great! That's an encouraging sign from the getaway driver.

I know from past experience that suggesting Crown or Clay do the driving instead will send my proud friend into an ice-cold silent treatment, so I keep my mouth shut and just show him the metal box hidden in the back of our closet.

"Come here, then." He sets his bucket on the dresser. I approach, giving him my back.

He fishes the clasp of my necklace from under my jacket and releases it for me, then holds the jewlery up to admire it in the light of the double lamps. From the otherwise plain chain dangles both mine and Cero's wedding bands, spinning slowly.

My wife designed our rings herself, sketching dozens of ideas before paying a jeweler top-dollar to bring her vision to life. "No look is complete without purple" was a motto Cero lived by, and so the rings feature alternating chips of charoite and glossy onyx set in delicate, sterling-silver bands.

"Cero had an eye for design," Ricket recalls, and returns my necklace for me to tuck inside the safe. Tonight's itinerary is far too rough for precious stones. I'd like to leave *something* behind for Tip to hock if I don't survive the night.

"Have I ever told you how much I appreciate that you *talk* about Cero?" I ask. "Everyone else acts like they think mentioning her will send "poor, fragile Magpie" on another bender. How can I know I'm doing a good job if we don't discuss all the changes I've made as leader?"

Ricket shrugs. "I like the changes. I felt strange giving those monsters money and letting them walk free. It didn't feel like a victory."

I feel validated, but Not-Cero is pissed. *He could have told* me *he felt that way!*

I'm not surprised he didn't. James Ricket isn't the type to make a fuss. I don't always notice, because I often motor-mouth and dominate the conversation, but he tends to keep quiet about himself; his thoughts and feelings.

I finish programing a digital code into the safe and turn to wrap my arms around my friend, breathing in the calming, woodsy scent of his cologne. He's really nice to hug; strong and soft and solid. Just to be silly, I give him a doglike nuzzle until he stills my head with his palm.

He returns my hug, but seems somehow distant. Catching my frown, he forces his smile to return. "There's something I need to discuss with you, dear. It's about your cousin."

"Did your dog eat his homework?" I joke.

We jump at Navier's boisterous knock on the door that connects our room to his own. "Come on, you two! It's dinnertime."

...

Navier and I, our bellies tight with steak (and a shot or two of melonball, for courage), dress and prepare for action. We've secured our hair into buns, covered up with caps, and on my outer thighs I wear holsters for my selection of trench knives.

Crouched in the seatless back of a beige van with all of our equipment, we and Rhys test our comms with the other three members of our party and find no issues.

Navier bounces on his heels like the puppy he is. I'm not faring much better. It's my time to shine; to show why *I* am the leader of this pack. I don't have Clay's resources, Ricket's brains, or Navier's mass, but I *am* a leader, I *am* a hero, and I will *always* take the risks the others wouldn't dare.

To Ricket, the phrase "drive it like you stole it" means "obey traffic laws like the world's most nervous granny." The fake license plates Navier welded are convincing, but wouldn't hold up under scrutiny, so he does his best not to attract attention.

Even drugged, Ricket is the best getaway driver we could ask for. Our van is nondescript, windowless, and *huge*. In the late-night traffic of this arterial highway, we may as well be invisible.

Rhys, laptop in hand, listens to the audio-visual transcripts provided by her programming and updates Clay on our progress.

Fifteen minutes prior, Clay and Crown dressed in local police uniforms (sewn by Clay herself, who once heard someone say it was impossible to pirate clothes and endeavored to prove them wrong) and went out to set up "road closed" signs around the major exit the Jacobis are scheduled to take.

They now direct traffic away from our route with orange cones, stop signs, and stern glares. Of course, if any *actual* cops became suspicious of this behavior...

I swipe my tongue over my teeth, withholding a groan when I taste copper. Are my gums bleeding *again?* My body keeps acting weird, but I *really* don't have the time (or money) to see a doctor.

When we reach the drop-off — Rhys's radar clocking the Jacobi brothers at less than two miles off — Ricket coasts to the shoulder and hits a button to raise the back of the van, then climbs out and pretends to putter uselessly under the hood.

Navier lowers the ramp while I straddle the loaner bike from Clay, securing my helmet. Hell yeah, night-vision goggles.

"No real cops nearby," Rhys reassures us, multitasking with an ear on her laptop and the other on her wife. "Navier?"

"Oui, cher." He mounts the second bike and idles beside me, fiddling with the slotted headlight covers that help us avoid detection. If my Ninja is a mule, then these bikes are racing stallions: thin, long, and slinky. I trust them about as much as I would a kelpie suggesting a dip, but I let them feed me their murderous energy.

We wait, muscles shivering, in tense silence until we hear the gravel-rumbling approach of the Jacobi's eight-wheeler.

The information provided from the last weight station implies that there are no extra bodies on board — not always a safe bet, as children are often quite small, but at least we're reasonably sure we're not about to endanger a vehicle full of innocents.

It must be the same truck they use for their moving business. It's bigger than the average mobile home, and tall enough to crouch under...

And it comes just a hair shy of hitting Navier head-on when he speeds their way.

"Moron," I hear Ricket grouch through the comm, but I don't think I'm imagining the note of jealousy in his voice. I didn't know him before his accident, but if Cero is to be believed, he was once quite the daredevil.

The truck damn near tips sideways as the driver — bets are up for whether it's Cash or Cotton — slams the brakes. I wait a beat before flicking on my siren and flashing lights, giving chase. At least my former career gave me plenty of practice for this.

The Jacobis floor it off-road, driving into the desert as we'd hoped. They move with such a panic that it trips my warning bells. Why would white guys run from cops if they have nothing to hide?

"Y'all are sure they don't have any kids yet, right?" I ask, doing my best to stay on their tail and speak into the microphone inside my helmet at the same time.

"No kids, but they're armed," Navier answers. He's vanished like smoke in the night. "Watch out for—"

The first gunshot half-deafens me. Aside from my helmet and thick black clothing, I'm wearing no protective gear. All these blind spots make me nervous.

"Magpie, be careful!" Rhys fusses, so I kill the lights (a custom feature I'd specifically requested from Clay) and attempt to disappear as successfully as Navier had.

Away from the road, my only source of illumination comes from the headlights of the Jacobi's truck, which makes navigating the dips, ruts, and vegetation of the desert nigh impossible.

"Right," I decide when a swarm of tiny rocks pelt my helmet like hail, disturbed by my tires. We'd planned to chase them further from civilization, but desperate times, desperate measures, yada yada. "This is stupid. I'm gonna stop 'em early."

I unsheathe the knife strapped to the outside of my right calf as I catch up to the moving truck, tilting so sharply my left handlebar kisses dirt.

With a powerful thrust that starts at my elbow and ends at the wrist, I slash the frontmost left tire of the speeding vehicle. The spinning rubber steals the blade from my hand in a blast of compressed air. I'm forced to release it immediately or grind the bones in my wrist into sand.

I'm nearly beheaded when the Jacobis fishtail, but I duck underneath their truck and out the other side, just avoiding the back tires. Navier about murders my eardrums with his whooping and cackling. Evel Knievel, eat your heart out.

With speed unchecked, I envision my body limp as overcooked pasta and hope for the best, sustaining some truly wicked roadburn and what I suspect is a cactus to the ass when I fly, crash, and bounce, the vacated bike grinding sparks a few yards behind me.

If I hadn't been wearing such thick clothes, gauntlets, and boots, I'd be one raw pile of hamburger. Not for the first time, I'm grateful Navier crafted such thick, sturdy holsters for my knives.

"Owie," I grunt, scooting to the crashed bike and killing the engine once I'm certain I haven't broken any bones — a miracle, and God knows how many of those I'm going to get in my career. Sooner or later, this shit will get me killed. "Navier, do something before I get eaten by *el Chupacabra*."

He says something in Creole that, judging by his sly tone, is probably an innuendo. Clay's tired sigh confirms my suspicions.

A moment later, there's a burst of light as Navier flings a home-made explosive into the side of the van. He must've ducked and covered, because I hear his grunt a second before the earth-shaking BOOM lights up the night.

"When life won't provide a door, you just have to make one yourself," he says, sounding both winded and smug. "Come, sha."

"My butt hurts," I complain, crawling until I can stand and approach the smoking truck.

Navier meets me in the cloud of gunpowder and dust, crushing me to his chest. I feel his heart thundering a baseline of adrenaline, so I take his wrist and direct his palm to my sternum, letting him feel our pulses sync.

These are the things we live for: the risk; the chase; the victory. Had we been born hundreds of years prior, we'd probably be high-waymen. Or pirates.

Clay and Rhys would never understand this rush. This is only a means to an end for them; not a journey they relish. And it would only make Ricket feel left out, so we keep it a secret between us.

I lift my helmet's visor to bite Navier's arm hard, and he reaches in to yank a fistful of my hair with his gloved hand.

Thus grounded, we help one another crawl through the hot, jagged edges of the overturned vehicle.

As expected, Cash and Cotton are disoriented and sloppy, staring dazedly at the great gaping void of what was once their truck. Navier offers them a smarmy bow as he hefts me into the hot, twisted metal can.

Cotton Jacobi aims his handgun our way, but his flabby arm is shaking badly. I doubt his vision is much better. He is no threat to us.

Navier pulls a Glock from his belt and fires, casual as blowing out a candle. Though the recoil barely rocks him, the splatter of Cotton's splintered skull and liquid brains on the windshield (*through* the windshield, as it is evidently not bulletproof) make me jump, hands flying to protect my ringing ears.

It's a useless gesture, as my helmet prevents contact.

I gape wildly at Navier, though we can't see one another's expressions through our visors. We've never carried guns; not even when Cero was in charge. Guns, gunpowder, cartridge casings... That's all traceable evidence!

"What was that?!" Rhys sounds almost as freaked as I feel.

"Magpie!" Ricket barks. He must think one of us has been shot. It's a logical assumption. What Navier just did has never before been a factor in our operations.

I wet my lips and force the scratchy words out before Ricket tries to send backup. "He... *Navier* shot Cotton. Cotton's dead." Very, *very* dead. Being shot at point-blank range with a .44 Magnum doesn't leave much to send home to mama.

Clay hisses. Ricket sighs; perhaps in relief. Navier ignores them all.

"Etienne, what the *fuck* do you think you're doing?!" If Rhys is stressed enough to drop first names and F-bombs, this situation is dire indeed. A dull panic creeps around the edges of my shock, intensifying the ringing in my ears.

Navier looks to the seat where Cash Jacobi slumps beside the twitching, near-headless corpse of his brother. He's fishing for something in the footwell.

Some*one* in the footwell.

The child Cash hauls up is sluggish; barely coherent as he's thrown into Cash's lap.

He's a barefoot, starved-looking tween wearing a filthy green t-shirt and khaki shorts, showcasing the brown sticks of his legs and arms. I clock his age somewhere between nine and eleven years old. Judging by the size of his pupils, the Jacobi brothers roofied him out of his little mind.

There weren't supposed to be kids yet! Didn't we intervene before they made the pickup? Didn't we send anonymous tips to the *policía* re: the location of the meeting point?! Holy shit; all the racing and crashing and shooting could've killed him!

Cash wraps a hand around the kid's throat; a final defense for the damned. His voice is thick; phlegmy. Spittle runs down his jaw. He must've hit his head hard in the crash; the skin by his right eye is split, bleeding and bruising already.

"Stay back," he threatens, voice trembling, eyes crazed. "Stay back, or I'll snap his pretty neck."

The boy turns to me. With his floppy dark hair and enormous eyes, he looks so fragile in the monster's grip. "*Por favor, señora,*" he gasps.

This isn't fun anymore. Where's the adventure in a world where vile, money-hungry pigs like Cash Jacobi commit such atrocities; where they get away with it again and again?!

I look at this abused boy, and in him I see every child an adult's ever taken, hurt, *used*, simply because they could. I see Crown; Tip; Cero; Omar... And myself.

From the holster on my thigh, I draw my only remaining knife. "Say goodbye," I advise Cash.

...

When I sleep, I dream of the winter I tracked down Cero's mother.

It took all the resources I had to find hints of a female toddler kidnapped from an unspecified Russian city in the mid-80s. That the toddler had noticeable heterochromia narrowed things down, but only so much.

Eventually I hired a private investigator to supplement my search. It cost a fortune. Back then, we had a fortune to burn.

Saint Basil's Cathedral, once a place of worship, now a museum, is eye-catching in wild, candy-colored architecture and fraught with storied history. That particular New Year's Eve, coated in softly falling snow, surrounded by raucous partiers carrying their traditional candles, it was a breathtaking monument to behold.

"What if she doesn't like me?" Cero was irritable from uncertainty; jaw tight, breath leaving her nostrils in short white puffs. She'd looked like an angry little olive in her deep green coat, her cheeks hot and red. "I don't know how to be anyone's daughter!"

We'd wandered the streets of Moscow all afternoon, hoping to trigger memories; a sense of home. There were none to be found. It was as alien a city to her as it was to me, recognizable only from Google searches and history books. Funny — of all the places she'd traveled, of all the people she'd met, she'd never before come within a thousand miles of this city.

It hadn't before occurred to me she might not *want* to find the family her kidnappers stole her from. Had I made a mistake? How like me, charging into things without considering someone else's feelings.

"Sometimes..." I began, uncertain whether relating to the issue would comfort her, or if it sounded as though I was making everything all about me. "I wish I had more of a culture to connect to."

I was born in America and raised by an old white lady. I've spent my whole life in California. "I don't know how to be Indian. I'm afraid if I tried, everyone would think I'm doing it wrong. Making a mockery."

Cero stopped under a streetlight to regard me with those mismatched eyes of hers. It was hard to look at her arrogant expression and flashy wardrobe, her aura of absolute confidence, and imagine her as a child trussed in the holding bay of a cargo ship bound to America. The decade of abuse and hard labor that followed ate away any softness long before the bones of her skull finished fusing.

"You're no fake, Miss Cop," Cero reassured, reaching to tug a lock of hair escaping my winter hat. "You're the most genuine person I know."

If I said *that* didn't make my heart give a little kick, I'd be a lying fool.

Our relationship had evolved from one of bitter enemies to a boss/employee type thing, and then to outright friendship as she seduced me over to her side of the law. I saw immediate, *wonderful* results in her work. I seldom saw any results at all — much less favorable ones — within the police.

And anyway, who was she stealing from but the rich pigs who didn't deserve their wealth to begin with? Robin Hood had always been my favorite folktale.

As time pressed on, as I became more and more entrenched in her capers, I fell in love with the adventure and danger — and, by extension, Cero herself.

She knew it. She was always flustering me by stealing kisses, by saying sweet things and pulling me close, by sharing private jokes with me that even her loyal gang weren't in on.

I'd never slept better in my life than during those nights our scheming lasted until we fell into her feather-bed together, her arms 'round my waist, her cats carelessly stomping over us. "Mags," she'd whisper, and kiss my fingers, my cheeks, my chin. "My Mags."

That night in Moscow, when she brushed snowflakes from my eyelashes, it felt as if there was more truth in my words than ever: "I love you, baby. I'd do anything for you."

The holiday fireworks raged every color of the rainbow, bright as dragon's fire, as they signaled the death of one year and the birth of another. The Russians danced and cheered for each report, their joy infectious.

When Cero kissed me, it felt as though time had coalesced into a single drop; an instant of limerence with all the secrets of the world at last unveiled. "You really mean it, don't you?"

I'd nodded enthusiastically, dizzy and kiss-drunk.

"When this is over," she'd whispered into my ear, warming her frosty lips on my cheek. "When we get home, will you do me the honor of becoming my wife?"

•••

I wake knowing with awful certainty that something is Not Right. The digital light of the hotel's alarm clock reads 4:16 AM. When I roll onto my side, the formerly soft sheets feel crusty beneath my legs.

The whole world reeks of dirty pennies. I'm forcefully reminded of all the roadkill I've seen over the course of my career with the police. Roadkill and people, too. One terrible night I'd even had to haul a gore and glass-filled baby carrier off the interstate.

I'm positive I've had all manner of human bodily fluids spattered on my person at one point or another. Spinal fluid, stomach acid...

Don't think about that.

I listen to Ricket's calm, deep breathing in the next bed over to wrestle down a wave of panic. I don't want to know. I don't want to see. I want to go right back to sleep and pretend everything is fine.

Get it over with, Miss Cop, Not-Cero commands. *Show me what's wrong.*

Like Ricket, I'd barely managed to strip down before collapsing into bed. We'd both passed out within seconds of each other, topless and fatigued. Gritting my teeth, I switch on the bedside lamp and stare down at my body.

I look like a crime scene. The entire surface of the bed is drenched in my blood; a crimson-black tide at the center that fades to dry brown rings 'round the edges.

It saturates my legs, my waist, my hands. My boxers could not have been more soaked if I'd balled them up and dunked them whole into a bucket. I'd even left a smear on the chain of the lamp when I pulled it.

We might have some difficulty explaining to hotel management how I managed to destroy an entire comforter and mattress, because no amount of cold water will ever save this thing.

Back when I was under Vince's thumb, I'd had a birth control chip implanted in my left upper arm. I could hardly trust a rapist to don a condom before undressing my semi-conscious body, after all.

As a result, my periods became spotty to the point of nonexistence, and I haven't had one in several years. One less thing to deal with, right?

Planned Parenthood warned me that the chip had the potential to wander and become ineffective. Holding my left arm out, I run blood-crusted fingers up and down the skin, searching for the tell-tale lump.

It's exactly where it's meant to be. So much for that theory, then.

I stand, then crumple to the floor with a cry, arms tight around my abdomen. I feel (and hear) a flood of liquid spill out of me and onto the carpet. My muscles are shrieking Ave Maria from my motorcycle crash, not to mention loading the corpses of two large men into the van to burn. Damn, damn, *damn.* I should've stretched before sleeping.

Ricket, who's probably been awake since I turned the lamp on, sits up and reaches for his glasses. "Mags?"

"No, don't..." I eek a protest, but it's too late. Ricket turns his own lamp on and studies the bloody mess I've become, his curly hair a bird's nest haloing his head.

"Where are you bleeding from?" he asks, voice hoarse from our long night; from inhaling the smoke of our evidence-destroying bonfire.

"Um." I clear my throat and try to smile winningly up at him. It must not be convincing, because he doesn't smile back. "My vagina, I think?"

He nods slowly, taking this in. "Has this happened before?"

"No," I reply miserably. I've had painful periods in the past, sure — cramps and nausea and diarrhea and all the fun stuff that comes part and parcel with possessing a uterus. But to bleed *this* excessively in just a few hours' time?! Absolutely not.

"Maybe this is just..." I start, struggling to invent some benign explanation. I'm forced to give up when nothing comes to mind. Whatever's going on is bad news.

"It's been years since my last menstruation," Ricket interrupts, reaching for his brace. "But I *know* this isn't 'just' anything, dear. And so do you. I'm taking you to Urgent Care."

I balk at this. "You *know* I can't afford—"

Neither of us are morning people. Once asleep, we prefer to stay that way. It's understandable when he's a little short-tempered. "I can. Please don't argue with me."

"Fine," I harrumph, more relieved than I care to admit. "I'll tell Navier where we're going. And, um... Maybe I should shower first?"??

Chapter Eleven – Magpie

i guess I've had worse morning-afters.

...

Living outside the law has a number of unforeseen consequences, such as having to drive three hours straight for medical attention. We want no record of our presence in Nogales.

Navier told us about a little place just past the border where we can get my "ouchies" looked at. We load Ricket's Jeep and begin our journey with little fuss.

"How long have you felt sick?" Ricket asks, handing me a bottle of lukewarm water he'd fished from beneath my seat.

I close my eyes and rest my cheek against the cool window. "A week, maybe? I keep getting nosebleeds."

He hums sympathetically. When he slides an arm around my shoulders, I lean into his warm side. Ricket has a real talent for making people feel calm. It's probably why his students like him so much.

We make it back into the States, flashing border patrol our fake IDs without a hitch before he finds a gas station. He parks; leaves; returns with two large travel cups of coffee.

I pretend not to notice him hiding a new pack of Camels in his pocket, aware that cigarettes and smoking make me uncomfortable. Life's hard for everyone. Sometimes we have to hurt ourselves so we don't kill ourselves instead.

With caffeine zinging our veins, we perk up considerably. Ricket tunes the radio to some dull AM talkfest. The moment his attention is back on the road, I flick it over to the sugary pop I can seat-dance to.

He holds a dark glare until I grin and twist the dial again, finding a classic rock station we're both able to tolerate. Ricket's husky voice crooning along to Aerosmith's "Sweet Emotion" comes as quite a surprise.

"You have a nice voice," I compliment.

His grin is genuine, turning wicked at the corners. In the morning sunlight, I notice his dark stubble contains flecks of gray to match his sideburns. "I used to be the lead guitarist and backup vocalist of a cover band."

"*You*? No!"

"During and just after high school. We were called the Snot Whales."

A surprised laugh bursts from my chest. "For real?! Did you have long hair?"

"Not only was it long; it was also blue. And I had a cuff piercing here." He touches the cartilage of his right ear. "I made everyone call me 'Bone.'"

I laugh until I'm coughing. "Hidden depths, much?"

"Don't make fun of me. I was extremely cool." He says this with a tiny, self-deprecating smirk.

"Stop, stop!" I wheeze. "I'm gonna gush blood all over, and you *just* washed last week's bloodbath from the upholstery."

Ricket cringes. "Charming. Someday I'll bill you for dry-cleaning."

"Don't be so cold, *Bone.*"

"I'm going to regret telling you that, aren't I?"

"Oh, absolutely!"

I think fondly of my own nineties teenhood, when I'd doodled "tattoos" on my arms with sparkly gel pens, then hid them from Gran's hawk-eyes under oversized flannels. I'd hidden my first girlfriend from her, too. And the second.

"Were *you* ever musical?" Ricket asks.

"Me? Nah. I snuck out to concerts all the time, though. I was into the Riot Grrrl scene, but I don't have a musical bone in my body. I'm sure Tip would tell you *all* about being tortured by my shower sonatas."

Which reminds me...

"Didn't you say you had something to tell me?" I ask. "About Tip? Now would be a good time."

"It's *not* a good time, actually, because it will upset you," Ricket replies blandly. "And when you're upset, you do foolish things that may or may not irritate your vaginal issues. But I promise I *will* tell you soon."

Well, that's ominous.

Is he wrong about the 'foolish' part, though? Not-Cero quips.

"Oh, hush up," I grouch.

"Pardon?" Ricket quirks his head.

"Don't mind me. Just talking to the voices in my head."

...

Apparently when people say they're going to the doctor, what they really mean is that they're going to wait in a lobby for several millennia, chat with some techs, wait another era, and then — if they're very lucky — a doctor *might* stroll in for a few minutes before peacing out forever.

"They make the DMV look time-efficient," I whisper to Ricket, looking around the packed lobby. Some people came prepared to park it all day, with blankets and snacks and portable chargers.

It's kind of depressing. We're all paying out the ass for health-care; medical debt is destroying lives; and still we're barely taken care of. "Let's move to Canada."

"Welcome to my life," Ricket retorts, and then I feel bad for complaining. He's always got something medical going on.

Tip, Crown, and I always used to be healthy people, up until Tip started using. We were so damn poor that on the rare occasions we *did* get sick, Gran coaxed us back to health with the magic of Vicks VapoRub and Campbell's Double-Noodle. I thought she'd weep when I broke my arm skateboarding and she had to pay for an X-ray and cast.

Maybe Tip paid for it.

Not wanting to dwell on this thought, I try and engage Not-Cero in conversation, but she seems to have retreated to the depths of my brain.

I can guess why. She spent the final months of her life trapped in facilities like this. No way she wants to be stuck here now.

I consider pestering the surrounding patients with jokes and conversation — hell, maybe even a singalong; why not? — but knowing Ricket, he'd probably find that embarrassing. Instead, I kill my phone battery reading an eBook, then am left with nothing to do but pick through old magazines. Good to know "Highlights for Children" is still kicking.

I'm so relieved when a ginger nurse calls for me that I could kiss him. He's tall, quiet, doesn't look a day older than twenty-five, and hunches over his tablet in a way that screams *don't yell at me; I'll cry!*

Ricket and I approach the doors that lead deeper into the UC. My nurse guides me towards a scale and some wall-mounted pressure cuffs. "Your husband is welcome to wait in the lobby," he mumbles without meeting my eyes.

Ricket isn't rude enough to smirk, but still I catch a hint of amusement in his eyes; there and gone in a flash. The last time we were mistaken for a couple, he'd had to endure me calling him "Shnookums" and "Honeybuns" all day.

"James is my friend," I explain in the sugar-sweet voice I use around all professionals. "We aren't married."

Not that Ricket wouldn't be an amazing partner. He's doggedly loyal, exceptionally competent, and hot enough to turn heads. I'd be down to mess around if ever he felt so inclined, but as he is very gay and I am very female, it's just not written in our stars.

Besides; unlike me, I don't think Ricket does 'casual' very well. He cares too much about his partners.

"Right." The unconfident nurse fixes his stare on the tablet as though it will instruct him on how best to converse with stubborn queers of color. "Well, uh, Alexis, because of your symptoms—" he rattles off the same list of gripes I'd given the receptionist upon arrival "—we're going to, uh... Take some blood for testing and conduct a physical exam."

Though the nurse had wanted me to come alone, Ricket remains at my side while Nurse Ginger checks my vitals, even carrying my boots and backpack for me.

An elderly phlebotomist, the kind of sassy old lady who probably gives out full-sized candy bars on Halloween, takes my signature of consent and then draws several tubes of my blood. We crack a few jokes about my diminutive height as the vials are filled. It's over and done with refreshingly fast.

She instructs me to hold a cotton ball to the tiny puncture to staunch the bleeding, but the fluff saturates into uselessness within seconds. Frowning, she takes out a roll of medical tape and secures a fresh wad to the crook of my elbow.

Then the original nurse leads us to a bare-bones examining room.

"I'll step out while you put this on," he explains, holding up a flimsy paper apron with dangling straps.

I want to tell him not to bother; that I don't give a damn who sees me naked. Bodies are incredible tools, but they're still just slabs of fatty meat suspended on a calcium frame. It's not like my squishy bits are unique or mysterious; especially to those in the medical profession.

He's gone before I can say so. I roll my eyes and strip, sighing when I see that the crotch of my clean boxers is already stiff with blood, despite the tampon I'd purchased from a dispenser before leaving the hotel.

Ricket, seated in one of the chairs beside the examining table with his pilfered stack of magazines, hisses through his teeth. I turn to frown at him. "What?"

He gestures to my backside, and I catch my reflection in the steel leg of the table. My skin is marbled with red and purple bruises; a few so dark they're nearly black. I'd had the forethought to bandage the roadburn on my arms and neck, but hadn't paid much attention to my butt.

I shrug, then offer a grin as I lace up my gown, shifting from foot to foot as the tile floor chills me. "Bet you ten bucks they'll pull me aside and ask if you're hitting me, darling 'husband.' They always assumed Cero and I were beating the shit out of each other, too."

Ricket doesn't seem to find that as funny as I do. What's his deal? Cero stopped hitting me *long* before we ever hooked up, and the few violent encounters early on in our acquaintance were just the natural result of two enemies colliding. I hold no grudges.

When the nurse returns, I'm sat on the examining table, legs dangling. He grills me with all sorts of "fun" questions, ranging from how often I smoke (never) to whether I'm sexually active.

"Sadly, it's just me and old Thumper right now," I sigh tragically.

The nurse blinks, unsure whether to tap "yes" or "no" on his tablet.

"Thumper is my rabbit vibrator," I explain, and he blazes fantastically crimson.

"For *God's* sake, Magpie," Ricket sighs, pinching the bridge of his nose like he's staving off a headache. I flash him a naughty grin until the nurse recovers and resumes his interrogation. And I hadn't even *mentioned* Buzz, Woody, or Cocksworth!

"What about alcohol? How much do you drink?"

I hem and haw and finally provide an answer that *might* be low-balling it, if just a little. Ricket frowns.

Q&A session completed, the nurse taps my knees with a little hammer. He presses a popsicle stick to my tongue and shines a nifty light around inside my mouth, up my nose, and into my ears. This isn't exactly fun, but it's a far cry from boring.

He rubs circles on the sides of my throat with his fingertips. After I lay down flat, spine to tissue paper, he repeats the motion on my armpits. My tummy is tender when he palpitates my liver, but I tough it out and keep my mouth shut.

"May I check the lymph nodes in your groin?" he asks. I nod.

There's nothing but professional courtesy as his gloved fingers skirt my pubic mound through the crinkling paper apron, yet I feel a sudden flare of anxiety very much at odds with my usual confidence. Fuzzy flashbacks of Vince's hands, so black from tattoos he may as well have been wearing lace gloves, has my tummy churning knots.

I sit up, meaning to say this needs to stop (preferably before I puke down Nurse Ginger's scrubs), but he's already finished. "Did that hurt?" he asks, stripping off his gloves.

I can't recall anything from the past few seconds. *Had* it hurt? Must not've been too bad. I shake my head no.

He types into his tablet for a long time. "Okay," he declares, looking at a spot beyond my left shoulder instead of into my eyes. "You can get dressed now. Doctor Paar will be with you as soon as she can, okay?"

He's gone before I reply.

"I feel like that didn't warrant a costume change," I grumble, glad to be back in my trusty boots and jacket with mine and Cero's rings warming against my sternum.

I still feel the slimy ghost of unwanted hands cupping my nethers, so I leave the table and cuddle against Ricket's side, needing some good physical contact to scare away the bad. "What are you reading?"

He tolerates my pestering for as long as he's able, then unearths a charger from his pocket and points me to an outlet in the wall, just above a sink stocked with jars of cotton balls and Q-Tips.

It's cute the way Ricket thinks of activities to keep me occupied. Reminds me of Tip. I bet he and his big sister Dee had to watch over their baby siblings all the time as kids.

Once my phone has some life in it, I see I've missed a call from Antonina and repress a groan.

I feel for the woman. She had nobody when we found her; nothing but the one-woman jewelry repair business she runs out of her apartment. That, and her mini-shrine to Cero's late father.

She and Cero got on like a house on fire, so it truly is nothing but Sucksville that my wife had to get sick and die. But she drives me *crazy!* Can't she go clubbing with drug dealers or stab child traffickers in the kidneys or take up drinking like the rest of us do when we're depressed?

As I'm debating whether to return my mother-in-law's call, an incoming call fills my screen. My heart flips when I read Rosa's name in digital letters. I rush to answer so quickly that I nearly drop the phone. "Good morning!"

Ricket blinks up from his magazine at my enthusiasm, an eyebrow arched.

Rosa has no time for such pleasantries. "Have you done anything about that asshole yet?"

Right. Vince. "I haven't really had the time to."

Nor the motivation. I was kinda hoping he'd consider me sufficiently rattled after that whole Omar thing and piss off for another year or so.

My answer, I deduce by her silence, is not good enough. I feel a pool of shame in my gut. She's right. This is my responsibility, and

I've been shirking it. "I'll look for him," I vow, and mean it. "Are you and Omar safe? Do you need anything?"

Rosa snorts, sounding like a disgruntled unicorn. "Magpie, I didn't get to where I am today by letting creeps and crazies intimidate me. We're doing just fine."

"I know," I reply, angling my body so the suddenly nosy Ricket can't see my soft-eyed expression. "That's what I—" *That's what I like about you.*

I'm interrupted by the door swinging open, pushed by a heavyset, olive-skinned woman dressed in the same pastel scrubs as Nurse Ginger. Doctor Paar, presumably.

Like her minion, the doctor's attention is focused entirely on the tablet she carries.

"Alright, Alexis," she says without looking up. "I've got some bad news. Your white cell count is concerningly high—"

In my sudden panic, my voice becomes a mouse's squeak. "I have to go now, Rosa! I'll talk to you soon!"

I never thought I'd ever hang up on Rosa Santiago. This is a low moment indeed.

Dr. Paar is watching me with nervous hazel eyes. She's probably wondering if her badly timed words count as a breach of HIPAA confidentiality.

Crossing my legs, I fix her with a tight smile. "What were you saying?"

She clears her throat and regains a semblance of professionalism. "Your white bloodcell count is very high. That, combined with your other symptoms, could have many causes. To screen for anything serious, we're going to schedule you an appointment at the UCSF Medical Center for a bone marrow biopsy. Would this afternoon work for you?"

In that instant, the air in my lungs solidifies to ice. I feel the constant presence of Not-Cero stir. Ricket and I lock eyes and have a silent conversation that may as well be made of screams.

He speaks, because I cannot. "What will they be screening for?"

"Well," Dr. Paar says, trying to sound both optimistic and businesslike. "We can't know anything for certain until we get those results, but there is a small possibility we're seeing some early signs of leukemia."

Chapter Twelve – Magpie

...

My Kawasaki might be a reliable old mule, but it's one of the early Ninja line, and so it has its share of problems. The ABS cable has a tendency to wander in front of the brake line, for example, which is a tad concerning for riders who like to keep all their teeth.

I have the bike on cinder blocks in my apartment's parking space. Gran would call this trashy, but I have nowhere else to work, so I ignore her disapproval. I've already got one imaginary ghost in my head. I don't need her, too.

"What's cookin', good lookin'?" a passing David asks, loyal Zelda trotting at his side. Judging by the paper bag he carries, they've just been to the nearby bakery that, in addition to traditional fare, also sells treats for canine customers. And judging by the bounce in Zelda's step, she's quite pleased with this development.

"Oh, the usual." I use pliers to pluck at the cable, careful not to snap it as I coax it back to where it belongs. "Maintenance."

David sits beside me on the white concrete guardrail that keeps people from crashing into their own front doors. Usually I like his company, but today I'm too high strung to enjoy him breathing down my neck.

"What's that on your hip?" he asks, tugging Zelda away when she tries to investigate my toolbox.

I refrain from touching the bandage he's referring to, visible only because I'm wearing low-rise jeans while bending over my work. "Radioactive bug bite. What do you think of 'Magsquito' for my superhero name?"

He reaches into his paper bag, producing a banana-nut muffin. When he breaks off a piece and holds it out, I ward him off by showing him my oil-blackened hands. He persists, bringing the morsel to my lips like he wants to feed it to me.

"Can you knock it off?!" I bark, dropping my pliers and swatting his hand away. "*God*, David."

His irises are so pale that when he's startled, all the light reflecting off of them resembles tears. "Sorry," he mutters, dropping his gaze and scuffing his feet. "Do you want me to go?"

I sigh, already regretting my harshness. Yelling at David is like yelling at a newly hatched duckling. "I'm sorry. Sometimes you get pushy, and I'm in a shitty mood. I can't promise I won't snap again."

"I'm sorry I'm pushy," he concedes, dirty toes curling in his hemp sandals like they're hiding from me. "I just... I like you, wild child."

I know he does. I've been taking advantage of it so I have somewhere to go when the emptiness inside Tip threatens to suffocate me. Does it really take a cancer scare to give my moral compass a kick?

I roll my thoughts around as I close the guard protector of my Ninja and put my tools away, hoping I can speak honestly without sounding mean.

"David," I say, looking candidly at my neighbor. "I'm not attracted to you, and I never will be. You're way too young for me, and I don't date guys—" Sleep with them? Occasionally. Date them? Never. "— And I just don't see you like that."

He boggles at me, jaw dropped. As I watch, a faint pink stains his acne-scarred cheeks. "I..." he stutters, and works to regain his footing. "I already *knew* that, Mags. I just like being friends with you, y'know? I didn't *expect* anything out of it..."

If that's true, then I really am a jerk. I've had harmless, unreciprocated crushes on plenty of friends, and they never called me out on it. I'd've felt humiliated if they did.

"Sorry if that was too much. I just don't want you feeling mad that I'm 'friendzoning' you, or whatever the kids are saying these days. Are we cool?"

Zelda, uncomfortable at our tenseness, whines. We both reach to console her at the same moment, and my knuckles smear oil on his wrist. I wipe the mark away with my somewhat cleaner thumb.

"We're cool," David agrees. "If you're done raking me through the coals. Damn, Mags."

I give him an apologetic smile as I haul my bike upright and scoot the cinder blocks out of the parking space, using a damp cloth to wipe a streak of oil from the worn seat. It's as good as it's gonna get.

David pulls Zelda's biscuit from the paper bag and has her sit and shake his hand for it, then scratches her cropped ears, cooing praises while she munches.

"Is there someone else?" he asks, would-be casual. "Not that it matters. Just. Curious."

"Yes," I admit. "There's someone I like, but I don't think she feels the same way."

Realization dawns in David's eyes — likely an incorrect realization, but I feel no need to tell him I'm not a lesbian.

It's not that I'm ashamed of my bisexuality. Far from it! But people have all sorts of weird, judgmental ideas about what multiple gender attraction entails. Why is it my job to educate them when they have as much access to internet search engines as anyone else?

"She'd be nuts not to like you," he says earnestly; perhaps *too* earnestly, now that he assumes my lack of attraction hinges on his gender.

Sweet boy. There are plenty of reasons people may not like me. I'm irresponsible and immature; I talk a mile a minute; I don't process negative emotions in healthy ways; I use my days off to chase men into the desert and butcher them...

Set into the wall between apartment doors is a spigot meant to connect to a garden hose. I rinse my hands under it while David hovers, fishing for conversation.

"I'm gonna go play Skyrim," he decides. "Maybe smoke some grass. Wanna come? I'll make coconut curry..."

With the morning I've had, I sort of *do* want to join in, but I reluctantly shake my head no. "Can't. I've got errands to run before work. Raincheck?"

He shoots me with double finger-guns, like our tiff is already a thing of the distant past. "Pow! See you around, wild child."

As I watch him and Zelda cross the lot and take the clanking metal stairs two at a time, I can't help but wish more people in my life were so easy to please.

I step into my apartment and see a bespectacled, shirtless Tip typing away on our laptop, feet tucked under his thighs. He's basking in the golden light of the late-afternoon sun, which lends him an angelic glow.

Suddenly I see him as nineteen again, handsome and strong and smelling of the sea, squealing euphorically as his hug steamrolls the breath from my lungs.

His consistent wins in local, amateur surfing competitions caught the eye of some bigwig, and in a matter of weeks, the CEO of Pepsi was offering to sponsor his training for state if only he vowed to clean up his act — and his track marks — on their dime.

On a nostalgic whim I ask, "I'm gonna visit Gran. Keep me company?"

He's never joined me on this errand before, so it comes as a surprise when he looks up, considers, and nods.

...

Five minutes later, we're on the road to Inglewood Park Cemetery. My Ninja isn't built to bear two passengers, but Tip is good at riding bitch. He moves fluidly with me, comfortable and easy, never stiffening against my spine as we weave and dip and sway.

Perhaps it's because he's spent so much of his life riding waves, but he trusts me to carry him as much as he trusts his boards. The thought makes a warm glow spread from my chest to my fingertips, lending wings to match my tattoo. *I can keep Tip safe.*

After I park before a wrought-iron gate, he dismounts and offers a gentlemanly hand.

Taking it, I dip in a silly curtsey that makes my pelvis ache where the marrow was drawn. Missing my grimace, Tip bows as he removes his helmet.

"You're in a good mood today," I observe, and any need to confide about the biopsy dies on my tongue. I'd do anything to keep that smile on my cousin's face. If the results come back positive — which they won't! — *then* I'll tell him. Otherwise, why stir the pot?

No sense causing a fuss for nothing. After all, *Tip* hadn't told me when *he* was tested for HIV until he knew for certain he was clean.

You were furious at him for that, though. Remember? Not-Cero reminds me.

I brush the thought aside, beyond pleased when Tip keeps hold of my hand, swinging our clasped fingers between us with every step. Such affection is rare enough to be treasured.

I feel the 'I love you' rise in my throat, and lock my lips against it. Any little thing could change his mood, and I want to preserve this as long as possible. Still it flutters between my teeth like a living thing: *I love you! I love you! I have always loved you!*

We walk together through flat, grassy rows of white marble slabs; prisms of chewing gum trapped in an emerald blister pack.

Cemeteries remind me of church. They're quiet and clean. The few people we encounter on the winding paths are dressed in their best. They greet us with little more than respectful nods. Everyone's on good behavior here.

I see a fresh grave as we progress, marked with a vase of pink plastic flowers. There's a lamb etched into the headstone, and by subtracting the DOB from the DOD, I realize its occupant had to be under four years old when she passed.

The thought drops into my stomach like lead.

I react poorly to death. On losing Gran, I threw myself into stalking Cero and her gang long after other officers declared them untouchable, stealing police resources leagues above my paygrade to track their every move.

Getting caught with an investigator's work was, ultimately, what cost me my highway patrol job. I'm lucky it didn't get me arrested.

Then, after *Cero* died... Well. I gave myself over to Vince's revelry, didn't I? Nights at the club. Mornings in his bed. Days too high and sick to count the minutes until it begin anew.

How well am I going to handle my own death, now that I see the Grim Reaper's approach on the horizon?

"What's the matter with you?" Tip frowns at me. "Your face went all weird."

I try to shake the icky feelings off. "I think someone just walked over my grave," I joke, then wobble, my tongue drenched in copper. *My* grave. *I will be in a grave!*

"Whoa! Don't puke." Tip escorts me to a stone bench; one of many that lines the paths. "Head between your knees."

He rubs my shoulders as I focus on breathing. It takes a while for the bars compressing my lungs to loosen. I wait for Tip to get annoyed, to tell me to snap out of it, but he remains calm.

I think about how he used to care for me when we were kids. Math and gym class were a breeze for me, but anything related to writing or literature was a nightmare; something I didn't get the hang of until recent years.

Tip worked for *hours* with me, using flash cards and diagrams, drilling spelling words and vocab into my stubborn, resistant head. He got me through all my worst classes; my strictest instructors.

"She's not stupid," I recall him snarling at the much-hated Mr. Stevens, who'd damned me to detention day after day when I couldn't sit still in class. "She's just hyper. If you'd let her get up and move around sometimes, or at least stop taking away her Play-Doh..."

"I'll be okay," I tell Tip, sitting up. "It just got to me. All this—" I gesture to the sea of graves surrounding us, nauseous when the sheer, inescapable magnitude of death strikes me again, harder this time.

Tip looks around, the evening breeze running fingers through his blond waves. "I like it here," he says. "Everything's lined up nice, and the grass is all the same height, and there are never any weeds. You always know where to find who you're looking for, and if you don't, there's a map by the gate."

It's such a Tip way of thinking that I almost laugh. Instead, I drop my head to his bony shoulder, inhaling the bracing, astringent bite of his burn lotion.

"Do you want to go?" he asks, stiffening to signal he's approaching the limit of his tolerance. I never know how much touching is too much, as it varies day by day, but he puts up with me more than he does outsiders.

"Nah." I stretch, stand, and paste a cheery smile on my face that doesn't fool him for a second, if the Look he shoots me is anything to judge by. "It would piss Gran off if we bailed now. C'mon."

I find her quickly enough, having walked this path countless times since her death.

"Oh!" I exclaim, looking at the bouquet of red roses obscuring her headstone. They're fresh, and very fragrant. "Crown must've come on his own."

But why would he spend so much money on this frivolous offering? Roses aren't cheap. It's not Gran's birthday, and while he's better off than we are, it still seems unlike our practical-minded cousin.

Kneeling, I lift the bouquet and pass it up Tip, the velvety aroma tickling my nose. The plastic cover crinkles as it changes hands.

Tip is correct about the cemetery grass being kept uniform, but sometimes the weekend mowers knock dirt or clippings onto the stones. Gran was such a tidy woman that I feel obligated to clean whenever I'm here.

Using the baby wipes I'd brought, I scrub the thing until the etched words shine wet and glossy in the setting sun. "Ethel Burbage." A name as fussy and old-fashioned as the woman buried beneath it. Just tracing the letters brings me back to the childish scents of peanut butter, Elmer's glue, and Crayola crayons.

Once upon a time, there were two boys and a girl who'd been kicked around the system so much we'd long since given up on a permanent home. Until we found ourselves placed in the care of an elderly foster mother, anyway.

It was an unorthodox choice for the state of California to make, and sure to be temporary. She had next to no money and could scarcely handle a houseplant, let alone a trio of abused problem-children too jaded to be cute.

Gran was pious and strict, forcing us three to church every Sunday and in bed by eight every night, but she fed us three times a day and ran our baths with bubbles and pressed firm kisses to ours scalps at least once every morning. She never hit us or raised her voice, even when we probably deserved it.

For better or for worse, she tried to do right by us. No other adult could say the same.

"Miss you, Gran," I tell the headstone, putting my cleaning supplies away. I reach behind my back for Crown's roses, but Tip doesn't give them to me. I turn to look at him, curling my fingers in a 'gimmie' gesture.

My cousin stands tense, unmoving. His eyes, now a shade of dusky violet I can't say I care for, are glued to the bouquet's thorny stems like he's trying to immolate them by sheer force of will.

I climb to my feet, craning my neck to see what has him so stuck.

From this improved angle, I notice a note tucked into the bouquet, written on a torn scrap of white stationary. I push at Tip's arm until he lowers it for me to see.

"I can send flowers too, Surfer-Boy," reads the note in Vince's spiked handwriting.

Chapter Thirteen – Tip

maybe it's a good thing i never had a mom.

…

"No!" Magpie barks, voice cracking. She grabs for the roses, but I shove her back, elbow locked, palm to collarbone.

"He came back for me," I whisper, my heart punching my ribs. Still holding Mags off, I fish the note from the plastic and flip it over, hoping for more. There's nothing but a Motel 6 logo.

Magpie uses the gap in our heights to duck under my arm. Taking my cheeks between her callused hands, she steals a moment of my attention. "Tip, *look* at me!"

I don't want to look at her. I want to scour the property until I find my boyfriend. I'll decide whether to murder or marry him once he's back in my arms.

Unfortunately for me, ignoring my cousin's fear is no easy task. I meet her dark eyes against my will.

"This is bad," Magpie intones, still holding my face. She speaks quickly, all too aware that I'm already half gone. "I *need* you to understand that. Vince hurts people. He hurt Crown. He hurt you! Don't go looking for him, Tipples; let *me* take care of it."

She strokes my cheekbone with her thumb, forcing a smile that's painful to witness.

My boyfriend assaulted both of my cousins; two in one day, likely with the same knife. I'll never know if his intent was to kill, or only to maim. I like to think it was the latter. That he was only sending a message, rather than declaring war.

That's what I tell myself, anyway.

Regardless, the truth is this: I am an addict, and Vince is my drug of choice. I've undergone withdrawals for the full two years of his absence, so constant that it's a background drone to my every waking moment.

By contacting me like this, he's brought it all bubbling to the surface. I am no more in control now than I was when I saw the syringes in James's cabinet. I want nothing more than to saturate myself with his poison.

"Tip, *please*," Magpie begs, voice thick with emotion. Her hands drop from my face to grip my arms, giving me a shake. She's stronger than me, and trained in combat. If she really wanted to take me on, I'd be no match for her.

I don't think she'd ever really fight me, but I'm barraged with intrusive thoughts of the horrors I've inflicted on others, applied in graphic detail to my cousin. I could break her face; gouge her eyes; rip out her throat with my teeth.

I could hurt her, and I would feel nothing doing so. I'm too good at turning my heart off when the going gets rough.

"Don't do this to me," she whispers, teeth grit, entire body shaking with the force of her conviction. "Don't you dare, Dylan Anthony Tippling. For once in your *goddamn* life, choose me first."

I realize I'm holding her cheek with my burned hand, four shriveled fingers lined along her scar. She has a hand on my wrist as she glares up at me. Her eyes are an infinity of brown; so dark I can hardly make out her pupils in this dusk light.

"I think," I tell her, our foreheads brushing as we stand before Gran's grave. "That *you* think I'm a better person than I really am. Give it up. I am only ever going to disappoint you."

It would be in everyone's best interest if she dumped my sorry, addicted ass. If she let me crawl back into the sewer I came from. Men like me aren't meant to last.

Her scowl intensifies, as does her grip. She squeezes hard enough to hurt; so hard that I hear the creak of my bones under her fingers. "I refuse to believe that," she snarls, fierce as any storm.

...

Trusting an addict is damn stupid. Magpie knows that.

She also knows she has no other choice. We desperately need money.

"You'll go to school, right?" she asks for the umpteenth time, changing into her work clothes. "I can drive you. Nobody will care if I'm late."

I force a tolerant smile onto my face. "Mags, if I hovered this much every time one of *your* exes was in town, we'd never get anything done."

I tell myself I'll eat tonight, but it's a lie. I don't need to eat. I'm clean, inside and out. Food would dirty me up and slow me down.

I think of *Turritopsis dohrnii*; a subset of jellyfish found in the Mediterranean sea. They're rendered biologically immortal by reverting into a polyp on an endless loop. So long as nothing eats them, there is no limit to their lifespan.

I wish I could be like that, living forever on sunlight, born anew until the stars burn out. Imagining such a clean, empty existence lulls me into a dreamlike state.

Eventually, Magpie leans over me, smelling faintly of the men's cologne she favors. Her silken hair tickles my neck. "We'll hang out soon, okay?" she asks. "Maybe after I get paid, we'll catch a movie at the dollar theater."

Perhaps nobody else could guess how nervous she is, but we've known each other for most of our lives. I've packed her lunches and stolen tampons for her. I've hauled her drunk ass off the floor more times than I can count. I know the good, the bad, and the ugly of Alexis Marya Magpie.

"Sure," I agree, voice smooth as a shark in icy waters. "That sounds fun."

Sometimes I think she doesn't realize how codependent we are. Codependency is common for kids who grew up in situations like ours — it's "us against the world" taken to the logical extreme. It can lead to isolation, obsession, and abuse. But it sure explains why she continues to trust me, even when all evidence points to the contrary.

She kisses my forehead. I touch her cheek, pressing a thumb into her dimple. Her smile contains enough sunshine to twang a guilty cord in my chest.

I listen to her leave, to the throaty growl of her bike fading around the corner, before rubbing my tired eyes. Every part of me is achy and drained. Food would probably help, but I'm stronger than such base needs. I'm. In. Control.

When I go, my bus takes me further and further north, leaving the sea behind. Crowded apartment duplexes become cookie-cutter houses as we breach the suburbs. Spotting a familiar, crook-backed tree on a darkened corner is my cue to tug the pull-cord.

The bus coasts to a curbside stop. If I'd stayed on for another few blocks, watching the houses morph from white to blue collar, then to Section 8 housing, I'd've reached Gran's old place.

My walk to a single-story brown-brick is a touch surreal. How many times have my feet travelled this path? Sometimes I limped along, pained everywhere below the waist. Other times I was so high I scarcely registered the pavement beneath my shoes. Regardless, this is such well-trod ground that I walk it in my dreams.

There's a statewide water restriction in place, so I'm not too surprised to see the house's lawn is yellow and dry. Sun-bleached garden gnomes judge me with chipped blue eyes as I climb the stoop, surpass the porch swing, and ring the doorbell.

The house is dark. It's too late in the night for visitors in these respectable neighborhoods. When a front-facing bedroom light snaps on in a spill of butter-yellow, I smile bitterly. It was just like this back in the old days, too.

I hear the hastened patter of footsteps before the door is flung open. A woman dressed in a feathery pink chemise, the material sheer enough to see her dark nipples through, gawks up at me, crestfallen that I'm not who she'd hoped for. Then recognition strikes.

"Tip!" she gasps like a vaudeville starlet, and flings herself into my arms.

"Hey, Eva," I greet Vince's mother, my chin atop her honey-blonde hair. She squeezes me, muffling squeaky kitten-mewls in my chest. "Thanks for answering the door. I know it's late."

She pulls back, her pudgy hands warm on my cheeks, and studies me with Vince's eerie green eyes. Her golden skin holds a few more wrinkles and freckles than I remember, but otherwise she's the same: Rubenesque and warm and smelling of cloves.

Also the same, I see when I'm drawn inside, is her house. Same bluebell-patterned wallpaper. Same overcrowded shelves of porcelain dolls and thrifted music boxes. Floors lined with braided rugs to match the cushy furniture. Even this late at night, the house is stiflingly warm.

Everything is draped with mismatched throw blankets and crocheted doilies. Even the hanging Thomas Kinkade calendar is the same; nearly two decades old and still open to December, with Vince's twenty-first birthday circled in blue ink.

The potpourri scent every cushion emits transports me back to my teenaged skin; bruised and dripping from every orifice; hoping for a shower and a pill or a bump (depending on whether we had school later) before I crept back to Gran's.

My feet want to head down the photograph-lined hallway; to take the second door on the left and slip into Vince's bed.

He always looked like an angel when he slept, bow-shaped lips pursed and pink, eyelids fluttering. My sleeping beauty, so clean and soft after my nights of filth. I'd cling to his side and kiss him awake, nudging and coaxing and warming. *Don't you have anything for me, Vincey? Something in your magic bag to make the night a little sweeter?*

"Can I fix you some tea?" Eva asks, snapping me back to the present.

I accept, not because I want any, but because I know she'll fuss until I allow her to play hostess. I approach her kitchen and sit at one of the counter's barstools, the hand-embroidered seat cushion a relief to my bony ass.

Eva pulls tea bags from a cedar box on her counter, holding up the options for my inspection. "Peppermint? Oolong? Earl Grey?"

"Whatever you're having."

Twin satchels of chamomile enter two empty mugs. She fills the ceramic kettle at the sink, sets it on the stove, and busies herself assembling ginger cookies on a plate. Her fluttering, French-manicured hands are hypnotizing to watch.

Finally, Eva has nothing else to focus on but me. "How are you, sweet boy?" she asks, eyes wide. She's too polite to say what she's really thinking — *wow; you look like shit, Tip!* — but that's what her words translate to in Eva-speak.

I won't let her bait me into a consult of woes. "Better than I could be. Have you heard from Vince?"

It's like I said something obscene. She flinches and nearly drops her mugs, quickly setting them down before gawking at me. That name holds weight in these walls.

"Well *no*, dear," she sputters. "I haven't heard a peep from my baby since he, ah, stepped away."

I know for a fact that isn't true. Though Vince cut his mom off as soon as he was able, I might be the only person alive who knows that he still calls her from payphones. He says nothing. He just likes to hear her hopeful little "*Hello?*" before he hangs up again — sometimes up to three or four times a night.

The one time I asked him about this strange habit of his, he hit me so hard my face swelled over the edge of my glasses. I had a beast of a time taking them off again.

Still, I don't think Eva's lying. If Vince *had* so much as sent a 'happy mother's day' card, I'm sure she'd be shoving it in my face, twittering her joy. Instead, she's avoiding my eyes, saddened over her lack of news.

My compulsion to see Vince's room flares overwhelmingly. It rolls through me, consuming my thoughts. I have mental exercises I'm supposed to practice when the OCD overrides my ability to reason, but I don't want to fuss with them.

I don't care that it's rude. I cave in and stand, hustling through the hallway. The doorknob feels exactly the way it should in my palm, but when I push the door open, my brain balks at the wrongness of the smell. *Not this room! The real one! Get it right!*

But it *is* the right room. There is no other, save for the bathroom and Eva's own bedroom further down the hall. It's just not how I remember, is all. It smells like Eva's cloves, rather than Vince's musk and smoke.

I reach to tap the touch-activated lamp, and my balking brain is soothed by the sight of everything as it should be; a time capsule of a nineties teenhood with navy-blue walls, beige window treatments, and polished wood floors.

The full-sized bed is made up with two pillows and a Lakers throw. As far as I'm aware, Vince was never interested in sports, yet that purple blanket is as familiar as the moon in the sky.

There's a hutch desk crammed to one side, making room for a now empty, wall-sized display terrarium where Dorothy, Vince's Brazilian rainbow boa, once lived.

He got her as a little kid. He has her still. She's the only thing he's ever put any effort into caring for.

It doesn't surprise me that the space is neat as a picture in a magazine. Though Vince himself is sloppy, Eva tidied up after him daily. Hell, I'm not even surprised when I tug the corner of the fuzzy blanket back to find the sheets crisp and clean. She probably still washes them every week, just in case.

I drop to my knees on the *rug* — hello, déjà vu — and pat around under the bed. Eva is ruthless in her war against dust bunnies. I find no magical duffel bag. My hand brushes *something,* though, so I drag it out.

It's a shoebox. Checking the label, I see that it's for children's sneakers, size six. It's decorated with a few Ninja Turtle stickers, and some Crayola doodles of various snakes.

Easing the lid off, I see several of Dorothy's skins on top. Vince only ever kept the whole ones, and complained that the snake often struggled to shed properly, no matter how careful he was to perfect the temperature and humidity of her environment.

Some of these skins are quite small, from her juvenile years before I met the pair. I pick them all out and set them aside, careful not to crush the delicate membranes.

The only other things inside the box are a handful of greeting cards, still in their torn envelopes. I spread them out on the rug. There are six total: birthday cards all addressed from someone named Irving Roth.

I flick open the one postmarked December 1986 and read the perfunctory, handwritten message. *Enjoy your birthday. Here is some money. Obey your mother. Take care of Dorothy. Love from Da.*

Well, shit.

I hurriedly put the cards and skins away, half-fearing that Vince might appear and see me looking at these forbidden relics from his father — someone he refused to ever, ever discuss with me; not even when he was high as a kite.

I can't help but notice small details as I stow the box back where I'd found it: that the address changed with every card, hopping from state to state and finally ending in '93 in Dál Riata, Scotland.

How Vince was always "Vincent" to this question mark of a man, though nobody else, not even Eva, calls him that.

I wonder if Vince ever attempted to write his father back. I wonder if Irving was the one to purchase Dorothy, perhaps as a consolation for his abandonment. Were he and Eva married? Had Vince had his mother's surname from the start, or was it changed later?

It's none of my business. Vince never pried into my lack of parentage. Why should I do it to him?

When I stand, I'm tempted to continue rifling through the room. To check the dresser for my old clothes. To scour the closets and air vents for any hidden smack. The feeling is just curiosity, though, with none of the life-or-death urgency of a true compulsion. I'm free to ignore it.

I leave the room and find Eva sat in her recliner before the television, tea forgotten, the satin of her chemise hiked to show dimpled thighs. She has the body of a half-melted cupcake; a softness I'll forever associate with motherhood because of her.

On her lap she holds an envelope of photos from a disposable camera, Sharpie-labeled with the year 2000.

"I knew I had this somewhere," she says when I approach, and offers me a glossy 5-by-7. I take it and see an overexposed image of myself sprawled on the same chair Eva sits in now. I'm wearing a formal cap and gown for my high school graduation, which means I must be seventeen.

Vince, twenty, is dressed in black jeans and a white tank. He has me in a playful chokehold, a frosty beer in hand. His lips mash my cheek. We're both wearing novelty sunglasses to mask our blown-out pupils, and my black eye.

It's a real punch to the gut seeing us young and happy — or high, at least, which for us is the same thing. I remember that moment; the way we wrestled on the recliner until he pinned my wrists and kissed me stupid.

I was underweight then. I wasn't healthy for another couple years; not until after my first round of rehab, yet I wasn't as bad as I am now. There was color to my cheeks and life in my smile.

Vince was coldly handsome as ever; wiry; his features model-sharp compared to the embarrassing pudge of my baby-face. His skin was ice pale against my surfer's tan. Though his felid eyes are covered, I see them on Eva when I look over the top of the photo at her.

"I'm surprised you have this," I say, and am proud to hear that my voice gives nothing away. "He stole all the pictures I had of him, and there weren't many to begin with."

"You're right," Eva agrees. "That boy hated the camera."

Vince has bewitched countless people, but Eva and I were the ground zero of his coming to be. Others may someday recover and move on from his influence, but I think the two of us are beyond help.

"Did he contact you?" she finally asks. "My understanding is that you're no longer seeing each other." She glances at my sleeve-covered left arm, then away again.

I shrug. "It's been two years."

Two years since Cero's death brought Crown and I home early from my tour. Two years since I caught Vince in bed with the fresh-ly widowed Magpie. Two years since we fought, and he retaliated by shattering us all.

"So you don't know where he is?" There's something sly in Eva's gaze that she tries to mask with maternal concern, but I know Vince — and therefore, Eva — well enough to see through it.

"If I did, I wouldn't tell you," I reply. "But I don't. I guess coming here was a waste of my time."

It wasn't, really. But maybe I want to be cruel. He's not here for me to lash out at. Eva makes a decent substitute.

Her eyes grow huge, and her mouth shrinks into a tiny O. She shrinks from me as though I've raised a hand to strike. With a derisive snort, I turn for the door.

Her panicked voice stalls me. "Was it because of me? Is that why he left?"

I know this game. She'll self-flagellate herself into tears, desperate to be told that, no. No, she's not a bad mother. No, Vince's delinquent teenhood wasn't her fault. He's a bad egg, is all, and isn't she just the bravest little ladybug for holding out hope?

Unfortunately for her, she's chosen the wrong comforter. I am a withered, ugly husk with no kindness left to fill her perpetually empty cup.

I could wreck her. I could tell her that yes, she drove him away with her cloying neediness — that no teenager wants his mother to crawl into bed with him and ask whether he thinks mommy is pretty; if perhaps he has any of those pills that made her head and heart feel so much lighter.

I could take it a step further and ask the questions that have plagued me for years — *if you're such a good person, Eva, why didn't you ever question the beaten, underaged whore creeping into your son's room night after night? Was it easier to look the other way and pretend you didn't know what was happening?*

I ask none of those things. "I don't know, Eva," I say instead. "How 'bout the next time he calls to pant in your ear, you ask him yourself?"

Her silence is absolute before I feel her wonder and joy tangibly fill the room. "Does he *really?*" she breathes euphorically. I grab the door handle and interrupt her.

"And when he does, pass on a message from me. Tell Vince his "Surfer-Boy" expects him to hurry up and keep his fucking promise."

I step out and close the door softly, although I want to slam it hard. I feel peculiarly numb all the way back to the bus stop.

Night buses in the suburbs are few and far between. I'm left waiting a long time and, when it finally arrives, find it's near-empty save for a few homeless people looking for a safe place to sleep. That's fine with me. I'm too lost in memories for company.

I was fifteen when Vince made his promise, but it lives in me still like a physical thing. It's the most intimate, romantic thing any-one has ever offered to do for me. I think I've grown around that promise the same way a tree grows around a knife in its roots. It's now incorporated in every facet of who I am.

We'd sat together in a secluded corner of beach. The occasional jogger who glimpsed us had no clue we were waiting for one of Vince's clients, Kyle, to approach. During a deal, he'd mentioned interest in some "young companionship," and of course shrewd Vince seized upon the business opportunity.

"Might wanna slow down there, Surfer-Boy," Vince had re-marked, a dramatic eyebrow arching, as I snatched the bottle of oxy from his duffle bag and upended two square pills onto a CD case, grinding them to white dust with a smooth, stone paperweight.

"*You* suck him off, then," I'd snapped, feigning anger to hide my nervousness, and bent to lick the eye-wateringly bitter case clean. I still wasn't brave enough to snort or inject things back then, but powder supposedly dispersed faster than whole pills. "And do it sober, too. I dare you."

He'd squeezed the back of my neck and shot me a stern look with those heavy-lidded, alien eyes of his, conveying without words that my attitude was not appreciated. I contemplated slugging him, but fighting with Vince never ended well. It was better to keep him sweet.

I'd softened my expression and tilted my face to kiss his wrist, still unmarked by tattoos, though not for much longer.

"He's not that bad," Vince promised. "He's not like the guys you find on your own. Just let me pick out your clients from now on. You really think anybody would hit you if they had *me* to worry about?"

It was a tempting offer. Street work was dangerous. I'd considered finding a pimp to do my screenings for me, but they charged a steep percentage and were often just as bad, if not worse, than clients themselves. In my short time doing this job, I'd already seen too many corpses. "You'd do that?"

"I found Kyle, didn't I?"

Vince ran a thumb along my cheek. I'd considered pushing him away. No need to give me a pimple, not when I'd worked so hard to keep my skin nice. The pedestal of youth my clients put me on was such a double-edged sword. The moment their fantasy was shattered by oily skin or a voice that broke, their desire turned into rage. *How dare you, Teenager, be a teenager!*

But the oxy was kicking in, and I wanted to relish the glow. I dropped my head onto Vince's shoulder.

"You're so pretty," I'd mumbled, studying his long lashes, the diamond-cut of his jaw. He was so elegant compared to me. Tall and clear-skinned with no baby fat to speak of. Everything about him was so controlled, so *perfect*. I admired and envied him in equal measures.

He snorted derisively, but I could tell he was pleased. "And *you're* high."

"Not high enough." I reached for his duffle again, and he seized my wrist, squeezing hard enough to hurt. I whined, straining. "I'll pay you back, just let me—"

"I'm all out of oxy, and you are *not* mixing shit. You wanna die, kid?"

"Kinda, yeah," I'd confessed. "Not from pills, though; you're right."

I couldn't do it yet. I still had three mouths to feed. Magpie needed new jeans, and the car was acting up *again* (add 'teach Mags how to do an oil change' to my endless to-do list). I'd done research about a wearable alarm to remind Crown when to use the bathroom, but *that* would cost some serious cash...

I dug the heels of my high-tops into the sand and watched the waves roll. The late-afternoon sun cast shades of gold on the ocean's surface. I wanted to stare at them until they made a picture for me. I wanted to fill my mouth with this magic sea. "I want to die *soon*. Wait until the kids graduate, and then maybe I can finally be done."

Magpie and Crown would always be "the kids" to me, even as Crown dwarfed us all and Magpie used her newly developed curves to sneak into underground concerts and grind on girls way out of her league. They weren't just "the" kids. They were *my* kids.

"How?" Vince asked, a fanged edge to his voice I was almost too high to notice. "Just fuckin' slit your wrists like all those pathetic Sylvia Plath bitches?"

"Sylvia Plath died with her head in an oven," I said, before remembering that Vince didn't like to be corrected. "And drowning is more my style. I'd paddle a board out past the breaker and keep going, until..."

Until dehydration and exhaustion and nature took its course. It could take hours. It might take *days*. Still, it seemed so peaceful to give up all illusions of control and let the ocean bring me home.

"Fuck that," Vince snarled, so harsh it startled me from my comforting fantasy. "You're mine; got that, you little fucktard?"

He'd shoved me. I'd fallen back in the sand and stared up at him, wondering what I'd done this time to earn his ire. He'd slung a leg over my waist and pinned me down, his knees on my arms.

"I don't understand," I'd said, hoping he'd see I wasn't giving him attitude; that I was truly confused.

"*You* don't get to kill yourself," he'd growled, his eyes searing into mine. "The ocean can't have you. I'll kill you myself when I'm good and ready. Until then, you'll just have to suck it up and deal."

•••

In my pocket, my vibrating phone brings me back to the present. I draw it out and see a text from James: *Are you alright*?

He must think I'm sick. Until tonight, I haven't missed class once in the two semesters he's been my professor.

I mull his question over. If I don't respond, it will look strange. Possibly strange enough to warrant a house-call.

From my other pocket, I withdraw Vince's carefully folded rose-note and squint hard at his words, trying to decipher any hidden message; to pick up on the intended tone. *I can send flowers too, Surfer-Boy*.

Is this jealousy? Anger? Amusement?

Stalking people is not unusual behavior for Vince. As far as I'm aware, he's never done it to me before. Why would he? I used to always be by his side. But it's clear he wants me aware that he's watching. *Why?!* Is there something I'm meant to be doing?

If I could only see Vince's face, I'd know. But how can I behave correctly when I don't know what he's trying to tell me? Yes, James sent me flowers. No, Vince doesn't normally do stuff like that. But it wasn't like I'd *asked* them to! I need flowers like I need a hole in the head.

I realize with some surprise that I'm worried for James; that I actually care, somewhat, about his wellbeing. What if Vince hurts him?

Sex isn't a problem between us; Vince sleeps around, too, which never bothered me until one of his conquests turned out to be my kid cousin. Getting upset because I fucked someone else isn't his style.

Then again, Vince never liked for me to have *friends*. And what was it that James said we were?

What was the last thing Vince did to the two people I most cared about?

Remembering the way blood spurted out of Crown's belly with every beat of his heart, the gurgles he'd made through the gash in his lung, I reply to my professor with a quick '*I overslept. Sorry.*'?

There. Nothing concerning about that — just a careless mistake. I'll email Bambi for class notes if I need them. Better yet, I'll drop out. I knew I probably wouldn't get to finish the program anyway, and if Vince is coming for me, school will soon no longer be a concern.

It's so easy to burn every bridge, every safety net I'd worked hard to build. To let go of dreams. It feels like freedom. It feels like giving up all control. It feels like paddling out into the ocean to die.

James replies within a few miles of road: '*Would you like to stop by and go over what you missed?*'

We've had sex several times since the beach party. Perhaps he's expecting more of the same, or maybe he really does just want to help. Either way, it's time to nip this mistake in the bud.

'*I'm not interested,*' I reply, and shut my phone off.

Chapter Fourteen – Magpie

...

I have to say, I'm not a fan of this whole 'feeling like shit all the time' thing.

I bend over my cash register (fuck the US and their damn respectability politics! There's plenty of places in Europe where cashiers can sit while working, but oh, no! Not *here!*) and rest my face in my folded arms.

My lower back throbs in time to my heart, and I feel each recently sustained injury throb — my bullet-grazed abdomen; my deep-tissue bruising from the crash; my roadburned skin; my biopsy stab; today's surgical cut on my left upper arm...

Maybe it's time I started being a bit gentler on myself.

On Doctor Paar's recommendation, I had Planned Parenthood remove my implant, since the added hormones might do more harm than good. My uterus has retaliated by flooding my boxers with blood and chunky tissue ever since. I've spent more time this shift *in* the bathroom than out.

Across from my register is a shelf of newspapers, which keep drawing my eye. "Burnt Human Remains Found in Sonoran Desert," a headline reads. "Foul Play Suspected. Mystery Child Found Alive At Scene."

Part of me is curious to read the official take on the Jacobi incident, but I know from experience that it'll make me feel anxious and paranoid. Better to remain as oblivious as possible.

"Wish you were really here," I say aloud. Cero used to fix me bubble baths and martinis when period cramps had me doubled up in bed, clutching my stomach.

I feel cold hands take my shoulders, cooling my overheated skin. There's a physical weight against my back that I can almost convince myself isn't imaginary.

Emotional and raw, I clench my teeth against a sob as Not-Cero kisses my shoulder. When her hands weasel under my shirt to hold my belly, I feel the cramps slowly ebb.

This has become too real to ignore; to pretend it's the result of sleep-deprivation and an overactive imagination. Auditory hallucinations aren't uncommon, but tactile ones are extremely concerning.

"Is it because I'm dying?" I ask. "Is that why you're here?"

Despite Gran's pious Christian teachings, the concept of God and an afterlife just seemed too alien for this rebellious foster girl. I've always considered myself an Atheist. But they say the sick and elderly often question these things; that the end of a life naturally has people wondering what comes next.

I didn't allow myself to ponder such thoughts after I lost Gran and Cero. I threw myself into alcohol and work and drugs and Vince until I was numb from brain to toes. It did me no favors, because now that I'm facing *my* demise, I don't know how to handle it. I'd always assumed I would die suddenly in a blaze of glory. That it would require no forethought on my part.

I'm not yet so far gone as to believe these hallucinations imply the existence of a God(s) (capital *or* lowercase 'G') or afterlives or deeper meanings. Far more likely, they're from too many head injuries; too much copper in our drinking water; maybe even a blood clot or tumor.

"I'm sorry," I whisper miserably into my folded arms. "I'm so sorry I wasn't with you when you died. I ran home for a *second* to shower and grab a sandwich and feed the cats—" and to see if Vince had delivered another magic baggie of sanity in pill form — "and you... couldn't wait for me anymore, I guess."

Cero hadn't died alone, thank the stars. Antonina had flown out to sit beside her at the end. She'd assured me that an hour of self-care would do me good; that she had everything under control. I'd only kissed my wife goodbye "for now," but it turned out to be goodbye, forever. No amount of drinking will ever take that away.

The arms around my waist constrict, drawing me into a clammy embrace reminiscent of standing before a refrigerator after being out in the sun all day. I shiver, but don't pull away.

The sound of a car door slamming outside has me straightening up fast, slapping on a shaky customer service smile. It would take only one bad Yelp review to be out a job.

I service a pair of stoners who load up on soda and powdered doughnuts. They're too blazed to do much besides giggle at each other and lose focus while trying to pay me. When I take the crumpled bills, count the amount myself, and hand the correct change back, I'm applauded enthusiastically.

I watch them from the window after they leave. They swing, hands clasped, under the many streetlights just outside. Their dozens of shadows dance alongside them. Just watching their easy joy makes me want to join the party. Perhaps they wouldn't mind a third wheel?

The bell above the door tinkles again, snapping my attention to the front. A young woman in a short, metallic-green skirt slinks in, looking around with wild, wide eyes before approaching my counter.

"Excuse me?" she mumbles, and I see how she grips her own arms, her manicured nails sinking painfully into her skin as she tries to hold herself together. "Um. This will sound *so* lame, but a guy's been following me around for a few blocks. Is it okay if I hide out in here?"

Immediately, my mind flashes to Vince. It's not impossible, but it could be any other creep, too. The world is full of them. "Of course," I reply. "Hey, it's not weird. I get people in here all the time for stuff like that. Make yourself at home."

She licks her chapped lips and finally meets my gaze, her brown eyes serious as a funeral. "I know," she tells me with a shy laugh. "Word on the street says this is the place to be. You've helped my friends out before."

It occurs to me that she's probably a sex worker. A street worker, too; less common nowadays than the more modern, somewhat less dangerous approaches to the profession. I'm not always quick on the uptake, despite having a former sex worker for a roommate.

"I'm glad to know people feel safe here," I say sincerely. "As long as I'm behind this counter, that's my priority."

If she knew about this, Brittanie the manager would have a cow, ranting that we don't want "those kinds of people" attracted to our business; that if I didn't stop, we'd have too many "undesirables" begging for handouts and protection.

Maybe it's the stubborn shithead in me that has me asking, "Want some coffee and a doughnut? Go for it. On the house." Suck it, Brittanie.

It does my soul good to see the timid woman give a shaky smile, edging her way towards the coffee station.

Suddenly, she flees for the bathroom on stiletto heels, slamming the door hard behind herself. I open my mouth to call for her when, just as quickly, the front door bangs hard enough to knock the bell off its hook. It crashes, rattles, and rolls to a halt under a display stand.

A man storms into my store, face tomato-red as he peers around. His eyes lock immediately on the bathroom door, skipping over me like I'm no more a deterrent than the display of phone chargers and wall adaptors. Rude. And a mistake, on his part.

"Can I help you?" I ask, drawing his attention as I study him. Late forties. White. Just shy of six feet tall; maybe two hundred pounds. Probably played football in high school, before office work softened him around the edges.

How average a monster can appear. I bet he's married. I bet his friends call him by affectionate nicknames, and have no idea what he gets up to for his midnight jollies. If pressed, perhaps his wife would confess to some uneasiness, some awkwardness from time to time. Moments where she fears he isn't *quite* who she thought she'd married.

He almost looks ashamed when he meets my eyes, and Cero and I zero in on the uneven cant to his hips and shoulders. Scoliosis? It's a subtle detail, and one he hides well, but he isn't the only predator in this building. We can't help but form a dirty plan of attack based on what we see. *Go for the kidneys first...*

"Uh, yeah." He touches his hair — thinning, but with a decent cut to mask it — and forces a smile. Bastard probably isn't used to women who aren't afraid to stare him down. "Did my, uh, girlfriend just come in here? Asian gal, about yay tall?" He holds a hand at chest-height. Offers me a beseeching smile. "We argued; she stormed off. I'm real worried about her."

"No," I lie, not even trying to sound convincing. I continue to stare challengingly into his eyes.

"Oh, but..." His smile becomes more genuine; warming as he packs his nighttime self away and brings on the daytime charm. "I could've sworn I just saw her..."

"You didn't." I pause, then add, "If you're not buying anything, you need to leave."

Surprise and confusion give his face depth, erasing yet more of the animal rage from before. I'm being openly hostile, and he doesn't understand why. It rocks his certainty. This will go one of two ways. Either he'll lash out at me to reaffirm control of the situation, or...

"I see. That'll be all, then."

... Or he'll cave like a house of cards. A shame, and a blessing. I'd been thirsty for a rumble, but my body isn't in the best condition for one.

Bravado sapped, he slinks out with his tail between his legs. I wiggle my fingers gloatingly at him when he glances into the window, and his face flames.

He swears and kicks the empty bike rack, his night's fun spoiled by one uppity brown bitch who won't stay in her lane. My smirk widens to jack-o'-lantern proportions.

I wait a few minutes, but when his car becomes a speck on the horizon, I leave my counter and approach the bathroom, tapping lightly on the door. "You can come out now," I say, chipper as a chipmunk. "Coast is clear."

I'm feeling so much better, physically and mentally, than I did ten minutes prior. I feel flush with vigor and life, having done the one thing I'm meant to. I was a *hero*. I defeated the bad guy.

The young woman eventually emerges. She looks around to ensure he's really gone before slumping against the door with an exhausted huff of breath. "Thanks. Nights like tonight are rough. Sorry to, um, leave you alone with him."

"I'm glad you did." I'm in full cop-mode now. I want to assess her age, her health, her social status. How long she's been in town; whether she has a pimp; whether this is a consensual career choice for her.

You can't save everyone, Mags, Not-Cero reminds me. *And you shouldn't try. She'd probably feel offended if you said something.*

Cero's always gotten huffy about my tendency to meddle. She'd had to do plenty of high-risk work long before she formed the gang. Maybe she thinks I'm being judgmental. I hope I'm not. But if someone had been there to help Tip...

That's different. Tip was a kid, and you knew his situation. You don't know hers. Butt out.

I *could* know her situation if I asked. If I don't, then I'm just as bad as those who hurt or ignored Tip. I open my mouth to do just that—

Alexis Magpie, I forbid you from hassling this woman. She knows now that she can come to you for help. If you push her too hard, she'll never do it, even if she needs to.

Fuck. She's right.

"I'd better... get back to work," the woman says cautiously, and inches towards the door.

"Hey," I stop her before she steps outside. "If you're ever grabbed, remember to SING— solar plexus, instep, nose, and groin." I demonstrate where to drive her elbows, her feet, her fists. A bungled version of this defense had worked on Navier the night I grabbed him by the balls, and he's practically a giant compared to me.

"Fight dirty. Your thumbs, his eyeballs. Your knee, his junk. Move your leg like you're trying to reach his throat — it'll tell your brain to kick harder. Puke on him, piss on him, make a huge damn scene. Remember, you're usually the smaller one in a confrontation, so stay low. You'll be harder to grab."

Not-Cero huffs a sigh. She probably thinks this five-second self-defense lesson is condescending. I'm assuming a lot here — that the woman doesn't already know this; that she doesn't have someone else to protect her; that she wants more help than she asked for.

To assume is to make an 'ass' out of 'u' and 'me,' Not-Cero snarks.

Better a cringey ass than an indifferent douche. I'm a hero. I *care.*

"Okay." the woman nods, smiles, her poker face so smooth I can't tell whether I've annoyed her or not. "SING. Got it."

"Be safe," I caution, and watch her slip into the night.

Chapter Fifteen – Tip

'enmeshment', definition: when your childhood was so fucked up that your familial boundaries are nonexistent.

...

Magpie's night terrors almost make me late for work. Again.

She seldom screams *loudly*, which is a blessing. We don't need a noise complaint on top of everything else. It's more akin to a ghostly moan pulled from somewhere deep inside her. Once she starts, she never stops without intervention.

I used to pull my pillow over my head to block her out, but it's useless. Her wails wind my bones, choking my heart with icy vines. Nowadays, I rise at the first whimper.

I snap her bedroom light on, nearly blinding myself at — I check the bathroom clock — five in the morning. She must've *just* gotten home from work.

"Where are you, you little weirdo?" I mutter, looking over her bed until I spot the blanketed lump near the foot.

I rip the comforter off, unearthing my broken doll of a cousin from where she's curled like a dragon around her hoard of books and booze. She's wearing gray boxer shorts and one of her polos from work. The latter is twisted uncomfortably around her torso, exposing the stretch marks and soft pooch of her belly; the wiry fuzz of her happy trail.

I toss books over my shoulder without a care for where or how they land. I chuck empty bottles into the graveyard of their own kind littering the floor. I am a sleep-deprived machine, going through the motions in the dim hope that I may soon rest.

When I grab Mags's ankles, she shakes so hard her teeth clack. "No," she begs; a little girl's plea. "Don't, please..."

"Yeah, yeah. 'Don't touch you.' I got it. Trust me, I don't *want* to."

This is usually the point where she throws a punch, but I've gotten good at dodging. Showing up to work with a bruised face once is awkward. Doing so repeatedly results in a "conversation" with my manager.

Tonight, Magpie remains relatively docile. I'm relieved by this lack of fight, until I notice the tears that wet her cheeks. She never cries when she's awake, but when she's asleep, all bets are off.

"Aw, Mags, don't," I mumble, my big brother instincts giving my heart a kick. Seeing her cry is painful, regardless of the circumstances. "You'll be okay. I'm here."

"Please no," she whispers as I struggle to roll her away from the edge of the bed. She tries to escape me by pillbugging up. I ignore this and bully her into a more natural position, shoving a pillow under her head.

"I'm sorry," she tells me, or whoever her dreaming mind mistakes me for. Her chin dimples like a kid's about to really let loose and bawl.

I bunch my sleeve over my hand to wipe her tears away. "I don't know what you're sorry for, but you should let it go. You didn't do anything wrong."

She stills. I might've gotten off easy tonight. Maybe she'll slip into a more restful sleep now.

I push her sweat-dampened hair back and straighten her shirt, but when I tug on the hem of her twisted shorts, her heel catches me hard in the chest. After watching her fists so closely, I forgot to check her feet!

Oh, and it *hurts*. I feel something inside me creak. I try to muffle my shout, but I needn't have bothered. She bolts upright, eyes rolling back to reveal only the whites, and *screams* like she's auditioning for a horror movie.

"Jesus *Christ!*" I slap a hand over her mouth, shaking her until her head lolls. "Wake *up*, you crazy bitch!"

She doesn't. After only a moment, she goes limp and silent as a dead thing in my arms.

Unable to support her weight, I set her down. Her grip on my sleeve is tight, and I'm too drained to fight her for it. I lay beside her, watching her face relax as her breathing evens out.

If we had the money, I'd take her to a sleep specialist. Or a psychiatrist. Fuck; I'd try an *exorcist* if she thought it would help. I don't know what the hell happened to her while I was away, but she wasn't always this damaged.

The room is cold as balls — I hope the AC isn't acting up again. The last thing we need is to get billed for something that isn't even our fault — yet Mags is somehow sweating buckets.

With a grunt and a sharp twinge in my kicked chest, I reach for the comforter and tuck it over us. Cocooned by her warmth, I close my eyes.

When I open them again, the sun is rising and I know I have to leave.

She stirs as I lever myself out of bed, reaching feebly for my hand. "Cero?" she asks, again speaking in the hopeful voice of a small child.

"Uh, nope. Sorry. Just me."

She mutters a string of incomprehensible gibberish, then flops with her back to me, stealing the warm spot I'd just vacated.

In our bathroom, I brush my teeth and wash my face, counting the strokes through my grogginess. I wince when I catch sight of my reflection in the mirror.

You're old and washed up and unlovable, I think unkindly, and sigh when I see the crescent-shaped bruise on my chest, already black as tar, where Mags kicked me. It hurts like anything when I rotate my shoulder.

Great. That adds a new layer of fun to the physical nature of my job.

I'd forgotten to prepare breakfast for myself the night before, but it's not like I have the time to waste eating, anyway. I set Magpie's coffee to brew, then head for the bus.

At work, after restocking the toilet paper in the bathrooms, there isn't much for me to do but pick up after the nighttime janitors. Blame it on the OCD, but to me there's the right way to do things, and then there's the way everybody else does them.

I push my yellow cart of supplies around the dolphin-patterned carpet and try not to let on how much I need its support just to stay standing.

Several specialists are testing the temperature and pH balance of the displays, using manual pumps to expunge poop from gravel. I enjoy watching cuttlefish, as their colors shift kaleidoscopically with every new emotion. The fact that they continue to change color in sleep suggests they dream.

Most customers at this hour are elderly folk, taking advantage of their seasonal passes to get some safe exercise by walking around. A head of dark hair in the sea of gray draws my attention. James stands before the manatee exhibit where Farah and her calf Josué drift sleepily.

I check twice to ensure it's him, unwilling to trust my eyes, but he's real as life. He's dressed in slacks and tweed, his smallest cane hooked over one arm. He adjusts his glasses, a faint smile gracing his lips as he watches the mammals swim.

Abandoning my cart, I storm his way and seize my professor by the shoulder. Passing guests gawk at us, but I'm fuming too hard to care.

James bends into the momentum, throwing my balance. In a fluid series of movements, he drops his cane and snatches my wrist with one hand, throwing me against his body. He uses his free hand to grip my throat, thumb to my jugular. When he squeezes, dark spots corrode my peripheral vision.

Through the sparkle and fizz, I see his calculating eyes rake across my face. In the split second he takes to recognize me, he drops his defensive stance.

I resist the urge to rub my throat; to gasp for breath like I've never been choked before.

"That's quite a greeting, Tip," he says, disapproval in his voice as he moves back and steps on the rubber base of his cane, forcing the handle to pop up and slap into his waiting palm. "I'd appreciate if you never approached me that way again."

It's not an apology, which suits me fine. I don't feel like apologizing, either. Sometimes I forget he used to be a SEAL. I won't that mistake again.

The fucked up half of my brain has awakened, flooding my system with longing for the punch that never came. *Come on, James; hit me! Hurt me! Break me! We both know I deserve it!*

I tell it to shut up, the irritation I feel towards myself manifesting as a scowl at the man before me. "Yeah? Well, *I'd* appreciate if you told me what the hell you're doing here."

"This is an aquarium," James points out, gesturing around us as though I'd somehow missed this fact. "And I'm a professor of marine biology."

"Oh, bullshit," I snap. My raised voice does nothing to quell the stares of passers-by. *Crazed Janitor Fights Disabled Man: More At Six.* "You came here because you know it's where I work."

"And this is a problem?" James asks, tone so dry it kindles my fury. The bastard knows exactly what he's doing. "I'm not permitted to visit my lover?"

To his friends, I'm a student. When it's convenient for his argument, I'm a lover. Tessa was right: sleeping with him *was* a bad idea. Not because it's dangerous, but because it's annoying.

Behind James, Josué rolls onto his side, trying to wedge his whiskered face under Farah's flipper to nurse. Farah pushes him away with her rubbery nose, telling her calf to stop being so silly; that he's big enough to eat solid food now.

I watch them, trying to regain my cool. I'd meant to ghost James out of my life, but it seems he won't be so easily deterred. Direct action is required.

"Come with me," I command, then lead the way further down the hall, listening to the muffled thumps of cane on carpet. The decorations and funky carpet patterns fade the further we walk, designed to discourage customers from taking this route.

There's a balcony above the fire escape where employees go for smoke breaks. On reaching it, I swipe my badge to open the door and meet the briny morning air.

There isn't room for two out here, but he follows me anyway, smelling of coffee and Camels and cologne. I try not to remember how much I *like* James's scent; the calming effect it has on my anxiety.

"I'm not interested in seeing you anymore," I say when the door clicks shut behind him. "I thought I'd made that clear, but apparently not."

His dark eyes study my hard-set mouth, my chilly expression, my foreboding posture. Nothing about me invites touch or radiates warmth. Questions are not welcome.

He wets his lower lip before speaking. For all the inflection in his voice, we might be discussing the weather. "I'd ask why, but I suspect I won't get any answers. Is that correct?"

I say nothing. The salt breeze fluffs our hair. It'd be a phenomenal day for surfing.

James takes a deep breath and exhales slowly, looking out to the endless sea below. "I can accept that."

What, he's giving me up so easily? Vince would've beaten me bloody for acting so bratty. If nobody hits me, how am I supposed to know they give a shit?

"What I can't accept is you skipping class," James continues, mouth a parallel line with his eyebrows. "I expect to see you at school tonight. And if you don't come, I *will* search for you. I'm excellent at finding people."

This sparks a thrill in my gut. I ask, almost eagerly, "Is that a threat?"

"It's a promise. You're a talented, passionate student. I won't insult your intelligence by tossing around nonsense words like 'fate,' but I believe that with time, you could become the scientist of your dreams. I won't allow you to forsake your seat at the table."

Moving no closer, he lowers his voice to something intimate. "Come to class, Tip."

I feel an electric spark at his order. My breath catches. He must hear it, because he cocks his head in curiosity, a scientist studying an alien species. I wonder if he'll kiss me. I wonder if I'll let him.

My Blackberry chimes with the alert that I'm falling behind on my tasks. Slamming my poker face on, I turn to swipe my badge and lead us back into the aquarium.

James stops me with a hand on the doorframe, cutting off my entry. I shoot him a hair-burning scowl that he ignores until I'm forced to meet his calm brown eyes. "Do we have an agreement?"

We stand in silence as, below us, the wind makes the palm trees dance. Finally I say, "I'll come to class so long as you leave me alone outside of school. No more 'just visiting' my aquarium."

My professor doesn't look sad, exactly, but that enticing, commanding heat fades from his eyes. Something like exhausted resignation takes its place. "Of course. We are nothing if not men of our word."

•••

I see Magpie's motorcycle parked out front when I get home, which sours my mood. She'd mentioned hanging out with friends this afternoon. I'd looked forward to napping in peace.

Once inside, I catch the tail-end of her speaking aloud from the cracked bathroom door: "If you *seriously* think we can scrape up that kind of cash, you're crazy."

This isn't what alarms me. Magpie is a chatterbox who frequently talks to herself. What has me freaked are the tears audible in her voice.

Magpie never cries when she's awake. She didn't cry when she broke her arm skateboarding and I had to carry her home to Gran. She didn't cry when her girlfriend dumped her for a college boy in the middle of Senior Prom. She didn't shed a tear during Gran or Cero's funerals. She's the type who'd rather drink herself numb than lose her smile.

As I stand in the doorway, I hear something even more unexpected: a low voice responding to Magpie's statement. I can't hear what it's saying, as it's far too muffled. But it's unmistakable: someone is in the bathroom with my cousin.

Since when does Mags bring people home? As far as I'm aware, she hasn't hooked up with anyone since Cero's death. Aside from whatever weird fling she'd had with Vince, anyway.

When she was twelve, Mags went missing for an afternoon; something she'd never done before. I'd come to pick her up from the after-school program she attended, only to be informed by baffled teachers that she'd mysteriously wandered off.

I'd phoned the parents of all her friends, prowling her usual haunts for a sign of the pigtails I'd braided that morning; of her denim vest with all its iron-on patches. I'd never experienced that level of fear in my *life*.

It took hours for some prick from my school to pull into our driveway in a shiny red Firebird, Mags stoned off her ass in his front seat. "I found this kid toking up with some punks by the light rail station," he'd explained. "I *thought* she was yours. You're welcome."

Thus began my relationship with Vince.

I'd considered beating him senseless for answers. Neither he nor Mags ever told me what happened that day. It couldn't have been good, because she avoided him like the plague ever after. Whenever he stepped foot in our house, she left. No "hi," no "hey, how are you?" Just poof! Gone.

It makes it all the more bizarre that she fell into bed with him. Grief makes people do weird shit, but...

Magpie sobs. I give myself a shake. What the hell is wrong with me?! My kid is crying in the bathroom, and I'm just standing here like an asshole!

Standing tall, I let myself in without bothering to knock.

Magpie, seated fully dressed on the floor of our shower, yelps and draws back. She's alone, without so much as her phone to account for that deep voice I'd heard. And yep; her face is wet with tears. I guess pigs really can fly.

I look around in confusion. The bathroom is tiny; scarcely larger than a closet. There's nowhere a person could hide in here.

"Tip?" Mags asks, recovering from the scare I'd given her. "Are you okay? You're acting weird."

I huff. *She's* bawling her eyes out, but *I'm* the one being weird? "Why are you crying?" I ask, sounding sharper than I'd intended.

For a moment, she's every bit the deer in headlights. I caught her doing something she doesn't want to admit to. How often does this happen?!

"I found a gray hair," she explains, and tries to play it off with a smile and some melodramatic flair. "I'm having a moment of vanity for my fleeting youth."

I scoff in disbelief. "You used to be a *way* better liar than that."

She pouts. "I *did!* Look!" She parts her blue-black hair and holds out a single strand for my inspection. I'd describe it as more white than gray, but tomayto, tomahto.

"So what? I find those all the time. Just rip it out." I'm *way* more bothered by my fading looks than she's ever been, and even I don't kick up a fuss for the occasional melanin-free strand. "Here, I'll do it for you."

I squeeze into the shower and pluck the hair, careful to do so by the root.

She takes it from me, absently weaving it between her callused, engine oil-stained fingers. Though she's stopped crying, her nose is still running. "Thanks."

"Gonna tell me what the *actual* problem is now?" I ask, and she shifts to press against my side. She's cold, her skin clammy where it brushes mine. I wind an arm around her shoulders, touching my cheek to her clammy forehead to gauge her temperature. Maybe she's feverish.

She drops her head onto my chest with a sigh. "It's just Cero."

Cero? It's not her birthday, the anniversary of her death, or that of their wedding. None of the usual days Mags is more melancholic than normal. "What about her?"

Magpie shrugs. "Sometimes I remember how bad things got at the end."

Ah. Leukemia is, indeed, a bitch.

"You were all alone, huh?" I ask gently. "I'm sorry I wasn't there for you. I didn't know things were so bad until..." Until I'd received her email explaining my in-law was dead.

I'd tried to atone for it by making myself useful, mailing Cero's ashes to Antonina on my own. It was my idea to have Nina weld Cero and Magpie's wedding rings together in memoriam.

But the fact remains that when Mags needed me most, I'd been thinking only of my career.

Magpie shakes her head no. "All of Cero's friends were good to me. But I wanted *her*."

She snuggles closer, taking my hand with her freezing one. Give her an inch of physical contact, and she'll take a mile. Kids who've been abused tend to vary in such extremes. Hypersexual; touch-starved; touch-*averse*...

"I thought you were in here with Vince," I confess. "When I heard you crying. That's the first place my brain went to."

I hear the surprise in her voice when she asks, "Were you going to fight him? You burst in really aggressively."

Wouldn't be the first time. "I don't know."

"For *me?*"

Again: wouldn't be the first time. "He hurt you. I never forgot." I gesture to her scarred face.

Magpie looks thoughtful. "Did you know I ripped out two of his orbital rings the night it happened? A scar for a scar."

A kiss for a hit, Surfer-Boy. Wasn't that the price for the first high he ever gave me? A brush of lips in an abandoned lot?

Vince doesn't always bargain with money, but nothing is given or accepted without payment. To him, there's no such thing as "free," or "gifts." His definition of fair value is different than most, but he adheres strictly to his own strange rules.

"Really?" I ask. Which rings were they?"

Vince has even more body mods than Mags, but I never got any. I can scarcely tolerate strangers touching me long enough for a haircut. Allowing someone to jam needles into my flesh sounds like actual hell.

She touches my ear to demonstrate, her thumb and forefinger pinching either side of the conch. I remember the thick silver hoops he used to wear there and wince, imagining how much tissue that must have torn.

"Did you do it before or after he cut you?"

"Before. He broke in while I was sleeping. I opened my eyes, and he was *on* me..."

Her voice trails off. She tucks her knees beneath her chin, like she's trying to protect herself from the memories.

"You're lucky he didn't kill you." Maybe not the most sensitive thing to point out, but it's the truth. He's butchered people for lesser offences, or had me do it in his stead. How she got away with nothing but a scar is beyond me.

"Did you really love him?" Magpie asks, her thumb stroking my knuckles.

"No." My lie is immediate. I loved him then. I love him now. I loved him when I made him laugh or smile as he did for nobody else. When he writhed beneath me, face pink, knees parting. When he used rubber tubing to tie my arm, smiling angelically as he waited for my veins to engorge. When he made his vow on the beach...

In a lot of ways, that promise saved my life. Had he not taken the choice of suicide away from me, I would have killed myself long ago. Sometimes I wonder if that wasn't his plan all along. If, in his strange way, he was protecting me.

"Heroin makes all the feel-good hormones throw a party in your brain," I explain. "It's the most blissed-out state you can achieve without dying." Sometimes dying is a side-effect, but no true junkie gives a shit. Sometimes, death is the point. "It's a package deal with all the mushy love-love feelings, so. Yeah, I thought I loved him."

"But you don't anymore? You've been clean for so long. Longer than ever."

I nod. Yes, I am clean. Yes, this is the longest I've *been* clean since I started using at age fourteen, with the pills Gran's landlord slipped me as I "convinced" him to forgive all her late payments — an arrangement that lasted until I was sixteen, and therefore too old to fit his preferences.

And when that landlord turned his greedy eyes on Magpie instead, I broke his fucking wrist.

"I'm proud of you," Mags informs me. "I see you growing and healing. You complain a lot, but you still listen to what Tessa says. And you're doing so good in school."

With that undeserved praise, I suddenly hate myself so much that it fills me completely; from the veins I'd once pumped with poison, to the tissue of my sinuses I'd shredded with grainy powder, and finally through the scaly flesh beneath my tongue, long since rotted with pills.

I'd destroyed myself one cell at a time waiting for Vince to take the final shot, but he never did. Instead, he tried to end the lives of the two people I'd sold my childhood to protect.

Magpie's thighs are so much thicker than mine, made strong by muscle and fat. Just looking at my matchstick legs against hers brings a great sadness to my heart. I'd once been strong enough to carry her. I may have quit drugs, but I never stopped killing myself; not for a second.

"I need to walk around." I jiggle my shoulder until Magpie sits up. "Do you want anything from the store, or...?"

She looks at me in sympathy, understanding more than she should. "I'm dying for a chocolate shake from In N Out," she suggests.

I nod. We shouldn't burn money like that, but a jaunt to the fast-food joint sounds like a fantastic idea right now. "Let me guess — fries, too?"

Her smile amps into something more genuine. "You know me so well, Tippy-Canoe."

Chapter Sixteen – Magpie

in my defense, he's hot.

...

It's official: I have cancer. Specifically, I have ALL. Acute Lymphocytic Leukemia.

"It's so rare in adults," the apologetic tech told me over the phone, but I know all about that. It killed Cero, after all.

ALL is a children's cancer. Adults seldom develop this particular strain of leukemia, and even more rarely survive it. The odds of my wife and I *both* contracting the same disease are astronomical, yet the proof is in the marrow. *My* marrow.

Ever since I received the news, I've spent my hours alternating between panic and numbness. I'd even been caught bawling by Tip. Talk about embarrassing...

Not-Cero hounds me endlessly. Even now, as I drive out to Navier's property, her voice circulates my helmet: *You need to start treatment.*

I wrench my bike's handlebars, teetering crazily. Great. I have cancer, I'm still hallucinating my dead wife, my rapist is prowling the city, and I nearly splattered across the Santa Ana freeway.

"Just drop it! Fighting fate didn't work for you; it ain't gonna do shit for me. Unless you want me to crash and die right *now,* let me drive in peace."

This shuts her up, however resentfully. I feel her settle in the back of my mind, seething over my thoughts like a vulture.

Chemo is a shitshow. No matter how much I drink, I'll never forget the life it sapped from my brilliant wife. How she became a shadow of herself, in body and in mind. There were days I'd look at Cero, and scarcely recognize the fragile, bitter shell she'd become. I think those memories frighten me more than the thought of dying.

Navier purchased a half-rotten farmhouse sometime in the nineties, though he sold most of the land to neighboring cotton farmers. Crown's commute to work takes him hours each day, but he never complains. Maybe he appreciates the privacy from SoCal city mayhem.

Regardless, it's a pain for me to drive out to the boonies. And it's taxing on the gas budget. I avoid it when I can, but nobody provides physical contact like Navier does. I need that comfort today.

He must hear the metallic purr of my Kawasaki half a mile before I reach the place. His visor-protected face peers from the detached garage as I skid to a halt in the tracks left by his Tacoma.

He waves a friendly blowtorch, having thankfully turned it off first. "Gimme a minute and I'll be right with you, darlin.'"

I nod, wiggle my helmet off, and leave it on the seat of my bike as he resumes his work. There's nobody around for miles. I'm not worried about theft. My hair is a rat's nest and, when I touch my nose, I find that it's bleeding. Again.

Hastening up the steep incline to the farmhouse, I spit blood into one of the many patches of dandelions that line the property. I even remember to clean my red fingers on my pants before pulling open the screen door.

Letting myself into Navier's home, I make a beeline for the kitchen. Like the rest of the house, the most that can be said for it is that it's spacious and filled with natural light, dust motes whirling hypnotically before the many large windows and skylights.

I nosy through Navier's belongings, admiring the odds and ends he's crafted since last I visited. He restored the cabinet doors and painted them fire-engine red. There's a bronze bull welded from forks and doorknobs and other junk, roughly the size of a bread loaf, that serves as a mail holder. Its horns are heavy with the weight of overdue bills.

It's in a creaky cabinet crammed with dollar store utensils that I locate a pack of paper towels to staunch my nosebleed. I've become quite the expert at this.

Apparently, Not-Cero's decided that since I'm no longer operating a vehicle, the time for lecturing is at hand. *You need to discuss treatment with a hematologist. And speak with Tip's case worker about applying for health insurance. If worse comes to worst, Ricket will marry you to give you access to his.*

"Oh, sure, I'll get right on that. 'Hey Tip, I'm gonna elope with your gay professor like we're in a modern-day Jane Austin novel so I can chase some bullshit fantasy of recovery. My dead wife told me to.' That'll go over great."

Other people have recovered.

"We're not 'other people.' Can't you feel it?"

Not-Cero emits a chilling, otherworldly snarl that has me quivering in my boots. At first I think her anger is directed at my overuse of sarcasm. My hands fly to protect my body.

For just a moment, I'm a twenty-something cop facing down a thief with mismatched eyes as she aims a punch towards my stomach. *Do you know what people like me do to little girls like you? You're in way over your head, pig.*

The flashback fades when I notice the three empty bowls on the floor beside Navier's fridge. I relax, then echo Not-Cero's rage. I don't send Navier money every month just for him to neglect our cats!

I lift all three dishes and dump them into the overflowing sink, cranking the tap to fill the largest with cold water. Then I search until I find the bag of dry cat food, randomly stuffed under a half-built kitchen chair. I scoop kibble into the remaining bowls.

It soothes Not-Cero when I arrange the dishes back where they belong. I feel the phantom touch of her arms around my waist, her forehead on my shoulder. She's shaking.

This is all my fault — *I'm* the one who asked Navier to watch the cats, despite knowing how irresponsible he is. *Stupid, stupid...*

The man himself strides inside and strips his sweaty flannel shirt off not ten seconds later, looking something like the Brawny paper towel mascot.

I don't want to start a fight, but something must be said. "You can't just leave the cats without water, Navier."

"Huh?" He uses his discarded shirt to wipe his sweaty face, then flings it into one of the piles that clutters his house like wreckage from a sunken pirate ship. "There's water in the bowl, see? They're fine."

"It's *in* the bowl because I just *put* it there. It's hot outside. Please try to remember."

Domesticated cats originate from Middle Eastern deserts, and seldom drink water in the wild. They're hydrated from their prey. Indoor cats who eat dry food, however, don't have that luxury.

"You got it, Fearless Leader." Navier shoots me a salute and a grin. "It's kinda hard to take you seriously when you've got a paper towel stuffed up your nose, though."

I know he'll forget what I said in seconds. I should continue to bring it up until the message sinks in. But I hate it when Navier says he *thought* I was a cool girl, until I started nagging "like every other bitch on the planet." If he doesn't think I'm cool, I doubt he'll continue to respect me as a leader.

I change the subject. "What were you working on?"

He makes a face and elbows me away from the fridge long enough to produce some orange juice, which he chugs straight from the carton. "Fixing the neighbor's tractor," he replies, belated, after a loud series of gulps. "Not my favorite kinda work, but..."

But. He clearly needs the money.

I have to grant him this: Navier knows where to find everything in his tornado of a house. He reaches into a cabinet beneath the sink and, amidst the jeans and boots and empty egg cartons, unearths a can of black olives, a plastic fork, and a can opener.

A pair of yellow eyes peep from the cabinet's depths. I wave hello to Ding. She ignores me, staring intently at a spot just beyond my left shoulder, until Navier shuts the little door again.

He hooks a finger through my belt and drags me to the dilapidated sofa the next room over, shoving a pile of disassembled boxes to the floor. When he flops backwards onto the room's only furniture, he drags me right on down with him.

The sofa springs scream beneath our combined weight. I make a face when a metal coil escapes a patch of duct tape and threatens to gouge my arm. My blood isn't clotting. I can't afford to get careless scratches and scrapes anymore.

Ignoring my wordless complaint, Navier opens the can, stabs a few olives with his fork, and prods my lips with them. Between the two of us, we polish the entire can off in less than a minute, juice and all.

Then he tugs at my leathers. "Off."

I strip. First to go are my boots, hitting the floor with twin thumps. My socks and jeans are soon to follow; then my jacket, though I wear only boxers and a ratty gray bra underneath. I leave that on, if only so Navier can't mock my lack of boobage again.

At blessed *last*, I'm cocooned in warmth; fuzzy belly on fuzzy belly. Skin on skin. I release a huge, shuddery breath and collapse like a soggy umbrella after a storm. Were I a cell phone, this would be my charging station.

"Better?" Navier asks, petting my hair.

"Mrphgle," I reply intelligently, and stuff my entire face into the darkened safety of his armpit.

It's easy to be comfortable with Navier, though we haven't gotten together like this in months. This is an aspect of our relationship that comes and goes when the mood strikes.

He's one of the few people I know who never thinks my touch starvation is "too much." Never says I'm weird. Never speculates about what childhood trauma may have made me this way. In my book, that's worth its weight in gold.

He tucks me beneath his chin, settling a hand on my spine as he reaches over the top of my head to flick on the TV, flipping channels until he finds Family Guy.

Not my cartoon of choice. I'd've preferred SpongeBob, or Bob's Burgers, or just about anything else. But this isn't my house *or* my television, so...

"We're the worst adults," I sigh resignedly.

Navier chuckles, patting between my shoulders in a forceful way that makes my chest boom hollow. "What do you mean?"

"How do you bring girls home to this dump?"

"I don't. I go to their place, then sneak out when they fall asleep."

"How gallant. When was the last time you ate a vegetable?"

"Olives are vegetables."

I'm pretty sure they're a fruit, but I don't care enough to argue. Soothed by the much-needed skin contact, and by the pressure of a heavy arm on my back, I doze through the rest of the episode.

When I again open my eyes, I find that Navier is watching me. He looks away when our gazes meet, but for a moment I'm struck by something alien in his eyes, and by the uncomfortable reminder that no two people truly know each other, no matter how close they are.

Not being prone to introspection, I ask the first question that pops into my head. "How did you and Cero ever become friends?"

It's hard to imagine Cero the Mastermind taking up with slovenly, easygoing Navier. It's hard to think of anything they had in common, come to that. How could such different personalities click?

You and Tip "click." You and I "click."

True, but perhaps I like irritating, difficult people. Puzzles. Challenges. Math always *was* my best subject.

Navier laughs, belly bouncing. "She never told you? I saved her flat little ass."

This ruffles Not-Cero's feathers. *He did not! I was the one who rescued him!*

I can't help but grin. "How so?"?

"Bar fight."

"When was this?"

"Hoo..." Navier rolls his eyes upwards as he counts, fingers drumming my neck with every year tallied. "Had to be... Fuck, almost twenty years back. Mags, am I old?"

It was seventeen years ago. I was still a teenager.

"You're never old til you stop stirring up trouble. Tell! Me! What! Happened!" I excitedly bounce my hands on Navier's chest for emphasis.

He gives my forehead an eye-watering flick. "Calm your tiny tits an' mebbe I'll tell ya."

His accent is always thicker when he's comfortably tired. When he's chatting amiably with friends. I want to protest the dig on my breasts, but I know it's his way of setting the tone.

"Me 'n some buddies was havin' a few rounds in this piddly truckstop watering hole, right? Kinda lousy; the beer was strong as chihuahua piss.

"I'm 'bout to suggest we blow, n' then I see this lil gal getting pushed around by some assholes in the back corner. I'm talkin' real redneck pieces of work; didn't have but three teeth between 'em."

I was hustling. None of them went home with their wallets.

"She couldn't've been older 'n sixteen, if that. An' she was real short, too. Little blonde kid; underaged lot lizard in the making.

Didn't have much booty to grab, but they was sure makin' an effort. So of *course* I step in, and..."

He recounts the smackdown he and his 'buddies' laid on said 'assholes.' Knowing Cero, I'm surprised my wife didn't take advantage of the hullabaloo to bail.

I would have, if Navier hadn't—

"Gotten shanked with a broken bottle," I say aloud, in time to Not-Cero's voice in my head. Navier blinks.

"How'd you know 'bout that? Yeah; right here." He lifts my upper body with one hand and points to a raised, circular scar on his stomach with the other.

I'd never paid special attention to it before. Not because it isn't gnarly, but because Navier has so many scars that no one in particular stands out.

Yeesh. It looks like the bottle nearly perforated his liver.

It did.

"So I'm bleedin' like a stuck pig. The assholes bail. My buddies left me for dead when the cops showed, when suddenly this chick — Cero — drags me to the dumpsters."

Navier gets a funny look on his face, struggling to recall the night's events. "She did *something.* Can't remember what. Hurt like a sonuvabitch, though; you can count on that."

Not-Cero supplies no commentary here. I prompt, "Did you lose consciousness?"

"Yeah. I woke at her place. A dinky studio apartment she treated like a castle. She looked at me with those freaky eyes of hers and said—"

'You have all the hubris of a hero. I want you for my own.' Not-Cero sounds wistful. I see the same emotion reflected in Navier's eyes.

I nod, thinking back to my first face-to-face encounter with the thief I would someday marry. "She said something similar to me."

Mere seconds after that initial punch struck true, in fact. "*'You carry the law on your shoulders, but it's weighing you down. Do you want to be lawful, or do you want to be a hero?'*"

Navier snorts. "Pompous little shit. She sure liked her grand statements."

There's enough fondness in his voice that I know he's missing Cero as much as I am. And even under Cero's muttering and grumping, I feel her affection spread warm through my cancerous blood. "She loved you," I tell him.

"You think so?"

"I know so. She loved us all, in her own weird way."

Navier's fingers skate beneath the band of my bra, following the lines of my tattoo. The wings were designed to correspond with my anatomy. The magpie's shoulder joints start at the arch of my own shoulderblades. The elbow joints frame each side of my intervertebral disc. Not an inch of my back is without ink.

In this quiet moment, I almost tell him about the cancer rapidly eating me alive. About my terror of dying. It won't solve anything, but it might make me feel better.

The impulse dies when Navier muses, "I always thought *I'd* be her second. I was her knight, y'know? But then *you* came along. She wanted you the second she noticed you stalking us like the goddamn Terminator. I thought she just wanted to fuck and kill you like all the others. Apparently, she wanted to hire you."

There's no malice in his words, but they ring my warning bells all the same. "I don't understand what you're saying." What 'others'?

"Oh, cher, you changed everything. We were Robin Hoods. We stole from the rich an' saved the poor. We were rolling in cash. The money we made launched Clay's whole career, an' *my* business was booming... Ah, it was a fine, rich time."

Navier would've been a poor commander, Not-Cero reassures me. *He has no ambition; no intuition. No ideas of his own. He's a puppet who only exists to follow orders. I chose you for a reason, Mags.*

"It was just a change in management," I try to laugh the discomfort off. "You all were thinking too much about the financial side of things. I had to bring our focus back to the kids."

I jolt when long-haired Roar pounces from the ether and walks along my spine to knead my ass with huge, smoke-colored paws. He sits on his haunches, batting at the empty air above us like he's trying to smack a mosquito away.

"Speaking of kids," Navier says, tone brighter than before. I'm relieved at the change in topic. He'd come dangerously close to ripping an ugly bandaid off our friendship. "Can you keep a secret?"

Well, that's concerning. "Did you knock someone up?"

"No, but Clay can't say the same." Navier's artist's fingers idly twist the chain of my ring-necklace.

My eyes widen as the implication takes hold. "*No.* Rhys?!"

"Totally preggo."

I think back to when I'd last seen Rhys. She'd looked fine in Nogales. Maybe a little tired. Had she had wine with dinner? I can't recall. "You're certain?"

Unlike Ricket, Clay hadn't begun hormone replacement therapy until a year or so ago. Gender dysphoria has never been a problem for her, and undergoing second puberty this late in life had seemed a big and unnecessary hassle.

I don't know what changed her mind. We don't have the kind of relationship where I'd feel comfortable asking. But the point remains: HRT often has the side effect of rendering the injectee infertile.

Often, but not always. And not always right away, either.

"I'd put money on it. It's all in the hips, if you know what to look for." He shoos Roar off my back, muttering, "It creeps me out when he stares at nothing like that."

Not for the first time, I wonder if Navier has a brood of curly-haired bastards running around somewhere. I can't imagine him paying child support, if that's the case.

"Do you think they'll keep it? Clay's in her *fifties*. That's old to be a new mom."

Navier shrugs. "That's why I said to stay quiet. If they don't keep it, they won't want this spread around."

Mostly, I feel excited. A baby! I might be an auntie! Any child with Rhys and Clay for mothers will be stunning and blessed with every opportunity in the world. But...

"You think they'll want to keep up our work, if they have it?"

Navier and I pull most of the physical stunts of our "night job," but those two are on the field with us, too. Arrest, injury, and death are risks we all face. What feels like a good time now takes on a new light when there's a child involved.

He has no answer to this, either. We'd be down a lot of members if the Gurira-Clays leave. Cero, Rhys, Clay... And soon, me. Who knows how long my health will hold out? I already feel like death warmed over. Have I run my wife's legacy into the ground?

Navier sits up to sneeze. I squirm when our bare bellies brush. He's hairy and muscular. I'm hairy and muscular, too, but he has excess testosterone to boost his growth. Lucky jerk.

"Gonna settle down there, sha, or you feelin' frisky?" he quips, his attention returning to the TV.

Just to see what he'll do, I writhe like an earthworm until he frowns at me, Family Guy reruns forgotten. "Mags?"

I meet his gaze and hold it, daring him to make his move.

It's like when we used to play Chicken in the desert, racing bikes or ATVs towards each other to see who would be the 'chicken' to swerve first. Clay forbade us from ever playing again after Navier had to be taken in for a minor concussion, and I wrenched my shoulder so bad it still locks up sometimes.

Navier's dark eyes sparkle, recognizing the challenge for what it is. He seizes me just under the bust and forces me up the length of his body, stubbled face grinding my stomach.

I slip and scrabble to brace my hands on the sofa's armrest, feeling his teeth nip just below my navel. All the blood in my veins rushes south fast enough to leave me dizzy. *"Jesus* fuck!"

"Tell me you want it." He pauses, big hands squeezing my hips, pretty mouth huffing hot breath onto my skin. I'm fortunate he's too used to bumps and bruises to question my biopsy bandage.

Are you serious? Not-Cero yelps, shocked by this turn of events.

Excuse the hell out of me if I don't allow the ongoing hallucination of a dead woman to dictate my sex life. Besides; free orgasms from a trusted, commitment-phobic friend? Hard to see a downside in that!

Navier is still waiting for my answer, motionless. Clearly, my consent is the trigger for this rollercoaster.

It's this gesture, more than anything, that cements my resolve. Navier cares about me. Navier is safe. It's been too fucking long since I had a good time. I can't allow the memory of Vince to rob me forever.

"What the hell?" I decide. Life is too damn short. Mine recently became a hell of a lot shorter. "Put your mouth where your money is, Cajun. Show me what you got."

...

"Wow!" I gasp, when I can again form human-sounding syllables. From this angle — Navier, seated; my head in his lap — I can see directly up his nose. He would benefit from some clippers. *"Wow.* I can see why you have a fanclub. Thanks, dude."

Navier rubs at his jaw. He seems a bit dazed himself; tousle-haired and flush-faced. "Glad to oblige. You're really loud, you know that?"

"It's a compliment," I insist, still basking in the afterglow.

Usually straight guys aren't all that good at oral, but the ones who bother to perfect their craft are worth keeping around. After his jaw became too sore to continue, he held me on his lap and split me open on three fingers, rubbing me off repeatedly until I had to cry uncle.

Pretty sure he replaced my guts with jelly in the process. How else to explain the wobbliness, the prolonged shaking? My teeth chattered for a solid two minutes after we stopped.

I fidget, uncomfortable with the angle; the uneven slant of his thighs. "Help me up?"

Still fully dressed, he hauls me into an upright position.

I pat his shoulder in thanks. "Want me to—?" I make a loose-wristed, up-and-down motion with my fist. I didn't miss the boner prodding me in the thigh for the last half hour, and I like to think I play fair.

Navier snorts. "I'll pass. I haven't forgotten the *last* time you got your hands on my junk. You're lucky my balls still work."

"Suit yourself," I shrug, refusing to be baited with what happened behind Rosa's bar. "Did you really *have* to throw my boxers halfway across the room?"

For once, timing is on my side. I'm just zipping back into my jacket when the front door opens and Crown, free from work, lets himself in.

He has to know I'm here, as I'd parked out front, but like when we were kids he heads straight for his room without so much as a howdy-do.

"Real social guy," Navier snarks, laying back and using the remote to crank the TV volume high. I wonder if he'll jerk off the second I leave the room, or if he's trying to will his erection down. My oversensitive nether regions twitch at the thought, hoping for a show.

"Don't be a dick. He just communicates differently than our noisy asses."

"If by 'differently' you mean 'not at all,' then sure."

That's unfair. Of us three cousins, Crown is by far the easiest to understand. He doesn't lie or manipulate anyone. He's never mean-spirited or petty. He communicates just fine.

"He's still my baby cousin," I warn Navier, edging towards the hallway. "I'll kick anyone's ass for talking shit. Even yours."

Navier looks neither intimidated, nor impressed.

With a scowl, I turn my back on him and make for the south portion of the farmhouse, forcing myself to stop by the bathroom to pee before continuing on. I don't know whether it's possible to contract a UTI from what we just did, but Navier doesn't wash his hands as often as he should. Best not to chance it.

Past the bathroom are Navier and Crown's bedrooms. Viewed together, the two spaces couldn't be more different. Navier's looks like the rest of the house: dirty; full of random trash and junk. Its smell, wafting into the hallway, reminds me of the gym lockers in high school.

Crown, on the other hand, runs a tight ship. Like Navier's room, Crown's floor and walls are impossible to see through the sheer amount of things packed inside. *Unlike* Navier, every inch of Crown's space is utilized with great thought and care.

He owns a ton of stuff; predominantly comics and related merchandise. It's all organized on thrifted shelves in an order that make sense to him, if nobody else.

Rather than a bed, he has a cozy blanket nest on the floor, neatly arranged with pillows of varying sizes. His two desks — a slanted drawing table for his work, and a flat one to hold his two desktop monitors — take up most of the floorspace.

The man himself is seated at his computer desk, eating a filet-o-fish from a paper McDonald's bag. Without Gran to fix his preferred fish sandwiches, this is his routine now.

Crown doesn't like people invading his space, so I stop at the doorway and speak to the back his head; to his short, tightly curled hair; to the raised pink rope of scar tissue that mars his burnished, walnut-colored skin and slithers down the neck of his knockoff Polo shirt.

I ask, "Can we talk?"

He removes the earbuds he's wearing; a clear invitation to speak.

As kids, my music used to drive him batty, but I don't remember him ever having audio preferences of his own. Maybe they're newly developed.

Maybe they were there all along, and I was too self-absorbed to notice.

I sit cross-legged on the hallway floor, leaning against the doorframe before I speak. With Crown, it's best to get straight to the point. "Some crazy shit is going down, my dude."

He doesn't turn, but his hand, dangling at his side, finger-spells Tip's name.

"Nope; not this time. He's fine."

No response but a signed letter 'M.'

"Not me, either. Well... Kind of me. I'm sick. Nothing contagious, but I'm afraid it's gonna complicate everything as time goes on."

I try to keep my voice steady, but it gives out on me. Surely he hears the way it cracks.

To avoid further questions I quickly add, "There's something you need to know: Vince is back in town. He threatened my gas station, and left a note on Gran's grave."

If I'd thought Crown was stiff before, it's nothing compared to the abrupt change in his posture. He could pass for stone.

It's only natural that Crown fears Vince. Vince *stabbed* him. Before that, Vince cut me. Before *that*, he raped me. I have no doubt Tip suffered years of similar abuse at his boyfrined's hands, even if he'd never think of it in those terms. Despite years of therapy, Mr. Don't-Pity-Me Tippling believes he's above victimhood just because he says it's so.

Vince stole into our lives when we were young; poorer than we are now. He was all flash and bravado, handing out expensive gifts like free samples at a grocery store. He could summon enough charm to pass for normal, but I think we all immediately sensed what a hellcat he is.

Tip thought Vince's presence would only bring pain to himself; not to the rest of us. He gamboled, and like any addict robbing his baby sister's piggy bank for drug money, we all suffered for it.

"For all Vince knows, you burned to death in Cero's Jaguar. There's no reason he should target you. But it's important you're aware of what's happening. Don't do anything risky without back-up."

With my spiel concluded, Crown and I sit in silence. I'd meant what I said to Navier; Crown communicates differently than I do. Than *most* people do. He processes things his own way, and the rest of us can get used to it or go take a hike.

Then an alarm on Crown's wristwatch chirps like a sparrow, and up he stands. He steps over my sprawled legs as he makes for the bathroom.

Crown has had self-care reminders since he was a kid. After losing a length of small intestine in Vince's brutal attack, the reminders are even more vital. He sets them himself, aware that he often becomes so caught up in work he doesn't register his body's needs.

The bathroom door shuts behind my cousin, and I'm left alone in the hallway. Staring absently into Crown's empty room, I take note of his computer screens.

I'd assumed he was designing yet another splash page for Ladybug Steals the Dime (the comic he's currently illustrating), but now that his body isn't blocking the monitors, I see he was reading the latest updates of a very familiar document, instead. It's the gang's compiled intel on Isaac Müller.

Page upon page of Isaac's movements fill the shared document. His employees, new and old, and where he found them; the dates of when he lets them take the fall and get arrested in his stead. His likely whereabouts. All our ideas on how best to crumble the empire he built on the blood of children.

It had come as such a shock the day Crown informed me that not only had he guessed I was in a gang (something even Tip, the *actual* genius of our family, remains in the dark on), but also that he wanted in on the action.

I'd thought it too dangerous a life for my mild-mannered cousin, but he'd already made up his mind. He shows us daily his commitment to the cause. Observing his vintage comics, those too old and valuable to leave their protective sleeves, I think I understand why: Crown not only admires the comics themselves, but also the stories of their artists.

Jewish refugees brought the American comic industry to fruition during the Great Depression. Their hopes and struggles are painted into every panel. The stories are full of unlikely heroes, underdogs, aliens and foreigners; repressed minorities of every ilk resisting fascism and fighting bigotry tooth and nail.

Crown and I don't have the superpowers we read about when we were young — no flight or time travel or animal shapeshifting for us. Instead, we had to change ourselves to sate our thirst for righteous victory, creating a life where we can drag the villains down kicking and screaming. Evildoers, beware!

Crown lives for it just as much as Navier and I. He simply does so more quietly. It's nice to be reassured in that much, at least. I have to believe someone will stick to the cause after I am gone.

I hear him wash his hands before exiting the bathroom and approaching my back. He plants an overwarm palm atop my head, petting me the same way he loves on Cero's cats.

"Hey, superstar," I smile, patting his hand. He continues to stroke my hair for a good minute. I close my eyes to enjoy it, calmed by his patchouli and printer's ink scent; by the dry heaviness of his touch.

As quickly as it'd begun, it ends. He returns to his desk. I know our conversation is over when he pops his earbuds back in and resumes his careful study against Müller.

He opens and closes his fingers over his palm when I stand to leave, offering ASL for 'goodbye'.

"I love you," I inform him, and tap his doorframe twice before returning to where I'd last seen Navier, intending to take my leave. I need to head back to the city in time for my shift tonight.

Navier isn't on the sofa anymore. The TV is off. He must've returned to his work in the garage.

I plop a kiss on Roar's head and leave the house, taking in the gradually lowering sun; the fresh scent of cut grass. "Hey, Navier?" I call towards the sound of power tools, walking to my parked bike. "I'm going home now. Thanks for having me."

I wonder if he's hiding because he fears the repercussions of sleeping with me. I know his track record with women: he runs away whenever he thinks they're growing too attached. I'd like to think he knows me better than that, but maybe he needs some distance to calm down.

I notice a folded slip of paper tucked beneath the visor of my helmet. We're too far from town to expect advertisements for babysitters or lawn care, so it must be one of the guys trying to be cute. My money's on Crown slipping me a mini-comic.

Grinning, I unfold the scrap and look with eager eyes, expecting to see doodles of the Magpie-persona my little cousin designed for me. As soon as my brain registers what I'm actually looking at, however, that smile falls straight off and smashes on the ground.

I'm not holding a friendly note. I'm holding a single piece of computer paper featuring two grainy photos, printed on a device that badly needs a replacement of ink cartridges.

The first image is one I recognize from a handful of days ago. It depicts James Ricket and myself, seated together in an Urgent Care waiting room. Ricket is engrossed in a magazine. I'm playing on my phone, head rested on his arm.

The second photo is of even poorer quality. The camera's zoom function must've been abused to the fullest to capture it. It features a white balcony jutting from a three-story building. It's centered on the people within said balcony, standing close enough to kiss.

Tip's golden curls are unmistakable, as is Ricket's blue cane.

There's something undeniably intimate about the image, even from such a distance. Without so much as touching, the two men create more of a charge than Navier and I ever could, even if we had sex on the roof during a lightning storm.

This is completely inappropriate for a teacher and a student. It's a despicable thing for my "best friend" to do to my highly vulnerable, volatile cousin. And he'd done it all behind my back, despite knowing what we've been through! I could spit fire!

"Damn you, Ricket," I snarl, flipping the note over for anything I might've missed.

Scrawled at the bottom of the page are the words **'It's not nice to keep secrets from family.'** The ink of the blue marker bleeds through the sheet.

It's not signed.

It doesn't need to be.

Look around! He might still be here, you stupid sitting duck!

From all directions I feel the itchy tingle of poison-green cat's eyes; feel long, cold fingers curling in my mouth, pressing flat to my tongue. I hear the phantom of a man's muffled grunts puffing hot against my ear...

But there's nothing here. Nothing but cotton fields and droning insects and the continuous echo of hammers, saws, and drills.

"Navier?" I call, hating how high my voice has climbed.

He peeks from his garage without a moment's hesitation, already frowning.

I try and dial my panic back; to distance myself from my emotions and speak like the confident leader Cero chose me to be. "I need to borrow some tools to check my bike, and I need you to watch my back while I do it. Now, please."

I doubt Vince knows enough about vehicles to cut a brake line, but I'm not taking any chances.

Chapter Seventeen – Tip

…

"You're coming to work with me tonight," Magpie says, her long hair imprisoned atop her head with an alligator clip. She stands at our kitchen counter beating pungent ingredients into what might become a stir-fry, or perhaps a chemical weapon.

I glance up from my homework, frowning. The cheap springs in my mattress whine under the shift in my weight. "Um, no? I've got school tonight."

"You're not going." She ruins a perfectly good pot of rice by dumping in a lethal dose of spices, giving it an aggressive stir. "I mean it, Tip. I need you with me."

Magpie is distractingly pretty when she's angry. The emotion transforms her cute, pudgy face into something powerful; something intense and fierce. She blazes like a second sun.

James threatened to get on my case should I ever miss class again, but Magpie wouldn't ask if it wasn't important. She helps pay for my schooling, so she has a vested interest in my attendance. Besides; I know of only one person who makes her this edgy.

"Does this have something to do with Vince?" I ask, adjusting my glasses in feigned nonchalance.

I know I've struck gold by the way she scowls at her plate of badly chopped peppers; by the way her fist tightens around the handle of her dull kitchen knife.

Well. That settles it, then.

I reach for my phone to text James an excuse, then shut it off without waiting for a reply. If there's hell to pay, then so be it. Let him beat down the aquarium doors. Once an addict, always an addict.

Mags and I go about our nightly routines; her in ever darkening spirits; me in such weak-kneed, jittery anticipation it feels like I'm coming down from Speed.

I duck outside to eat tomato slices with shaking hands. Fun starvation fact number one: the constipation is relentless. Not as bad as what regular heroin usage does to your bowels, but when starving or shooting up, MiraLax is always your best friend.

Fun fact number two: people rarely die from starvation itself. It's all the other stuff — the weakened immune system; the damaged organs — that winds down the clock. Someone like me is far more likely to die of a heart attack than of mere hunger.

Maybe it's the anxious excitement talking, but my racing heart makes that feel like a distinct possibility just now.

I suck tomato juice off my fingers, then feel dirty for needing the calories so bad. Who's in control here; me, or the food?

I *do* feel more capable of staying on Mags's bike when we leave, though, which was the point. I rest my helmeted head on her shoulder and close my eyes, feeling and mirroring the tiniest shifts of her muscles. It's not surfing, but it ain't bad.

Upon reaching the gas station, I stand outside as Mags clocks in and relieves the evening cashier of her duties. I don't wander in until I see the woman's VW leave the lot.

I've visited this dingy stoner's paradise before, taking advantage of Mags's employee discount to stock up on school supplies. Almost everything is the same as it was then, save for a frightening, man-sized display of the green M&M posed provocatively atop her wares.

I don't envy Magpie's being leered at by the candy's creepy bedroom eyes every night. Suddenly maneuvering my yellow cart through the aquarium's crowded hallways doesn't look as bad. At least none of the seahorses threaten to melt in my mouth.

"Are you babysitting me?" I ask Magpie suspiciously, watching her count the previous employee's drawer, frown, and count again, stacks of green whipping through her deft fingers like cards at a Blackjack table. "Or am I here for a real reason?"

"A real reason. Go sit in the manager's office and don't touch anything."

I do, spinning in the computer chair of the "office" behind her, watching my cousin work her way down a stream of bored customers. I pretend I don't notice when she takes a covert swig from her hip-flask. The fluorescent lights above cast white-blue rings in her shiny black hair.

After a half hour of this, a curly-haired guy I'd describe as "sex on legs" wanders in and leans against the counter. His torso is shaped like a YIELD sign. He has a jawline that could cut glass, stubble for days, Princess Peach lips, and wide brown eyes.

Paging Disney studios: we found your lost Prince Charming.

As I'm drooling over his enormous hands, he reaches across the register to ruffle Magpie's hair, mouth quirked in a warm, crooked smile. She giggles in a most un-Magpie way. My eyebrows rocket sky-high at the sound.

It's only when he glances at me that I feel a spark of recognition. This dude was Cero's best man at the wedding. He'd stood behind her at the altar, while Mags walked down the peony-strewn aisle on my arm.

Magpie glances over her shoulder at me, a grin on her face and a sparkle in her eyes. "You remember Navier, don't you, Tipples?"

She pronounces it the French way. Three syllables that ignore half of the consonants present. *Nah-vee-ay*.

It hits me that, at some point in time, Mags must've slept with this dude. Either that, or she *wants* to. I barely refrain from wrinkling my nose in disgust. It's never fun realizing you have the same taste in guys as members of your immediate family.

"Hey, man." He does that awkward half-wave thing straight guys always do when greeting men they aren't familiar with. "Tip, right?"

I can't make fun of him too much. I have no idea how to talk to men. While other teens were learning basic social skills, I was turning tricks, acting as my boyfriend's personal loan shark, and being the closest thing Crown and Mags ever had to a father. "Hi."

"Did Crown come?" Magpie asks, which nabs *all* of my attention. I sit up in my chair and stare holes into the back of her head.

"I told him Tip would be here. So, no."

Mags sighs, shoulders drooping. "I figured."

I'm on my feet in an instant, hands braced on the counter, getting all up in Monsieur Tall-Dark-and Handsome's business. "How do you know Crown?"

Magpie is about to scold me for knocking into her, but more customers approach. She has no choice but to reapply her customer service smile and print their money orders.

I scuttle around the counter and take Navier's arm, dragging him with me to the aisle of diapers and aspirin. It doesn't matter that he's taller than Mags and I put together; I suddenly have the energy to fling him into the moon.

"Spill," I demand, all pleasantries evaporated. My fingers don't leave his arm.

He doesn't beat around the bush. "Crown is my roommate. I needed someone to help with the mortgage. He needed a place to stay. Mags hooked us up."

I nearly slump into the shelf, and not just because moving so fast made me dizzy. There was once a time when Crown refused to even sleep until I'd crawled back through our bedroom window and into the bunk above his. Now I don't even know who he's living with?

I fucked up when I let Vince hurt him. It doesn't matter that I did the best I could to stop it; that I fought for his life long after Vince had jumped ship.

I'd brought Vince into our home. Into our lives. I was the one who ignored all common sense to keep him away. Crown had trusted me to prioritize his safety above my love life, and I'd let him down.

I'm still letting him down. He and Mags both. He's right to hate me.

"Why are you here?" I ask, hating how hoarse my voice has become. "Why am *I* here?"

The last of the customers, a mother and her child, leave with two shopping bags between them. I hear the little girl call, "doggie!" as the station door closes.

Navier glances over the shelf-tops. With a grin to rival the devil's, he fumbles a phone from his pocket, zips through the apps, and cranks the volume as high as the tiny speaker will allow.

'When I Kissed the Teacher' by Abba blares as he holds the device above his head, swaying like his phone is a lighter and he's enjoying a live concert. "All my friends at school had never seen the teacher blush; he looked like a fool!"

"I am forever astounded by your maturity," James snipes, approaching from the door.

I feel my stomach drop right into my shoes. My mouth is dry as paper.

James is here. My teacher, whom I have indeed kissed. He's using his cane, wearing a tweed vest, and looking at Magpie and Navier like he's known them all his life.

He doesn't glance my way.

I can't move. I can't move. *I can't move.*

Navier gloatingly sings along to the music, shimmying his shoulders and hips. "Leaning over me, he was trying to explain the laws of geometry. I couldn't help it; I just had to kiss the teacher!"

"That is *so* not funny," Magpie scolds. "Turn it off!"

James and Hero circle the cashier's station. The leashed dog is wearing her service vest. She hops into James's lap after he sinks into my vacated office chair.

Navier silences and pockets his phone, then spreads his arms wide, inadvertently knocking packages of Pampers off a shelf. "Are you joking right now?!"

"Etienne, please." James's apparent exhaustion is contagious.

"Nuh-uh! This is hilarious! *Perfect* Ricket; *genius* Ricket; Ricket who's never fucked up once in his *life...* Schtupping his student! And not just *any* student. Magpie's jailbird-junkie *cousin!*" He laughs uproariously, deep and rich, and wicks moisture from his eyes. "This is the best day ever."

James briefly meets my eyes, then lowers his head again.

I look between him and Magpie, then duck out from under Navier's arm. I brace my hands on the counter to loom over my cousin's small, dark form.

"What the hell is this," I ask, but it's not really a question. My arms are shaking. My chest is hot. The ocean in my veins surges until it drowns out the world, pickling the air with brine and salt.

Magpie, unflinching, holds my stare. From her pocket she draws the apology card James sent me alongside my hyacinths—proof she'd been rifling through my belongings. Then she adds two more scraps to the pile.

One, I recognize as the note accompanying the roses on Gran's grave. The second, however, is new.

I study the pictures, the message, and feel a tingling coolness creep from my brain to coat the rest of my body, silencing my ocean with eerie finality. *Disassociation,* Tessa calls this state of numb calm. The gift life grants to some trauma survivors.

It's dead silent in the gas station when I finally look at James, pointing to the photo of him and Mags snuggling in some random lobby. "Were you ever gonna tell me you're buddy-buddy with my family?"

"Ooh," Navier eggs me on, clearly enjoying James's discomfort. He reminds me of the annoying "little sibling" architype found in every popular sitcom.

"It wasn't relevant," James replies, voice tight. "She's my friend. You're my student."

"Did you teach him some good 'lessons'?" Navier baits, and is ignored by everyone.

"Was this a joke to you?" I demand. "Coming into our home, carrying Mags to bed, pretending you were total strangers? Did you two have some good laughs, talking about me behind my back?"

"Wait; he did what to me?" Magpie asks. Her confusion sounds genuine, but I can only focus on one thing at a time, and right now that thing is James.

James seems to shrink further into himself with every word I say. "I didn't want to complicate things. I didn't want to involve school in the other parts of my life. What happened between us was a—"

He cuts himself off so completely it's like someone hit the 'mute' button on the remote control of life.

I arch my eyebrows, then laugh. "It's okay; you can say it. I was a mistake, right? How did Pepé Le Pew over there word it? 'Schtupping Magpie's jailbird-junkie cousin' wasn't in your five-year plan, huh?"

He was the only person I ever slept with sober. The only one I ever had any sort of connection with, untainted by drugs or money. I'd made the mistake of thinking he meant it when he said he cared about me; that he saw me as something more than a warm mouth and a pair of pretty, color-changing eyes.

Vince is right; I really *am* stupid.

James doesn't contradict me. He only looks at the dog in his lap, confirming every word with his silence.

My lip curls in disgust. With him, certainly; but mostly with myself. It's amazing how I have the lowest expectations in the world, and still people manage to dig a hole and limbo right on underneath them.

I turn back to Magpie, still holding onto the printer paper featuring two photos and Vince's handwriting. "When *was* this?" I demand, clipped. "Where were you?"

Oh, that's not a question she wants to answer. I see it in how her arms cross. Her lips flatten, trapping her secrets behind their barrier.

I'm about to really lay into her when the bell above the door jangles *again*, and a cool hand settles on my shoulder.

I twist back to see a tall, rail-thin woman with electric blue eyes holding me. It takes me a second to recognize her as Jane Clay from that fancy farmer's market where James and I had our not-a-date. Her soft-looking wife isn't far behind.

"Fantastic!" I throw my hands up, knocking her grip off me with the motion. Of *course* a world-renowned formalwear designer and her blind wife are involved, somehow. This may as well happen. "Super! Welcome, ladies. Come join the circle-jerk of bug-fuckery!"

Spittle flies from my mouth at the 'p' in 'super.' I'm too keyed up to care.

Jane Clay's aristocratic mouth pinches. She looks like a disappointed boss; a scolding mother. "There's no need for that attitude. We can talk everything out like rational adults."

I want to rip my hair out. I want to rip *her* hair out. I want to snatch the keys from Mags's pocket and book it on out of here.

Instead, I watch as my cousin leaves to scrawl a note on a sheet of printer paper, taping it to the inside of the glass front door: *STORE CLOSED FOR INVENTORY.*

She locks up and turns out all the lights, save for the one in the office. She produces a metal folding chair from said office, opening it for Jane's wife, and then hops to sit on the counter. Her legs dangle, booted heels drumming cheap plywood.

"Alright," she says. "Let's talk."

...

"Is everybody caught up?" Magpie asks, when everything has been laid bare.

"I understand that my cousin is in a *gang*," I snarl, slumped on the floor behind the counter. To my left, Navier munches his way through a third doughnut. "And that you dragged Crown into it. Great, Mags. Really responsible."

"Kinda, yeah," Navier agrees easily, sucking frosting from his fingertips. "Glad we're on the same page."

Magpie scowls at him until he holds up his sticky palms, playing the innocent. "What? We steal stuff. We kill people."

"We don't kill *people*," Mags corrects haughtily. "We hunt *monsters*. We're heroes."

Jane Clay, leaning against the wall with her arms crossed tight, gives her head a shake. "We can't think of it like that, sweetheart. The individuals we target are still human beings."

It's endlessly strange seeing someone of her clout slumming it in a place like this. Like spotting Oprah at a laundromat.

"We're not doing anything wrong," Magpie argues. "We save kids from "human beings" who *are* monsters. What's the difference? Call them whatever you like, but I don't lose any sleep taking out trash like them."

Doesn't she, though? I knew better than anyone how broken her sleep has become.

"Magpie?" Clay says, looking my cousin dead in the eye. "Last week, you stabbed a man to death. We helped you dispose of the body; the evidence. He had a brother, a job, a home, and three dogs. His mother is now in police custody with no idea what happened to her sons. All because *we* decided it was time for them to die."

Magpie draws away from that intense blue stare, shaking her head in denial. Not of the statements, but of the intent behind them. "But they were *evil!*" she insists. "We were right to do it."

"I am not arguing with you. And I'm not sorry, either. But I *am* saying that we need to take responsibility for our actions."

"You never had a problem with it before," Magpie points out, voice growing more bitter by the second. "You launched your career on stolen art; built your empire on the work of others. Why wait til *now* to be 'responsible'?!"

If she wants to hurt Clay with this barb, the hooks don't land. Jane bows her head in humble acceptance. "What I did hurt countless artists. I can't change my past wrongs, but I *can* use my platform to help people; to bring good and beauty into this world."

Whatever point she's working up to, it's one that she's put considerable thought into. I can already tell Magpie won't shake her resolve.

"What are you saying?" Mags asks, sitting up. At my shoulder, her dangling ankles uncross. "Do you want us to *stop*? Hundreds of people are kidnapped and sold into trafficking every day. It's awful!"

"It is. The cruelty of our species knows no bounds." Clay leaves her perch against the wall to cross the station, her mile-long giraffe legs blocking my view when she takes Magpie's face in hand.

"Aren't you *tired,* sweet girl? We didn't start this war, and it won't end with us. We're not getting any younger."

Magpie closes her eyes and takes in a shuddery breath, then slowly lets it out through pursed lips. She's the picture of a soldier waiting for the bomb to drop.

"It's time to move on," Jane whispers, her words meant only for my cousin, yet still heard by all. "We can't keep chasing your — *Cero's* — fantasy of a world cleansed in blood. We have to focus on new growth now." She looks over her shoulder at her wife.

Rhys clears her throat. "I am seven weeks pregnant," she announces in her sweet little voice, drawing the room's attention.

Navier twitches against my side, something like triumph flashing in his brown eyes. James blinks rapidly. He's the only person present who actually looks surprised. "Congratulations?"

"Thank you." Rhys rests a hand on her flat belly. "It came as a surprise, but after a lot of thought, we've decided to have this baby. Parenthood is the next step we want to take in our lives."

"I'm so happy for you," Magpie says, but her voice wavers. Is she about to cry *again?*

Jane tilts Magpie's chin up, then presses soft lips to her forehead. "Magpie, I think you're wonderful. I think you have so much to offer the world. Cero fell so deeply for your fire that all the rest of us did, too. We just couldn't help ourselves."

Navier ducks his head. James's eyes have gone terribly soft. Magpie hiccups. Yep; she's crying. Twice in one week? Must be a record for her.

Jane continues. "I mean no disrespect to Cero, but it's time to let the dead rest. You don't need to keep living her dream. You are allowed to be your own person now, Magpie."

Tears slick down Magpie's cheeks, glossy under the singular light still shining overhead. "You're leaving me, aren't you?"

Hearing how tiny her voice has become transports me ten, twenty years in the past; back to a little girl in my lap, feverish with chicken pox, groaning miserably as I rubbed topical lotion into her angry red blisters. *Everything hurts, Tipples. Can't you make it better?*

My heart throbs, aching and hollow. We've come a long way from when some cream and popsicles could solve our woes.

Clay nods. "It's time for us to part ways, sweetheart. I hope we can do so as friends."

James makes a small sound in his throat. I recognize his grief, however quiet it may be. I fight the instinct to take his hand. That's not my place anymore. I doubt it ever was.

"We'll *always* be friends," Magpie promises solemnly, and Jane kisses her again before straightening her posture.

Rhys stands too, smoothing the ivory lace of her dress, and pulls a bundle of paperwork from her pocketbook. "A token of our friendship," she says, and hands a bank check each to Magpie, Navier, and James. "We wish you every happiness."

Magpie's eyes go very round at the amount of zeroes she sees written in Clay's tidy penmanship. "We couldn't possibly—"

"You can," Rhys interrupts firmly, her pointy chin set in stubborn insistence. "We're not taking no for an answer."

She and her wife make the rounds, saying their goodbyes, while I try to sink into the shadows and be as unobtrusive as possible. This moment isn't meant for me.

"We had some good laughs, didn't we, you old hound-dog?" Jane smiles when Navier hops to his feet and crushes her to his chest. He sniffles loud enough to make *my* nose hurt.

"Godspeed, you funky little lesbian," he chokes out. "Give Junior some love from uncle Navi." He inclines his head towards Rhys's stomach.

James looks numb when Clay kisses both of his cheeks. It's not proper to distract a service animal at work, but she pats Hero's ears anyway. James doesn't say a word against it.

Only then do the two women depart, leaving us four in the dark. I watch as the shiny Lexus they'd arrived in pulls from the parking lot and shoots off, silent as a dove's wings, into the night.

Navier is the first to move. He lurches to Magpie, scooping her off the counter, holding her in his thick arms as they share their pain in a very extroverted way.

I glance at James, who only looks down at Hero.?

"That was rough," I mumble, though I'm not the best at the whole 'empathy' thing. I'm trying. He must know that I'm trying.

"Yes," he agrees. "Clay and Rhys have been a part of our lives for so long that losing them will be a major adjustment."

I shift closer. I don't touch him, and he doesn't reach for me, and we are *certainly* not extroverts, but maybe we, too, are sharing something.

The moment doesn't last. Magpie squirms in Navier's hold. He sets her back down, remaining stalwart at her side.

She swipes at her face with her sleeves, clears her throat, and pulls her hair into a bun, securing it with a ballpoint pen she nabs from the cash register.

With that simple bracing motion, she cuts her losses and compartmentalizes her priorities, like a true leader is expected to do. "Well... that sucked. It looks like we've lost two more members of our party. What about the rest of you? Navier?"

"I'm in," he agrees without hesitation. "You know I'm always up for an adventure."

"What sort of 'adventure' are we talking about?" James asks before he can be questioned.

I wonder what he thinks about all this; whether he blames me for his being stalked and photographed by my sort-of ex. Hadn't this been exactly what I was afraid of when I'd rejected him?

Magpie paces the short space behind the counter, avoiding my outstretched legs on each turnaround. "We're in agreement that

James, Tip, and I are being menaced by a dangerous man. He somehow followed us to Nogales and back to Urgent Care. What does that tell us?"

"And why does he want us to *know* he's doing it?" James adds. "Fear-mongering? Blackmail?"

It feels weird to discuss Vince like he's the killer in some bad cop procedural. *Suspect is a white male sadist in his late thirties...*

"It's a threat," Magpie responds, pointing a Slim Jim from a bucket on the counter at James. "He wants us to know he doesn't like that you're dating Tip." She pauses. "Neither do I, come to that. What the *hell,* Ricket?"

"Then you'll both be very pleased to learn that Tip and I are no longer involved," James sighs, shifting Hero on his lap to rub the bridge of his nose. Navier cocks his head curiously.

"I don't think it's a threat," I interrupt, causing everyone to look at me. I clear my throat. "Vince never cared who I messed around with, so long as I wasn't actually dating them."

I don't know how else to say 'so long as I never forget who owns me' in a way that doesn't sound bad. So much of mine and Vince's relationship doesn't make sense when explained to outsiders, which is why I prefer to keep it to myself.

James frowns. "Is *that* why you—?" He doesn't finish his question. I'm unspeakably grateful.

Magpie points her Slim Jim at me. "Keep talking. Why do *you* think he's doing this?"

I feel put on the spot, and it makes me cranky. I want to say something mean to end this conversation. They're poking their noses into stuff that's none of their business, no matter what those photos show.

"He wants me to know he's here," I mumble, and I don't know until I say the words how *warm* they make me feel. "That he's watching. That he cares, and notices, and…" I clear my throat. "The day he left…"

Don't think about Crown's bleeding body. Don't think about the explosion.

"I told him he doesn't care about me. That he never came to my competitions or my sobriety celebrations, and he shouldn't have slept with… Well, anyway. This is him showing me that he *gives* a fuck now; that he's involved and invested in my life, and he's trying to change."

The other three people in the room stare at me like I've gone stark raving mad. The quiet makes me fidgety; makes my scowl grow.

"So these are love letters?" Navier asks, holding up the two notes Vince has left so far.

I snatch them out of his hands. It's one thing for me to criticize my boyfriend. Hell, even Magpie has a right to, after all that he's done to us. But the rest of this uninvolved party is not allowed a voice in the debate.

"Fuck off if you're gonna be judgy," I grouch. "He gave me *flowers.*"

"No; he put roses on our grandmother's *grave,*" Magpie argues, barely keeping her cool. "That isn't creepy to you?!"

"I'm just impressed he found the grave, considering he didn't go to her funeral or anything. Don't you see? This is him showing that he *knows* me. That he cares about what's happening in my life. He's trying to fix things."

"He. Set. Crown. On. *Fire!*" Magpie bends over me, close enough to kiss, literally screaming her pent-up rage in my face. As usual, her breath smells of cheap vodka poorly masked with coffee. "So please *try* to pull your head out of your ass, and—"

James gently taps her shoulder. "I hate to interrupt," he says, calm in the face of so many emotions; so many strong personalities.

In all the hubbub, I hadn't noticed him stand up. "But it appears we have company."

We turn to look out the glass door. Sure enough, there stands a very large Hispanic woman and a skinny black teenager, both frowning at the sign Magpie taped up.

Chapter Eighteen – Magpie

...

"Who's she?" Navier asks, a hand sliding into his denim jacket. I recall the gun he'd so shockingly brought to the Jacobi confrontation, and shove his elbow hard.

"They're my friends," I tell him sternly, scowling until he relaxes his posture, hands once more at his sides. "Everybody got that? No being mean to the nice people."

He and Ricket nod. Satisfied, I cross the floor to unlock the door. "Hey, guys."

"Are you crazy?" Rosa snaps, shepherding me right back into the station. Omar follows like a lost puppy at her heels. "You just open the door like that when some psycho is prowling around after you?"

I blink. "This is a public business. Vince already knows where it is, so if he ever feels like waltzing in to buy some Tootsie Pops, there's not a hell of a lot I can do about it."

It's a worrisome fact of life, and it makes the more vulnerable tasks of my job — hosing off the cement, taking the trash out, putting new receipt paper rolls into the gas pumps — pretty nerve-wracking. But living under constant stress while being unable to act on it quickly fatigues a person into indifference.

Rosa doesn't look happy with my explanation. She crosses her arms and glowers. It's a fearsome expression, but I'm just happy to see her.

"Guys?" I say, turning to speak over my shoulder. "This is Rosa. She owns Buenas Ruedas."

Rosa jumps when her eyes adjust to the darkness and she sees the three men crouched around my counter. "*Hijo de puta*!" she yelps, and though the situation is far from funny, I fight a smile.

"While they are indeed *putas*, they're also my friends. The big guy is Navier..." At my introduction, he slinks to my side. He and Rosa stand close to the same height.

"I know you," she accuses. "You scared Magpie outside *my* bar. You tried to drag her away."

"Only the once," he protests with a winning grin. "Mags likes to be dragged."

He demonstrates this by hooking an arm around my neck, wiggling me back and forth like a loose tooth. Rosa's eyes narrow into tiny slits.

Before this can develop into a problem, I laugh and shove Navier off, pointing to the others. "Blondie over there is my cousin, Tip. We live together. And the dude with the service dog is James Ricket."

"A pleasure to meet you, Miss Santiago," Ricket greets politely. At least I can count on *one* person not to inflame the situation. "Our Magpie speaks very highly of you."

Rosa ignores him. With Omar still hiding behind her bulk, she points a red-manicured fingernail at Tip's chest. "You!" she barks. "*You* are the one who loves the devil."

He balks, confused and affronted. "The fuck, lady?"

In answer, Rosa reaches behind herself to fish Omar out, hauling him forward to stack her chin atop his head. Her thick arms wind his shoulders. "Your boyfriend tortures *niños* for laughs, yet still you defend him?!"

"Tip is half blind without his glasses," I explain before he says something rude. "He's too vain to wear them outside the house, but it's dark in here. He can't see what you're talking about."

Rosa huffs, then scoots herself — and a very uncomfortable Omar — closer. Tip looks like a cornered cat. I'm torn between a lifelong desire to protect him, and the comparatively new urge to please Rosa.

"Look!" she demands, fierce and unrelenting as ever.

Tip looks. He stares for a long time at the stitches dividing Omar's face.

Omar grimaces and drops his eyes. "C'mon, man," the teen complains when Tip climbs to his feet and approaches, breathing hard.

"That's..." Tip looks from Omar to me, his startled eyes following the curve of my scarred jaw. "When did..."

"I think we'd all like to hear this story," Ricket remarks. He's looking at me when he says it, eyebrows arched. He'd been the one I'd called when Vince flayed my face open, after all.

Navier reaches into the heated cabinet for a fresh doughnut, tearing it in two and stuffing half in his mouth. "You'd *better* fill us in," he says through a mouth full of pastry. "This sounds like some prime-time drama."

Get everyone on the same page, Not-Cero agrees. *These are your allies.*

"Why don't you sit?" I suggest, and direct Rosa to Rhys's vacated chair. She declines and points Omar towards it, instead.

As he sits I ask, "What brings you two here? I'm always glad to see you, but isn't it a Friday night? The bar should be busy."

"I closed it, because I'm tired of this lack of action. I'm tired of looking over my shoulder every minute, wondering if this 'Vince' will come and attack us. If there's a problem, we need to take care of it. No more screwing around."

She's right. There's nothing else for it.

I end up keeping the gas station 'closed' longer than I'd intended. We tell our stories for the second time in one night. It feels good not to have to hide anymore; to prove that we really *are* taking action; that none of us are sitting idly by.

Finally, Rosa stands. "Fifteen bucks on pump twelve," she snaps, and reaches into her bag to pull out a wad of cash, tossing it onto my register before storming outside. Omar hastens after her.

The guys and I regard each other long after the ring of the door's bell fades. Navier breaks the spell by laughing, head tipped back, chest hitching. "You sure know how to pick 'em!"

I dive for my counter, punching in Rosa's order before she can start the pump.

Navier follows me and playfully grabs for the cash inside the register, wincing when I move to shut the drawer on his calloused fingers. Then he just leans into me, squashing my back against the wall. "After marrying such a shortstack, s'kinda cute to learn Mags likes 'em *big.*"

Je-*sus!* I grab my Slim Jim and whack him repeatedly with it until he lets up. "I like people for their *personality,* not for their size!"

"Aw," Navier teases, evading my attack. "I'm flattered."

Ricket, who had been ignoring our antics until that moment, whips around to look at us. Double hell. Can't Navier *ever* keep his big mouth shut?!

I force a huge smile and punch him in the arm. "Yes, Navier, I even like *you.* Personality is important in friends, too."

Ricket doesn't buy it, not for a second. I see it in his eyes: disappointment. Judgement. Concern.

I meet those eyes in direct challenge, then look pointedly to where Tip is reading the nutrition facts on an economy-sized bottle of mustard.

Ricket drops his gaze, message received. If he'd wanted to throw stones, he shouldn't have put his hands on my trauma-ball of a cousin.

I leave the station and go to the pump where Rosa fuels her bike. Omar is looking worlds better than the last time I saw him. He's wearing clean clothes that fit him, and he's put on a few pounds. The stitches still hold his cheek together, but they'll need to come out soon.

"Hey, buddy," I greet. "How're you liking the bar life?"

He shrugs, hands in his pockets. "S'okay. Rosa has me in the back doing dishes. She pays me."

"I'd meant to hire a dishwasher anyway," Rosa dismisses before anyone can accuse her of charity. "Business is too good to stay a one-person gig."

"That's great," I enthuse, giving Omar a little nudge. *"And* it's almost June. Is someone gonna graduate?"

He smiles; a white slash in the dark that makes the world a thousand times brighter. "Yeah," he admits. "Finals are next week."

"Tell me when and where the shindig is!" I insist. "I wanna cheer your skinny ass on."

He looks at me a little funny. I guess it *is* weird to hear that the woman you held at gunpoint wants to celebrate your high school graduation. But I was a foster kid. I know how much adult support means.

He huffs a laugh, his tense posture at last relaxing. "Yeah, why not? I'll snag you an invite."

From the station stalks a grouchy Tip, who approaches with hand outstretched. "Keys. I'm going home."

Tip doesn't have a motorcycle license, and I don't have a student bus pass like he does, but I reach for the keys anyway because I never claimed to make good choices. Ricket's voice stops me: "I'll drive you home, Tip."

He walks with cane in hand, leash in the other, balancing a stolen cup of coffee between his forearm and his chest. I glance at

Tip to ensure it's okay. If Tip doesn't want to be alone with Ricket, I *will* intervene.

"Might as well," Tip shrugs, facing Ricket. "Trying to keep you safe didn't work out, since apparently you're in the middle of all the bullshit anyway, so sure, why not?"

Ricket doesn't flinch, but I see a crease form between his brows. "Tip…"

"No, it's fine. Why should I care that you were lying?"

"Ooh." Navier leans out the door, jonesing for a fight. He bears the wicked grin of one who's never experienced relationship troubles by virtue of not sticking around long enough for them to develop.

Rosa, who definitely didn't sign up for my cousin's drama, rolls her eyes and drops a helmet onto Omar's head. "We're going home, too."

"Call me," I say when she slings a leg over her Harley and waits for Omar to do the same.

"*Ooooh,*" Navier repeats when she nods. Good Lord; he's like a thirteen-year-old who never learned how to shut up. I ignore him and wave as the two depart.

Tip slides into Ricket's Jeep, looking like he's done so a million times before. Hero, freed from her leash, leaps in after him. He shuts the door and pulls her onto his lap.

Ricket glances to ensure Navier is out of earshot, then leans in close. "I meant to ask you," he whispers. "About your biopsy results. Is everything okay?"

Tell the truth! Not-Cero insists. I swat her away like a pesky fly. If I tell the truth, Ricket will try to nag me into accepting treatment. When I refuse, he'll *look* at me with those big brown eyes of his, and I'll feel like I seriously let him down.

Because you are *letting him down!*

"It was nothing," I tell Ricket, ignoring the phantom voice of my wife. "Just a little anemia. Thank you for taking me to see a doctor."

He *is* worrying, though. "Magpie..."

Please drop it, I beg silently. *Please.*

Tip leans out through the Jeep's window. "Can we *leave* now?!" he asks irritably. "Sometime tonight, maybe?"

"Better go," I urge, relieved to be let off the hook. "He gets cranky."

"Oh, I know." Ricket's smile is both wry and affectionate. "I am very aware."

Does he like Tip more than I'd assumed? Whatever happened between them is still objectionable on every level, but I'd feel better knowing Ricket's feelings towards my difficult cousin were (are?) genuine. "Get home safe, okay?"

He nods and returns to his Jeep. I watch him take my cousin away.

Might you consider not *standing around alone while there's a violent rapist stalking you?* Not-Cero suggests.

"I'm not alone," I retort, and return to my station. "I have Navier."

The man in question sprawls in a chair with his size-fourteen feet on my counter. I let myself in and make for the breaker box, plugging all the lights back in until the station no longer feels so isolated in the night.

"What's on the agenda, cher?" he asks. I grin at him.

With cheerleader levels of false enthusiasm, I trill, "Not to brag about my glamorous cashier life, but I'm doing inventory and stock! Then if you're *really* lucky, you'll get to see me scrub the toilet! How does that sound?"

It's entertaining watching him actively try not to wrinkle his nose. He doesn't succeed. "Can't you at least get robbed, or something fun like that?"

My laughter echoes off the tile floor. "You never know. Stick around; maybe your wish will come true."

He grins, pleased to have amused me, but loses it all too quickly. "Can't. Got somewhere to be."

I knock his boots off my counter, then glance at his clothes. There aren't any holes or grease-stains on his flannel, and his jeans are borderline tolerable. That's about as fancy as it gets for us. "Booty call?"

"I fuckin' *wish*. Nah; just business."

Business this late at night? Did a vampire hire him to fix their hearse?

I nudge him out of his chair so I can put it away, getting the store ready for customers. He surprises me by catching me against the office door with a hand on either side of the metal frame. "You gon' behave yourself while I'm gone, darlin'?"

I'd expected Navier to pretend our impromptu sofa hookup never happened. I'm no Victoria's Secret model, so I didn't think he'd consider me good bragging fodder. Guess he's still got a few surprises up his sleeve.

"Have I *ever* behaved myself?" I counter, jutting my chin. I enjoy flirting as much as the next guy. I flash my dimples and laugh when he hip-checks me into the wall to mouth at my neck. It tickles.

The bell above the door jangles as a customer lets herself in. Panicking, I shove Navier off a little harder than necessary. He stumbles ass-first into the counter and fixes me with a wounded puppy-dog pout.

The customer, an elderly woman in a motorized scooter who heads straight for the humming fridge in the back, pays us no mind. "Sorry," I mouth silently to Navier, who shrugs it off.

"I'd better go." He checks his pockets for keys, then abruptly hauls me in by the neck to plant a kiss — our *first* kiss! — on my lips. It ain't no *two-Mississippi's,* either. There's spit in my mouth that did not come from my salivary glands.

When I gawk at him, he grins broadly and flicks my nose. He doesn't seem to register that I did not kiss him back.

"Call me sometime," he purrs, and lets himself out, a swagger in his step. I listen to his Tacoma rumble from the parking lot.

"Wow," I mutter, and wipe my mouth off on my shirt sleeve. I'm trying not to compare apples to oranges, but the last person to kiss me was Vince, and *he* hadn't asked for my permission, either. Navier is making a lot of assumptions about my comfort levels.

The elderly customer, driving her scooter to my counter with an Arizona tea and a bag of Doritos in hand, gives a knowing shake of her jowly head. "Girl, that boy is *trouble...*"

Chapter Nineteen – Tip

mr. sandman, kindly fuck off.

...

"I dreamed about you last night," I inform Tessa, immediately upon seating myself in her cramped, chai-scented office.

It's too early in the morning for the sun to have baked the ocean's fog away. It cloaks the windows in hazy gray gloom. I can scarcely glimpse the empty parking lot, so many stories below.

If I'd hoped to disarm her by getting the first word in, I am sadly disappointed. She only looks up from her notebook and fixes me with those nonplussed owl eyes of hers.

"Good morning to you, too, Tip. I *know* you know I don't do dream analysis. Dreams are nothing more than the brain processing disjointed bits of information as you sleep. They carry no deeper meaning, positive or negative."

At least we agree on *something*. My last therapist, Arnie, made me write down all of my dreams for him to pour over in excruciating detail. Apparently everything from my teeth falling out to a jazz-singing bearded dragon signified a burning desire to "procreate with the fairer sex."

I guess "I strongly prefer dudes" was a concept he couldn't wrap his bald head around.

I should probably feel guilty for driving Arnie into an early retirement, but I don't. That hack had it coming.

"This one was different," I insist, waiting for Tessa to set her things aside and look at me properly. If I keep her talking about dreams, there won't be time to grill me on James, or the weight I've visibly lost since last we met.

Ours is a game with confusing rules and a clock to beat, and I've come ready to play. "I was lucid enough to pull myself out when it got too weird."

"But not before?" She crosses her legs, her layered skirt trailing when she leans an elbow on the side-table. She lifts a pencil, ready to take notes. Good; I caught her interest.

From my perch on the floral sofa, a pillow clasped in my lap, I shake my head no. "It was interesting. I wanted to see what would happen."

"Hm." She inclines her head, a lock of sand-colored hair falling over one shoulder, and takes my bait. "What happened in your dream?"

I recount what I can: how I drove Magpie's motorcycle to Tessa's home. In my dream, said home was a large stone building adjacent to a private lake. How I let myself in and found her in her kitchen, insisting, *demanding* that I needed her immediate help.

"You were wearing pajamas," I remember; an insignificant detail that would nevertheless have made Arnie shit his polyester pants. They weren't particularly sexy pajamas; just matching yellow shorts and a top decorated with a pink rosebud print, but the recollection strikes sharply enough that I say it anyway. It's one of very few definitive details in my otherwise fuzzy memory.

Tessa has no interest in my sleeping brain's fashion sensibilities. "What did you need me for?"

"We went into your office. You have a really nice desktop PC, by the way. You sat in your chair, and I..."

Damn it all! I'd been doing so well playing the passive observer, but the catch in my voice belies my true intensity. The dream had rattled me, alright, clinging for hours afterwards like a film of scum. I *need* Tessa to rationalize it away so I can feel normal again. "I got in your lap."

If that revelation makes her feel uncomfortable, she doesn't show it. She merely scratches out some notes and meets my eyes without a trace of shock or judgement. Her posture remains loose;

calm. "Do you interpret this as a sexual act, or perhaps a parental one?"

The question stumps me. "Both, I guess. Is there a difference?"

Oh, *that* makes her scribble some notes in my file. That's what annoys me most about therapy. Every stupid little thing is treated like a significant window into my psyche, when in reality it doesn't "mean" jack shit.

Now, because of that slip, I bet my next session will feature pointless questions about my biological parents, neither of whom I know anything about.

For now, though, she lets it go. She asks, "Did anything else happen in your dream?"

"I asked you to cut me."

She looks up sharply, fixing her owl eyes on my face. Maybe she thinks I'm making this up, but I'm really not. My exact words were, *'please, ma'am. I need it bad.'*

In my head I stack the possible questions she might ask like cups in a pyramid. Has anyone ever cut me in the past? Not in an intimate setting like that. No, I've never been a cutter; my self-harm is outsourced. No, knives have never been particularly sexual for me, save for—

"I used to date someone who…" I struggle to word this next bit in a way that won't encourage her to give my parole officer a call. "Enjoyed violence. Uh, sexually."

It feels like a betrayal, giving this piece of Vince's private information away, but whenever he pulled a blade on someone, I knew rough sex was sure to follow. "He *really* liked it when I hurt people *for* him. I was his weapon; his favorite knife."

What a good dog you are, Surfer-Boy…

Tessa studies me closely. The way she uses her thumb to adjust her glasses reminds me of James. Maybe that's what gives me the second wind I need to finish recounting my dream.

"You wouldn't do it. You refused, even after I—" *begged you to hurt me, crying like a little bitch.* "You handed me a box-cutter and told me to do it myself."

Tessa's office is one of many, honeycombed on a psychiatric floor of fucked up people paying strangers through the nose to be un-fucked. Is there a point to any of this? Does anyone *actually* get better, or is all of this a rambling joke without a punchline?

When Tessa uncrosses her legs and leans forward, I realize she's close enough to touch.

At the end of our first session, she'd asked whether we had a "touching relationship." The question confused me, so she'd explained that she would only initiate handshakes and hugs if I felt amenable. I was quick to say that no, we *don't* have that kind of relationship.

So far, she hasn't betrayed my wishes.

Is that about to change? Will she reach for me? Hands on my face, fingers hooking my mouth, reeling me between her knees to—

"Tip?" Tessa asks, and her voice is sharp enough to break through these intrusive thoughts. "You're breathing very hard right now. Let's try to take some slow breaths, okay?"

She does not touch me. We breathe. I am in control.

"That's when I woke up," I finish, my voice thick. Yes, I'd jolted awake, but not before dream-me dashed my dream arms and legs and face on the end of Tessa's blade, blood running freely from me and onto her. I'd hacked myself to flowing red ribbons; felt each stinging slash. The entire world reeked of copper; like Vince's skin and breath and Magpie's face and Crown's chest and the bodies of every addict who'd ever crossed my boyfriend.

"Tip. Breathe."

I'm dizzy from all this deep breathing. I brace my elbows on my knees and duck my head.

We sit in silence for a few solid minutes. Tessa sweeps her hair into a bun and spears it with her pencil in a gesture so reminiscent of Magpie that the tight fist of my anxiety contemplates loosening its hold.

"Tip." *Why* does she keep repeating my name?! "Let's address some things. You understand that what you saw was only a dream, and not a representation of reality?"

I snort. I'm not a delusional child. "I got that, thanks."

"Good. Next," I hear the drum of her nails on a file folder. "Do you think your past trauma with authority figures might've influenced these thoughts about me?"

Authority figures…?

"Your grandma's landlord. Your tenth grade history teacher. Your youth pastor. Kyle. So many others."

I flinch. Whenever Tessa remembers things I've told her in the past, it serves as a reminder that I need to better keep my mouth shut. Most people don't really listen. I've gotten sloppy about letting tidbits slip.

"They abused your trust by being sexual with you. They saw a vulnerable teenager who needed help, and they took advantage of your situation."

This annoys me in ways that are hard to articulate. "They didn't. They never had my trust to begin with. I get to decide if I was hurt or not, so I choose not to be." The very definition of control; plain and simple.

"Tip."

"I'm done talking about this." Let her tell my parole officer I'm non-compliant. I don't *care*.

"You've been failed so many times by those who should've known better, but chose to hurt and use you anyway. It's possible that your dream about me, and even the attention you seek from your professor, reflect some learned survival instincts. You think offering yourself sexually to us will buy you safety."

Wow. Every word in her pathetic little speech is dead wrong.

"I can't believe they call psychology a science," I sneer. "You're no scientist. You just invent shit cuz you get off on fucking with peoples' heads. Maybe you want to make your joke of a job easier on yourself."

She regards me coolly, unfazed by my degrading her profession. "And *you* are lashing out because you feel threatened. I'm touching a raw wound you've hidden for so long it's festered. You will never heal if you don't treat it."

Isn't she just chock full of wisdom today! I wish she'd take her hair back down and let all this bullshit die. It was a mistake to bring it up in the first place.

"That what you think you're doing?" I ask, when the silence grows too strong to tolerate. My voice is no longer harsh; only tired. I am a shark with no teeth; starving; drowning. *"Fixing* me?"

Her eyes are sad. Compassionate. Somehow, that stings worse than any judgement. "I can't do it alone, Tip. It has to be your choice, or nothing I say will ever help you."

...

I've missed my last two classes. A third absence will automatically drop me from the program, though even that's not necessarily permanent if I make a good case with the dean. College is a lot more forgiving than high school ever was.

I've kept up with all my online coursework, but the moment I walk into our classroom, Bambi is upon me with a vengeance.

"Where have you *been*?" she demands, meeting me in the doorway. Today the loose dress she wears is an eye-catching shade of emerald, while her hijab is silver and black. Her necklace is a twisting metal snake I vaguely recognize from the Harry Potter franchise.

"Sick," I lie, hoping the threat of germs will keep her at bay. "Thank you for emailing me your notes."

She plants her hands on her hips, scolding with no real heat. *"Astaghfirullah!* Tariq and I had to present all of our trawling data without you. Take better care of yourself, lunkhead! Finals are just around the corner."

Try as I might, even I can't hate Bambi. Twenty years old and already such a brain. James was wrong when he said *I'm* the one meant to go far. By the time Bambi is my age, she'll have changed the world.

I instinctively move my arm away when she makes to take it.

"Oh, sorry." She grimaces, dropping her hand before it can brush my sleeve. "I forgot about the no-touching thing. Come sit, okay?"

Our classroom comprises six rectangular tables with three stools beneath each. It's tightly cramped, in order to make room for the lab and all its merrily bubbling saltwater tanks.

I follow Bambi to the table she shares with Tariq, listening to her babble about a krill shortage off Key Cove, at odds with the high number of gray whale deaths this year. "Shouldn't it be the other way around?" She ponders. "Kill the predator and watch the prey overpopulate?"

I pull out a tall stool and sit.

"Hi, Tip," Tariq greets in his low voice, and I give him a lazy wave. Like Vince, Tariq is attractive enough to stop traffic. He's lean and wiry with prominent cheekbones, eyes closer to gold than brown, and a jawline chiseled by diamonds.

He emphasizes his beauty with makeup. Even under the harsh classroom lights, highlighter and glittering eyeliner lend his warm brown skin a rich glow.

He's soft-spoken, yet almost as accomplished as his girlfriend. Still, he lacks the drive I see in Bambi and most of our other classmates. I sometimes wonder whether marine biology is truly his passion, or if he's simply content to follow Bambi across every ocean.

"Tip's been sick," Bambi informs her boyfriend, plonking into her seat. He grimaces in sympathy.

I plug the unwieldy, ancient laptop Magpie and I share into the table. It looks stupid compared to the surrounding students with their tiny MacBooks, but if I want to keep up despite my damaged left hand, I have to type on *something*.

I connect to the school's Wi-Fi, and my browser defaults to Facebook.

"Who's that?" Bambi asks, shamelessly peeking over my shoulder at the screen.

I grunt, glancing at Magpie's newest selfie. She takes the blurriest photos, and always gives them asinine captions. Today it's a bathroom mirror selfie, all pajamas and bedhead, with her lips pouted like a fish's. The caption reads, *'Don'tcha wish ur cashier wuz HAWT like me!?!!?'*

"She's my roommate."

Bambi isn't the judgmental type, but it's a pain to explain how an Indian chick is related to a dude as fishbelly-white as me. People feel awkward when you tell them you were raised in foster care.

I'm about to leave the website when Haleigha, pouncing on the little green dot that indicates my online presence, shoots me an IM: *Hey, shark! You comin to the wedding tomorrow?*

I puzzle over how to word my decline. Tessa implored me to seek healing through friends and hobbies; to combat depression by physically forcing myself out of bed and into the world; but I consider tonight a victory just for making it to class. A wedding sounds *exhausting.*

That said, maybe I'll go just to show Tessa how full of crap she is. *I followed all your stupid advice, and nothing improved.*

Spite is my favorite motivator. I ask, *Can I bring my cousin?*

Haleigha sends me a long line of random letters and symbols. It looks like he pounded the keyboard with his fist. *Hell YEAH hell YEAH BRING THE WHOLE FAM!!!!! Everybody's welcome at a Hawaiian wedding.*

I don't have a 'whole fam' to bring, but I appreciate his enthusiasm. *Location? Dress code?*

As I send this, James pushes the classroom door open. It's a struggle doing so while juggling his bag, coffee mug, and cane, but we know better than to offer help.

I have to go now, I tell Haleigha. *Send all the info you can.*

I leave Facebook and open the online classroom. I glance up in time to see James watching me from his desk. When we lock eyes, he offers a cautious smile.

Does he have a right to smile at me, after everything I learned? Why does he even *want* to, now that he knows more of the skeletons in my closet?

He lied to me. He's embarrassed to be seen with *Magpie's jailbird-junkie cousin.* And hey; who could blame him?

Despite it all, I want to go to him. I want to put my head on his chest and rub my cheek against the abrasive material of his sweater — a sweater! In *May!* — and take one of his big hands to guide between my legs. *'Good boy,'* he'd call me, and I'd be putty in his arms.

Is Tessa right about me? Are all these feelings due to the shit I got into as a kid? Am I still, mentally, a stupid teen using myself as collateral?

"Feeling better, James?" Bambi asks. "You canceled our last class super last-minute."

He turns his enigmatic smile onto her. "I am, thank you. I apologize to those who didn't receive my email and arrived to an empty classroom, but there was an emergency."

If "hang out in a gas station to discuss gang activity" qualifies as an emergency, then sure.

"Everything okay?" someone else asks.

"It will be fine," he promises, and launches into lecture mode while we scrabble to keep up. That's James, alright; why share anything when he can deflect?

Unphased, I type along to the lecture; my right hand fluid, my left, stiff and inaccurate. The noisy keys clack beneath my fingers until Susan, a bespectacled mother of four, twists around to scowl at me.

I deliberately type all the louder just to get under her skin. Bambi rolls her eyes.

I'm thankful today isn't a lab day. I feel too shaky from hunger to stand for very long, and I don't have the mental capacity to measure silt in samples of ocean water like I'd been doing for the past few months.

A silent email notification pops into the bottom right corner of the screen. It's addressed to Magpie. I'm prepared to ignore it until I notice the sender's handle: Superstar.

Magpie's nickname for Crown.

With my heart in my throat, I click on the notification to read what he sent her.

From: c.karuna@freelancesplash.net

To: sexilexxi@aol.com // ricket_james@ucla.net // ragincajundesigns@yahoo.com

Subject: A Parting Message
Greetings, friends and family.

I write to you from LAX. I apologize for emailing this rather than telling you in person, but I am short on time and it takes too long to communicate in a way we all understand.

I am going home to the Ngāpuhi.

This is a decision I made years prior and have been build-ing my savings towards ever since. I've arranged every-thing with my elder, my surviving kin, and my work. I will get to keep both of my jobs, which I will now con-duct online.

I am asking you all now not to retrieve or stop me. I leave of my free will to live the life I should have been grant-ed from birth. I am righting a wrong committed against me. I am seeking happiness.

My actions were, in part, spurred by Vincent Ras-mussen's return. That man is dangerous and deranged. He nearly ended my life for reasons I still don't under-stand. I feel very concerned for my safety, and for yours.

It saddened me to learn of Jane and Rhys's choice to leave our work unfinished, though I understand their reasoning. I wish them the best with their child, but re-spect their need for a clean break. I will not be contact-ing them.

Etienne: I have left enough money in my desk to cover my half of the utilities for the next two months. You are welcome to do with my furniture what you see fit. Thank you for being my housemate.

James: though we were never close, I enjoyed our work together. You have an interesting mind. I had so much fun with you and Rhys on all the little details of our work. I hope you find happiness.

Magpie: I can only ask you not feel too saddened. I've left you some comics from our childhood; the ones I know you favored most. You will always be Jessica Jones to me.

Attached, you will find all the information I have compiled on Isaac Müller. I'm sure you won't be surprised to learn that I've done plenty of research on my own. Whatever you do about him, be mindful — he has many supporters in the underground.

In the words of my people, *E noho rā*. Goodbye to you all. I hope we meet again in better times.

Crown

I stare at the screen, struggling to comprehend how my littlest cousin has abandoned me without so much as a goodbye.

I can't deal with this. This is the type of shit heroin was invented for. Good God *damn,* I need it bad. The pinprick scars along every vein in my body seem to open; little mouths pleading to be fed so we can rest. So we don't have to feel so bad.

"Tip?" Bambi whispers, leaning in close so only I can hear her. "Tip, are you okay?"

Fuck, no. When am I *ever* okay?

"May I touch you?" she asks, and I open and close my mouth like a landed fish, unable to breathe the unfiltered oxygen of the world.

When I process her question, I shake my head no. If anyone but Vince puts their hands on me right now, I will dissolve into a flood of sea-foam to drown the world.

Bambi hands me her pen instead; a textured thing that surprises my fingers. She'd wrapped alternating shades of blue and green yarn around the plastic to make it pretty.

She nudges her spiral notebook my way. "Write something," she commands.

I want to protest that my handwriting is terrible. That it will ruin her beautiful notes. But she's insistent, so finally I touch nib to paper, cementing my tsunami-brain onto this one simple action.

I'm okay, I write in the margins. *I'm in control. I am okay. I am okay. I am okay. I'm in control.*

I scrawl the affirmation until it comes true. Then I write one final word: *thanks.* I set the pen down to show that I'm finished.

Bambi nods and accepts her returned utensils, focusing again on James's lecture as though what'd just happened *wasn't* weird as all hell. Like I'm not an absolute freak.

I try to do the same, but I can't help but sneak a peek at Bambi's soft face. How did she know doing that would help me? Come to that, how had she known I needed help to begin with?

The email isn't so scary now, but it makes me feel heavy inside. *Crown left me. He's gone.* Why had I been so certain we'd have a chance to make amends first?

'Gone' is better than 'dead'. I was so sure he was already dead when I'd hauled him out of Cero's Jaguar, not yet feeling the flames licking me; not yet knowing I was on fire. All I could see was his blood, everywhere, staining my vision whether my eyes were open or shut.

I know very little about cars, but I'd smelled heavy gasoline, and heard the rapid-heart ticking of the overexcited engine. *Explosion,* my brain knew, and my body responded accordingly.

Vince did that to him. I know he did, and I know it was to punish me for arguing with him. I know it's my fault.

Crown's leaving is a good thing. It will keep him safe from us.

When the lecture ends, I stand up and leave, then hide in the nearest bathroom until I'm reasonably sure the classroom has emptied. As grateful as I am to Bambi, I want no well-meant questions about my mental health.

As I'd hoped, when I return to the classroom, James is the only person inside. He's at his desk typing into his laptop, and seems surprised to see me again. "Tip?"

"Check your email," I tell him, and shut my eyes tight. "Please."

Chapter Twenty – Magpie

cute first date idea: hunt a violent drug dealer with your beloved.

...

Heatwaves ripple off the tarmac. I watch them dazedly from inside the diner on Belmont, fanning the neck of my top to circulate air onto my sweat-sticky chest.

SoCal can be beautiful, and I know Tip wouldn't survive without the ocean in his pocket, but the state is hot, expensive, and has a troubling tendency to be on fire.

Gran wanted to go somewhere landlocked, fearing the sea would swallow our sinful state upon the second coming of Christ, but we couldn't afford the move.

"Are you ready to order now?" a teenaged waitress asks, notebook in hand.

I've been sitting in the same spot, nursing the same iced coffee, for close to an hour now.

"My friend should be arriving any minute," I force a smile and will her to go away. It's not like the place is crowded. They can tolerate my butt a minute longer.

It's rude not to order, Not-Cero nags, as though I'm too stupid to know eatery etiquette. But I *did* order. I'm paying three bucks for some coffee poured over ice. And what if I *did* arrive too early only because my apartment is unbearably hot this time of year?

You can afford AC, my wife reminds me as the waitress shuffles off to refill a trucker's glass of orange juice. *Clay paid you off before betraying me.*

She had. I'd fearfully stored the check in my underwear drawer, as though even touching it would decrease its value. It's hard not to feel like Clay bought my silence for her crimes. But that's exactly what happened, right?

At least she'd remembered to make the check out to 'Georgia Byrd', one of my false names — 'Byrd,' because I'm a magpie, and 'Georgia' for Cero's snobby taste in modernist art.

When, after a few glasses of Merlot, I'd claimed Georgia O'Keeffe, queen of yonic symbolism, for my patron saint, my wife had contracted an adorable case of giggles. Thus, my pseudonym was born.

Georgia Byrd receiving large sums of money is far less suspicious than any deposits into Alexis Magpie's bone-dry account.

You can afford chemotherapy now, too.

"I'd rather drop dead," I snap, fed up with all her pressure. The startled trucker glances over his shoulder at me. I give him a weak smile until he returns to his OJ.

Jeez. If I start referring to my wedding rings as 'my precious' on top of chatting with the voices in my head, someone's gonna have to knock me down a volcano before I snack on some fingers.

Chemo is a *shitshow*. If I believed it would help, then *maybe* I'd give it the old college try, but there's less than a 25% survival rate for A.L.L in adults. I don't want to blow this windfall on an agonizing treatment that won't even work.

You're scared.

Of course I'm scared. How could I not be? My only coping mechanism is to avoid thinking about it; to seek distraction, preferably in liquid form.

Cero must sense that I'm too tense for conversation, because we drift into our own worlds: me, staring unseeingly at my cracked iPhone and she, resuming dark musings on Rhys and Clay's desertion.

Though she doesn't direct the thought at me, I feel it running like hot tar between us: *traitors!*

"But they're pregnant," I remind her. If I were responsible for an infant, I'd feel obligated to cut my gang ties, too. Parenthood and first degree murder don't make for good bedfellows.

That child should belong to the gang. We could raise it collectively.

"You get a little possessive sometimes, sweetie. Let them go."

They! Are! Mine!

She doesn't say it, but I know what she wants: for me to drive to their house and bargain with the mothers-to-be. To see if I can win back their loyalty.

If I can't, she wants me to find another way to take it — through violence or blackmail; the method doesn't matter.

She knows I won't do it, and so she doesn't ask. But I feel her tangled desires all the same.

They wouldn't have left if I was still alive.

The accusatory 'they wouldn't have dared to' is pointedly implied.

"Oh, so now I'm a bad leader because my *friends* aren't shit-your-pants terrified of me?!"

Leader, first; friend, second. That's how it has to be.

I finger my left clavicle. It didn't heal quite right after Cero shattered it against the hood of her Jaguar the very first time she caught me snooping around. It juts against my palm.

That was back when I was the cop and she, the thief. She'd done nothing of the sort once we became allies. It wasn't like we had an abusive romance...

My phone lights up in my hands. I pounce on the text from Navier, grateful for any reason to end this imaginary conversation.

The photo I receive depicts a part of Navier's anatomy I'd not yet familiarized myself with. I've never seen a veiny, erect penis dressed in a lobster bib before, but it's not a sight I'll soon forget.

Propped against Navier's naked hip is a bottle of red wine. Perhaps for set dressing, but more likely to compare sizes. 'Dinner for 2?' reads his caption.

It's by far the crudest, most ridiculous proposition I've received in my thirty-mumble years of life. I snort so hard my sinuses ache.

'Sorry,' I reply, still snickering to myself. 'I have plans. Maybe another time?'

There's a pause. He never was a quick texter. Then: 'Cmon.......
U O me 1'

Oh, *yikes*. Smirk falling, stomach dropping, I blink at the hurtful message. He's probably just joking around, but I'm *so* not a fan of manipulative language like that.

I type a rapid, 'Guess I'm not hungry,' and power my phone off until the only thing I can see is the reflection of my joyless face in the black screen.

As far as Navier is concerned, my "maybe another time" has just become a "no; not ever."

How fast a mood can turn. It's not even eleven yet, and already I want a stiff fucking drink. I clench my teeth against the ever-present memories of Vince's unwelcome hands.

Fuck this. Fuck him. Fuck everything. I slam back the last of my coffee and crush the ice between my jaws.

It's hard to read Not-Cero's reaction. She rustles like a vulture in the alcoves of my mind.

"What?!" I demand, braced for accusations. "Just say it."

Did you expect anything different? You know what he's like. What were you thinking?

Do I sense another layer to her reprieve? We're discussing Navier, but in the back of my mouth, I taste the acidic syllable of a sharper name.

Did I expect anything different from Vince? I knew what he was like. What was I thinking?

Fuck fuck fuckfuckfuck *fuck!* I need a drink I *need* a drink I NEED—

"Hey, Magpie. Am I late?"

Rosa blocks my view of the window by standing at my table. In concession to the extreme heat, she's exchanged her leathers for denim shorts, gladiator sandals, and a sleeveless yellow blouse to showcase her arms. *Someone's* been lifting weights.

Some might say I'm great at compartmentalizing. Others would argue that living a life of denial has stabbed my mental health into swiss cheese. Regardless, I eagerly latch onto distractions. Rosa happens to be an ideal one.

Her left thigh features a tattoo above her right knee of three fist-sized lemons dangling from a leafy, thorny branch. The way they're shaded brings to mind a fifties magazine advertisement. The warm yellows and greens are gorgeous against her rich brown skin.

Stop ogling her legs, Not-Cero sighs, exasperated. *Don't make fuck-me eyes just because you feel like shit.*

I offer Rosa my biggest smile, trying not to wince at Not-Cero's read of my flaws. "Not at all! I got here early. Please sit."

The pleather-padded bench squeaks loudly when she slides in across from me. The table lurches into my chest. Her face flames red. "Oh, oh hell... I'm so sorry!"

I wave her off. These things happen all the time with Crown. "Dude, no worries. Everything is jammed too close together, anyway. Lemme fixit."

Bracing my feet on the ground, I arch my spine and force my bench back a few inches, dragging the table with me to give her thicker body more space. "Better?"

Rosa nods, avoiding my eye.

I don't want her to feel awkward! I flash through things to talk about to put her at ease. She always puts a lot of work into her appearance, so maybe... "Your makeup looks great," I compliment. "Is that, uh, gloss?"

She blinks at me.

Crap. I probably just said something epically stupid. That's what they call the stuff, though, right?

To my immense relief, she laughs; a smoky curl of sound. "This *heat*. It melts all my makeup! I'm glad you like the look, but I can't do *anything* with my hair..."

"You're radient," I tell her, because I'm exceptionally gay and it's the truth.

Her eyes soften. Her smile warms. "You're very sweet."

Our teenage waitress returns. Rosa confirms they're still serving breakfast before ordering a special. "Put us on the same bill," she tells the girl. "My treat."

My eyes bug. No *way* — I'm not some leach! And this isn't a date... is it? If it was, shouldn't somebody have told me?

The waitress looks expectantly my way, pencil poised.

"Um." I glance uselessly at the menu, then away again. "I like waffles."

Ladies and gentlemen: the most intelligent sentence I've ever uttered, right after 'is that, uh, gloss?'

Thank the Lord and every saint for sympathetic youth. The kid guides me through an order, though I'm so embarrassed I just agree with whatever she says. I wind up with two waffles and a side of scrambled eggs, in addition to a refill on my coffee.

I bury my face in my hands the moment she walks away. "I promise I'm not usually *this* dumb," I tell Rosa, peeking between my fingers as she smirks at me.

"I don't know," she teases. "I've seen you on tequila night."

I groan. "You don't have to pay for me."

"You can pay next time."

Next time? Well, *that* hits like a swarm of bats in my tummy. Now I'm fighting to conceal a goofy grin as I emerge from my cave of mortification.

"How's work?" Rosa asks.

"Good. Hopefully, I don't get fired for hosting gang meetings during business hours, but you know how it goes. You?"

She fills me in on bar gossip until our food arrives. I see the way Rosa's eyes *spark* at her stack of pancakes, drizzled with chocolate. She makes a dive for the Maraschino cherry in her shake.

"Sweet tooth?" I ask.

"*Sí,* not that I need it."

I don't know whether I'm meant to argue or agree, but I know that insisting I think she's perfect will sound patronizing, despite how true it is.

"My salt addiction is worse," I promise, reaching for the shaker even as I speak, though it's far from the worst addiction I have. "But it puts the 'yum' in 'sodium.'"

"That's just like Omar. Did you know I caught that boy putting salt on *watermelon?* I think I should hold an exorcism. That just seems unholy."

"No, it's delicious!"

We banter and eat. Rosa is *funny*; sharp as a whip and twice as quick. Apparently she plays the electric cello. I have no idea what such a thing could look or sound like, but I make a mental note to Google it as soon as possible.

She's a big fan of reading, too, with an emphasis on classic lit. "That's where my cat got his name," she supplies, and I recall the noisy, deaf critter haunting her home. "After Victor Hugo."

"Oh!" I exclaim. "I recently got into reading, after..."

After a few casual date rapes courtesy of one Vincent Rasmussen made me reconsider clubbing as my favorite pastime. Nothing to keep you cozy while you drink yourself into a stupor like a good book! "Just in the past couple years. I check out *stacks* of library books at a time. Mostly nonfiction."

And fairy tales, and comic books, but I'd feel embarrassed to share *that* level of nerdery.

Rosa wrinkles her nose. "Nonfiction? Never romance, or poetry?"

"I might get into romance, if it's written well. Poetry is a little too abstract for my brain." I tap my head with my knuckles. "No artistry in this noggin."

"Hm. You haven't listened to the good ones yet, then. Poetry is all about how it sounds when it's read out loud. Somebody should read you some Maya Angelou, or Sandra Cisneros, or Julia Alvarez..."

"Rosa *Santiago,*" I gasp, mock-scandalized, popping the last bite of waffle into my mouth. "Are you offering to read me *poetry?*"

She juts her chin boldly. "Maybe I am. You have some serious gaps in your education, young lady!"

Oh, bury me in a field of wildflowers; I'm doomed. I melt like the whipped cream in her shake, and smile like the most twitterpated fool in all of California. "Name the time and place, and I'm yours."

Only a bite of pancake remains on her plate. She spears it on her fork, swirls it in chocolate, and holds it out to me like a challenge, or a reward. "Eat. I'm full."

Meeting her eyes, I do just that.

...

We pay and depart, taking the crosswalk as we head to our real destination: the Motel 6 across the street from the diner.

I'm just thinking, rather nostalgically, that it's been a *while* since I took a girl to a motel (hello, high school prom), when Rosa shoots me a cocky grin.

"Are the rest of your family so short?" she asks, indicating the way I stand well over a foot below her.

It's not the first time I've gotten this question, and it won't be the last. "You've met Tip. He's big compared to me, but petite for a cis guy. Our little cousin Crown is close to seven feet tall."

Rosa whistles in amazement. "For real? Damn!"

We wait at the intersection for the traffic signal. Cars stream all around us, smelly with exhaust. "So Tip is really your cousin? How…" She trails off, catching herself.

I playfully nudge her side with my elbow. "How is he white?" I tease, thinking of the film 'Mean Girls.' *God, Rosa, you can't just ask people why they're white!*

"You don't have to tell me," she's quick to reassure, but I can tell she's curious. "If it's too personal."

I shake my head. "It's not."

It *is* personal, but it's not a secret. "Tip, Crown, and I are technically foster siblings, but we prefer the term 'cousins'. I was in the system since infancy, and was eight years old when the same caregiver took us all in. I've never met any of my biological relatives."

I wasn't technically a "dumpster baby," having been abandoned at the Santa Cruz fire department at just a few hours old, but that didn't stop Vince from making shitty Family Guy references when we were in high school.

Rosa nods. "Gotcha."

"I'm glad you asked," I say warmly, in case she's worried she pried too much. "I like talking to you. Tip and Crown are my family, and you're important to me. I'd like for us to be friends."

I'd like to be a lot more, and normally I'm not shy about making that clear, but as my life expectancy is now less than five years…

"Aren't we already?" Rosa asks as we hustle across the street, and I nearly trip. *Really? We are?!*

Usually tall people have trouble keeping up with me. I've got fast little legs. To this day the best compliment I've ever received is that I walk 'like I'm going to war.' But Rosa walks with a purpose, and so we stay perfectly in stride.

"What about you? Your family?" I ask.

We reach the front doors of the motel, and Rosa waggles a manicured finger at me. "Ah-ah-ah, not so fast. You have to reach at least a level five in friendship before unlocking *my* tragic backstory."

Oh, so it's like that, is it? I incline my head in acceptance and follow her into the dimly lit lobby. I wonder what level our friendship is at now. Pancake-sharing has to be at *least* a two, right? Did Omar's rescue push us into a three?

The motel is disappointingly generic. Dark-carpeted floor; plain desk; two chairs on either side of a table holding a water cooler and some plastic cups.

There's nobody working the counter. I take childish pleasure in slapping my palm down hard on the ringer of a silver bell. It's the little things in life...

From the back, we hear the raised voices of a girl and a man, arguing. "Screw you, Uncle Bill! You can't keep calling me in on my day off."

"We're understaffed, Iris. You said you needed more hours..."

"Not so last-minute! I had plans. I had a *date*."

"Young lady..."

Whatever 'Uncle Bill' plans to say next is cut off when a sour-faced blonde, maybe nineteen years old, storms from the back to slam herself aggressively into the desk chair.

"What?!" Iris barks, scowling at the both of us like we've personally wronged her.

Rosa and I exchange a glance. Man, and I thought *my* customer service was lacking.

"We're here to ask about a guest," Rosa says, bracing her elbows on the desk.

The reminder of why we're here knocks the levity from my system. I glance around, half expecting to see Vince lounging in one of the hard plastic chairs, sipping water from the cooler.

"Yeah?" Iris asks, cracking her gum. "Who?"

It's my turn to step in. "His name is Vincent, but that's probably not the name he gave you. He's tall and dark-haired and has a lot of tattoos. He probably paid you in cash. I think he stayed in room twelve?"

Iris brightens. "*That* guy? Yeah, I remember him! He was hot."

I cringe, warning, "He's a rapist, and he attacked at least one local minor in the past month."

I've slipped back into cop-mode without meaning to, voice low and gaze intense. Iris's blue eyes bulge in shock.

"For real?" she asks, losing her brassy tone.

I nod gravely.

"Jesus..." She falls quiet, probably thinking back to all the times she'd interacted with the charming customer. All the times she was alone with him. "You guys undercover cops or something?"

It's as good a cover story as any. Banking on the hope that she'll believe me without proof, I say, "I need all the information you have on him."

"Uh, yeah, uh..." She turns to her PC and types rapidly, the chipped black polish on her nails glinting in the late-afternoon sun. "He called himself 'Dylan Tippling.'"

I stiffen. He'd used Tip's name? Does he have a fake ID under that name, like I have a 'Georgia Byrd' ID and social?

Does he have a reason for this, or is it yet another mind game?

"Yeah, he *was* staying in twelve," Iris reads off her screen. "Single-bed, smoking room. He checked out two days ago. Yep, paid in cash. He had a wake-up call set for five every night of the two months he spent here."

Two *months?*

Iris's pale cheeks heat. "I liked being the one to make his wake-up calls," she confesses.

"It's not your fault," I reassure. "He was probably sweet to you, right? You couldn't have known."

"A customer grabbed my butt one night while I was walking down the hallway," she says, staring down at her keyboard. "That kinda thing happens all the time here. But Dylan — uh, Vincent — defended me. Told the guy to piss off, and made sure I was okay"

This isn't about me, but it's hard not to compare Iris's experiences with my own. Oh, I knew Vince was a dealer. I knew he'd abused Tip. I knew he'd been making me feel uncomfortable since I was a kid.

But I was dealing with the slow death of my wife, my boss, my *leader,* all on my own. Tip and Crown were gone. Gran was dead. The gang avoided us, as though fearing cancer or depression were contagious.

Vince was the only one who came to me.

You want a night out, don't you, Squirrel-Face? I've seen how much you love to dance.

We'd gone to the most elite clubs in the nicest of cars. We'd partied with celebs in Hollywood, though I wouldn't have cared if we were dancing alone in a dollar store parking lot. I'd just needed to *move.*

People, even well-known, influential people, just can't get enough of what Vince has to give. What chance did I stand?

It wasn't like I'd never taken party drugs before. Molly, mostly. A teenhood of underground mosh pits does that to a person, though I'd behaved myself since academy days. When he'd offered colorful tabs on his index finger, an eyebrow arched in challenge, it'd felt only natural to lick them off.

They'd made the lights brighter; the dances faster. They'd made the acute feeling of *wrongness* in my chest fade to happy confetti when his hands squeezed my hips or tangled in my hair. He wasn't charging for it, so what was the harm, right?

If you're not the buyer and you're not the seller, then you're the product. Wasn't that the first thing I ever taught you, Miss Cop?

"People fall into Vince," I tell Rosa and Iris, ignoring Not-Cero. "Like he's a disease."

Tip came to him for drugs when he couldn't bear his life anymore. And so did I, for the same reason. "You want to please him. When you're with Vince, the entire world feels like a joke."

I wonder if writers base the fairy tales I read late at night off of people like Vince. The heartbroken and the downtrodden give themselves over to devils and find, when the dream ends, that they're aged; changed. That they now have holes in their hearts that can never be filled.

"You think you can show us his room?" Rosa asks.

Iris is hesitant. She glances over her shoulder, at the back room where she'd been arguing with her uncle. "I don't think that's allowed..."

"Please?" I meet her eyes. "He's sending threats to people. We need to learn all we can about where he might have gone before he harms them. You'd be such a help."

The girl lights up at the prospect. "Oh, why not? I hate this job, anyway."

Room twelve is on the first floor of the South wing of the motel. We exit the lobby and step out back where the air smells of chlorine from the pool. I can hear kids there laughing and splashing each other.

Iris, electronic key in hand, takes us to the room. There're a few old ladies playing outdoor chess who wave at us when we pass. Based on their outfits, I assume they spent the day at the nearby casino.

She unlocks the door, marked in chipped paint with the number 12. The room is as basic as the lobby. There's a window covered by flimsy curtains above a rusted heating/AC box; a king-sized bed sandwiched between two nightstands; a wall-mounted television; doors leading to a closet and a bathroom.

I smell nothing but cleaning solutions, and hear only the occasional gurgle of cheap plumbing.

Propping the door open with a rock from the step, Iris plants her hands on her hips. "What do we do now?"

I'm working out how to politely tell her to get lost, when a distant man's voice interrupts us: "Iris? Where did you go?"

She groans and rolls her eyes. "I'm *helping* our *guests,* Uncle Bill!" she shouts back, injecting every syllable with pure teenage disdain.

"You're supposed to stay at the desk!" There's a whine in his tone. It's clear who wears the pants around here, regardless of who technically owns the place.

"Ugh!" Iris stomps for the door.

I stop her, zipping to the closer nightstand where a pad of stationary rests between a landline phone and a stack of religious texts — Quran, Torah, and the King James Bible. Props to Uncle Bill for inclusivity.

"Let me give you my number." I reach for the pad and pen, then pause, considering.

Setting my backpack on the floor, I fish out an old In N Out receipt and scribble the digits on that, instead. I add Ricket's number for backup, making sure to use our real phone numbers instead of the burners we've accumulated over the years.

A real cop would have a proper business card to give her, but Iris looks a few sandwiches shy of a picnic. I'm not too worried about her piecing my lie together.

"If Vince ever comes back," I instruct, handing the scrap over, "Make sure to never be alone with him. Try not to let on that you know who he is. Call him 'Dylan,' like he told you. Then text one or both of these numbers. We'll help you, okay?"

Iris nods and takes the receipt, then opens her mouth to say something else.

"Iris!" Bill interrupts, sounding closer now.

She sighs, shoulders slumping, and leaves to address her uncle. Rosa waits until her footsteps fade before quietly closing the door and turning the lock. "Let's get started."

"Do you have a pencil?" I ask, setting the motel pen aside. "I need one."

She digs in her own bag for the requested item while I begin a search of the room. Obviously they cleaned it after Vince left, but with employees like Iris, I doubt it's been cleaned *well*.

Kneeling to peek under the bed — the frame is solid wood, so nothing can get too deeply lost under there — I groan when I find three gray socks, a bottlecap, loose change, a colony of dust bunnies, and a handful of crumpled tissues.

Any of this could belong to Vince, but it could just as easily not. No useful clues here.

"Pencil!" Rosa triumphantly holds the implement aloft — a classic, yellow no. 2. Perfect.

"You got paper, too?"

Rosa huffs an irritated sigh.

I bat my eyelashes winningly and, with a dramatic roll of her eyes, she resumes rifling in her bag.

I make a note to carry better supplies from now on. Then I get up and open the closet door.

"Jackpot!" I exclaim. The dust bunnies here have bred alarmingly, ignored by vacuum cleaners. More importantly, I see a battered blue backpack held together by duct tape. The name written in Sharpie across the front pocket reads "OMAR."

"Don't do that," Rosa protests when I carry the bag to the bed and upend it over the blanket, knowing the tan fabric will catch any small odds and ends that would otherwise be lost on the dark carpet. "That's not yours."

"Just checking to see if Vince put in anything nasty. One time he hid an eightball of coke in my jacket pocket. That was one awkward surprise at my friend Alina's sleepover, when I *thought* I was pulling out some fruit snacks..."

Rosa joins me on the bed, sorting through Omar's textbooks and laundry; the wallet and toiletries and utensils and bedding. He was right: this bag holds everything.

There's a home address printed on his student ID that I don't allow myself to look at. If I don't know what it is, then I can't disrespect his wishes by going there and demanding to know what his family's beef is.

"There's cash in his wallet," Rosa observes. "Why didn't Vince steal it?"

"What would he need it for? He's loaded." So why stay in such a shoddy motel for two months, then? Just to be close to my apartment? And what made him *leave?*

There's nothing out of the ordinary in here. No body parts or drugs. As far as I can tell, Vince just kicked the pack into the closet and forgot about it.

It's weird, how he can be so meticulous about some things, yet utterly careless about most. I don't think he's ever faced a repercussion in his life; not even a speeding ticket.

Rosa has no paper in her bag, so I flip Omar's spiral notebook open to tear out a single blank page, then hand over the rest for

Rosa to pack away. I twist my body around on the bed to reach and turn on the lamp, then drop the stolen paper on top of the motel's stationary pad.

Bracing my right elbow on the nightstand, I use Rosa's pencil to scribble a layer of graphite over the entire sheet. The places where a pen nib pressed down in the past now stands out in white contrast to the pencil's silver.

"You pick up that trick from Jigsaw Jones?" Rosa teases, watching over my shoulder.

"Excuse *you*. I learned my expert sleuthing skills by being a highly trained agent of the law!" I gasp, a mock-offended hand to my heart. Then I let my grin shine through. "But yes, Gran read Jigsaw Jones to me at bedtime. And Nancy Drew, and Hardy Boys, and Encyclopedia Brown..."

"That's a phone number," Rosa points to the paper.

It is indeed; nine digits scrawled with a generous hand. The area code is local.

Anybody could have written a phone number on the previous page of this stationary. It could've been from Vince, or it could be from a guest twenty years prior.

Rosa jostles my arm, sounding excited. "Call it!"

I'm hesitant. "What if it's nothing?"

"What if it's *something?*" There's a fire in her eyes. "Just stay quiet if someone answers. It'll be fine."

I'm still unsure. "Google it first," I advise. "See if it pulls up a pizza place or something."

I hand Rosa the paper and stand, making for the bathroom as she pulls out her phone to do just that.

The bathroom is as average as the rest of the place. It's superficially clean. There are thin white towels stacked on a wire rack above the toilet.

To the left is a sink with a tiny box of bar soap helpfully waiting to be opened and used. To the right is the shower, where Vince assaulted Omar.

With a heavy heart, I approach the toilet, pulling up the lid and seat to see exactly what I'd expected. Vince did an okay job cleaning up after his crime, but around the porcelain hinges are rings of brown. Oxidized blood. Even the runniest of diarrhea wouldn't be so thin, streaking in layers like the legs of weak wine.

If I were to take a cotton swab, dab a sample, and take it to a lab, I'm certain it would show Omar's DNA. But I already know who was cut, and where, and by whom.

What's more, I know exactly what it feels like: the terror of a rapist crawling like a demon through your window and into your bed and holding his knife to your face and—

I let the seat drop. Then I slap the two rolls of backup toilet paper off the tank. I kick the wall, leaving a dent and a black smear from the toe of my boot. I curse in barely restrained rage.

The best option is to feel nothing at all, but when given the choice, anger is far more palatable than sadness, or fear.

I smack the bar of soap from the counter. It hits the floor with a satisfying clatter. Next to go are the towels, which flutter daintily downwards. There's no relief to be found in their graceful descent, so I seize the lid off the toilet tank, grunting, prepared to smash it to pieces against the mirror, the lightbulbs...

Something silver glints inside the toilet tank, submerged beneath the float. I lean the heavy lid against the wall to free my hands and reach for it, shaking the water off before examining what I hold. It's a simple butterfly knife; black handle, silver blade.

Butterfly knives are flashy little tools. Those who collect them are fond of flipping them; a dance honed over months of practice with a dull blade.

Vince, partial to anything beautifully threatening, showed this skill off as far back as high school. My face throbs, recalling the cold slice of an identical blade.

This discovery tells me nothing I don't already know, but it somehow sinks my heart in a grief so profound I lose all the strength in my body. My legs wobble. My head hangs. I want to cry, but the tears won't come.

"Magpie?" Rosa calls. "I can't find the number online. I'm calling it now."

"No!" Knife in hand, I sprint for her.

It's too late. Rosa holds the landline's plastic receiver to her ear, listening. "One ring," she says. "Two, three..."

I hop onto the bed and crawl over to her. She shifts to one side so I can hear, too. We sit, cheek to cheek, hearing a fourth ring; a fifth.

Then Vince's deep voice crackles into our ears. "Dude, I'm busy. The fuck do you want now?"

The bottom drops out of my stomach. Rosa looks at me. I force my lips to form his name.

There's a pause on the other line. "Who is this?" Vince asks. He's lost his tone of familiarity, suspecting we aren't who he'd originally thought.

Burner phone, my cop-brain supplies. *Likely one that only a single other person knows the number to, or he wouldn't have answered so confidently.*

"Mom?" Vince asks, voice going softer, sweeter. "Mommy, is that you?"

I retch, acid spewing upwards to coat my tongue. I squeeze the knife until my knuckles pop.

Rosa wrenches the phone from my hand and slams it back into its cradle, then watches as I shudder and curl in on myself, pulling my knees to my chest and burying my face in them.

My breakfast threatens to make a reappearance. I fight it valiantly.

"Magpie?" Rosa asks. "I'm going to take the knife out of your hand, okay?"

I feel her fingers work mine open before pulling the tool away. She sets it on the table with a clack. Then she shifts towards me. "Is it okay if I put my arms around you?"

"Please do," I rasp. I need to feel something, *anything* that's not Vince's weight crushing me. I stopped breathing, sometimes, when he was on me. When he pressed a knee to my diaphragm. An elbow to my throat.

Rosa is warm and soft. She smells of limes and salt and good whiskey. I melt into her chest. She envelopes me entirely, and isn't afraid to squeeze. I never want her to let me go.

"He did more than just cut you, didn't he?" Rosa asks.

I nod. She's the first person I've ever confessed that secret to.

Rosa sighs. The sound goes on forever as she pieces the puzzle together. "Oh, *cariño.*" She nestles her chin atop my head. Some of the unbearable weight finally lifts from my heart.

"Distract me?" I request. "I promise I'll be okay in a second, I just..."

She plucks at the necklace I'm wearing, lifting it to examine the two wedding rings welded together. "You said your wife made these?"

"She designed the rings, then a jeweler made them. Cero's mother, actually. After Cero died, Tip sent them back to her mom so Nina could bind them into a necklace."

"I didn't know your wife was a necromancer."

"Excuse me?" I blink at her, my trauma laid aside for this oddity. She may as well have said, 'I didn't know your wife was a goldfish!'

"See these markings?" Rosa tilts the pendant my way. I peer at the two rings, seeing the swirly designs that decorate the silver bands. "The mark on this ring is Namtillaku's sigil. He's a Sumerian Lord with the power to raise the dead."

I see nothing but lines and hoops on the ring Cero once wore. It looks like anything else she'd ever designed: abstract, but deliberate.

"Are you sure?" I ask dubiously. "It looks like a doodle."

Rosa gives a disdained huff. "Yes, I'm *sure*. Nobody 'accidentally' carves the summons for a lord of death. And even if I *wasn't* sure, look at this sigil on the other ring. I don't believe in coincidences."

She flips the pendant over to show me the ring I'd worn for years; first on my left hand, now around my neck.

In the direct lamplight, if I squint and lean in close, I can see similar markings etched into the diamond itself.

"My eyes aren't good enough to see much without a loupe," Rosa admits, referring to a jeweler's magnifying device I'd only ever seen in Antonina's toolbox. "But I'll bet you that's Asarualim's sigil."

"The who's what, now?"

"Look, based on that line right there. Doesn't it look like an arrow? This should give the wearer secret knowledge over death, excellent counsel, and resistance to trickery."

"And that's on *my* ring?" I goggle at the diamond, willing the miniscule scars to provide better clarity. "I guess it didn't work. I don't know shit, and I'm gullible as hell. How do *you* know all this?"

Rosa smirks, dropping the pendant back onto my chest. "Oh, you know. Closeted lesbian bookworm in a strict Mexican-Catholic family? I had to annoy my Abuela *somehow*. My studying witchcraft drove her loco. She hung so many crosses around my bed..."

This gives me a smile, imagining teen-Rosa in her grungy concert Ts, pouring over dusty occult texts to get a rise from her family. As one who specializes in being a little shit, I can relate.

"Was she really a 'necromancer', or did she just like the designs?" I ask. "Cero was all about aesthetics."

Rosa shrugs. "She's your wife. You tell me."

"Is a necromancer..." I pause at the strange word. "What *is* that, in the witchy world? Can they like... Heal dying people?" I think of poor Navier, glassed through the liver.

"Nope. It's mostly focused on the after-death stuff. *Preventing* death is a whole 'nother branch."

Maybe I should dig Cero's sketchbooks out of storage for curiosity's sake, if I can be bothered. But why should I? So what if she put some funky designs on our rings? She was just an odd duck, not a *necromancer.*

"It's getting late," I tell Rosa, struggling to my feet. "Soon your bar's gonna fill up, and you don't want poor Omar wrangling rowdy bikers all by himself, do you?"

"We should go," she agrees. "When things settle down, maybe we can do this again? Preferably without the, uh, sleuthing for violent drug dealers, but I'm not picky."

Oh, my heart. "Let's," I agree. "I like talking to you. Can I hear you play your cello sometime? It sounds badass."

"It is," she agrees. I see a twinkle in her dark eyes. "Yes. Then I'll read you some poetry."

Maybe I should just tell Rosa that I'm terminally ill, and let *her* decide whether I'm worth pursuing. I don't know how much longer my tenuous health will hold out. Eventually, my symptoms will become impossible to ignore.

But it's just so nice, this. I want to enjoy these moments while they last.

Rosa stands and stretches, then holds her hand out for mine.

I reach for it, then pause, smiling sheepishly. "I wrecked the bathroom," I confess. "I'd better fix it. You go on."

Rosa shakes her head. "We'll fix it together. I won't leave you here."

With more gratitude than I can express, I slip my hand into hers. We clean the bathroom and sneak from the motel in silence. We return to the diner and don our leathers. I wave goodbye as her Harley roars from the parking lot.

Once home, I'm just parking my Kawasaki when Tip throws our door open, hands on his hips in a posture I recognize from Gran.

"Why don't you *ever* answer your phone?!" he demands as I approach.

Oops. I'd shut it down after Navier pulled his weird crap on me. I reach to power it back on. "Is something wrong?" I ask while it boots up. "You're not usually awake at this time."

"Huh? No." He takes my helmet from me as I step inside. "Would you... This is gonna sound so stupid."

I wait. I'd do pretty much anything for Tip, so long as it didn't involve drugs.

"Wanna go to a wedding with me?"

Chapter Twenty-One - Magpie

if nautical nuptials be something you wish...

...

Standing at the bathroom counter as I apply sunblock and braid my hair, I listen to the messages in my voicemail. There's two from Tip, each less than five seconds long: 'Hey, where are you?' and, 'Call me back,' respectively.

It doesn't escape my attention that Navier never texted back after my rebuttal. Radio silence all around.

There *is* a message from Antonina, however. Scarcely a day goes by when I don't hear her frantic voice. 'Alexis! Oh, please answer me! I have made such terrible mistake. Please, oh please; you are in a danger and I cannot pay the travel monies to come to you!'

That one, I'm quick to delete. I can hardly blame the lady for going a little batty, but she's driving me up a wall. Can't she find somebody else to rave at?!

There's only one voicemail remaining. The gas station's phone number in my history makes my tummy clench. It's probably nothing — maybe they found the hat I lost at work a while ago, tucked in a shelf somewhere. Or they just want me to cover Melody's morning shift again.

I know better the second I hear Brittanie speak.

'Yeah... Lex? So like, here's the thing. I'm getting tons of complaints about the station being closed at night sometimes? And apparently there's like, hookers and whatever hanging around? It's scaring people off. Our night sales aren't looking great. Like, way, *way* worse than usual. *Please* fix this, or I'll have to cut your hours.'

She ends the call. My voicemail helpfully informs me that it is now empty.

"Yikes," Tip says, echoing my thoughts. I turn to see him standing behind me, one of Cero's sunset-colored Hawaiian shirts in hand. When he holds it out, I button it over my lilac tankini. "Trouble in paradise?"

"Don't worry about that. Why are your surf buddies getting hitched *here?*" I ask, adjusting my shorts. Not the greatest gear to ride a motorcycle in, I'll admit, but do terminally ill people really *need* to bother with road safety? "Why not Maui?"

"I asked the same question," he informs me, applying lotion to his burn scars before donning a pair of sky-blue hiking sleeves. They match his board shorts. "I guess they wanted to go to Disneyland for their honeymoon."

I smile, recalling how I'd begged Cero for the exact same thing. Neither of us had ever been there before — me, because I'd grown up poor. She, as a victim of child trafficking, hadn't had much opportunity for theme parks.

"I'm happy for them," I say warmly. "Tell me how to say the bride's name again?" I repeat Leilani's name aloud several times, determined to get it right.

We leave once I Google the route. There's a section of cabin-filled beach reserved for military functions — meaning that it's not open to the public, and thus is ideal for parties.

Tip hops off the bike while I park, watching me swap my boots out for sandals. We walk in the direction of military cabins on the sand, then up a rocky slope towards colorful umbrellas and awnings where the distant strains of music and voices carry.

It worries me how out of breath he is as we hike said slope. I knew he was out of shape, but his face has gone a chalky white, and I hear him struggling to hide his wheezing.

"You okay, Q-Tip?" I ask, masking my concern with flippancy. "You ate today, right?"

"If I had food inside me right now, I'd be spewing it across this *fucking* path," he snarls through clenched teeth, pearls of sweat beading on his forehead.

I give him my sternest face. "You'll eat once we get to the party, right?"

I know it does no good to force food on people with disordered eating issues, but I wish I could find the highest calorie drink at the party and dump it down his throat. I don't know how to help him with this aspect of his life. For me, food is delicious fuel. Never an enemy.

He fixes his sea-eyes on me. Today, they're blue as the horizon. His voice loses some of its edge when he replies, "If it makes you happy."

It sounds like concession. Resignation.

"It does," I say, though I don't want him relying on me for sustenance. I want him to eat because *he* wants to eat.

Everyone wants what they can't have.

We eventually make it to the top of a cliff overlooking the sea. I gaze out at the ocean; at the setting sun dazzling the water. Tip, at my side, emits a longing sigh.

The area is shaded by an enormous tent that people mill in and out of, their animated chatter tossed and distorted by the breeze. The tent is open on both ends: one towards the path we just climbed, and the other leading to a tall, flower-woven arch ensconced by some hundred plastic chairs.

The far-reaching aroma of smoked pork has me drooling, combatted by that of the hundreds of flowers climbing every object; tied into every head of hair. Their perfume alone is enough to get drunk on.

And the *music...!* I search high and low until I find its source: two beaming Hawaiian girls, surely no older than twelve, absolutely *shredding* on a pair of ukuleles.

My jaw drops at their skill. "I didn't know ukuleles could *sound* like that," I gasp to Tip. I'd only ever heard the plinky-plunky melodies from white kids on YouTube. That stuff is as distinguished from this as a chihuahua is from a dingo.

Some people are already dancing in and out of the tent — children festooned with flowers, clasping hands to form a chain; elderly couples swaying with startling grace, their foreheads pressed.

Tip grins. It softens the hard lines at the corners of his eyes.

"Dance with me?" I reach for his hand, stopping just shy of taking it.

His grin fades, but he nods. "I will. Later, though. Not now."

Because he *wants* to, or because I'd asked? I recall his words from earlier: 'If it makes you happy.' How much of what he does is just to placate me?

"Come on," I say, careful not to touch him; afraid that any excessive contact will deplete his reserves before I get that dance. "We should find the groom and say hi, since he's the one that invited you."

And now Tip's grin is back in full. I try to commit it to memory while it lasts. He has a face made for smiling and sunlight; it's a shame it sees so little of either. "Haleigha's not a hard man to find."

He inclines his head towards the middle of the tent, where a man rivalling Crown in mass holds council with as many guests as can gather 'round him.

Some of these guests are dressed formally; pantsuits and button-downs that clash with the crowd's muumuus and swimwear. Some of these sore thumbs hold cameras; others, microphones.

"Is that a news crew?" I ask Tip, scanning their gear for a company logo.

"Looks like it." Tip watches the cameramen like he might a colony of ants devouring a carcass. "Haleigha is pretty well-known in our circle. I'm not surprised Surf Network wants a special on this. Maybe they cut a bargain and paid for catering."

If they did, it was an offer well taken. Once inside the tent, I see that most of the space is occupied by a ring of collapsible tables groaning under the weight of jewel-bright foods and drinks.

"I need all of that in my mouth immediately, if not sooner," I inform Tip.

"That's what she said," he retorts, quiet enough that only I can hear. I scoff and elbow him in the ribs.

It doesn't escape my attention how he presses to my side the more we're crowded in. I wonder if touching has a hierarchy in his mind; if all touching is bad, but I'm still a step above touching strangers.

It's probably selfish, or pathetic, to be pleased by that thought.

"Don't forget," Haleigha is saying to the crowd and crew. "Surfing belonged to the people of Oceania long before white folks got their hands on it. Isn't that right, Shark?"

He directs this last bit at Tip, somehow spotting us in the kerfuffle. The cameras, and those who wield them, swivel towards us.

I duck out of frame so quickly I fear I've cracked a rib. The last thing I need is for one of Müller's goons to spot my face on television and connect my identity to Tip, the biggest chink in my terribly flawed armor.

"Absolutely," Tip agrees smoothly, unbothered by the attention. "You're looking sharp, Haleigha."

The large man smiles, holding his arms wide and twisting his torso to show off his loose white outfit; the lei of maile leaves and tuberose that drapes his shoulders.

"That's never Dylan *Tippling*," gasps the female news host, her bleached eyebrows disappearing into her hairline. "My goodness, Tip, it's like you're back from the dead! Care to shoot a quick interview for the network?"

"I don't consent to that," Tip says firmly, more accustomed to dealing with the press than I am. "This is Haleigha's wedding. Focus on him."

The male host is unsatisfied with this answer. He presses through the crowd to push his microphone into Tip's face, camera crew tailing loyally behind. His eyes are round and spaced too far apart, giving the appearance of a tall baby in pancake makeup. "What about the rumors? Did you really try and kill your foster brother? What *really* happened to Crown?"

Tip and I both go still. Me, bursting with molten lava. Tip, frosting straight to subzero. Perhaps an inclination towards extremes is in our nature, but who could blame us? We three cousins are all we've ever had. To cheapen our bond with gossip and speculation is the worst flavor of nasty.

I open my mouth to say something — what, I can't begin to guess — but Haleigha is faster. He plants a massive paw on the anchor's shoulder.

"You weren't invited today to make my guests feel uncomfortable," he reminds him in an achingly polite tone that bodes murder.

The anchor blanches the exact color of sour cream, then forces a laugh. "Roger that, big guy. I got carried away. Too many daiquiris, you know!"

"That's what I thought." Haleigha releases him and launches back into an enthusiastic retelling of how he and Leilani met. The crew refocus their cameras on him.

I'm still angry. I can tell Tip is, too. Angry and guilty and sad.

He tucks all that away fast, though, and gives me a nudge. "Go play. I'm gonna stay and listen."

I'm reluctant to leave him after all that, but he knows me well: I *do* want to explore and mingle.

Squeezing through the crowd, I admire colorful outfits and listen to snippets of excited conversation. Children press close to the news crew, making faces at the cameras.

Beyond the tent, there is an empty fire-pit and a small stage. Behind the stage, I see a guardrail to protect inebriated guests from taking a plunge into the rocky sea below.

A little boy drops a pink lei from his basket over my neck — a lei made of real flowers, soft as bunnies and scented like heaven — and kisses both of my cheeks. "Aloha," he tells me proudly.

I wish like anything I'd known about this wedding beforehand. I'm sure one of the libraries I frequent carries books about Hawaiian wedding traditions. I want to know the hows and whys of *everything*. "Aloha," I echo, and he smiles.

I watch him, and a herd of other children, plant pink leis on all the guests. By the time I reach the buffet table, I've got a pile up to my chin. The intense perfume makes my head spin.

"This is wonderful," I sigh to a very tall Hawaiian woman in a flowing cream gown with scarlet accents.

She smiles enormously. I'm treated to yet more cheek-kisses, which doesn't help with the dizzy situation. "I'm so glad you're enjoying my wedding!"

Her wedding...?

She's wearing the most formal outfit of anyone present, and her hair, filled with flowers, is intricately braided into a crown. Who else could she be but the bride?

"Leilani!" I exclaim, feeling stupid.

She cocks her head. "Do I know you?"

I fill her in on how I came to be here.

This is what I'm good at — talking to people; making them like me. I pause at all the right moments, touching her arm to draw her in. My face is animated, my tone bubbling with an excitement I can't quite feel. My relatively mundane story soon has *her* laughing, too.

"Well, I am just so glad you've stumbled into my happy day!" she says, and sweeps me towards a table. "Have a drink, have some lau lau. I should go speak to my mother; excuse me..."

I have no clue what lau lau is, but I want it. I want everything.

This part of me — the Indian girl raised by an old white woman; the girl who never got to experience her own culture — can't help but ache when I see others fully immersed in theirs. It's obvious that Haleigha and Leilani take great pride in who they are.

I grab a drink. It's delicious, so I end up knocking back a few more until I feel too good for my pity-party to last; until I can only smile, and my walk becomes a dance.

At some point, the group migrates towards the mouth of the tent, spilling onto the vine-covered arbor where the officiant — an elderly woman I'm informed is Leilani's grandmother — waits.

The crowd chuckles when she bodily drags Haleigha into a hug. He flails helplessly with a cheeky grin, apparently overwhelmed by this tiny old woman's strength.

I don't know the man personally, but already I like him. It makes me feel good to know Tip has friends like that.

We sit at random. I search for Tip, and find him close to the front. I don't get socially anxious the way he does, but I miss his presence all the same.

The officiant wastes no time in getting started. Soon the happy couple are exchanging vows. Though I don't understand their language, I can hear their passion, their devotion. They touch foreheads and inhale deeply.

Not-Cero glides against my back, her chin hooked on my shoulder, her cheek bumping mine. *You smiled like that for me,* she murmurs, admiring the way Leilani glows at her husband. *I was so nervous...*

She was?! She'd looked cool as a cucumber in her tailored tux, a single prairie gentian tucked in her front pocket. *I* was the one who was a nervous wreck when Tip walked me down the aisle.

Of course I was. I always wanted to keep you happy.

I know it's not healthy to humor these delusions, but it soothes the empty ache in my heart. Just for now, I snuggle into her hold and feel lips brush my forehead; a hand slip into mine.

In that moment, I think I'd do anything to have her back.

Do you really mean that, Miss Cop? Think carefully, now.

I taste the now-familiar copper of my own bleeding gums and sigh, swallowing it back. I guess if there *is* such a thing as an after-life, I'll be there with her soon enough.

The ceremony closes out, and the officiant takes Haleigha and Leilani aside to make it all legal. Several family members stand around them, acting as witnesses to them signing page after page of documents.

The rest of us are ushered to the tents; back to the food and the music. I wash the taste of blood from my mouth with another drink, and am promptly invited to dance by the same little boy who'd given me the first lei.

I dance with him, and with other children — one of the girls who'd been playing the ukulele among them. "You're very talent-ed!" I inform her. She beams, showing off a mouthful of rainbow braces.

I'm passed from hand to hand, hardly caring who my next part-ner is, caught in the frenetic energy that demands I *move* until I can do nothing but smile. My bare feet kick up whorls of soft sand. I even find myself in the bride's arms for a moment.

My touch starvation hasn't been *this* sated since I last went clubbing.

When the festivities take me out of the tent, I notice the moon has climbed high in the sky. A bonfire crackles, ringed on all sides by paper lanterns. As I'm admiring this, hands take my waist.

"Found you." Tip is gentled by darkness. I think it's the proximity to the ocean that has him so doe-eyed and dewy.

God almighty, after all this time, after all that we've been through, he still can catch me off guard with his beauty.

"What's up, Maggie-the-Riveter?"

"Hi," I breathe, delighted to see his smile.

"You promised me a dance," he reminds me, and works his hand into mine. It's his burned hand, I realize at the rough rasp of scars. "Not backing out on me now, are you?"

"Dylan Tippling," I lecture, waggling a mock-stern finger before gripping his good shoulder. "I would *never* break a promise to *you*."

He dances so formally that I'm charmed. I can almost hear him counting steps in his mind as he carefully, precisely navigates us around the fire. That's the way of Tip: learning the theory, making it a science.

"I love you," I say, so quietly that I'm not sure he hears me; not until he meets my earnest eyes. His smile goes tight at the edges. "Tip, I really..."

I have always loved him, from the first time he gave me his own breakfast when mine wasn't enough. For our entire childhoods, I'd had no way to repay his sacrifices *except* with unconditional, blind love.

Maybe it's too much to state the obvious, because he leaves soon after, stating the need for a beachside walk.

I let him go, my hands feeling empty and cold without his.

There's a point in every party when things drop from wonderful to terrible; euphoric to desperate. It's something to do with energy and balance, I'm sure: for every high, there must be a low.

The best high-empathy party girls anticipate that moment and leave just before it hits, but I'm rusty and out of practice. It rushes upon me hard when I'm approached by a stranger. The only way I can describe it is being plucked out of boiling water and plunged into iced.

"You must be the infamous Alexis." A thin man with long, colorless hair sidles into my sightline. He appears to be in his late sixties, with skin like sun-baked leather. I startle at the bold hand cupping my lower back, and gaze up into cornflower-blue eyes.

I don't like him. I don't know why, exactly; it's not that he's handsy (though that certainly doesn't help), but something about the way he cornered me alone makes my hair stand on end. This is not how strange old men should behave if they want to be perceived as benign.

It's not an accident. He wants to intimidate. Men like this always know.

"Actually, I go by my surname," I correct, regaining some footing with my chin held high. "Call me Magpie."

"Like the bird!" he laughs, revealing a mouthful of gold caps. "I'm Kyle Aristarkhov, but that's such a tongue-twister. We'll stick with my first name, hm?"

He leans in conspiratorially to tell me this, and while it might be to bridge the gap in our heights, I don't care for the way his free hand clamps my upper arm, like he's trying to lock me in place. "Dance with me."

It's not a request.

Easy, Not-Cero cautions when my muscles tighten like springs. *Don't get your hackles up yet. Find out how he knows you first.*

Normally I'd tell "Kyle" to piss off, and smile savagely when I got called a bitch for it. But this is a nice wedding. I shouldn't make a scene unless I have to.

"I have time for *one* dance," I unhappily agree.

Maybe it's the daiquiris talking, but the music seems stuck on a loop. I've stopped being able to differentiate one song from another. Because leading is what I do, I take his hands and place them firmly where *I* want them to stay: at the very tops of my shoulders. Then I take his waist.

We must look ungainly. I am, after all, "fun-sized." But he asked for this, so he can suck it.

He only laughs at my chutzpah, swaying obligingly with the music.

"So, *Kyle,*" I say when his laughter dies. "You say I'm 'infamous'?"

"Oh, yes," he grins. His hand oozes low on my shoulder, thumbing the strap of my tankini. "Tip and I go *very* far back. I suppose I could say I knew him before he was famous, if I wanted to brag."

"Are you a surfer?" I jimmy my shoulder, popping his hand back up to where it belongs.

"Only recreationally. I deal in boards. I supplied Tip with his very *first* board, actually."

I remember that board well: a powder blue Takayama that bridged the gap between sea and sky. Tip loved it like I love my Kawasaki, and babied it to a ridiculous extent, waxing and covering it every night like he was bathing and tucking in a child.

I knew even then that professional boards were expensive, but only as an adult did I learn the cost tiptoes close to a solid grand. And this stranger just *gave* him one? *Why?*

"He talked about you all the time. You and little King."

"Crown," I correct. "It's short for—"

"'*My cousin is incredible!*'" Kyle interrupts, doing a bad impression of Tip's salt-rasped voice. "'*She's so brave. She wants to be a police officer!*' He thought the world of you, kid. It was adorable."

I don't understand this conversation at all. Why does Kyle have the tone of smug boasting?

Mags, Not-Cero breathes, disgusted, piecing it together mere seconds before I do.

When it clicks, my heart freezes solid and plummets to my knees. *"You* were one of his clients!" I gasp, horrified.

I think of the cigarette burns on Tip's arms. I think of the bruises, the vomiting, the meltdowns. I think of the weekly shouting matches he had with Gran while I cried in bed, covering my ears to drown out their hateful words.

How *old* was he when he got that blue board? Fourteen? Fifteen?

Easy! Not-Cero repeats. I barely hear her over the sound of blood rushing in my ears.

"I thought of myself as his mentor. Even a father figure." Kyle smiles nostalgically. "Poor boy; never had one of his own..."

With a noise of revulsion, I shove the man off of me, watching him stumble to keep his footing. He opens his mouth. I drive my fist into it with every ounce of my strength.

Punching someone in the face isn't a smart move, in terms of combat. It's far more likely to hurt the puncher than the punchee. The twenty-two bones of a skull, built to protect the brain, are far denser than the twenty-seven spindly, delicate ones inside a hand.

I'm aware of all this, but I'm still a hot-headed idiot. There's something viscerally satisfying about that *crunch*.

He reels and bellows like an ox, covering his face with both hands. A spray of blood spurts between his fingers. Either I split his gums, or I broke a tooth.

Glancing down at my bleeding hand, I see that it's the latter. I grimace and pluck the chip of incisor from my knuckle, flicking it aside. Fight bites are nasty. I make a mental note to clean it before it gets infected.

Kyle screams again, and the wedding party falls silent. Surfers gawk, wide-eyed, from the tent at the strange woman who up and decked an aging, well-liked member of their community for no clear reason.

I'm too pissed to care. Shaking my hand out, I start for Kyle again, watching in grim satisfaction as he lurches away with panic in his eyes.

"Pedophile! Rapist!" I accuse, and am promptly seized around the neck by two bony arms.

"No!" Tip hisses in my ear, half throttling me. "Hell no, Mags; hell *fucking* no. Are you crazy?!"

I gag when he presses on my windpipe, using his height to knock me off balance.

I'm stronger than Tip. I could throw him like a horse bucking its rider. My body knows what to do: duck down low, kick his feet from under him, slam him chest-first into the ground, and finish him by crushing his neck under my heel. It'd be over in a millisecond.

But *because* it's Tip, I fall still, hands hanging limply at my sides. I'd sooner stop my own heart than ever harm him.

"He hurt you," I wheeze as the crowd emerges to surround Kyle. "I'll kill him. You know I can."

"Shut up," Tip snarls, and takes a step backwards. I choke. He reluctantly loosens his grip.

The camera crew pushes excitedly forward, chasing newsworthy events like sharks sniffing blood. "That's Dylan Tippling!"

"Who's he with?"

"Did that chick say 'pedophile'?"

The party is suspended in a state of alcohol-softened shock, but soon someone will think to phone the police. This is our chance to move.

Arriving at the same conclusion, Tip charges forward, exchanging his grip 'round my neck for one on my wrist. He bowls violently through their shouting number, and then we're sprinting on, unhindered.

There's a strategy to running on sand that neither of us knows, but we make decent time to the table of purses. Tip snatches my backpack and, still running, fumbles the keys to my Kawasaki from the front pocket. "Go," he hisses, giving my shoulders a shove. *"Go!"*

Caught in his frenzy, I do. We scramble down the slope we'd had such a rough time climbing, tripping and sliding and sprawling towards the parking lot. The petals from our leis leave a fragrant pink trail behind us.

It's illegal to ride a motorcycle barefoot, especially after too many cocktails. I do it anyway, painfully clicking the brake with my toes, slamming the helmet onto Tip's head, peeling from the beach at breakneck speed. Tip's hands crush bruises into my waist as we swerve onto the busy road.

Well. That was stupid, Not-Cero lectures. *Vengeance is best seized in stealth, my love. Never before witnesses.*

I'm too frantic to bicker with ghosts. I just committed aggravated assault at a wedding filmed by a news crew.

I'm not a person who can afford to stand out like that, considering my 'extracurricular activities' with the gang, and the fact that I'm legally responsible for Tip under his parole. If I'm deemed unfit for the job...

But Kyle hurt Tip! He'd knowingly used him; a lion content to lie with his mouth open wide, flaunting his money to force lambs between his teeth. To keep his friends and admirers looking the other way. *Monster!*

I don't *just* want his teeth scattered like pearls in the sand. I want him dead and rotting. I want his head on a pike, tongue lolling, crows plucking at his eyes. Let him stand as an example for every rapist there ever was: *this is what you deserve.*

Perhaps that thought is monstrous in itself. Perhaps I don't give a fuck. Perhaps my need to be a hero is second only to this other need; one I don't have a name for yet.

Mags! Not-Cero screams, breaking my introspection.

Cars slam warning horns. Tip shrieks something inaudible, his fingernails piercing my skin. We're coming in fast on a cement roadblock, shiny with yellow caution stickers. I'd driven straight from my lane and into danger without realizing it!

I dip to the right, low enough that my shoulder kisses asphalt. The fabric of Cero's Hawaiian shirt shreds to ribbons, with my skin following close behind.

There's an ear-bleeding squeal; a crunch of metal and gravel as the roadblock shaves my left mirror off. We wobble drunkenly, fighting to regain momentum.

I think it's willpower alone that maintains our center of gravity; that allows me to speed to eighty, ninety MPH before straightening out. I outpace the gut-twisting seesaw motion and achieve smooth sailing, soaring straight over a curb and into an orange grove.

We slow by swerving between tree after tree, bouncing and jolting over dirt and roots. My right foot crushes the rear brake so hard I fear either it or my cuboid will shatter.

Sparks fly when I knock the kickstand with my heel, bare toes digging into dense green grass. The bruised-citrus perfume wafted with every motion is overpowering.

Behind me, Tip quakes so violently I fear he may be seizing. I hear him take tiny, panicked sips of breath through clenched teeth. He has his helmeted head buried in my neck. When I try to turn around, he doubles his grip.

What remains of the mirror dangles from its stem like an eyeball from a socket, throwing light from the headlights over dozens of painted-white tree trunks.

"M-M-Mags..." Tip's fingers flex. The overheated engine ticks like an insect in a tree. I take the keys from the ignition so it can cool. Without headlights, all we have are the stars and moon.

"Are you hurt?" I ask, and am proud when my voice emerges steady and calm.

"My *leg...*"

I have to look at Tip's leg. Good; a task. Do the thing, Mags.

I take both of his wrists and, with difficulty, pry his hands off of me. Then I climb from the bike and all but collapse. My legs have locked up. My shredded shoulder screams.

I take my phone out of my pocket. I shine its light as I bend and look at Tip's left leg, seeing nothing unusual. I circle to the other side and find, branded on the back of his calf, a long red burn. It glistens, seeps, the fine blonde hairs all around crisped to a scraggly black.

The exhaust pipe. He must've nearly slipped off the back, searing his flesh against the metal. He could've *fallen...*

He jolts when I touch his ankle, skittish as a colt. "How bad is it?" he asks through gritted teeth, trying to quell his panic. "I can... *smell* it, just like when..."

Just like when he'd been hurt in the Jaguar's explosion.

I am, beyond question, the worst cousin in all the world.

No time for a pity-party, Not-Cero scolds. *The epidermis and dermis are blistered and swollen. There's some white, but only at the edges. It smells burnt; not charred. That means...?*

"Second degree burn," I state. "Bordering on third, but not quite."

And?

"It covers a surface area smaller than three fingers. I don't think he'll need to see a doctor."

He would benefit from one, of course, but we can probably stave off infection by ourselves.

Tip swings his damaged leg over the bike and stands without looking at me. "Yeah," he mutters, peeling his helmet off and setting it on the saddle. He resembles an awkward, floppy-haired teenager as he avoids my eyes, picking at his old scar tissue. "I'm gonna go, Mags."

Huh? He can't *go*. We have to boost the bike from this grove before somebody catches us trespassing. We have to drag it home without getting pulled over for the mirror situation. We have to...

You're losing him.

My instinct is to reach for Tip, to keep him present. But Tip doesn't respond well to touch. I need to appeal to his logic with words.

"I need you to stay with me," I say, trying not to sound frantic. My phone goes back to its screensaver, bathing us in darkness. I've never been in a grove after dark before. It's nothing like a forest — too tame, too orderly — but the presence of trees all around has a similar effect.

"I *can't*." his voice cracks. He swallows thickly. "This is too much. *You're* too much! You hit Kyle and almost killed me. That's not something you're allowed to do."

"I punched a monster who *hurt* you because I *love* you. How is that not obvious?!"

"Maybe you should love me a little less, then. Kyle was one of the decent ones. Never cheated me or hit me..." Tip laughs, cold and terrifyingly empty. "He paid for *your* school trip to the state capital, by the way. You're welcome."

It's like being slapped repeatedly, each time harder than the last. I *remember* that seventh grade trip; the long bus ride, the boring lectures. I'd taken it all for granted; a hamburger lunch, a notebook from the gift shop...

"You were *fifteen*," I manage, my voice barely above a whisper.

"Well, I'm not anymore, but you still act like a child. Thanks for alienating me from the only people who ever liked me. Good luck with the bike."

He turns and limps away, using his phone as a flashlight. He follows the bike's path of destruction towards the road.

He's *leaving* me. I could vomit. It feels like he won't ever come back.

Panic gives my legs wings. I fly to him, flinging my arms around his waist. "I'm sorry!" I blurt, pleading shamelessly. "I'm sorry you got hurt, I'm sorry I'm irresponsible and immature and a complete dumbass, I'm sorry I didn't listen to you... What do you need from me, Tipples? How can I fix this?"

"You can't," he snaps, and tries to fight my hold. "Let go of me!"

Let go, Not-Cero echoes. *Cornered animals bite, Miss Cop.*

I can't. Let him bite. Leaving is the worst thing Tip could possibly do to me. Any injury sustained in preventing that is just collateral damage. "I'm coming with you."

If Tip is surprised by my declaration, he doesn't show it. He elbows me hard in the stomach and shrugs away, then continues walking. "I don't care."

"Wait!" I demand, and look back at my bike — my *custom* bike; a unique relic of who I used to be. Daredevil Mags: bright as a laugh and fast as sin. I love my Ninja like a *vaquero* loves their horse. To me, it is freedom and joy.

I screw up my courage, and my face, so that I don't sob. "Give me ten seconds to take the plate off. We don't need cops beating down our door."

This is, apparently, enough to startle Tip into stillness.

"I need your help," I coax, darting back to my bag. "Come here and hold your light steady? I know I have a screwdriver in here somewhere..."

I find one by digging through all the crap I have and hold it aloft, relieved to see that Tip is watching me. When I meet his eyes, he approaches, curious to see if I mean what I say.

Stop this, Not-Cero protests as I pop the clasps on my license plate. *This has gone far enough.*

No. There's so much further to go.

"You're bleeding," Tip informs me.

He's correct. Blood sluices down my shoulder, coating my chest and arm. My knuckles never clotted after breaking Kyle's teeth, either. Damn leukemia.

"Don't worry about it," I dismiss. I unscrew the gas cap and dip two fingers inside, wetting them, then beckon for Tip to follow me to the front.

I tilt the handlebars, squinting at the steering neck until I find the neat line of numbers and letters etched into the green metal. I smear gas over the length of them. Then I spin the lighter's dial, and introduce its flame to the VIN.

The gas catches immediately. Tip takes a hasty step back as it burns itself out in a white doe's tail, leaving only tarnished black metal and no VIN to be seen. It stinks badly enough to turn my stomach.

Even with these precautions, it'd be easy to link this bike with me, if anyone was truly determined to do so. There are only so many Kawasaki dealerships in SoCal; surely one of them remembers my expensive modifications.

But abandoning a vehicle on private property isn't *so* illegal that anybody would go that far, I don't think. They're likely just to tow it and forget it.

I hastily don my socks and boots, fix my ponytail, and tuck the license plate into my backpack. I carry my helmet underneath one arm as I turn my back on my treasure.

Not-Cero seizes upon the hot burst of grief that threatens to overtake me. *Don't leave it, then! This is* stupid. *What does it prove?*

It's atonement, of course. A grand gesture twenty-five years in the making: I stand with my cousin. Now that my own life is drawing to a close, he is my utmost priority.

Would you have chosen me, *back when I was still alive? Did you love me this way, too?*

"Yes." I reach for Tip's hand. "Without hesitation."

Chapter Twenty-Two – Tip

*the human body contains 2.5 family-sized soda bottles of blood.
it's a real bitch to clean.*

...

It's been a doozy of a day. I've been depressed since that email from Crown, and the events in the orange grove didn't help. I butchered yesterday's calc quiz. Today I woke with a new compulsion to cluck my tongue at regular intervals, which earned me several stares on the bus.

Though I'd prepared meals for myself, my bizarro brain lost its grip when I tried to eat them, seeing nonexistent filth in every grain of rice. I haven't eaten since yesterday. When I try, my entire body rejects the food, gagging and heaving and filling my mouth with stomach acid.

The heat is downright oppressive. The sun beats violently over all of SoCal; triple-digit temperatures uncut by wind or humidity. Magpie was too heat-exhausted to do much after work but melt on the kitchen floor, her bare torso to the cool tile, and that was *before* the sun rose.

I sweated my way through my canvas uniform at work today, the fabric chafing my burn scars. I'd been more irritable than usual for the swarms of small children — two large birthday parties! *Two!* — leaving cake crumbs all over the café, fingerprints on the exhibits, and water on the bathroom floors; all to be cleaned by yours truly.

The horrid day isn't done with me yet. On the blissfully air-conditioned ride home, a new, astronomically strong compulsion takes hold of me: *Get out at the next stop.*

Why would I do such a thing? I'm miles from the apartment, and the next bus won't be along for hours.

You have to.

The itch won't leave me be, though I use Tessa's tricks to try and control it. I breathe in counts of four while reasoning my way through the irrational fears of what might happen if I disobey. Surely the bus won't crash, weighing a dozen passenger deaths on my conscience, just because I failed to comply!

There's a young mother and toddler in the seat before mine. When I look at them, my brain strobe-flashes. I see hyper-realistic images of the little family, mangled and smashed and twisted, teeth broken, fragments of glass glittering like diamonds in their bloody box braids. It's my fault, my fault, *my fault!*

You have to.

You have to.

You have to.

Tip!

I am not in control.

I lunge to my feet and seize the stop-cord so aggressively it all but snaps in my hand. My panic is instantly soothed by the squeal-hiss of brakes. I can breathe again.

The compulsions always win. Isn't it better just to obey them right away?

The people on the bus probably think I'm high for how fast I book it, moving like the devil is chasing me. Oh, if only they knew... I've never been more sober in my life. Is that where the problem lies? Maybe things were *better* on heroin. At least then I could calm the fuck down!

I watch the bus pull away in a cloud of exhaust and think, *maybe I just saved everybody on that thing.*

But I know in my heart I didn't. The only thing that's changed is that I now have to *walk* home when I can barely stand.

As I plod along the sidewalk, I dream that I'm a little fish following the ocean currents. That the palm trees I see are really anemones, and the speeding cars are predatory fish to avoid.

Mount San Antonio, looming hazy on the horizon, is an underwater volcano no longer dormant. It would explain the extreme heat making the air wriggle and writhe, the tarmac going soft and sticky as gum beneath passing tires...

I don't know how I make it home, but I do, and I'm glad for it. The windows are open. I smell bleach as I approach the door. Magpie must be in a cleaning mood. I hear her tuneless singing through the cracked window. She's been on a Smashing Pumpkins kick lately.

Suddenly she stops singing and turns the music down, speaking, her voice lilting up at the end like she just asked a question. I hesitate with my key almost to the door.

A deeper voice replies. A guest.

Shit; I am not at all fit for company. But what can I do; stand out here until I die of dehydration?

"Not putting in the effort to keep yourself alive is as good as suicide," Magpie's guest says, and I am startled — first by the words; then the voice. I *know* that voice, strained and hoarse as it is.

"I am not committing suicide," Magpie rebuffs. "I'm accepting the inevitable. It's my body, my life. You had your own. You don't get to dictate mine, too."

"I took thee to be my wedded wife," the deep voice says, with the formal air of a quote. "'For better, for worse; for richer, for poorer. In sickness and in health.' Well, you're worse now. You're poor and sick."

"You're forgetting something!" I see Magpie through a gap in the blinds. She whirls until her back is to me, confronting the speaker with renewed vigor. "'Til death do us part.' You *died*, Cero. I loved you with all that I am, but I can't live *for* you! I'm not your second chance at life!"

Cero. *That's* where I know that voice from. Cero and I were never close. She came into Magpie's life when I was busy competing, and from what little I know, it was a tumultuous whirlwind of a relationship.

None of this accounts for how Magpie is conversing with a dead woman in our kitchen.

I creep close to the window, trying to see the speaker. I can't piece together an explanation for what's happening, though my overheated, unmedicated, starving brain isn't providing any assistance.

I see an elbow and shoulder when I crane my neck, but most of my view is blocked by the cabinet we store canned foods in.

That leaves only the door. So much for stealth.

The conversation halts when I use my key to let myself in, looking towards the corner where the speaker should be — where she *was*, where I *saw* her — and see only our broom and mop propped against the wall. No guest in sight, dead or otherwise.

"H-hey, Tippaliscious," Magpie stutters, surprised by my interruption of her intense conversation. She wipes her dish-soapy hands dry on her cutoff jean shorts, which her thick thighs are slowly reducing to fibers. "How was work?"

Every surface in the kitchen gleams. The dishes are washed and stacked. She organized the contents of the fridge on the counters. Mags doesn't go on cleaning sprees like this often, but when she does, it's damn impressive.

I open my mouth to compliment her, then fall silent, going very still. An icy cold, completely at odds with the weather, floods my insides.

Mags had pulled all the shelves from the fridge and scrubbed them clean. They're now propped vertically against the walls to dry, giving the whole kitchen a funhouse mirror effect. I catch my reflection in the furthest one, stretched tall and thin as a scarecrow.

That isn't what turns my blood to slush, suffocating the words in my throat. No, that honor goes to the squat figure I see reflected just behind me. It's a blue-black silhouette of a person, flat and staining the air as a bruise does skin.

It's utterly featureless, blurry 'round the edges, devoid of face or clothing, yet I see the way it cocks its head; intelligent; *sentient*; divorced from any source. Everything about it is *wrong.*

My sweat-dampened neck and back chill. I'm frozen to the spot.

"Tip?" Magpie takes a step closer, oblivious to this impossible intruder. The thought of her stepping into danger unlocks my muscles, and I shake my head to stop her. Around her throat, the dual wedding rings clink on their chain.

She reaches towards me with a dish-soapy hand, concern etched in every line of her face. "You look rough, hon."

The figure behind me moves in sync with my cousin, stretching its own arm out. They both touch me at the same moment. Magpie's hand is firm and familiar on my left shoulder; a rough grip good for throwing baseballs and climbing ropes.

The cool touch on my right shoulder is so faint I mightn't have noticed it, were I not watching it happen in the reflection.

Magpie gives me a little shake. "You're really freaking me out. What's wrong? Do you need to sit?"

The creature leans closer. Its head appears just behind my neck, and I feel its chilly breath there. It smells like wet dirt.

The heat, the hunger, the ill-advised walk, and now *this* new shock all catch up to me at once. My vision floods with a galaxy of lavender clouds, and down I go like a sack of bricks. I feel the fall, but not the landing.

When I come to, I'm sprawled on the kitchen floor with my head in Magpie's lap. Her face is ashy. Her hands shake.

We lock eyes. Through clenched teeth she demands, "When was the last time you *ate?!*"

I close my eyes to escape her judgement, but it does no good. Her words circulate, slow and insistent, through the echo chamber that is my brain. "Where did the ghost go?" I ask. My voice is a frog's croak.

"You almost bashed your *goddamn* teeth in on the freezer door."

The very teeth that Vince paid "the big bucks" to fix. When I was a kid, they were irregularly spaced, with an extra row in the back; sharp, pointy...

My good hand is resting on Magpie's fuzzy ankle. I give it a squeeze, grateful that she caught me.

"I thought you were doing better," she accuses. "When did it get this bad?"

I have no answer. It's always bad, isn't it?

"Is it because of Vince?" she speculates. "He's back, and suddenly all your hard work goes to shit?"

She's not wrong. I always develop new (or worsen old) compulsions when I'm particularly stressed. Some come and go; some stick. Some lie dormant for months before resurfacing.

"Don't make me bury you, too, Tip. Please don't do that to me."

Oh, that's not her angry voice anymore. That's her *sad* voice. Insects of guilt squiggle beneath my skin.

"Will you eat now?"

My throat is dry as a desert. "No."

"Then I'm calling an ambulance."

That one call will plunge us into a pit of bankruptcy so deep we'll never be free. "I'll eat."

She nods once. Props my back against the stove. Stands.

I listen to her fuss. She fills a glass of water at the sink-filter before passing it down. I sip the water, though it sits weighty and tasteless on my tongue.

When she hands me a plate of sliced banana, I balk.

"It's dirty," I whisper, staring at the fruit. It's chopped into uneven chunks and riddled with spots of brown, a string of phloem snaking over the top like toilet paper on a bathroom floor.

"What?" Magpie frowns. "No it's not. Eat."

Of course she doesn't see how filthy it is. Her brain isn't broken like mine is. It's all I can do not to hurl the plate into the wall.

"I can't," I whisper miserably.

She looks away, scratching at her mouth while she thinks. She used to do that as a kid, rubbing the same patch of skin until it was red-raw. I want to pull her hand away before she hurts herself, but I can't reach high enough.

"What *will* you eat?" she asks, a note in her voice I'm not at all accustomed to hearing: desperation.

I think of the sushi from James's house. Cold. Fresh. Clean. Perfect. I remember how good, how *alive* I'd felt after eating it. Energized for hours. Borderline happy, even.

I say nothing.

Nor do I resist when she takes the cup and plate away, then ducks down and pulls me over her shoulders. The back of her head fits neatly in the hollow of my gut. Her arm hooks between my knees to grasp my dangling wrist.

I don't fear her dropping me; not even for a moment.

We go outside. She crosses the alley between buildings and climbs the rickety metal stairs affixed to the neighboring apartments. She walks carefully to avoid jostling or banging me into anything.

She releases my wrist long enough to knock on a door, then takes hold again. I hear a muffled dog barking. The door opens.

"What happened to *him*?" David the stoner asks, befuddled.

"Do you have any food that isn't dirty?" Magpie replies.

···

I sit on a barstool and watch, dazedly, as David scrubs his hands and sets to preparing a late lunch. Zelda the pitbull grinds a mangled squeaky toy into Magpie's stomach, demanding attention.

Once she sees that I'm okay, Magpie explains that she has to put our perishable groceries back into the fridge. I lay my head on the counter when I hear the door close behind her. Zelda rests her chin on my knee.

I already feel a little better, because David can afford air conditioning.

"Spinach okay?" he asks, holding up a bunch. It looks fresh. "I'm gonna steam it."

I nod, watching him fill the bottom half of a steamer with water. He crams the entire bunch into the top basket, drops the lid, and plonks the whole thing on the stove. Then he gets out another bag and a frying pan.

"Thoughts on pine nuts?" he asks, showing them to me just as Magpie returns with an armful of spare clothes. The pine nuts look fine: tiny, round seeds like popcorn kernels. I nod again. David flashes a triumphant smile. "Protein *and* fat!"

A moment later, I'm stiffening at the application of grease to pan. "What's that?"

"Just coconut oil." David pushes the jar my way.

I read the nutrition label, mentally calculating how many calories two tablespoons contains. t's a lot, but the amount never bothers me. I just need to know.

I open the lid and examine the opaque liquid inside. It smells okay. I relax.

David toasts the pine nuts into fragrant crispness.

The spinach shrinks to a quarter of its original size when steamed. David fills three bowls with it, adds sea salt to two, then looks my way. When I nod a third time, he salts mine as well. Then he tosses in the pine nuts and divvies the bowls out.

"I don't mix food," I mumble, poking at it with my fork, then push some into my mouth anyway. I *can* eat this, so I'm obligated to do so. For Magpie's sake, if nothing else.

David looks chagrined. "Sorry. I should've thought to ask."

It's good. It's so good I could cry. It's so good I forget I have an audience.

I close my eyes and am transported to a better time, back when I was clean and healthy and had my OCD under wraps. I'd made careful meals for myself so I'd have the strength to surf my heart out. Why does every castle I build have to crumble?

"Vegan food isn't *all* bad, I guess," Magpie concedes.

David laughs. "It isn't, but I rarely go to this much effort. Usually I eat junk."

Magpie finishes eating in a few huge bites. "Thank you, David," she says warmly.

He pretends not to notice her dimples. "Mi casa, and all that jazz. Hey," he leans across the counter, fixing earnest eyes on my face. "Does grass help you at all? You know; munchies? Pull that stick outta your ass?"

Now that my head feels less swimmy, I remember that I don't care for David. I try not to speak with too much derision. "Can't say I've ever used *pot* to force myself to eat. Seeing as I'm on parole and get drug tested every week, that doesn't sound like an awesome plan."

There *are* places in California where weed is perfectly legal, but the laws are a little stricter for ex-cons on drug watch.

Magpie is considering the suggestion, though. I can see it in her creased brow. "Do *you* think it would help?"

David shrugs.

"I could take his next two drug tests *for* him," Magpie muses. "And if it *does* help, we could try getting him a medical marijuana license..."

Wait... Is she serious?

Even David looks impressed. "Damn, wild child. Hardcore."

She'd already proven in the orange grove that she'll go to dramatic lengths for me. Still, this grand gesture catches me by surprise.

How much of my childhood did I lose providing for Magpie? When did she start returning the favor, piece by tiny piece? When she spoke for me at my trial? When she let me live with her?

"If you're up for it," is all she says, and leaves the decision in my hands.

What the hell. My entire life revolves around bad choices made in desperation. "Sure."

The matter settled, David goes into his bedroom to gather supplies, calling Zelda with him. He shuts the door on his way back, leaving her inside.

In that moment, I find I like him a fraction more. At least he isn't one of those assholes who tries to get his pet high for kicks.

"Are we really doing this?" I mutter to my cousin. "I *am* a junkie, you know."

She inclines her head towards my mostly full bowl of food and, sighing, I take another bite. Chewing is such a pain.

"If you have a better plan," she says, "I'd love to hear it."

I have nothing but a headache and a lifetime of fuckups. "Fine, but for the record? I hate pot. It makes me feel like a slug."

"Maybe stop bitching when someone else is footing the bill, sunshine," David suggests, returning with a dime bag of bud and an Altoid tin of rolling papers. He sets to work on the kitchen counter. "And this is Sativa. It perks you up."

"Makes you paranoid, more like."

"Has anybody ever said that you have all the charm of a menstrual cramp?"

Despite myself, I laugh, though loath am I to give this underfed Puli any encouragement. I see him smirk before he licks his thumb and seals the white tube over the carefully measured flakes.

It's a well-rolled joint. The guy's clearly had a lot of practice, though I would've pegged him as the type to hoard a collection of glass bongs. Maybe he didn't feel like busting out the fine china for the likes of me.

"Wild child, you might wanna give Zelda some company," David warns, clicking his lighter. "If you're gonna be the one pissing in cups for a while, you don't want a contact high."

Magpie heeds his advice, shutting herself in his bedroom with the pitbull.

"Stay out of the nightstand, okay?" David calls after her.

"Okay!" she replies innocently.

Now it's my turn to smirk. "You know she's gonna look, right? If you'd wanted to protect your Fleshlights from her nosy ass, you should've kept your mouth shut."

David, lips now occupied by the joint, flips me the bird as he lights up. He takes a drag to get it started, then passes it to me by the crutch.

I'm lucky to not be one of the obsessive compulsives distressed by germs. Nope; it's only the things meant to keep me alive — food; human contact — that *I'm* averse to. I've shared needles with strangers. A smoke with a neighbor is nothing.

Holding the joint between my index and middle finger, I inhale and feel velvet grow inside my lungs. Bye-bye, sobriety.

It really is unpleasant, but I'd promised to give it a fair shake. I hold my scratchy lungful for four Mississippis, then duck to exhale before repeating the process. I cough down the neck of my shirt.

David stands, tugs the joint from between my fingers, and directs me to the sofa. I don't miss the way he hopefully snags my bowl of spinach as he goes, setting it on the armrest.

His checkered sofa is covered by a plastic sheet, likely to protect it from pet stains. It squeaks unpleasantly as I settle down and watch David toke up.

"Mind if I—" he gestures to the sound system by his gym equipment, no doubt feeling as awkward as I do.

I nod. Even hipster music is preferable to silence.

When he clicks his remote, we're serenaded with acoustic guitar that rumbles our feet before rising.

"Slo-o-o-w," he cautions, ashing the joint into a little dish before slipping it back into my hand. "You're right — Sativa *will* make you paranoid if you overdo it, and you've already fainted once today. And you probably don't have good tolerance anymore."

I'm used to the group etiquette of keeping a cycle going, but it's just the two of us. Slowing the hell down is acceptable.

I close my eyes and try to let the music calm me. David hums along, leading me to wonder if he does this a lot. He must be lonely, living here all alone. No wonder he's always puppy-dogging after Mags.

"Do you actually have a job?" I ask, each of my words dripping molasses-thick from my lips. If *I* didn't have to work, I think I'd sleep myself to death. That's how empty *my* life is.

"Does your job give your life any meaning?" he counters, which is close enough to what I'd been thinking that I feel a spike of anxiety in my guts. Had he heard my mind?

It takes a long time to puzzle out a response. "There's Agwe," I offer, and tell David all about my manatee. Her name is so precious; it flows straight from my vocal chords to be cradled by my tongue.

I've never before spoken about her. Not out loud, at least. Doing so now makes my eyes sting, then run.

He smiles. It's a huge, doggy thing, half his teeth capped by shiny silver crowns. "Fuckin' sweet, my dude. You know this is the first time you've ever sounded human to me? 'Grats."

"Sometimes I think about doing camwork instead. Maybe phone sex, but that sucks if you're not working for an agency. Camwork sucks *worse,* though, cuz I'm—" I gesture to my inadequate body, which speaks for itself. "But there's an audience for everything if you search long enough."

David cringes. "That sounds like one shitty Google search. Stick to the phone sex."

He talks like it's easy, but phone sex is a difficult branch to be stellar in. It requires conveying a believable narrative of emotion and fantasy in a single conversation with a stranger. While it's physically safer than most forms of sex work, it's emotionally draining as hell.

"I'm not skilled enough at emoting to be 'good' at it," I admit. "But there's plenty out there happy to beat their meat to some whiny twink calling them 'daddy.' It's not the worst if you need a quick buck."

David cringes again, throwing in a little shudder for effect. "I literally cannot imagine *you* doing that."

It's easy to do distasteful things when you can turn your heart off at will. Drugs help.

We've puffed and passed our way down to the roach, which David grinds into his ashtray. I feel no calmer than before. At least, I think I don't. I don't really feel *anything* but tight in the chest and messy in the head.

When it hits, it doesn't last long. And when it fades, I'm *manically* hungry.

David snorts, watching me wolf down the contents of my bowl and then get up for a refill from the stove, mixing spinach and pine nuts and salt with wild abandon and helping myself to some soda crackers, too.

"Take it easy," he warns from where he's flopped across the sofa, stealing my spot. "Your stomach is smaller than your fist right now. Or is it two fists? No, that's your brain. I was right the first time."

The fist-sized stomach in question doesn't want to listen to him. I am starving, starving, *starving*. I feel the spinach take root inside me, blooming fresh and green as algae in an underwater forest.

I am alive. I am present. I am okay, and that makes me laugh out loud — I'm *okay*! When was the last time I was okay? Sure, I'm jittery and keyed up — fucking Sativa and its high THC content — but still!

"Sit down before you fall down," David advises, eyes closed. He probably has too high of a tolerance to be deeply affected.

I return to the sofa and look at him for a long time, his funky-smelling hair like long ropes of cauliflower escaping a bun, his head so much bigger than his skinny body, save for his enormous feet. He looks like a Pez dispenser. His socks are Scooby Doo-print.

I loved Scooby Doo as a kid. I loved figuring out who the bad guy was long before anyone else could.

I step onto the sofa's arm and stand there a minute, admiring the room from this taller vantage, then bend my knees to sit like a cat in a too-small box. I take David's arm and pull it — and him — on top of me.

He groans, dismayed. "Of course *you'd* be like this. Why am I not surprised?"

I pull away fast, sensing rejection, but he hauls me back and props an elbow on my ribs.

I don't know what to say after that. Do I thank him? Insult him?

This is the part where someone pins me and shoves a hand down my pants, I think. *This is the part where I'm handed a blade and told to cut myself. Why else bother to get me high?*

I must've been thinking too loudly again, because David looks at me with concern in his blown-out eyes. "I'm seriously not interested, dude."

I want to explain that that's not what I'd meant; that my words are of relief, not complaint. My tongue is enormous and heavy. I'm so *tired* of being hurt.

Time comes in snapshots after that. David eventually wriggles out of my hold. Magpie takes his place, climbing onto my chest and tucking her head beneath my chin like that's where she belongs.

She's compact as a boulder when I braid my legs with hers. Her hair, spilling onto my neck, is blue-black ink; too silken to be tickly. I work my fingers in it and hold on tight. This is good. This feels right.

She's your baby cousin.

I don't care.

"Am *I* dirty?" She asks, voice tiny. Her eyes are the quicksand I've spent decades struggling not to fall into. "Too dirty to touch, like those bananas?"

It's impossible to explain myself, to put it into words. The dirtiness I so fear isn't something other people can give. It's something that was bred inside me, built up over time.

If I stretch my memories far enough, back to a time of crying instead of speaking and leaky diapers that never got changed, I see a house, a small house, with shattered windows and exposed drywall and no furniture save one bare mattress.

I see men who grabbed with bruise-knuckled fists, and women with teeth that fell out one, two, three at a time like keys off a broken piano. White and black and white again.

And if I stretch back further, I recall a child who may have been a boy, and may have been my sibling, but that doesn't matter because they swallowed the pretty snow from a plastic bag and then spat foam and went gray and cold and then stopped moving altogether no matter how hard I prodded or how loudly I screamed.

I want to say that Magpie *can't* be dirty, because the dirt lives beneath *my* skin like mold in the walls of that crackhouse. Filth and I are inseparable. It's all I'll ever be.

So I swallow it whole, all the decay of the world; gallons and gallons pouring like raw sewage down my throat, and I bloat and I fester and I rot, all so the rising tides can never touch her; can never reach Crown.

I don't know if I say any of this aloud or not. The snapshot goes off again and when I open my eyes, the window is a yawning mouth to the starlit sky. I expect to be cold, but I'm not; it's a California summer, and Magpie is my breathing blanket. Were it not for the AC, I'd've died of heatstroke.

A woman looms over the armrest, gazing blankly down at me, and I see her eyes: one blue, one brown.

"Shh," Cero warns, her breath hot, moist graveyard dirt bathing my face. "Shhh*hhh*..."

The sound crashes like the sea breaking shore. It thrusts me violently into a sleep without dreaming.

I wake to the lightening of sky that heralds the dawn, my tongue an enormous brick in the drought of my mouth. The sound of incessant barking drills my stuffy skull.

Magpie has slumped sideways on the sofa, curling in on herself. There are small dots of brown on my shirt that I realize stem from her nose, which is crusted with blood.

I to use my sleeve to wipe her face clean, but she scrunches and bats me away. The bleeding has already stopped, so I guess it's fine.

Zelda is still barking.

Funny; as long as we've been neighbors with David, I can't remember her ever making this much noise. She's a good dog, as long as she gets some exercise in. Maybe she's hungry?

I wriggle out from under Magpie. Predictably, she doesn't wake. When I stand, I'm pleased that my wobbly legs hold me.

David's tiny apartment is identical in layout to ours: the front door opening to a kitchenette; a sitting room with a guest closet; a single bedroom containing the only bathroom.

I rap my knuckles on the bedroom door. "Yo, stoner," I call. My mouth is cotton. I choke on the words. "Can you shut your dog up before we all get evicted, please?"

No answer. I pound the door some more and hear the faint click of claws on tile. Did he trap that huge animal in his tiny bathroom?

"You'd better not be naked," I warn, and swing his bedroom door open. Once inside, I grab the door-handle to the bathroom where Zelda whines and howls.

She explodes out, winding my legs like she's *trying* to knock me over, and then clings close. What's making her shake so hard?

"What the hell?" I grumble, trying to push her away. It's like scooting a brick wall. I don't like dogs at the best of times. Definitely not a fan of ones big enough to render me infertile.

She smashes her face into my thigh.

I sigh and rub her cropped ears with my good hand. "What's the matter?" I ask, trying to gentle my tone. "You need to pee?"

Her next whine ends in a low growl that has me backing away, instinctively covering my junk.

My butt hits the foot of David's bed, which is crammed into a corner to make room for his huge entertainment system; the sixty-inch television hooked up to all the gamer bells and whistles.

I glance over my shoulder, return my attention to Zelda... And then stiffen.

As though sensing my oh-shit-o'meter rising, the dog also stills, mouth open and head cocked.

David is lying prone on the bed. I glimpsed his long, narrow bare feet, ten toes pointed downwards, when I first came in. But now I notice that he's not making any noises; no sleep-deep breathing or soft snores.

My sense of smell is half dead, but Zelda's isn't. I at last catch a whiff of what's bothering her so. The velvet musk of blood is unmistakable. Sharper still: fecal matter and piss.

"Oh, God," I whisper. "I'm about to see something horrible, aren't I?"

I can't stand here forever, my back to David, staring into his little bathroom with a tub of vegan shaving cream on the counter.

Bracing myself, I turn around and look at the mess head-on.

Arterial spray is one crazy bitch. The human body contains so much more of it than most people know. Even a twiggy dandelion like David is full of the stuff.

Was full of the stuff.

Now it crusts the lamp, walls, sheets. It puddles on the floor, where his limp hand dangles off the mattress. I'm positive it's everywhere; in the vents, in the carpet pads.

I see why David didn't hear Zelda's racket. Kinda hard to do that without a head.

Chapter Twenty-Three - Magpie

...

I don't know how long Tip shakes me before I wake, but he's gotten rough by the time I open my eyes and stare into his. Today they're a flat, iron gray.

Something is seriously wrong.

He holds tight to Zelda's collar. I don't think I've ever seen him willingly touch a dog before.

"What is it?" I ask, sitting up.

"David's dead." His words are clipped. Flat.

I'm incapable of doubting my cousin when he looks and sounds like this, but the rush of numb confusion makes me feel woozy.

Tip grabs my hand and pushes it through Zelda's collar. I clutch the woven band, and he releases both of us before crossing the room to the window above the kitchen sink.

It's wide open. He wrestles it, and the curtains, shut.

"Did you open this?" he asks, his back to me.

I'd considered it, wanting to clear out the smoke, but it'd seemed like too much effort. "No. It was closed when I came out here. Maybe David..."

No. Not David. He'd flopped into his bed beside me and was asleep in seconds. He wouldn't have had the presence of mind to open or shut any windows. I hadn't felt comfortable sharing a bed with David, so I'd gone to join Tip on the sofa instead.

"Let me see the body," I say automatically. I worked highway patrol before moving up to detective work, so my forensics training only covered the basics, but maybe I can still configure a time and cause of death.

Then I realize what I'm saying, and my stomach roils. *The* body. David's body. *David* is...

Tip shakes his head no. "It's very violent. There's a lot of blood. You can't go leaving footprints in it."

Violent? *Blood?*

I struggle to understand how David could have left a mess like that. "Did he fall in the shower? Hit his head?"

Tip's eyes sharpen. I think I see pity in their depths. "Mags, this wasn't an accident. Someone murdered him."

The world stops. My *brain* stops. I stare at my cousin, barely processing his next words: "— Can't believe we heard nothing. I know I was stoned, but—" and, "—Looked everywhere for the head, but he must've taken it with him—"

That creeps slow as a stop-motion monster through my fog. "Who?"

You know who, Not-Cero says. She doesn't sound at all surprised by any of this.

I answer my own question. "Vince."

Tip grunts and tosses a white envelope at me, then gets up and crosses to the kitchen, where he roots through cabinets. He finds an enormous bag of dry dog food. "How much does that thing eat?" He inclines his head to the dog.

Math. I can do math. "She weighs about eighty pounds," I calculate. "Should be three cups. David feeds her twice a day."

I hear Tip scooping food into a bowl, which catches Zelda's interest. I check David's bedroom door to confirm it's shut before releasing her collar, running my hand down the short, oily fur of her back as she passes.

"He didn't hurt her," I realize, listening to Zelda munch her breakfast. We're the humans. As far as she's concerned, it's our job to handle the problems. "Why?" *And why* didn't *he hurt us?*

"Vince is good with animals. He probably talked sweet to her, and the dopey mutt waltzed right into the bathroom. Maybe he had food."

So much for a guard-dog.

"Where the fuck does David keep his bleach?" Tip demands, still digging through cupboards.

"He doesn't." I'm motionless on the sofa. Even Not-Cero is quiet. "He uses vinegar and baking soda to clean."

Tip punches a cabinet. I hear the cheap wood splinter. *"Fucking* hippie!"

It's just shy of a roar. He's really worked up. Funny — Tip being the emotional one, while I'm running on empty? It's like we've swapped roles.

Look down, Not-Cero advises, so I do.

The envelope in my hands is standard in size, and unsealed. There's a brown half-moon of a thumbprint on one corner.

Upending the contents into my lap, I see a note on yet more Motel 6 stationary, snarled in angry slashes of black ink: *Bad form screwing with Eva,* reads the first line and, on the back: *Come earn your promise.*

The next item is a Greyhound bus ticket destined for Strawberry, Arizona. It's dated for departure the morning six days from now. June fourth.

That's a lot to unpack. "This was a punishment? Vince is punishing you for..." *Who is Eva?* "Something, just like when he attacked Crown?"

"Yep."

"And he wants you to go to him."

"Looks that way."

"But you're not going to." I try to make it a command, not a question.

Tip doesn't answer. Having abandoned his search for bleach, he leans his back against the front door and rubs his haggard face with both hands.

It strikes me that this is probably not the way normal people react to a murder, let alone the murder of a friend. But I'm a hero and sometimes a killer, and Tip's been in and out of hell since birth. We're not exactly poster children for normal.

Sometimes it feels like we're so accustomed to trauma that we don't know how to function without it.

Zelda whines at the door, interrupting my introspection. Tip uncovers his eyes to look at her. "What now?"

"She needs to go potty." The childish word slips from me before I think to hold it back, but Tip isn't in the mood to jeer. "Nobody will think it's weird to see me walking her. I do it all the time."

"Wash the blood off your face first."

I touch my lip and feel a now-familiar crust. Another nosebleed; just what I need.

Wait... A nosebleed? Blood? *My* blood, at a crime scene?

I look to where we'd slept, touching the cloudy stains on the plastic sofa cover.

"There's no point." Tip shakes his head. "Our DNA is everywhere. Our fingerprints. Probably some hairs. There's fuckall we can do about it."

He's right. I can only focus on one issue at a time, and right now that issue is washing my face off so I can walk David's dog without drawing attention. Or at least, no more attention than a pittie always draws in a pitbull-hating world.

Feeling like a zombie, I stand and shuffle to the sink, turn the cold faucet on, stick my mouth and nose under it, and watch red water swirl down the drain.

When I straighten, Tip takes my chin in his good hand and tilts my head back and forth, examining my face. He uses a rag to swipe one final streak off my cheek, then tosses it into the trash.

I've never been so thankful that David keeps Zelda's leash and harness by the workout equipment, and not in his bedroom. The pitbull offers a paw at a time for me to strap her in, knowing a walk is coming.

As I do, Tip puts her empty bowls into a reusable grocery bag, also grabbing a few of her toys.

"Leave her at our place," he advises, busying himself by filling a paper bag with scoops of dog food. "I don't want her getting in the way, tracking evidence everywhere. Bring back bleach. Plastic bags."

I should've caught on to his plan the *first* time he said the word 'bleach,' but my brain isn't working at top capacity just now. "You want to clean the scene."

"That's the idea."

"Why?! Vince killed David, not us. Let *him* swing for once."

Tip shakes his head. "You don't get it. Vince has never been busted. For anything. He's never gotten so much as a speeding ticket. His prints aren't in the system, but you know who's are?"

I don't answer, though the truth of his words lands like a stone in my throat.

"A junkie violating parole by getting high, and an ex-cop who apparently 'slept through' a homicide; that's who. We're fucked, Mags, even if we *prove* we weren't the ones holding the knife."

"So we cover it up, like it never happened? David has a *family*, Tip. He's my friend."

I recall Clay's soft voice that final night at the gas station, trying to make me feel remorse for killing Cash Jacobi. She'd mentioned his mother, his dogs... She might've saved her breath. Jacobi was evil, and therefore he deserved to die. I regret nothing.

David is different. He never hurt anyone in his life. More importantly, I liked him.

Tampering with the scene of a murder could earn us life without parole, easy. This isn't *as* daunting as it should be — I'm strong enough to defend myself. I make friends easily. I have almost nothing to lose, what with my gang falling apart and everyone I love dropping like flies.

What's more, I'm dying. I probably wouldn't be in there for very long.

Maybe it'd be nice to just give in. To go someplace with regular meals, shelter I don't have to pay for, free medical care... In some ways, prison offers me more than my current life does.

But then there's Tip. Frail Tip. Moody, prickly, broken Tip. Tip with his debilitating OCD; his need for "clean" foods. Tip, who rolls over and takes it from anyone because he's got it in his head that he deserves to be hurt.

They'll split us up, just because Tip happens to be a man. Without me to protect him, he *will* die there. It's only a matter of when.

See, Miss Cop? There are always shades of gray.

There Not-Cero goes again, smugly criticizing my moral code. "Shut up!" I snap. "You *always* put yourself first. At least I'm doing it because I care about other people!"

"*Excuse* me?" Tip narrows his eyes. I wave him off.

"I'm not talking to you." I snatch the handle of Zelda's leash and reach for the grocery bag in Tip's hand. He holds it above my reach, blocking the door.

"Who *were* you talking to, Mags?" He demands, studying my face with keen eyes too sharp, too *knowing* to meet.

I fish for a lie that doesn't arrive in time, leaving only the truth. "Sometimes I talk to Cero," I confess awkwardly. "It's not *that* crazy. I bet tons of widows do it."

There's something in his expression I don't like. He gazes at me like he does the ocean's waves, mapping out how best to traverse them, how to get past the initial rush until they accept him as their own.

"I'd better go," I mumble.

He nods, stepping aside, allowing me to take the bag. Then we're out the door, the morning sky a pat of cheerful butter melting on a baby-blue pancake.

Zelda is eager to trot down the stairs, tugging me towards her preferred walking path.

Tip knows, Not-Cero informs me, after my cousin closes the door on us. *He's seen me.*

"What the hell does that mean?" I demand, earning me the double glare of two older women out for a power-walk.

I hold a hand to my ear like I'm adjusting an earpiece until they outpace me.

He's seen me. Clever boy.

Maybe I *am* going crazy. My hallucination has progressed from criticizing my life to making nonsensical comments. "Seeing as you don't exist, I doubt it."

Black and white and so damn stubborn. You suit your name well.

Zelda pees twice and defecates once. I carry the poop baggie all the way to the corner trash bin, where she gazes longingly at the traffic light leading to the dog-friendly bakery.

"Not today, baby girl," I murmur, scratching the spot on her ribs that makes her back leg kick. "We're gonna hang out for a while, okay? Sleepover at Magpie's place?"

She looks dubious, but her stump tail gives a wag, and she comes willingly as I lead her back to my apartment.

Once inside, I remove her harness and allow her to roam, snuffling everything. She hops onto Tip's bed and makes herself comfortable in the blankets.

At the sink, I fill her water dish and set it on the floor with her toys and half-gnawed chewie. Then I gather the things Tip and I will need: plastic grocery bags, duct tape, the bottle of bleach we use for laundry.

It's not enough. Speaking as someone who's disposed plenty of bodies, this isn't going to work.

Zelda grunts when I flop down beside her and dredge my phone from my pocket.

The battery is nearly dead, and I've got a metric crapton of missed calls: three from Antonina (crap), one from Tip's parole officer (double crap), one from work *(fuck!),* and a final call from an unknown number.

As the cherry atop my shit sundae, there's also this charming text from Navier: *It ain't gonna suck itself.*

I ignore everything and instead call Ricket. He's remarkably good at fixing my messes, and this one's the messiest mess that ever messed.

The reliable man answers on the third ring. I'm so thankful I could, and probably *should,* kiss the ground he walks on. "Good morning, Magpie."

"Hey, Professor Nerd," I reply, forcing a smile so that I hopefully sound less wretched. "Sorry if I woke you, but I'm screwed six ways to Sunday. Please come rescue me?"

Chapter Twenty-Four – Tip

...

With gloves on his hands, a food service net covering his hair, and plastic bags duct-taped over his shoes, James strides into David's bedroom and surveys his headless corpse.

"I see," he muses, then turns around and walks back out. "Let's get to work."

One trip to the hardware store later and we're coating the bloody walls with paint guaranteed to hide ugly stains.

David's aversion to traditional cleaning products apparently did not extend to a single bottle of pet stain remover, found beneath his bathroom sink. Mags uses it to make the carpet look less murderey.

Our efforts would not hold up under the scrutiny of a forensics team. Hopefully, it never has to. No corpse, no crime, and this gang knows how to lose a body.

"Rent is due on the first," Magpie fusses. "If he doesn't pay it, the landlord will come looking for him."

Typical. The residents and staff here ignore months worth of Magpie's night-screaming, but the moment money is short, *that's* where they draw the line.

James digs around until he finds David's checkbook and, with a steady hand, copies the information and handwriting from the carbon paper of a previous rent check. The forged signature looks perfect to my untrained, nearsighted eyes.

He hands the check to Magpie, who pockets it. "Turn this in with your own."

Bodies release unpleasant things when orifices relax, and the reek of shit and gas radiates from the bed. Still preferable to the sickly-sweet stench of rot, which will come with bacteria and insects.

James lifts David's elbow and examines it closely, then its twin. He beckons me to look, as though showing me an unusual sample of richelia under his microscope.

"Rigor mortis has come and gone," he points out, causing David's hand to flop. "In this heat, I'd say maybe eleven, twelve hours dead."

Considering how early we'd fallen asleep, and how long we'd remained that way, that holds up.

He shows me a puncture in the pallid flesh atop a green vein. I know a needle's pinprick when I see one. Those are the veins junkies destroy first before turning to the ones between our toes, beneath our tongues, inside our sclera...

"If I'm not mistaken, Vince drugged David shortly before killing him. That's why you didn't hear a struggle."

His theory holds upon studying the stump of David's neck; the clean slice. How level the protruding fragment of vertebra is. "Piano wire," I guess, and James nods.

He'd given no fight, despite the force of bloodspatter suggesting he'd been alive during his decapitation. Corpses don't hemorrhage.

"Vince doesn't play fair, does he?" James asks, a note of disapproval in his voice. "This was a coward's kill. He couldn't even look the man in the eye while he took his life."

He gestures to David's prone position, something I wouldn't have thought twice on had it not been brought to my attention.

I consider the thought. Is Vince a coward? He seems fearless, but perhaps that's only because he knows he'll never be punished.

James's eyes are still on me.

"What?" I ask, self-conscious. I'm not exactly looking my best here, wearing yesterday's sweaty work uniform and all.

"What in his life did David value most?" James asks.

Why ask me? It's not like I really knew the guy. This feels like a particularly bizarre object lesson. *Hey Professor, will this be on the final?*

"His dog? Pot? Gaming? Maybe Mags; he had a Kentucky-sized crush on her."

James nods. "Find representations of those things and bring them here, as well as any important paperwork or documentation. All finances, contracts, leases, forms. If something strikes you as personal, bring it here."

Grateful for something to do, and someone to tell me to do it, I obey.

I wander the apartment and find all that was asked of me. Bongs and family photos and tax forms; sex toys and immunization records and a frayed baby blanket carefully stowed in the back of the closet.

I collect David's life in bite-sized pieces and drop them all on the bloody sheets for disposal. The sad thing is, David has more to show for his life than I do, and I'm a decade and some change older than he'll ever be.

James has raided the bathroom, but not as thoroughly as I would have done. He grabs the daily necessities — toothpaste and brush, soap and shampoo and razor — but leaves all the rest.

"David left in a hurry," James narrates, sitting on the bed beside the corpse without an ounce of squeamishness. He pokes through all the paperwork until he finds a handwritten page of passwords, using them to log into the gaming system. "Maybe he meant to come back, but never did. It helps that you live in a complex that's particularly..."

"Shitty?" I suggest.

"Disreputable. His drug use and unemployment are in our favor."

He tosses me David's ancient iPhone. "Try '021392' for the password. His sister's birthday. If that's not it, try '624743', which spells 'Magpie'. If *those* don't work, we'll examine Zelda's paperwork for a date of adoption."

Mags, scrubbing the carpet, makes noise in her throat; the broken warble of a dying bird. This likely goes against all her copper ethics, yet she *must* see it's the only way. We can't be tangled in a murder investigation. We're barely hanging on as it is.

I'm okay with being selfish and underhanded if that's what it takes to survive. Besides; this is hardly the first mess of Vince's I've had to clean up.

James's first guess at the phone password is correct.

"Well, that's terrifying," I inform him, trying to sound candid and not at all turned on. "You're good."

He smiles without joy and navigates his way through various multi-player games, updating David's status as "online" and offering text responses to the players most pleased to see him.

"Message his dealer," he instructs. "Inform them you are no longer in need of their services."

I do just that, finding badly coded messages to someone by the name of 'Starr.' I try to copy David's speech patterns as best I can.

Starr is *pissed*, but I don't argue with them. Let them think David found Jesus.

Shit; I *hope* he did.

"His family will look for him eventually," I point out, showing James the texts between David and his mother; his sister. "Look. They love him."

"Which is why you'll be keeping that phone for a while. You'll continue to be David until Magpie's disappearance is well underway."

Magpie and I both gawk at him.

James looks from the game to us, a furrow in his brow. "Well," he says, like it should be blindingly obvious. "You couldn't expect to stay *here*, could you?"

...

"You're really sending Mags to live with your *parents*?" I ask, still not over the thought. It doesn't feel real to me yet.

All of this day has a surreal cast to it, actually. If it turns out I slipped into a coma while watching the Twilight Zone, I won't be surprised.

"Only for a while." James limps alongside us as we take Zelda on yet another walk.

The dog hadn't appreciated being left alone in our apartment all day. She'd thoroughly explored the contents of our garbage can before vomiting half of them on my bed.

"I've never even met your family," Mags points out, clucking her tongue to discourage Zelda from sniffing the mangled remains of a pigeon in the crosswalk. "I know nothing about them — wait, really? They're scientists, too?"

James gives her a funny look. "How did you know that?"

Magpie clears her throat. "Cero told me," she says, avoiding his eye.

My impossible theory on my cousin's deceased wife grows yet another layer. I think I saw something unnatural in the kitchen yesterday, and I *know* Cero was standing above me last night.

The fact that I'd been high, dehydrated, and suffering from moderate heat exhaustion throws some doubt on these observations, but Occam's Razor states that the most obvious solution is often the correct one.

Something foul is afoot. I need to gather more evidence.

"Did she?" James's frown grows. "She wasn't in the habit of sharing my secrets."

"I'm her *wife*," Magpie snaps. *"Was* her wife. Whatever. Anyway, so your family are scientists. What else?"

Evasive Mags, huh? She only gets like that when she's hiding something, like that time I'd caught her buying E from Vince in seventh grade, or the Sophomore pregnancy scare, or her current drinking issues...

My big-brother instincts are tingling. I'm tempted to force some answers out of her, but it's best to wait for when we don't have an audience.

"I have three siblings," James says. "Only one of them still lives with my parents, as the rest of us don't care to spend our days in the middle of the Sonoran Desert, peering into cacti with magnifying glasses."

At Magpie's blank expression, he explains, "They're well-credited entomologists."

"Famous bug scientists," I clarify, before she can ask us to speak English.

How *funny* — if his folks are so into the creepy-crawlies, I wonder what drew him to all things oceanic. Is this his nerdy form of rebellion?

James nods his approval. "Precisely. They and my sister Lettie travel in a camper van, so locating them can be difficult. And dangerous. They're... Protective of their work."

"So I'm just supposed to drive around the desert at random, searching for bug scientists who might kill me because they'll assume I'm trying to steal their research?"

When *Magpie's* questionable sense of self-preservation kicks in, something must really smell fishy.

"Yes. See, your ill-reputed cousin was having an affair with your best friend. The scoundrel left you for his professor, and you couldn't afford the rent without him."

I blink. That's low, even for me. "I did *what*, now?"

James's smile is small and self-depreciating. "It fits your reputation. The best way to deceive the world is to do exactly what they expect."

"Bully for me!" I snap, trying not to sound *too* sarcastic. "I always knew my enterprising career as a child prostitute would serve me well."

Magpie walks quietly between us, no doubt feeling like a third wheel in this awkward turn of events.

What James proposes makes sense. I'll move in with him. Mags will skip town. If anyone hunts her down to see if her friend David is with her, either they won't find her, or they *will* find her living nomad-style with the Rickets. *No, officer; I've been here all along!*

"So, like, since I'm That Asshole," I say, taking Magpie's elbow and hauling her away from the busy street. "I've got to ask. Is this cuz I ended things between us? Is this a way to keep me in your debt?"

Magpie shoots me a wide-eyed *'shut up!'* look. James is offering us a way out of our troubles, and she probably thinks her friend is too good a man to take advantage of that.

I've been around the block enough to know there's no such thing as a good man. Myself included. Myself, *especially*.

To James's credit, he doesn't take offense. "I assure you, I will not lay hands on you while we live together. You are free to come and go as you choose. We can stage a breakup after a few weeks, if you like."

I'll hold him to that, even if a part of me wonders if I should. I can't afford to live alone, and scouting Craigslist for roommates really isn't my thing.

If left to my own devices, I know what will happen. It involves needles, and a stranger's bed to pay for them. I may resent the claustrophobic living conditions with my cousin, but the truth of the matter is, she keeps me from sinking too deep.

Rather than voice any of this, I ask the obvious question: "What about Vince? If he was pissed about the flowers, just imagine what he'll do if I move in with you."

Finally James looks up, a gleam in his eyes. "Let him come," he says sweetly, and I see how it lights him up inside. He *wants* to goad Vince into action. "I suspect he'll find me a more challenging target than poor David."

"You know, some might see your bloodthirsty side and call it a red flag," I remark as we double back towards the apartment.

"But not you," James replies, far too knowingly.

I feel the blush in my chest before it crawls up my neck, staining my cheeks. No. Not me, indeed.

We discuss our plans as Magpie leads the way over the grassy courtyard of the complex, past the mossy fountain that serves as a centerpiece — disabled, because California drought laws are in effect — to the wall of mailboxes.

She unlocks ours and scoops all our mail into a plastic bag, then does the same with David's. He must've been lazy, like us, letting it accumulate for days at a time.

"Ugh," Magpie groans, holding a yellow slip of paper that informs us we have a package waiting in the landlord's office. "Tip, did you order something?"

I shake my head no and take Zelda's leash when she hands it to me. She crosses the courtyard to the office and lets herself inside.

Zelda tangles my legs with her leash. James watches in amusement as I step out of its confines, only to be immediately trapped again. "Haven't you ever walked a dog before?" he asks.

"No," I grouch, almost losing my footing when she wedges herself between my legs. I could probably sit on her tank of a body, and she wouldn't even bend under my weight.

James laughs and offers Zelda his hand, which she snuffles before allowing him to rub her ears. "Maybe we should collar Tip," he jokes in the same sweet voice he talks to Hero with. "Keep him out of trouble."

I have a brief, vivid mental image of myself wearing a dog's collar, with James's name stamped on the metal tag. All of the blood in my body rushes south, fast enough to leave me reeling.

He cocks his head, an eyebrow crooked. "Oh? It's like that, is it?"

I scowl, mortified to be so transparent.

Magpie returns. She's got a large box in her arms, which I trade for Zelda's leash.

It's heavy, and held together with duct tape. I look for any sender information, seeing nothing other than Magpie's name and address typed on the sticker.

It must be too big a box for its contents, because the weighty thing inside rolls around as we resume walking.

It doesn't escape my attention how Magpie takes James's free arm, cuddling into his side. Mags doesn't handle death very well, so I'm sure there'll be fallout once her shock wears off. For now, she clings close to the only member of our party who will tolerate physical affection.

I make a mental note to touch her later, for as long as I can bear. Hell; maybe I can smoke some more of David's stash, and then I'll be fine to snuggle all night again.

She's your baby cousin. Don't ruin her with your filthy hands.

I know. I *know.* I've never once been able to forget.

We return to Magpie's apartment to get Zelda some water, and because I don't know if James can handle more stairs right now.

He stands in the doorway, watching as I fold my bed up and put down the sofa cushions. Then he sits on it, stretching his leg out.

"Can I trouble you for some water?" he asks, but I know by the fatigue in his voice that what he really wants is coffee.

I pour him a glass from the sink, then spoon some grounds into a paper filter. While I'm there, I also scoop three cups of food into Zelda's dish.

The movements have a nice synchrony to them that pleases my brain — *pour, clink, spoon, spoon, scoop, scoop, scoop.* The burbling coffeemaker adds a distracting rhythm.

I feel a moderate compulsion to keep going, but we don't have a lot of dog food, and she'll need to eat more tomorrow. "Can you tell me to stop?" I ask, already reaching for more. "I'm getting stuck."

James looks puzzled for only a moment before understanding dawns. He knows about my disorder, as we've had similar experiences in class.

"You can stop now, Tip," he says, kind and authoritative. "That's enough."

I hadn't expected it to help, but it does. I'm able to put the food back under the sink and bring him his water before I'm struck by what happened.

I'd given James my control — not a lot, but some — and it had turned out okay. *This* time.

Vince would've physically forced me to stop, grabbing me and shoving me down, or just tightly covering my mouth. *"Why are you like this?!"* He'd demand whenever I became stuck on a thought or a sound or an action. *"Are you fucking retarded?!"*

I perch as far from James as the sofa allows, every line in my posture tense to convey *Do Not Touch.* Maybe I'll warm up later, but right now I feel too muddled to be friendly.

I listen to the coffeemaker gurgle, watching from the corner of my eye as my professor pulls a pill bottle from his pocket, taps two capsules into his palm, and swallows them down with his water.

The toilet flushes. Magpie returns from her room carrying scissors in one hand and a bottle of whiskey in the other.

She sits between us, snuggling into James's side, and glugs from the bottle in a way that has us both gawking. Whiskey is *not* meant to be consumed multiple gulps at a time.

"Jesus, Mags," I manage, as she chokes and wipes at her streaming eyes. She probably doesn't know it, but my drug tests sometimes randomly scan for alcohol. If she really plans to take them for me...

"You can shut your face," she snaps, setting the bottle aside, bending to lift the mail package from the floor. "Today sucked ass."

"In that case," James says, pulling a pack of cigarettes from his shirt pocket. "Do you mind?"

Our apartment has, up to this point, been non-smoking. I remember from Gran how long the scent lingers in a place — forever, basically. But after all he's done for us today, I think we'd've let him host an orgy and snort lines off the kitchen sink if he felt so inclined.

Mags nods. I stand to pour James's coffee, bringing back an empty yogurt cup for him to use as an ashtray. I sit on the arm of the sofa so that my knees touch Magpie's hip.

For a while, the only sounds are Zelda munching her dinner and Mags hacking at her box. James exhales a lungful of smoke over his shoulder and washes it down with a slurp of coffee. He looks as content as I've ever seen him.

I would be okay if life was always like this, I think. *Just the three of us, right here, doing nothing. Saying nothing.*

It's a wretched thought, considering what we've already done; what we're *about* to do. Still, I feel calmer now than I have since the last time I was in James's bed. Maybe I'm only capable of feeling good after bad things happen.

At last Magpie wrestles the package open. Its contents are wrapped in a white garbage bag, a dark stain showing through when she holds it to the light. On seeing this, my heart sinks with dread. It knows what's up seconds before my brain figures it out.

"Mags, don't—" I reach to take the bag away, but with a final dash of her scissors, she splits it open.

The stench hits us first, stronger even than the fumes of alcohol; the curling heat of cigarette smoke. We recoil in unison.

David's milky eyes stare at us from his severed head. It's nestled atop a mat of his own dreadlocks, which are stained a streaky brown from dried blood and cerebrospinal fluid.

The thing looks like a tacky Halloween prop. I can't stop staring at the black veins in his eyelids; the way his dried tongue pokes from between his colorless lips.

Silently, Magpie closes the flaps of the box over her dead friend's head. She stands and carries it to the door.

We follow her back to David's apartment.

•••

"What's in his mouth?" James asks, once we and the box are back in David's bedroom.

I squint and, even without my glasses, see the way the dead man's sunken cheek puckers around a foreign object, trapped between flesh and molars.

"Nope!" Magpie exclaims, throwing her hands into the air and stalking to the relative safety of the hallway. "Nope, nope, nope. I draw the line at digging around in there."

James looks at me, a request in his eyes.

I switch off the part of my brain that feels fear and disgust, and plunge two fingers into David's cold, spongy mouth. His incisors lightly scrape my knuckles. The objects clink together as I withdraw.

Resting on my palm are two silver rings, hinged and hooked.

Magpie gasps from the doorway. Her hand covers her mouth, as though hiding rings between her own two lips.

"Care to let us in on the secret?" James prompts.

In response, Magpie carefully removes a golden hoop from her own ear, holding it up for us to see. Aside from the color, it's a match for the ones I hold.

"Vince is reminding me of the time I ripped out his orbital rings," she explains. "Guess he *is* still pissed."

I don't want to hold the jewelry a second longer, so I drop them back into the box and go to scrub my hands at David's bathroom sink.

James sets the box down on the ruined mattress and leads the three of us back to the main room of the apartment, firmly shutting the bedroom door behind us.

"Vince's games are growing tiresome," he sighs. "We *understand* that he wishes vengeance on Magpie. That he intends to resume a relationship with Tip. His point has already been made, and now he's just playing cat-and-mouse. Distasteful."

I see Magpie's jaw drop; hear the squawk she emits as she struggles to form words. "That's all you have to say about this? It's 'distasteful'?!"

James blinks, wearing the same expression he uses when a student asks an obvious question. "Well, yes. A true artist knows the line between enough and excessive. *This* man is little more than a bored, spoiled child."

I nudge James as I sit down beside him. "Don't talk like that. You sound like a sociopath." *I* understand his point, but someone like Magpie never would.

James frowns. Argues, "I experience empathy. I'm simply stating—"

"I know. But Mags is freaking out, and you're not helping."

James looks at how Magpie watches him. She's holding together pretty well, but I can tell by the wild-animal glint in her eyes that implosion is imminent. Hopefully James knows her well enough to see what I see.

He ducks his head. I watch him piece himself back together, putting away the scientist, the pragmatist, the — it must be said — *criminal,* and bringing forth the mask he wears to placate normal people. He reaches for her.

She hesitates only a moment before giving him her hand, which he squeezes. "My sincere apologies, dearest," he says, his smile as gentle as his voice.

Now that David is out of sight, I'm feeling more than a little affectionate. I press the back of my hand to James's good leg, and am delighted when he takes it, running a thumb across my knuckles.

He holds us both and tries to find a more palatable way to word his thoughts. "Vince is sloppy," he tells us. "And sloppy criminals make foolish mistakes. He has a few loose threads he could've hidden better, I think."

There's a knock on the door. James calls, "Come in, Navier."

Chapter Twenty-Five - Magpie

things can always, **always** *get worse.*

...

It's odd to say that I have a preferred buddy to dump bodies with, but it's the truth. Navier and I have done this so many times that loading a corpse and all of its trappings — in this case, David's mattress and head — onto the Tacoma bears the comfort of ritual.

He's practically whistling as he ties a tarp down over the truck bed. I check to ensure he exchanged his real license plate for the one his persona uses, just in case.

We both carry the fake IDs and social security cards for our alternate selves, and Navier sanded down the Tacoma's VIN years ago. Tonight, Alexis Magpie and Etienne Navier have been replaced by Georgia Byrd and Robert Gray.

If any neighbors are watching, they'll assume we're just moving some furniture. We climb in and get the engine rumbling.

"Someone's been naughty," Navier grins, doglike, as he pulls from my parking lot. "Shitting where you eat, sha?"

"I didn't kill him," I snap, curling in the seat and hugging my knees to my chest.

"Right, right." Looking as though he couldn't care less, Navier cranks up the radio and speeds to the highway that will, eventually, lead to empty desert.

"Watch it," I glare at his speedometer. "You wanna get pulled over? Remember the cop adage — 'eight, you're great; nine, you're mine'!"

Back when I was a traffic cop, I had a strict nightly quota of tickets to hand out. Some guys pulled people over for peanuts just to *meet* said quota. Anyone who thinks American police forces care about anything other than money prove that ignorance really is bliss.

"You worry too much. Didn't that one guy get pulled over with a *bunch* of bodies in his car, and nobody ever noticed? And that other *homme* — shoot; a teenager ran naked an' bleeding from *his* house, and the fuzz just handed him right back over! Cops don't notice fuckall."

He's referring to serial killers Ted Bundy and Jeffrey Dahmer, respectively. And while he's technically correct — those unforgivable oversights *did* happen, to devastating consequence — it's too much to expect we'd get such a lucky break.

"That's still no reason to attract attention," I grumble, leaning my head against the window. "And I don't appreciate being compared to a serial killer."

Navier glances at me, driving in that easy way of his with one arm slung over the wheel, his elbow poking from the window. "How many victims does a serial killer make?"

"Typically three."

"And how many people have *we* killed?"

"If I have to *explain* this shit to you, I don't think you'd understand." I reach to crank his radio volume higher. "Be a serial killer if you want, but I'm not."

We drive for an hour in peace, watching the city landscape gradually wink out until cacti outnumber palm trees ten to one, and the houses become trailers, then nothing.

"Hey, Navier?" I ask, remembering the sketchbooks I'd dug out while cleaning yesterday, shortly before Tip collapsed. "Weird question, but did Cero ever talk about occult stuff with you?"

"Hm?" He flicks the radio off. "Cher, I'm Cajun, not Creole. An' don't call Voodoo 'occult'; it's just a religion."

"No, I mean like... Witchcraft? Demons? Whatever the goth kids in high school were into?"

I'm probably being offensive, but this is so far out of my lane I barely have the vocabulary for it. I know numbers. I know combat. I know the lyrics to every Bikini Kill song. I don't know this.

Navier shrugs. "It's possible. She was a *femme aux nombreux talents.* Nothing was off limits to her."

"What about when you got shanked at that bar?" I ask. "Do you remember what happened after?"

"I told you. I lost consciousness. I woke up in Cero's apartment. I liked her, so I stuck around. And here we are!" He wiggles his fingers. "Ta-da!"

Something doesn't feel right. It rubs at my mind like a pebble in a shoe. No matter how good Cero is — was — at treating injuries, a perforated liver would require immediate invasive surgery.

"We're here," he says, parking and hopping from the Tacoma. 'Here' being an area of the desert Ricket and Crown mapped out for body disposal. We've planted more than our fair share of men in these grounds.

We get right to work. Shovels are produced. Hydrofluoric acid from UCLA's stock is poured.

"Navier!" I realize, almost too late. "You used rope on David's wrists and ankles!"

"So?"

"*So,* you know nylon dissolves faster than meat and bone. His hands and feet will float right to the top!"

We don't have time to dig a *very* deep hole, so we rely on the acid to take care of the evidence before scavengers come along. If David's extremities float, however...

The look Navier shoots me, illuminated by headlights, is less than pleased. He so hates criticism. "Picky, picky, picky. Nobody's gonna find him out here! Dump him in; we don't have all night."

I cross my arms stubbornly. The last thing we need is a coyote dropping a human foot on the side of a road, or a vulture-culture nut prying open some hawk's belly to find fingers. Fingers with traceable prints.

When he sees that I'm not going to budge, Navier swears and straddles David's corpse. He uses the knife from his boot to hack the ropes off the dead man's ankles. "There's zip-ties in the glove compartment. If you care so much, *you* get 'em."

"Thank you. That's all I wanted."

Apparently he still wants the last word. "I swear, Mags. Sometimes you're alright, but then you go and nag as much as any stuck-up bitch."

My jaw drops. I want to demand he explain himself. I want to punch an apology out of his stupid face. It's not that I've never been called a bitch before. It's not even that *he's* never called me a bitch before. But that *tone...!*

Not-Cero urges me to get moving. To punish his disrespect later. Navier was right about one thing: we *don't* have all night.

I stomp to the truck and climb inside, spitting curses under my breath as I violently wrench the glove compartment open. The contents tumble into the footwell. Parking tickets, loose condoms, a tool kit, a car manual, a million fast-food receipts...

The packet of zip-ties bounces under the driver's seat. I have to lay flat to fish them out, dragging them and some McDouble wrappers from the shadows.

Since when does Navier let the Tacoma get sloppy? Just last month he yelled at me for putting my boots on the seat. This thing is supposed to be his pride and joy!

I sit up and make a face as I peel a paper from the plastic packet, glued with what might be mummified mustard. A warning bell buzzes in my head when I see the Motel 6 logo printed in green ink.

Flipping the paper over, I see a phone number scrawled across it; ten digits copied with a hasty hand. The warning bell becomes a siren.

This looks like the number Rosa and I called while investigating Vince's motel room. Identical, in fact. There's not a doubt in my mind.

Navier has Vince's phone number. Navier has the number to Vince's burner phone. Navier is the *only* person Vince gave that number to. Vince... *Gave*... Navier...

The note in your helmet, Not-Cero breathes, sounding as numb as I feel. *With the photos. And wasn't he the one to suggest which Urgent Care Ricket take you to, that day you bled all over the bed?*

I want to protest; to say we shouldn't jump to conclusions yet. But...

But Rosa doesn't believe in coincidences. Neither does Cero. Neither do I; not anymore.

"Mags!" Navier barks. "Can you hurry? The hydro-whatever is makin' me dizzy."

I stand. Tuck the stationary into my pocket. Carry the zip-ties to the person I thought was my friend.

"Took you long enough," Navier grumbles, and sets to securing David's limbs properly.

It sure did, Not-Cero agrees, still dazed. *We almost missed it.*

We finish our work quickly, survival instincts keeping my mouth shut tight. I am in the middle of the desert with an armed man more than twice my size, surrounded by plenty of body-disposing materials. Navier makes me feel lots of emotions, but until this moment, fear was never among them.

Keep your head on straight, my wife commands.

She's right. I've just got to hold it together until we get home, and then Ricket will know what to do.

"Whew. I think that's about everything." Navier leans against his shovel and wipes his brow.

"Looks like it," I agree, proud that my voice remains light; calm. "You did a good job. Wanna head back?"

We load the truck and bounce and jostle through rough desert until we find the road. Then we wait a while to confirm there's no traffic before flicking the headlights back on and rejoining society.

"What do you think, cher?" Navier asks, a grin in his voice, which he pitches comically low. "You wanna?"

"Huh?"

He holds up one of the condoms from his glove compartment and waggles his eyebrows.

"What part of 'my friend just got his head lopped off' are you missing?!" I demand, furious. "I'm not in the mood, thanks!"

I refrain from adding 'you absolute child,' but it's a narrow miss.

He loses the easy grin. Tosses the condom over his shoulder to land in the backseat. Focuses on the road. Concedes, "I guess that *is* shitty timing. Sorry, Mags."

I want to scream at him, but Not-Cero pipes in. *Play along, Miss Cop. Keep him happy.*

I don't want to. But I'll be stuck with this creep for the long drive home, and I'm scared. Sure, I can take Navier down when he's unprepared, but my odds don't look great in an actual fight, especially considering we were trained by the same person.

You think I haven't had to play nice before? You think Tip *hasn't? Ricket? You can be angry later. You can smash all the toilet tanks you like. But for now, you must play dumb!*

I give Navier a smile, reaching to tuck his curly hair behind one ear. I run my thumb over the shell until he leans his stubbled cheek into my palm, docile as a hound.

"I thought you never ate at the same restaurant twice," I point out, using one of his cruder metaphors. "*And* I thought I wasn't your type."

Navier barks a laugh. "Yeah... But I kinda think we have something. Maybe you were what I was missing."

And he'd decided this all on his own. Why ask my opinion, right?

I barely keep my smile when his hand drops onto my thigh. It stays there until we're close to home again.

"Oh, shit!" I exclaim, wide-eyed. "Oh, hell; I forgot I have to make a call. You got a burner? I lost mine."

"Hm?" Navier shifts in his seat and pulls a cheap flip-phone from his back pocket, holding it out. Careless as ever.

"Perfect!" I open it, making a beeline for his call history, and scroll back as far as I can. Navier has called Vince several times a week as far back as two months back.

Amateur mistake, not even bothering to delete this. Didn't Cero teach him to cover his tracks?

I check the texts, but there are none, so I dial the first number I can think of. I need to keep this ruse going; need to keep the phone in my possession.

"Hola?" Rosa asks. "¿Quién es?"

"Hey, beautiful."

"Magpie?"

"Just wondered if you got that stuff for me."

"*What* stuff?"

I smile brightly as Navier settles into a parking space. "You are the absolute best, babe." I blow kisses into the receiver. "Knew I could count on you. Love you!"

"Magpie, *what*—"

I hang up and hop out of the truck, dancing up the stairs to David's front door before Navier can try to take the phone away from me. "Can you load the moped into the back?" I call down, flashing my deepest dimples.

Navier glances at David's vehicle with disdain, but sets to work.

I knock on the door in what I hope is a cheery fashion. Tip, still dressed in the clothes I nose-bled on, opens it.

He opens his mouth, probably to scold me for taking so long, before frowning at my expression. "What's wrong?" he asks.

I muscle into his chest, pushing him back inside the apartment. He grips my arms, looking over the top of my head to glimpse whatever is troubling me.

From where he stands in the kitchen, still wearing his hairnet and gloves, Ricket goes very still.

"Act normal," I tell them, and kick the door shut behind me. It's not until Tip takes my hand that I realize I was scratching at my mouth again. "Ricket? You armed?"

"Always. Aren't you?"

No. I should be. I'm an idiot *not* to be. I vow to never leave home without my knives again.

"Let him in. Cut off access to all exits," I command. Ricket may be the only loyal member of my gang remaining, but I'm still the leader.

"Are you talking about Navier?" Tip looks annoyed. That's par for the course, but I see the subtle worry in the squinch of his eyebrows. "Did he hurt you?"

Ricket meets my gaze. He doesn't look at all surprised. How long has he suspected the shift in Navier's loyalties?

"He might be carrying a gun," I warn, voice low. "He had one that night with the Jacobis. And at the gas station."

Now I see some worry in those dark eyes. "Magpie..."

It's too late. Navier swings the door open and strides inside.

Once, Cero took me to a college production of Beauty and the Beast. I'd never been inside an actual theater before, and had been so impressed by the enormity of the place; the deep colors of the curtains and the fabric-covered seats.

The acting and singing had amazed me so much that I'd forgotten it was only a story. I'd felt like I was part of the unfolding events, a silent witness to its reality, until Cero grounded me by leaning into my side.

"Does Gaston remind you of someone?" She'd whispered, a grin crooking her lips. "And I'm not *just* talking about the accent."

I'd muffled a giggle, thinking she meant the arrogant way both Navier and the character strutted; the deep timbre of their voices. And they weren't dissimilar in appearance, either.

Now, however, I see other similarities. The boorish way Navier talks over people. How he views women — especially women he's slept with. He acts like his crassness is a joke, but is it really?

He flops onto David's sofa, dragging me down with him. His thumbs slips up the hemline of my shirt, rubbing circles on bare flesh.

The taste of acid, once only associated with Vince, floods my mouth. How fast things change. I feel nothing but disgust and hurt for someone I used to love cuddling.

Focus, Mags.

I see the way Tip, actually wearing his glasses for once, narrows his eyes. He looks first at Navier's fingers creeping up my shirt, then to my face, assessing my reaction to being fondled. I try and give him a reassuring smile.

He scowls, not buying it for a second. He always could see right through me.

I get to work before Tip can make a scene, leaning my head against Navier's shoulder. My hand idly strokes his chest, searching.

Bless Ricket and his inscrutable poker face. He approaches, dragging a barstool from the kitchen to sit on. He plants himself across the room from us, 'coincidentally' blocking the front door.

"Did everything go according to plan?" He asks. "You didn't use the drop by the solar farm, did you? I told you that one might be compromised."

Navier frowns. "You *never* told me that! What's wrong with it?"

At last I find Navier's cross-chest holster. The thick leather strap fits around his right shoulder and, presumably, connects somewhere below his left arm.

I'd trained with and carried a piece as a cop, but I never enjoyed it. Guns are bad news. They're messy and noisy, they leave traceable evidence, and the potential for oopsies is high.

People accidentally shoot others, or themselves, all the time. I've never accidentally stabbed anyone. Every death from my knives is calculated, deliberate, and controlled.

Navier feels out of control. Mine, Cero's, and possibly his own.

When Ricket's eyes flick to me, I raise a finger in the guise of scratching my nose. *One gun.*

Maybe just the one. I didn't feel anything at his waist, but I'm not brave enough to paw his legs.

Tip catches my gesture and stands, stomping out of the room like a moody teenager. David's bedroom and bathroom doors slam in quick succession behind him. *Bam! Bam!*

Navier, who doesn't know Tip well enough to guess what is and isn't his normal behavior, hardly bats an eyelash. He's too busy arguing with Ricket. "I didn't see any construction!"

Minutes of bickering pass before I hear the muffled sound of running water.

When the door creaks open, I cough to mask the sound of Tip's approach. He's probably about to do something very stupid, and I don't want him to get hurt.

Sure enough, he leans over the back of the sofa, hooks one rubber gloved arm around Navier's throat, and violently jams a dripping rag against his mouth and nose.

Navier flails, his cry muffled in the fabric. One hand reaches back, grabbing for Tip's face, while the other dives down the neck of his own shirt.

I tackle him, snatching his hands, pinning them between us with my full weight. He stares at me in shocked disbelief. I scowl right back.

Even working in tandem, Tip and I can't overpower this much thrashing muscle for long. It'd take forever to smother him; full minutes astride his bucking form.

For a wild second, I think Navier is crying. I'm so shocked I nearly lose my grip, until I register that his eyes are running from the noxious stink of the cloth. The excess fluid spattering my arms and chest stings, then burns.

Navier gags, choking. His stomach heaves against mine, as though struggling not to vomit. He tries to wrench free, but Tip yanks a fistful of hair to hold him steady.

In movies, bad guys often drug people unconscious with chloroform. The victim blacks out in seconds, waking later to plan their daring escape.

In reality, losing consciousness by inhaling toxic chemicals can easily kill someone. There's a reason anesthesiologists are paid the big bucks to keep patients alive.

Navier's eyes roll back, lids at half-mast, shivering in their sockets. He makes a gurgling sound and goes limp between us, twitching and jerking sporadically. A seizure?

Not yet. Let go.

I do. Tip meets my eyes and does the same. Navier's wet lips part for fresh air, a pinkish trickle of froth dribbling down his chin.

Even then, my priority is to unbutton his flannel shirt and retrieve the pistol, checking its safety before sliding it across the floor to Ricket. Further patting down reveals no additional weapons.

Ricket takes the gun, then climbs gingerly to his feet, reaching over our heads to open the window. It's a good thing, too; Tip and I are coughing hard from proximity to the fumes. Tip strips the yellow dishwashing gloves off and throws the rag aside.

I notice Ricket watching my cousin, a heat in his eyes I've never seen before. "Was that chlorine gas?"

Tip is breathing hard, high on adrenaline, when he nods. "If he dies from that... Sorry. Wasn't my intention."

"*Good* boy."

I was a passable chemistry student in high school, and I remember some lessons. To create chlorine gas, Tip would've needed bleach — presumably from the bottle we'd brought from our apartment — and ammonia.

"Tip, sweetie?" I ask, standing to douse myself under the kitchen faucet. "Did you *piss* on that rag?"

His ghoulish grin speaks volumes.

...

I fill the guys in on everything as we haul Navier to David's bedroom, bind him tightly, and dab his face with a concoction of aloe vera and honey. Tip rubs it into my skin, too, until the burning subsides.

Tip wanted to take Navier's gun into the room with us, but at that, I'd put my foot down. A single gunshot in a moment of high emotion can never be undone. He holds a kitchen knife, instead.

"If he lives, he'll need to go to the hospital," Ricket says. "His lungs are damaged. Hear him wheezing?"

Tip harrumphs. "What do you *mean*, he's working with Vince? He'd better wake the fuck up and explain." He kicks Navier in the ribs. "Yo!"

"If you didn't know why you were attacking him, then why did you do it?" I ask.

Tip shrugs, savagely calm. "He was touching you, and you didn't like it."

Navier whimpers. The raw skin of his face is hardening into blisters. His lips and streaming nostrils, especially, are swollen and cherry-red. When he opens his eyes, they're bloodshot to match.

He tries to speak, but all that comes forth is a prolonged rattle. He tries again and immediately begins to cough, chesty and deep. "What did you *do* to me?!"

"I make it a point not to educate the willfully ignorant," Ricket says crisply. Since David's mattress is gone, he leans against the bathroom door. Tip and I take the floor.

"The real question is, *why* did we do this to you?" I hold Navier's phone in one hand and the motel stationary in the other. "And I've got a few questions for you, too. For starters, why are you in contact with the man who tried to murder me and Crown?"

Beneath the goop on his face, Navier goes very pale.

"And don't lie," Ricket advises. "Do you know what will happen if you don't receive prompt medical attention? Perhaps you'll only develop pneumonia, but more likely you'll wake to find that your lungs have perforated."

Navier gawks at the other man, dumbstruck. He's no coward, but the pleasant, matter-of-fact cadence to Ricket's voice is chilling.

"Does your chest itch, Navier?" Ricket hums. "Does your trachea sting? Imagine bile pumping through all those little holes in your airways... Your body produces an excess of it to wash all that junk you eat, so it shouldn't take *too* long for you to drown."

Navier's breathing speeds up, as though he's already feeling the effects of said drowning. He tugs at his bonds, lightly at first, then with more force, panic building.

"It was the money, okay?!" He rasps. "I need it bad. My truck, my business... I was gonna lose it all! I didn't *mean* anything by it..."

We aren't thieves anymore. We *spend* money doing our vigilante work, rather than pocketing cool thousands per gig. It's no small wonder...

"So you've been helping a rapist terrorize your friends for *weeks?!*" I demand. Hot rage has me shoving Navier until his head bounces off the wall. The only thing worth fuckall in this God-forsaken world is loyalty, and he went and spat on my trust. *"Look* at me!"

He does, his eyes following the ugly scar that dents my face. *Guilty, guilty, guilty.* He knew exactly what he'd set us up for.

I ask, voice shaking almost as viciously as the rest of me, "How much did he pay you? What are our lives worth, you think?"

"Thirty," Navier whispers, when it becomes clear my question isn't rhetorical. "Thirty grand. Enough to pull me out of debt."

"Oh, well. In that case, I *understand,*" I snarl, bitter and biting. "My *mistake.* That's totally reasonable, then."

"Mags," Tip points to my face. "Your nose. What's up with that?"

I touch it. My fingers come away wet and red. "Oh, this just happens sometimes," I wave his concern off.

"Does it?" Ricket frowns.

"It bled last night, too." Tip points out. "It never used to do that."

"We're getting way off topic here." I hold my arm to my nose, willing the flow to stem. "Navier, you royally fucked us over. I'm so disgusted I can't see straight. Just tell us everything, and someone will drive you to the hospital. After that, I never want to see you again."

The wise choice here would be to eliminate him entirely — he knows too much. He has dangerous contacts. There's no reason to believe he won't come back for revenge. But unlike Navier, I *am* loyal. Killing him would damage my heart beyond repair, no matter how satisfying it would feel in the moment.

He needs to die. I will not allow him to live.

The first words Not-Cero has spoken in a good while do not comfort me. They're stiff; formal with resignation. With certainty.

Navier spills everything. How Vince had approached his garage a few months ago under the pretense of a car repair; had chatted him up, gradually steering the conversation towards me and Tip.

Vince is good at acting personable when he needs to. I can see how a friendly guy like Navier would take a shine to him.

"And that didn't set off any warning bells?" Ricket asks acerbically. "Someone just showing up and asking questions about the leader of your gang?"

"It did!" Navier is insistent. "I damn near held a welding torch to his face, but we got to talkin'... He'd been spyin' on us; he wanted payback for some 'unfinished business.' None of you were gon' get *hurt* — he just wanted to scare you some."

"So he gave you a gun to *scare us some?*" I repeat, endless reserves of anger flaming anew. "And this seemed like a reasonable idea to you?"

"When you say 'unfinished business'..." Tip frowns, leaning forward, knife in hand. "Did he specify what he meant? I thought he was just punishing me before things went back to normal."

Back to normal! As though having a boyfriend who punishes him at all — much less by stalking and threatening him, and beheading those who get too close — can ever be called *normal.*

Navier shakes his head. "He didn't say."

"No; he just waved some cash at you, and you smiled and nodded your empty little head like the puppet you are," Ricket surmises.

"I'm not proud of it," Navier confesses, begging with puppy-dog eyes for us to understand; to see things from his perspective. "But I *needed* the money!"

"And you think I don't?!" A hysterical laugh brims in my chest. "I'm hallucinating voices, one bad week from homelessness, *and* dying of leukemia. You can take that excuse and shove it up your ass!"

Giving him one final push, I stand and stalk out the door. Ricket can finish the interrogation if he wants. I'm done.

Chapter Twenty-Six - Tip

called it.

...

In the days that follow, I'm thankful that they cut Magpie's hours at the gas station. That I get this time with her, before she goes to stay with James's parents.

It turns out I don't *need* pot to hold her through the night, now that I know she's dying.

Magpie stirs in her sleep, shifting onto one side. I move with her, leaning back until she settles, then wrap my arm around her waist. Her hand clutches my sleeve, same as she did when we were kids and she didn't want to lose me in a crowd.

My eyes sting. She's not losing me. I'm losing *her*.

I am beyond drugs. I am beyond *Vince*. When Magpie dies, I will have no more reason to live, Vince's promise be damned. There *are* no more waves in my ocean. The moon has dropped from the sky.

David's phone buzzes in my hand, which causes Zelda, resting at the foot of my sofa-bed, to grumble. David's sister, Claire, is an insomniac. Sometimes they do nothing but text random emojis back and forth for hours.

Claire, June 4, 2:25 AM: [skunk emoji]

David, June 4, 2:25 AM: [skull emoji]

Claire, June 4, 2:25 AM: [Narutomaki emoji]

David, June 4, 2:26 AM: [paw-print emoji]

The phone is silent after that. Either Claire fell asleep, or she got bored. Probably the latter.

Being Digital-David is a role I fell into easily. I compliment his mother's Instagram selfies. I promise someone named Jackie that I'm still looking for a job. I play Claire's Facebook games. So far, nobody has realized that he's dead and buried.

Zelda whines and rests her chin on my ankle. I wriggle my other foot out from beneath the sheets, stroking her side with my toes.

When I register a spreading dampness on my chest, I sigh and tilt Mags's face so the blood flows onto me instead of down her throat. There's no sense trying to stem it. It'll stop on its own.

"I did *everything* for you and Crown," I tell her sleeping, bloodied face. "And now you're both gone."

She squirms. I feel a swoop of panic in my gut. She's such a deep sleeper that I hadn't thought my voice could wake her, but her eyes open all the same.

"Come, now," she says, voice rich and husky. "Don't be so dramatic."

I freeze. Those aren't Magpie's chocolatey eyes looking out from her face, glassy in the light from David's phone. The left eye is a dark, cavernous void. The right is the blue of a freezing lake.

I cannot move. I cannot speak. I can only watch as Cero sits up and stretches Magpie's arms above her head, spine popping leisurely. She smacks her lips, rubs her streaming nose, and examines the blood on her hand before looking back to me.

"What's with the face?" she asks, a smirk most unlike Magpie's curling her lips. Her teeth are stained red. "You already *knew*."

"This is impossible," I inform her, my mental glitch unthawing enough for me to switch on the bedside lamp. I sound irritated, as though I'm trying to scold reality back into coherence. "You died."

"That I did. And yet..." Cero inclines Magpie's head, plainly amused. "You are a scientist. When presented with new information, what do you do?"

Record. Adapt. Accept, but not before testing.

"You are Sonya Vasiliev."

"I am, though I prefer my chosen name. I wasn't 'Sonya' until adulthood, and never had the chance to acclimate."

When she stands and walks into the kitchen, I follow. I watch as she flicks more lights on and gathers paper towels to hold against Magpie's nose. She fumbles one-handedly for a glass, fills it at the sink, and chugs it.

"It is *nice* to have a body again," she says decisively, once her thirst is sated.

"No." I brace one hand on the stove and the other on the counter, trapping her in a corner. "You *don't* have one. Yours was cremated. Your mother has your ashes. *This* body is Magpie's."

"Not for long, it's not," Cero says, and shows me the wad of bloodied towels. "Magpie said it herself: a body is nothing but meat and bone and electricity. Her vessel is becoming *quite* damaged, I'm afraid. Soon it will no longer be able to hold her."

She's referring to the cancer that eats Magpie from the inside out; an invisible enemy I can't fight, not in the time it would take to make a difference.

I could hook her up to a cell saver; pump cleansed blood into her veins with every beat of her heart. I could spend millions on bone marrow transplants. It doesn't matter. It won't correct the error; the bug in her programming that causes this malfunction.

"Did you do this?" I ask, voice low. Is *Cero* the bug? "Are you killing her so you can have... What? A pile of dead, diseased flesh?"

Despite the bleakness of my question, I feel invigorated by the prospect. I can't fight cancer, but perhaps — in this indisputable new evidence that there is, in fact, a self, a spirit, a *soul* — perhaps I can fight Cero, and *that* will correct this malware.

Instead of answering, she reaches for me.

I take a step back. Magpie is allowed to touch me. Someone wearing her skin like a costume is *not*.

Cero smiles thinly, like she'd known I would react that way. She ducks under my arm and walks deeper into the apartment, heading straight for Magpie's bedroom.

Again, I follow. What choice do I have?

She's stripped naked, save for Magpie's necklace, in the time I take to catch up. I see her considering a sports bra, which she foregoes for Magpie's jacket atop a men's flannel shirt.

When she catches my eyes in the mirror's reflection, she gives a knowing grin. "She finds you just as pretty as you do her, you know. I'd guessed *that* much even before I died."

Scowling, I look away, staring at the mess that is Magpie's bed. As always, it's covered in books and booze. No wonder she prefers mine.

Cero produces a harness from the dresser and slides long, thin knives into its many pouches. She buckles the leather straps around Magpie's thick-muscled calves. Only then does she don boxers and jeans.

"Help me with this," she orders, holding a bunch of loose hair. "It's annoying."

"Why should I? I want to know what you're doing."

"I'll tell you, but only if you take care of this. I know you know how."

I take her into the bathroom.

She sits on the closed toilet lid as I pull Magpie's comb and elastics from a drawer. I don't want to touch her, but so long as she doesn't touch *me*, I can manage.

I comb Magpie's mane as gently as I'm able, wetting the tines at the sink every six strokes. When I find tangles, I hold the roots and pick them loose. "Talk," I command.

"I'm going to Navier's home to take his life. I'd appreciate if you helped."

"Oh, is that all?" I no longer have the dexterity needed to weave intricate plaits like I did when we were kids. Instead, I braid a single, chunky rope down her back.

"Well, Navier is in possession of my two cats. I'll need you to collect them. But yes, that is 'all' for tonight."

I wait a beat. "And if I refuse to help you?"

"Then I'll go by myself. My control over Magpie's body is tenuous; I've never had full possession before. I'd prefer if somebody who loves her is present to ensure she gets home safely."

Hmmm. Smells like a threat. But it's good to know Magpie *is* still in there. "What if I trap her here? Tie you up so you can't take her anywhere?"

Her voice takes on a condescending edge. "If you want to fight me, by all means, do. Her body is strong, and I am exceptionally skilled. You are weak, and unwilling to harm her. I have the advantage."

She's right, on all accounts. Fuck.

I take an elastic and twist it around the tail of the braid. "How do you know he'll even be home? James took him to the hospital. Maybe he's still there. Or maybe he skipped town to hide from Vince."

Cero shakes Magpie's head. "I know Navier. You've disfigured his pretty face, so I can't imagine he's out and about. If I'm wrong, what skin is it off your back? Humor me."

I rub my tired eyes, glance at the clock, and sigh. There's less than four hours remaining before my shift at work begins, but I can't leave Cero to do God-knows-what with Magpie's body.

"She's gonna be pissed," I warn. "She told James not to kill him."

I know what Cero's answer is going to be before she gives it. "*That* is your problem, darling."

We return to my 'room' as I change out of my pajamas. Cero's mismatched eyes rake up and down my front with detached curiosity. "You've been destroying your own vessel, I see. It's even worse than Magpie knows."

"That's not your place to judge."

"You're right." She waits until I'm dressed to continue, slipping Magpie's backpack over her shoulders. "I think I like you, Tip. You are an iron soul in a brittle shell."

I snatch up Zelda's leash. Excited by the prospect of a late-night walk, she hops off my bed and flounces over, lifting a paw for her harness. "What's your point?"

"I want you."

I raise both eyebrows. "Pardon?"

"Be mine."

"Do you always talk in conversation hearts?"

She ushers me and Zelda out the front door. "I want you to agree to belong to me, permanently and exclusively. Through Magpie's memories, I see that you can be quite servile. I *need* a good dog, now that I've lost Navier, Rhys, and Clay."

Will she ask me to kill those women, too? I don't think I can do that. Navier is trash, but they haven't wronged me or mine.

Side-by-side, we walk down the street, Zelda trotting at our heels. "What's in it for me?"

Cero has her answers prepared. She ticks them off on Magpie's fingers. "One, you'll never have to make another choice again. You'll have me to do it for you. It's obvious you crave to be owned — why not by me?"

I was an idiot to ever think my heart was a secret.

"Two, I will help you handle your compulsions, depression, and disordered eating. You will achieve physical and mental stability. You will surf again, if you like."

My voice cracks, though I try to keep it impassive. "That all you got?"

"Finally, I will provide for you financially. I will support you through your schooling and onto your career as a biologist. I will handle your troubles with the law. Cops are easily bribed."

She's put a lot of thought into this. It feels like everything I've ever wanted: a promise that someone can take the world off my shoulders. That all I have to do is follow orders, and life will be handled for me. The offer is more seductive than it has any right to be.

"Where is Magpie right now?" I ask, wanting to give myself time to think.

She touches her forehead. "Asleep. I will attempt to resurface her once we finish this task — you have my word."

We walk for several blocks until we find a dinged Corolla parked on a curb. Cero leans against the sidewall, watching as I jimmy the window with a wire hanger from Mags's backpack. I crawl beneath the dash and hot-wire the vehicle, nearly electrocuting myself twice.

"See?" Cero says, pleased, climbing into the driver's seat when the engine turns over. "You *are* a good dog."

"Gee, thanks," I snark, using sarcasm to hide the blooming warmth those words spike inside me. She's good at playing people like a flute; I'll give her that much.

I boost Zelda into the back and buckle her leash. Unused to cars, she kicks up a fuss. I find beef jerky in the glove compartment and pass a piece back to her.

Cero adjusts the seat and rearview mirror to fit Magpie's compact body. She chuckles when she finds a pair of knockoff Aviators on the dashboard. "You favor this style, don't you?" She drops them in my lap.

I pass them right back. "Cover your own eyes up," I advise.

She glances in the mirror. Frowns at the sight of her heterochromia in Magpie's face. Dons the glasses. "I wasn't expecting that little holdover. My eyes have always been an inconvenience. It's difficult being an anonymous thief with such a distinguishing feature."

"How did you do it?" I ask, coming back to the only question that matters. "How did you transfer yourself into Magpie's body?"

This earns me a pitying look. "You'd have to be mine for a *long* while before I'd trust you with that information."

I grit my teeth and scowl out the window. She eases the Corolla onto the empty road before flicking on the headlights.

"So," I say, as the miles and silence drag on. "Fill me in. We're murdering Navier *because...?*"

"He betrayed my orders. My command was for Magpie to lead in my absence. I don't agree with the direction she took things, but it was her right to do it."

I pass more jerky to Zelda, rubbing her ears when she takes it. "So, if I was yours, and *I* did something you didn't like..."

Cero looks at me. The answer is plain: I would be a dead man walking. I can accept *that,* but... "Crown isn't yours, is he?"

"No. I allowed him in to keep Magpie's trust; nothing more."

Cross *that* off the list of worries. "I can't see Mags ever agreeing to belong to someone."

To my surprise, Cero *laughs*. "You were there for that arrangement! She signed it in her own hand."

What does she — *oh*. "You have a very old-fashioned view of marriage," I say, derision dripping off every syllable. "You know that wasn't what she meant when she said 'I do.'"

"Then perhaps she should have asked more questions. She's a simple woman, Tip; nothing like you."

"If you're trying to endear yourself to me, maybe *don't* call my kid 'simple'. Just a tip."

Navier's house is fairly isolated. Ramshackle though it appears, no property in SoCal is inexpensive. The more I look at his life, the more I see why money was such a problem.

The moment I unclip her leash from the seatbelt, Zelda bolts inside the open garage and hides by Navier's truck, watching me reproachfully.

"No running off," I tell her, though I don't know whether she's trained to understand that command. To Cero, I say, "Not sure how much you know about me, but I'm just a janitor. This stuff is Magpie's gig. I don't do a lot of breaking and entering, or torture, or murder."

"But you have, in the past."

"Never without my boyfriend, and only towards his clients."

She regards me as though I'm being deliberately stupid. "Do now what you did then. Follow me, like you followed him. You are a student, so *learn*."

Well. Fair enough.

The back door — we walk around to avoid being seen from the street — is deadbolted. No wire hanger will solve this.

Cero watches me think. I've seen tutorials on how to crack deadbolts online, but they require manual dexterity and small tools, neither of which I possess.

Navier's a careless guy. I bet he loses his keys all the time. Not only that, but he's *tall*. What if...?

"Boost me?" I request.

Cero kneels, offering Magpie's knee, and her hand for balance. When I step on, I'm tall enough to pat along the doorframe. My hand encounters a spare key. I triumphantly present it to her, and she lowers me.

"What a smart boy you are," she purrs, taking it. Unlocking the door.

My heart kicks. Though I know she's not Magpie, *those* words from *that* mouth are a natural high.

The house is dark and still. We stand in the doorway and observe everything before Cero takes a step inside. The jingle of a tiny bell has me snatching her hand, dragging her back.

She turns to regard me, sunglasses glinting.

I let go, ducking my head, expecting her to hit me for interfering.

"It's only Roar," Cero reassures. She bends to lift a large, long-haired cat, stroking him affectionately. Cooing to him until he purrs like an old motor. "Here."

"Oh..." Embarrassed by my slip, I take him. Since I'm a stranger, I expect him to squirm in resistance, but he butts his face into my shoulder instead. Friendly boy.

"There's a carrier over there." Cero points to the corner of the garage, where I see one buried under a pile of odds and ends. "Put him in that, and then go look for Ding. I'll take care of Navier."

"Yes ma'am," I reply, causing her smile to grow. Most of the world can go fuck themselves, but there *are* a handful of people I feel compelled to impress. I guess Cero is now one of them

Sometimes I wish I could be more open with my therapist. *Hey, Tess? My dead sister-in-law possessed Magpie, gave her cancer, and triggered my submissive side.*

I unearth the carrier and slip Roar inside, then take it on my hunt for Thing Two. I hear Cero's footfalls down the hallway, and am surprised when she switches lights on as she goes. Apparently we're not angling for stealth.

I turn lights on, too, as I search the living room and kitchen. Poking through cupboards yields no results, but at last I spot a pair of yellow eyes watching me from underneath the sagging old sofa, comprised of more duct tape than fabric.

I kneel to fish Ding out. He puffs and hisses, raking his claws down my arm when I grab him. I bite my tongue against the pain.

Cat scratches are riddled with bacteria, so it's best to wash up while the blood is fresh.

I get him settled in his carrier, then cross to the sink to do just that.

This had been Crown's house, I recall, peering at the mountains of clutter and laundry. I feel a familiar pang of regret, wishing I'd explained myself better, or at least *tried* to earn his forgiveness.

Maybe I didn't try because I knew I didn't deserve it. Him. The only real apology is changed behavior, and I could sooner lasso the moon than kick my Vince habit.

"Tip?" Cero calls. "Come here, please."

Dripping water, I follow her voice to the end of a hallway, where she stands before the only open door. She removes her sunglasses, expression deliberately blank. "Apparently we weren't the only ones with a grudge against Navier."

When I glance over her shoulder, my insides frost.

The room is in shambles. Everything is broken and strewn, as though flung in a violent frenzy. The mattress hangs off the bed, stuffing spilling from deep gouges. Two of the three overhead lightbulbs are shattered, and the blades of the fan have been plucked and thrown like flowers.

Still, it's hard to focus on the décor, because there are puddles of meat and bone-chips sprayed on every flat surface, including the window and ceiling. Judging by the screaming black mass of flies all around, this has been the state of things for several days now.

It looks more like ground hamburger than a human being, but there are recognizable fragments here and there. A glistening pink coconut shell of a scalp slithers down a lampshade. An eyeball, optic nerve attached, sways gently on the hinge of a cabinet.

Somehow, I smell no rot. Blood and shit and stomach acid, yes, but no decay.

It only gets stranger from there. The blood on the walls is shiny and fresh. The offal spilling over the carpet pulses regularly. The remains of a heart, visible in the cage of snapped ribs, pulses in rhythm. The ripped lungs, separated by an upended dresser drawer, inflate and deflate. Inflate and deflate. Inflate, and...

This meat *lives*.

I leave the carrier in the hallway and pull my shirt over my nose and ears, making a hood. I have no gloves, so I pull my hiking sleeves over my hands like mittens. Belly exposed, I pick my way through maggoty flesh marred with little bites — the cats, probably — and look over what used to be Etienne Navier.

Flies ping off every inch of me like hail in a storm, their discordant hum vibrating my bones. My glasses provide a minimal barrier against their wings and legs. Under the noise, I can faintly hear Navier's inner workings; the ticks and squelches and gasps of a corpse that somehow isn't dead.

This makes no sense. The veins are shredded. They have no blood to carry; no pathway to carry it *in*. No blood, no oxygen. No oxygen, no burning of fuel. No burning of fuel, no energy, and there *is* no life without that. It's impossible!

My heart whispers a different word, though: *magic.*

"There are more things in heaven and earth, Horatio, than are dreamt of in your philosophy." Cero smiles and kneels across from me, wearing latex gloves she pilfered from Magpie's bag.

I blink. She huffs. "Hamlet; act one, scene five. Goodness, are your studies *so* narrow? There's nothing more pitiful than a limitless brain cursed to follow a single track."

I say nothing, so she nods at the window. "Break that. Create enough space for my cats to slip through. Forensics will assume they've run away when they discover the scene, a day or a decade from now."

I go and do just that, holding the broken curtain rod like a javelin to smash a pane, then using a decorative stone bowl to smooth out the jagged bits. I linger a moment to gulp some fresh air.

When I turn, Cero has rolled the largest slab of Navier's torso so that his spine protrudes, white sharks in a red sea. I see a flash of pelvis; sacrum and coccyx and pubis.

Cero gives it another roll. It now rests on its side, facing her. She plunges her gloved hand between tattered strings of abdominal muscles and creamy yellow fat.

A rib cracks. Bubbly maroon froth, the remnants of an insect-riddled liver, wells between her fingers to dribble on the floor.

"What are you doing?" I ask, curious, crouching to watch.

In answer, Cero holds up a large coin, coated in gore. When she does, Navier's remains shiver and shudder and sigh, and then fall still.

I stare at the man's exposed heart, waiting for it to pump, but it never does. His lungs remain deflated bags. The blood on the walls starts to dry.

Navier is dead. The flies drone on. Cero pockets the coin.

I'm startled by the heaviness that overtakes me. We'd come here *to* kill him, after all. I have no reason to regret his passing.

Perhaps Cero echoes my odd mood. She lays his torso down, heart up, as though Navier is lying in a coffin. She looks around until she sees a fragment of femur, which she rests below his pelvis. It's like she's trying to assemble an unbelievably macabre jigsaw puzzle.

Helping a ghost put Humpty Dumpty together is easily the strangest thing I've ever done, but it feels right. I scoop intestines into his chest cavity. Tuck a collarbone beneath his mandible, and cover them with scalp. Pluck teeth from the carpet like pebbles out of peas.

As we work, Cero's voice takes on the dreamy cadence of a bedtime story. "Once upon a time, there lived a young woman with blood on her hands and ambition in her soul. She'd survived the worst humanity had to offer, and intended to replace every scrap of life that had been stolen from her. To demand what was rightfully hers."

I give her a *look,* willing her to talk straight. She ignores it.

"This woman knew that the world was full of followers. People who couldn't know their potential until she taught it to them. People who *needed* her. A bishop with the funds and prestige to seduce the world. A rook to plan, and a knight to fight. A pawn who thought she was Queen."

Did she just call Magpie a fucking *pawn?!* "Shutting up is an option," I remind her, squeezing a fistful of molars.

Now it's her turn to give me a *look,* haughty and proud. "Fine. Then I *won't* tell you how I travelled to and from the underworld, my thread uncut by Fates. *Or* how I tricked Charon himself into dragging Navier from Styx."

I scowl, frustrated by my own ignorance. "I *barely* understand what you're talking about. That's Greek mythology, right? Not my area of interest." Much closer to my area of disdain, actually.

"Then someone has homework to do. The important part is this: from the moment I cancelled his death, Navier existed divorced from time. Not quite alive, but unable to die. Until now. I have revoked my gift."

Again, she shows me that coin from the dead man's liver.

"You *want* to be mine, Tip," she concludes, eyes bright, in awe of her own cleverness. "That cat you love may know a trick or two, but he is nothing compared to me."

"And you've lost me again." I make a show of disinterest, returning to the task of forming Navier's skull. "You're more into cats than I am."

As though to illustrate my point, Ding gives a piteous mewl inside his carrier.

Cero laughs, a rumbly sound that seems to echo inside her chest. Then she stands, brushing off Mags's jeans. "You'll come around. For now, it's time to go. We're done here."

Excuse me?

I lurch to my feet and chase her to the door, careful not to step on anything too squishy. She stops me with a raised hand, pointing to my ruined high-tops. A length of what might be a tendon dangles from an eyelet.

Grumbling, I grip the door's frame for balance and peel them off. My bloodied sleeves, too. There's no time for shyness about my scars; Cero already knows I have them.

She does the same with Magpie's boots, passing them to me. We leave the room in just our socks. We weren't *very* careful about hiding our tracks, but Cero doesn't seem worried, and I don't have the energy to care.

"What do you *mean,* we're done?" I ask, watching her lift the cat carrier. "We don't even know who did that to him!"

"You don't know your own boyfriend's handiwork?"

Vince? What had his murder weapon been; a pack of wolves?! Navier was a large, muscular person. Even with Magpie's help, I'd scarcely been able to restrain him for two minutes.

While Vince is tall, he's also slender and lazy. I can't fathom how he did *that* much damage. While he's certainly not above torture and murder, his weapon of choice is other people. People like me.

Then again, I have no reason to believe he'd made someone else behead David. And now this? Why has he changed?!

"Please explain," I beg as Cero walks through Navier's home, ensuring we leave it as we'd found it. "Please. I need to know."

I think this is the most alive I've felt in years. I am a child breathlessly watching a Scooby Doo mystery unfold on a Saturday morning. I'm a scientist struggling to comprehend what I see under a microscope.

Cero waits until we're back in the garage before giving me a gentle smile. A promise: "Agree to be mine, and I will tell you everything."

I almost accept her offer on the spot. What do *I* need autonomy for? All I do with my life is screw it up. Let someone else take the reins!

But Magpie...

Until I figure out what this spirit is doing to my cousin, I can go no further. It's the only loyalty I have left. I love her more than I hate myself.

Cero removes her glove and reaches to cup my cheek. I pull away before she makes contact.

She sighs, disappointed, and drops her hand. "Soon, then," she decides, and returns Navier's key to where we'd found it.

Loading Zelda and the cats into the Corolla, Cero drives us silently towards home. With the Aviators masking half her face, I can't begin to guess what she's thinking.

We ditch the Corolla two blocks from the apartment, stopping first to bury my shoes and sleeves at the bottom of a public trash bin. Magpie's boots are made of waterproof leather, so we can hose them off.

We walk the rest of the way home. Cero with the cats and back-pack; me with the boots and Zelda. Both of us watch the pavement, avoiding puddles and broken glass. Much of the world is asleep; the houses dark, the cars empty. Only the streetlights keep us company.

Cero is the first to break the silence. "Because it's irksome to watch you dance around the obvious, I will give you one freebie tonight. Your boyfriend *is* a rapist."

I nearly drop Zelda's leash. "What?!"

I *had* wondered why Magpie called Vince a rapist that night we interrogated Navier. As far as I'm aware, he's done no such thing. Granted, he's done some stuff to *me* while I was unconscious or unwilling, but that doesn't count. *I* don't count.

And why *would* he ever rape someone? He's attractive; strikingly so. And charismatic. And wealthy. Luring people of all genders to his bed has never been a challenge.

A blocked-off corner of my brain, one I never acknowledge if I can avoid it, gives a prolonged, shaky sigh. *It's because rape isn't about sex, or even attraction. Rape is about violence, and entitlement, and hate, and power.*

My heart sinks, slow and sure as a boulder through molasses. I know. I know. *I know.* I only *wish* that Cero was lying.

"Who did he..." I swallow around the lump in my throat. Throw the question away. It shouldn't *matter* who Vince attacked. The fact that it happened, at all, to *anyone,* should be more than enough to earn my letter of resignation. Goodbye, relationship. Goodbye, feelings.

But *does* it change anything? I've supported him through every other crime under the sun. It's not like this one is any worse than those. No less monstrous. No more devastating. There are more ways to hurt people than there are stars in the galaxy, and he has mastered every one.

Cero shoots me a pitying glance. Wearing those sunglasses, it'd be hard for anyone else to tell it's not Mags under there. To me, everything about her feels wrong. The way clowns are wrong, and dummies, and dolls, and corpses.

"I wonder," she scoffs, tapping her chin in a mimicry of thought. "Think *really* hard, now."

My feeble grasp on denial crumbles and dies. I hadn't wanted to know, but now I have no choice.

My boyfriend raped my cousin.

"*There* we go," Cero pats my shoulder, reading the answer in my eyes. "Knew we'd get there in the end."

I can't even bristle at her mockery. I feel every screen inside my brain surrender to sleep mode, closing each pathway to my heart until I feel nothing but tired; heavy. *tip.exe has stopped working.*

From far away, I hear myself ask: "When did this happen?"

"Many times after I was sent to hospice. Occasionally she knew what was going on; usually not. You know how it goes."

I do.

Maybe that's why I'm reacting so severely. I've told myself, all my life, that the choices I've made are to keep Mags, and Crown, safe. Provided for. Comfortable. That it didn't matter who I hurt and used, because protecting them was the only important thing.

But I couldn't even do that much, could I? I'd led the wolves right to their door, and then looked the other way each time a red flag waved. There were so many opportunities to step in, and I took none of them.

I have completely, utterly, and profoundly failed my cousins in every way possible.

"Why did you tell me this?" I ask Cero, head hanging in shame. "What do you want me to do?"

She shrugs Magpie's shoulders. "Do whatever you like. I simply despise elephants in my room."

We walk all the way to my front door. Cero waits patiently as I rummage the keys from my pocket and let us in. Once freed from her harness, Zelda bolts for my bed, tunneling under the blankets until only her stumpy butt protrudes.

"I gave you my word I would return Magpie to you," Cero says, following me inside and setting her cat carrier on the floor. "And I never break a promise. I *do* hope you'll think carefully about my offer, Tip, because I won't make it more than twice."

She stands in the center of the kitchen, arms hanging loose at her sides. Then, like a puppet with its strings cut, she collapses.

I dive for her, catching her shoulders, but she's too heavy to hold. The best I can manage is to slow her fall.

We sink to the floor, legs tangled, her head on my shoulder. It feels like a strike of lightning when I notice she's not breathing. "Mags?!"

I touch her throat with my damaged hand, realize it's not sensitive enough, and switch to the other. I hold my fingers to the soft place behind her earlobe, praying for a pulse.

I feel nothing, and then I feel *something*, but I can't tell if it's my own panicked heart or hers.

I've laid her flat, tilted her chin up, and made a knot of my hands to pump her breastbone when she sucks in a great, rattling lungful of air. Her legs kick out. She coughs; harsh, chesty barks that echo through our tiled kitchen.

"Oh, fuck," I hear myself moan. "Oh, *Christ...*"

Mysteriously losing all strength in my limbs, I lay down before I can fall, too. The tile is cold on my ear. The two cats gawk at us, bewildered, through the slats of their carrier.

Between coughs, Mags sputters, "Why is it so dark? Where are you?!"

The noise I emit may be a laugh, or a sob. I reach to pluck the Aviators from her face, beyond relieved to see her brown eyes staring fearfully at the ceiling.

"Hey," I whisper, gazing at her through a shimmering veil of tears. Does she understand that surface tension is the only thing keeping my face dry? So long as I don't blink, I don't have to admit I'm crying.

She stares back at me, visibly shaking, face ashen. "What happened to me? Where did I *go*? Tip, I'm scared!"

An old memory surfaces. Magpie, eleven, curled on Gran's sofa, delirious with fever and dehydration. She'd been even tinier then than she is now; a disappearing slip of a girl.

How embarrassingly I'd fussed, fetching ice; Vix; Aspirin. I'd taken her temperature so often Gran feared I'd break the thermometer.

What had I called her, then?

Oh. Right.

"My baby bird." I stroke her cheek. Smooth her braid back. Guide her hand to my mouth so I can kiss her palm. "I'm here. It's okay. I've got you."

And I'm never letting go again.

Chapter Twenty-Seven – Magpie

...

I've been doing so much sleeping the past couple days that my rhythm is out of whack. Tip passed out hours ago; a still, silent lump beneath my bi-pride comforter.

I fiddle with the envelope Vince left on David's body, pulling out the Greyhound ticket to examine it again.

The internet turned up precious little info on Strawberry. It's a tiny area on the Mogollon Rim boasting nothing more than a few cabins, a one-roomed schoolhouse, and a sledding hill. As far as I'm aware, it holds no personal significance to Vince.

He wants one of us — presumably, Tip — to go there tomorrow. He'd left no further instructions. Ricket was right; he *is* just playing a sloppy game of cat-and-mouse. Why else send us to Randomsville Wherever, population zero?

What really gets my goat is his certainty that we'll follow such an absurd prompt. What possible incentive is there for walking into a trap? Does he think we're *that* stupid?

Yet here I sit, curled on a mountain of my wife's old sketchbooks, contemplating doing just that. Maybe I'm a sucker for punishment. Or maybe this just *looks* like a more straightforward path than the other puzzles I'm trying to solve.

I peek at a sketchbook, at the Sumerian writing surrounding images so similar to what is etched into my wedding ring. Then I look to mine and Tip's laptop, open to a translate-to-English program. Its glow is the only light in my room.

Cero was involved in the occult. Cero *is* living — *not* living? *Un*-living? — inside me, though I've heard nothing but radio silence from her since she took control of me, plunging me into a sleep so deep I neither saw nor heard what my own body was doing.

It's unsettling, feeling alone in my head after so many weeks of chatter. Is she sleeping? Hiding? Did the complete takeover exhaust her reserves, or is she just biding her time?

'Biding her time' sounds so nefarious. I shouldn't think ill of my wife. She wouldn't *really* hurt me...

Nope. That's bullshit. I refuse to deny that I've been harmed. Wronged. Used.

"My wife hurt me," I say aloud, speaking quietly so as not to wake Tip. Snoring at the foot of the bed, Zelda's ear twitches. Ding's yellow eyes glow from where he's curled in the bathroom sink.

It feels wrong to say the words. Abuse is obvious from an outside perspective, but it's harder to spot when it's happening *to you*. When it's administered by someone you love.

"My wife broke my collarbone because I touched her car. My wife isolated me from everyone, save for her own friends. My wife gaslighted and manipulated me for years."

I don't want to keep doing this. I want to grab the nearest bottle and pour its contents directly down my throat, glugging and gargling like a cartoon lush. But first I need to push past that; to see where this road takes me.

"I love my wife," I continue, voice wobbly. "I think she loves me. But..."

I can't force myself to speak the fears aloud. I roll onto my side and drag the laptop closer, opening the notepad app. I type:

I'm afraid my wife is killing me.

That isn't my biggest fear, though, is it?

*I'm afraid she's been planning this for a while; maybe as far
back as when we first met. I'm afraid our marriage was all
a lie.*

And, because I'm really in it now:
I think my cancer is really Cero's cancer.

A.L.L. is very, *very* rare in adults. It's called the *children's* cancer
for a reason. What are the odds of my organically developing the
same anomaly that killed my wife? Lightning seldom strikes twice.

"I don't believe in coincidences," I sniffle, wiping my damp eyes
on my pillow.

Somehow, repeating Rosa's words lends me some of her
strength.

If a soul is a transplantable, like a kidney or a heart, is it really so
strange to believe Cero tied hers to mine? According to her sketchbooks, she'd been dabbling in necromancy for a long time, exper-
imenting on oblivious people like Navier. If anyone could cheat
death, it would be my wife.

Tip sighs in his sleep, expression troubled. Even dreams bring
him no peace. I carefully remove his glasses and put them on the
nightstand, smoothing wavy hair behind his ear.

I lift his head from the notebook and onto a pillow. I pry his
stiff, burned fingers from where they're clenched around a pencil.
Fussing over him gives me the illusion of productivity as I struggle
to organize my thoughts.

I glance at the notebook as I set it aside, noticing the last few
things he'd written before passing out:

Charon's obol + Styx = **Greek**
(Coin in liver, not mouth????)
— Rings made from Medusa coins
Souls tied to coins?
Significance of onyx?

*Asarualim + Namtillaku = **Sumerian***

1. Cero bastardizes death culture

2. Cero would NOT have shown her hand if she could be stopped.

The final lines chill me. Cero 'bastardizing' mythos from every culture is so like her. She believed all folklore, every religion, held a pearl of truth. She was willing to crack them open like oysters to find it, before throwing all the rest away.

I'd glimpsed notes in Cero's sketchbooks on death practices from Egyptian to Hindu to Muslim to Christian. Diagrams of mummification processes. Dried marigold petals taped to incense sticks from Día de Muertos. A splinter of the true cross.

She stole treasured beliefs and sacred practices the world over to MacGyver herself a one-way ticket out of the grave. Apparently, she'd cracked the code.

I reach for our conjoined rings and flick on the bedside lamp to peer at the secret designs — designs I found echoed a dozen times over in these very sketchbooks. Would destroying them help me regain ownership over my body, or would it make everything worse?

Tip sighs again. In less than two hours, the alarm clock will chime. He'll leave for work, likely more tired than he'd been before he passed out. Watching Cero pilot my body must've spooked him fiercely, because he's been clingy ever since it happened.

Not that I'm complaining.

The bus pass continues to watch me from where it pokes out of the envelope. I try to ignore it; to lock my attention on reading about Styx and Charon and ghostly possessions.

It's no use. I'm a person driven to move. When the options are research or action, I prefer the latter. So what if this is all a trap? It's better if I'm the one to fall into it. At least I know how to fight my way out, right?

What's more, I need to leave behind a world where my cousin can heal. If Tip runs to Vince when my death leaves him hollow, same as I did after losing Cero, the hopeless cycle will have no end. Best to take that option off the table while I still can.

Carefully, so as not to jostle the bed, I stand and change from my pajamas into street clothes. I strap every knife into place, don my leathers, and stuff the ring-necklace into my pocket. Turning Tip's notebook to a fresh page, I scribble a lie, saying work called me in for a shift.

I leave the note on my pillow, weighed down by the silver Medusa coin we'd washed Navier's fluids from, then kiss both Tip and Zelda on their foreheads. I close the door slowly as I leave, trying to keep it from creaking.

In the kitchen I collect my backpack, then open the fridge for a snack and a bottled water. There's a pile of Tupperware inside, each marked with a post-it that Tip wrote a timestamp on: 5:30, 8:30, 11:30, 1:30, 4:30, 7:30, and 10:30.

Curiosity has me opening the 5:30 Tupperware. Inside I find, not only a cup of white rice and sliced zucchini, but also a paper liner holding pine nuts from David's kitchen.

He's feeding himself tiny meals at regular intervals in order to get stronger. He's forcing himself back into a semblance of health so that he can shoulder more for the both of us. He's trying. *He's trying.*

For the second time that night, tears prick my eyes. I put the food back into the fridge. Tip never did let me down, huh? Right from the start, he'd only been trying to care for me.

My turn to take care of you, Tipples.

I step outside and start walking. The only mode of transportation I have left is my legs. I should make it to the Greyhound station in under three hours.

I'm going to the man that hooked my cousin on heroin and pimped him out. Who'd carved a child's face open. Who'd split Crown down the middle. Who'd turned one friend against me and beheaded another. I'm going to the man who raped me, cut me, and left me for dead.

I'll find him, and then I'll kill him. He'll never hurt anyone again.

There's no reason I can't multi-task, though. From my pocket I draw my phone and punch in a number I'd been avoiding for weeks. If she doesn't answer, it'll be what I deserve. But she's there on the first ring.

"Alexis?" Antonina asks, in her timid little voice.

"Hey," I reply. "Listen. I'm so, so sorry for the way I've treated you. I shouldn't have ignored you. You were right all along. I understand if you can't forgive me, but please—"

"Are you ready to *hear*, now?" She doesn't sound angry. Only grieving. Lonesome. How could I have been so cruel to this woman?

"Yes, Nina," I promise, walking at a brisk clip. "I'll hear anything you say."

•••

This bus, like all of its kind, reeks of piss. It's crowded, too. A surprising number of people apparently want to go to Arizona on an early Thursday morning.

A tall teenager, wearing leggings and those fluffy boots the kids today favor, approaches. "Can I sit here?"

The only other empty seats are beside men, so this is probably her safest bet. Mine, too. When I nod, she takes the aisle seat, pops in some earbuds, and tunes me out.

From my backpack I grab a book of fairy tales. In my terminal condition, I've become less self-conscious about who might judge my reading choices. I flip to the chapter on *siabhra* — lesser fey spirits known for evil and mischief. The restless dead; how fitting.

When I try to read, however, my vision goes swimmy. Fatigue from my long walk, and from general sleep deprivation, is catching up to me. I've been eating poorly, too — too much booze, too many carbs. No wonder I'm out of shape.

It's foolish to relax at all on this mission, but if I must, this is the time to do it. I lean my cheek against the window, brain echoing with snippets of mine and Nina's conversation.

Blinded by grief — *"to have only just found her, and now to lose her twice!"* — she'd agreed to follow Cero's last wishes, using the tools from her career as a jeweler to fuse an ounce of Cero's ashes between the bands of our rings.

I suspect she flubbed the truth of her motivations when she'd recited Cero's chants, bathing the metal in moonlight. I don't care how sad someone is; collecting graveyard dirt to bury wedding rings for nine months in is too specific for mere grief. Nina had hoped something would happen, and happen it did.

"She came, Alexis. As I soaked the rings in father's blood and mother's milk—" presumably not Cero's, as her father is dead and Nina is well past menopause — "she taunted me. Ghostly figures haunted my sleep saying *'you are a failure. You let your husband sell me. Everything is all your fault.'*"

I'd had no idea it was Cero's father who sold her into trafficking. I wish she'd told me. I wish she'd told me a lot of things.

"So you sent *me* the haunted rings and then decided, what, that you were sorry?" I feel bad for the lady, but holy shit! What was she thinking?!

"Blood of a father, milk of a mother, dirt of the grave, light of the moon, ash of the body—" here, Nina'd taken a great breath. "And life of the wife, combined to be reborn. If I completed the spell, she would return."

"But you were cool with taking *my* life." My short-lived sympathy for her situation evaporates.

"She is my *daughter!*"

What *is* it with everyone screwing me over? First Cero, then Navier, now Nina... Clearly, I need to pick better friends. I struggle to keep the anger out of my voice. "So, what made you decide that hey, maybe sending people some cancer in jewelry form *wasn't* a great plan?"

"She continues to haunt me still. What happens to you happens to me, also. I am ill, Alexis."

"You have leukemia, too?!" My mind whirled at the thought. Had Cero been possessing Antonina the same way she possessed me? Did Nina, too, converse with a voice inside her head?

I don't understand this jury-rigged necromancy. I don't think *anyone* could understand it; not even people who practice witchcraft. This is like inventing a new language by combining every previous language in existence.

"I am very sick. We help each other, now."

Nina insisted I come to her, and bring my haunted rings with me. When I'd suggested I just destroy them myself, she'd panicked, insisting that to do so would kill both her and me. Not to mention leaving Cero as a half-formed spirit to wander the earth forever.

"I can show you how is fixed, but you must come to me."

I don't want to go to Moscow, to the woman who'd caused me so much trouble, but I don't want to die, either. I guess cashing Clay's check and purchasing passage to Russia will be my next move, right after I kill Vince.

I must've drifted off juggling all these thoughts, because the next thing I know, a hand is shaking my shoulder.

I open heavy eyelids. My teen seatmate relaxes her grip. "We're in Joshua Tree. This your stop?"

Joshua Tree National Park is less than a third of the way to Strawberry. We've been driving for about two hours. I rub the crust from my eyes and smack my dry lips. "No."

"Oh. Sorry to wake you, then."

"S'cool."

There's a fifteen minute gap before we hit the road again. I stand and make my way to the station, where a bathroom and some overpriced coffee sing my name.

I have to shade my eyes with an arm for the short trek from the parking lot. The sun is a blazing disc that bakes the landscape of cacti and mountains. My vision adjusts and my warming limbs lose some of their stiffness when I stretch, pacing the dirt road.

They'd named this park for its Joshua trees; squat plants twisted and bent into bizarre shapes. I remember Gran telling me Mormon settlers named them that because the tufted trees called to mind the biblical Joshua praying to make the sun stand still.

In the distance, their tiny silhouettes creeping up Quail Mountain, I see a trio of hikers. I shake my head. You couldn't *pay* me to hike at this time of year. Every summer, "experienced" hikers wind up dead or missing or, at best, airlifted to the hospital because they underestimated the severe conditions.

I return to the bus with my coffee and churros, intending to offer one to my seatmate, but she's nowhere to be found. Instead, my fairy book is splayed across both seats, open to the chapter on *cait sídhe*.

Of all the fair folk, they unsettle me the most. Though beautiful, the illustrations make my skin crawl. These felid *sidhe* are all dark-haired and moon-pale, leering with claws popped and fangs bared. Their eyes are green as sin.

Phrases jump out at me as I take my seat and reach for the book. *Manipulative tricksters. Shapeshifters. Entertained by acts of extreme violence.*

I shut the book and stuff it back into my bag, then take an enormous chomp of my churro. I'm out of time for fairy tales. I have a score to settle.

Chapter Twenty-Eight – Tip

…

I'm not used to eating so much. My shrunken stomach protests this constant, painful fullness. I'd planned for the nausea by preparing tiny portions, and yet…

There *is* no control in starvation, not really. I hate when I'm forced to acknowledge that. I need help if there's any chance of me fixing this issue long-term. What I'm doing now is only a band-aid on a bullet hole.

"I'm not gonna puke," I tell Agwe, who mushes her blunt nose against the medical pool wall to make goofy faces at me.

I grin. She always makes me feel better. "That would make all this effort counterproductive, and I just don't put up with that shit; not even from my own digestive system."

"That's the spirit," remarks an older East Asian man in the far back corner. He's tall, graying, and the tightness of his black wetsuit reveals a physique tight with wiry muscle. His fingers flit busily over the screen of a tablet.

I jump, flushing furiously. I hadn't known I had a human audience to my nonsense.

I quickly hide my empty Tupperware behind my back, but the man doesn't seem to care that a uniformed janitor is blatantly shirking his duties to dine with a manatee.

"I'm doctor Kevin Lin," he introduces himself, his Chinese accent faint and pleasant. He puts his tablet away before rolling on a pair of thick rubber gloves that extend halfway to his armpits. "On loan from Florida Aquatic Preserves to look over *this* gorgeous girl."

He climbs a platform to dunk his hand in Agwe's water. Despite her shy nature, she doesn't seem to mind his presence, even approaching for a pat. She snorts irritated bubbles when he grips her head to examine the socket of her missing eye, but doesn't otherwise protest.

This man is living my dream. This is a marine mammal veterinarian; likely very high on the ladder to be sent for a job across the country.

I'm sure if I were to look up his name online, I'd find page upon page of his accomplishments; his travels and published works. It's hard to tear my eyes off him. My heart tangibly compresses with envy. With grief for a life I might, in a kinder world, have lived.

I could still—

No. I will never have this, because Magpie is going to die. After that, either Vince will kill me, or I'll do it myself. I'm tired of waiting. There's nothing left to wait *for.*

Why I hurt myself by asking, "How is she doing, Doctor Lin?" Is anyone's guess.

"She's gained some weight, which is excellent. She had a fungal infection on her nostril valves, but we've cleared that up with medication and washes. We hope to breed her with Poncho, the largest bull in Florida's preserve, before releasing them all in Crystal River."

My heart, oh my *heart.* It drops straight through me and shatters on the tile floor. My vision goes dark around the edges, but only for a second.

It's not that I'm upset they'll rehabilitate Agwe — that *is* the oft impossible goal of caring for any wild animal. It's just that, someday, I'll no longer be a part of her journey. It'll break my promise to care for her.

The doctor runs his hands along Agwe's sides as she swims for him, checking for lumps and abrasions. She seems to enjoy the attention, closing her eyes when he circles his thumbs 'round her tiny ears.

I laugh. The sound comes out as a sharp sob. He shoots me an alarmed glance.

I go to grab my cart of cleaning supplies, face burning, eyes stinging. *Way to play it cool, Tip.* "Don't mind me; I'm just nuts. Have a great morning/day/whateverthefuck."

"Are you well?" He asks, descending the platform.

I laugh again, digging for an excuse. Allergies; bowel trouble; a death in the family...

What comes out is this: "I'm losing everyone else I love. She might as well go, too."

Could I sound *any* more pathetic? I make for the elevator, intent on escaping the basement. Hopefully this specialized expert won't narc on a crazy parolee found weeping out of bounds.

"Wait," he calls to my retreating back. "What's your name?"

Welp, that's it. He wants to report me by name. I might as well go turn my badge and uniform in now. "Dylan Tippling."

The rarely used syllables trip oddly on my tongue. It's not that I hate my given name. It's that I'd once looked up the etymology, and had been shaken to discover it means "son of the sea." How could someone like *me* carry such a title?

"Dylan," Doctor Lin repeats, circling me to speak to my face. His eyes are kind; gray-lashed and surrounded by laughter lines. "When does your shift end? Perhaps I can tempt you with some coffee in the café?"

I blink, a residual tear licking down my cheek. Dear God above; *please* tell me this isn't a pickup. I know there's a fetish for everything, but crying, emaciated janitors with dirty mop water soaking their jumpsuits is pretty niche, even in SoCal.

He lowers his voice conspiratorially, eyes twinkling. "I'd enjoy talking about Agwe with someone who loves her so much. And I have no human friends here. I'd greatly appreciate the company."

He's only patronizing me, I'm sure. Either that, or...

No. He doesn't want to sleep with me. He just pities me. Kind people supposedly exist, right? And even if he did, I could still say no. Probably.

Or maybe I should go for it. Tell him I'll blow him for the right price; fuck him for more. Ask him to drive me to the docks, where Vince's inferior replacements hustle. They'll regurgitate knotted condoms of fine beige powder, hot and slick with stomach acid, and...

"My shift ends a quarter past noon," I answer, feeling like a crumpled umbrella left to molder. "I'll meet you there."

...

It's not like I've never performed this way before.

No. It's the fact that I *have* that has my guts in knots.

I don't want us to be like this. What we have — what we *had* — was something better. Something real.

I'm offered on his desk, pants unzipped, an entrée to be consumed.

He's bowed over me, a hand up my shirt and the other, lower. His stubble rasps my neck.

He smells the same — coffee and cigarettes. He feels the same — solid and warm and controlled.

But this is not the same.

When he glides up to kiss me properly, I avert my face, unseeing eyes on the far wall. This will all be over soon.

James frowns, stilling. "Tip? Are you there?"

I say nothing. I *am* nothing. I am the smallest rendition of myself.

My professor moves to gives me space, but it's too late. The classroom door opens. Bambi and Tariq stride inside, smiling cheerfully. "Hey, James. We..."

They stop. Stare.

James straightens, fumbling the button of his pants, swiping his swollen lips with the back of a hand.

"O-Oh," he chokes, playing the pervert, caught. Pretty good actor, for a teacher. "This isn't what it—"

Tariq seizes his girlfriend's hand, hauling her back. The door slams behind them. I hear them speaking frenzied Arabic in the hallway, voices rising in crescendos of rage.

Though I don't understand their words, I can tell they're disgusted with the professor they'd trusted so completely. With me, too, probably.

With a shaky sigh, James sits in his chair, bracing his elbows on the desk. He removes his glasses and hangs his head, massaging both temples as though to stave off a migraine.

•••

It should be impossible for Bambi to surprise me anymore. She's proven herself a brilliant, kind young woman. Still, she manages to catch me off guard.

When I return home and boot up the laptop, I see that I've received a message from her. I expect to be called all sorts of names: whore, slut, cheater. I'm shocked instead to see a very different email.

She asks if I'm okay. Whether I'm being pressured into sex. That she wants to report James to the schoolboard. She even apologizes that she and Tariq hadn't stuck around to protect me.

I leave the computer and snatch Tiny Meal no. 7 from the fridge, taking the time to put a new pot of rice on the stove for tomorrow.

I can't think of a good response to Bambi's email, but I have to come up with something fast. We want James's reputation tarnished. We don't want him *fired*. I have to get across that *I* wanted this liaison; that *I'm* the one who initiated it.

It's the truth, but would she believe me? Would I believe *her,* were our situations reversed?

Probably not. She's so much younger than me, and she's also a girl. Maybe I'm a giant misogynist and hypocrite to feel that that changes anything, or maybe I just watch the news enough to know the statistics of sexual assault.

I stir my rice, empty the litterbox, and feed the animals. Two cats and a dog have transformed our apartment into a miniscule, hairy zoo.

"Hey, Mags," I greet, pushing open her bedroom door to leave food for Ding. He hasn't forgiven me for our rough introduction at Navier's house, so I'm not surprised when he hisses. "Think if I try to sell the cats on Craigslist, Cero will pop out to kick my ass?"

Magpie isn't there.

Ever since her hours were cut at the gas station, she's become a bit of a shut-in. Discovering that one's dead wife has made you terminally ill in a bid to steal your body will do that to a person.

She was called in to work last night, but surely she should be back by now...

There my big brother instincts go, tingling too little, too late. As I look around Magpie's empty bedroom, I get the uncomfortable feeling I'm missing something important.

"What is it?" I ask Ding, who's eyes glow from the depths of the closet. "What am I forgetting?"

I set his bowl on the bathroom counter, push Zelda away when she tries to steal it, and drum my fingers atop her head as I think.

It comes to me like a mallet to the skull. The bus ticket. It was for today, wasn't it?

I've been so distracted by the proof that there is life after death, and the effort to keep my cousin's heart beating, that it utterly slipped my mind. Vince would be so pissed...

Zelda mashes her chilly nose into my stomach, whining, so I press her head against my thigh and rub her ears. She's pricking them in the way that indicates she's on high alert, or she just needs to pee.

"Wanna go for a walk?" I ask, still kicking myself for forgetting something so important. I don't make mistakes like that — I'm Dylan fucking Tippling!

She gives a low "boof," so off we go to find her harness. I turn off the stove. We make it to the end of the street before she finds a patch of dirt somehow superior to all *other* patches of dirt. Here she circles and squats.

"You're weird," I inform her.

A charcoal-gray BMW briefly bathes us in headlights as it passes, making Zelda's eyes glow. *Tapetum lucidum,* that pretty blue-green layer behind the jelly of an eyeball, is one of the flashiest differences between humans and animals.

Zelda stands, and we head for home. She could benefit from a longer walk, but I'm not up for it. "You don't think Magpie would *really...?*"

I don't finish my question, because she *would*. She must have. She *did*. This was the girl who started moshing at age thirteen. This is the woman who takes on child traffickers with nothing but a bike, some knives, and a smile.

Shit, fuck, and damn.

Snatching my phone from my back pocket, I dial my cousin. My call goes straight to voicemail without ringing once. "Where the hell are you?!" I bark. "You'd *better* not be doing what I think you're doing!"

Sometimes I wish we hadn't upgraded from flip-phones. Where's the satisfaction in hanging up if I can't violently clap the stupid thing shut?

I pocket it in dissatisfaction and wonder what to do next.

That BMW from before circles back and pulls alongside the curb, idling just in front of Zelda and I with hazard lights blinking.

The tinted window lowers. Leaning an elbow on the frame, Vince smiles winningly out at me. His eyes are faintly glowing. "Want a ride, Surfer-Boy?"

Chapter Twenty-Nine - Magpie

gran always said motorcycles would lead to trouble...

...

I don't know what I'll find when the bus rolls to a halt in Strawberry, but I'm so overheated and crabby that I haul ass off the thing with no hesitation. I'm not snatched up or shot upon entering the station, so that's encouraging.

Maybe I've been inhaling too much exhaust, because the mental image of Vince waiting inside, sunglasses on, Starbucks in hand, waving a sign with Tip's name on it, makes me snort. He's less intimidating when the sun's still shining.

Much like California, Arizona is devastatingly hot; a dry heat that relentlessly beats one over the head with brass knuckles. The only difference is the lack of salt-smell; of ocean breeze.

My leathers don't help matters. I pinch the neck of my top and flap it, directing airflow to my sweaty chest.

Then I straighten and survey the surroundings, paying special attention to the station employees. I haven't forgotten how Navier bribed (threatened?) someone at Urgent Care to snap that pic of me and Ricket.

I'm gonna come out of this with some serious paranoia issues, aren't I?

Well, assuming I come out at all. Even if I manage to beat Vince, there's still Cero waiting in the shadows.

How would *she* handle this situation? Where would she go? I'm almost certainly being watched, so enclosed spaces should be avoided. Perhaps the sledding hill, tucked into the woods...?

I leave the station, walking in large strides. I'm small, but tough, and it's always fun seeing the alarm in big men's eyes when they realize a 'little lady' like myself ain't gonna yield.

It's gorgeous here; I'll give it that. Woods. Cabins. Hiking trails. I bet the property makes bank when snowbirds flock for the winter, but in summer heat, it's a ghost town.

"Where are you, creep?" I mutter, wishing I had six more eyeballs to watch every tree, every cabin. "I'm not a pretty blond boy, but you know you're curious about why I'm here."

Assuming this whole thing wasn't just Vince trying to get me out of his hair, that is.

I stop, feeling fear's icy hand seize my spine. Why the hell hadn't I considered that possibility before?!

Vince knows how contrary I am. He knows I throw myself headfirst into trouble, relying on my friends to do the planning. It wouldn't be the first time I'd waltzed between his waiting jaws.

He might've predicted I'd do what I did. He might've *counted* on it.

I dig my phone from my bag and power it on. It's four o'clock here, so it's three in California. This long gap between Tip's shift ending and his classes beginning, where he usually naps the afternoon away, is ideal for danger to strike.

The stupid phone takes forever to boot. I fidget, cursing, earning glances from a cabin dweller relaxing on her balcony.

Just as I pull up my contacts list, movement catches my peripheral vision.

I tilt my phone to catch reflections and, with a jolt, see that the woman is staring at my back, intent and still as any predator.

Tilting the phone in the other direction reveals two more people across the street, heading my way. One speaks into a phone. The other's eyes never leave my back.

Shit.

I resume walking down the long line of unoccupied rental cabins, my combat boots tromping twigs and pinecones on the uneven dirt path.

I make like I'll keep walking straight all the way to where street signs point to the sledding hill. Then, when I see two A-frames built close together, a motorcycle parked out front, I take a sharp left. The cool, scrubby gap between buildings hides me from sight.

That's when I heed my instincts and *run*.

My body is not built for speed. I spend far more time lifting weights than I do jogging laps. If this becomes a race, I've already lost.

That leaves me with two options: stay with the cabins, or make for the woods? Based on the clatter of approaching footsteps, I've got seconds to decide.

The sight of an open window makes the choice for me. Ponytail whipping, I sprint half a lap around the occupied cabin and leap, grabbing the white metal window-frame to vault myself through.

I land with a jolt and roll across dingy shag carpeting, momentum halted by the scarred wooden legs of a pool table. I'm heaving, gagging, sputtering for breath. 'Stealth,' perhaps, is not my strong suit.

Mounted on the wall, across from an ugly green sofa, a TV projects a Telenovela. I'm the only one in here to watch it. When I quirk my head, I can hear the pattering of shower water from another room. A male voice tunelessly warbles, *"Dime tú que hago vida mía..."*

I hope the guy is living here alone. All I need is for his wife or kid or friend to catch me and sound the alarm.

Pocketing my phone, I stand and steal a billiard ball from the table — number six; green like my Kawasaki. I close the window and creep into the hallway.

Judging by the outdoorsy clutter all around, this resident is a nature lover who's been living here a while. He must really love it, to tolerate this heat. Probably not one of my stalkers, then.

I'm at an impasse when I reach the hallway. Where to go; bathroom or bedroom or kitchen?

My gut tells me to keep running. This dude can't shower forever. Eventually he's gonna come out and question why a short Indian chick is creeping 'round his cabin.

Someone raps on the front door, loud enough to stop my heart. That's not a howdy-do knock; that's a knock that means business.

Seconds pass. Then there's a *boom!* as something big hits the door. I can hear the wood splinter; the screws in the hinges pinging free. The man in the shower yelps.

Without another thought, I dart for the steamy bathroom to see his wet, wrinkled old face peering fearfully from the seashell-patterned curtain.

I snatch his discarded jeans off the floor. As he cries out, speaking so frantically that I lose any hope of translation, I search his pockets. I unearth a wallet, crumpled receipts, and a ring of keys. *"Lo siento, señor!* I will lead them away from you!"

He stares in gray-faced shock as I climb his sink, sending a cup that contains a comb and toothbrush skittering to the floor.

The round bathroom window is much smaller than the one in the game room, but it opens on easy hinges. I stuff my torso through and wriggle free, though it takes some doing to squeeze my hips and butt through. I belly-flop on the splintery deck of the cabin hard enough to wind myself.

There's a reason Gran let me quit ballet after only one class.

While my body struggles to breathe, I see there are four casually dressed men at the door, all armed. One wields a battering ram; the same model we'd trained on at the police academy. Another grips his arm, providing counterbalance. The others keep watch.

The door itself is on its last leg. It held up admirably to the attack, but three tons of impact force per strike is too much for mere wood to withstand.

If these men run in Vince's circle, I know they'll have no qualms murdering an old man who happens to be in their way. I'd promised to lead them off, and so I shall.

The man's bike, a sexy vintage Aprilia RSV with wires exposed and headlights larger than my tits, is exactly where I'd seen it last: parked to the side of the cabin.

"Hey!" I shout, and bolt. I shoot a quick promise to God that if I survive this stunt, I'll go back to church and try to cut down on masturbating. Maybe.

The men turn my way as I baseball-slide down the dirt driveway, shredding my jeans. The impact of body against bike nearly sends us both sprawling, but I do manage to throw a leg over the saddle while fumbling for the keyhole.

The bike is significantly larger than I'm used to. *Too* large for me. 'Oversized' works for t-shirts and waffles. Not so much for modes of transportation where nothing but gyroscopic forces are keeping the rider upright.

The men drop their ram and move. I notice that not a single one of them draws their gun. If Vince doesn't want me dead, what else could he have in mind?

That thought scares me more than anything that's happened this year.

"Come on, *come on!*" I kick out the stand and crank the key until the engine turns over. My attackers are close enough to count the buttons on their shirts. I recognize one of them as a passenger on the Greyhound.

"Alexis!" He calls. Only then do I notice the tattoo on his grasping hand: the dark silhouette of a monitor lizard, its tail maypoled around his thumb.

What the hell? What are Müller's lackeys doing *here?!*

He grips a fistful of my shirt and attempts to unseat me. I swing with the billiard ball, my weighted fist connecting solidly with his cheek. I hear the crunch of bone before he crumples. I don't see him hit the ground, as the Aprilia and I are hurtling recklessly over the dirt road.

The bike roars, its voice similar to Rosa's Harley. I'm jounced and throttled over dips and ruts, clinging with all the strength of my thighs just to stay seated. I lose the ball almost immediately, as it's all I can do not to be thrown over the handlebars.

"Cero?" I try, hating myself for wanting her after all she's done. Hating *her* when I receive no answer. I'm all alone in here.

"Okay," I say to myself, though I can barely hear my words over the motor and wind resistance. "Isaac Müller is here. Didn't see that coming."

But why? Are they and Vince connected, somehow? Vince is a dealer, not a *trafficker...*

The bike lurches off the side of the road. Similar to the orange grove incident, I bounce down a steep incline towards a gorge of pine trees. Unlike that night, none of my panic is softened by alcohol.

There is no time to brake; no way to swerve. I feel the acute, horrific sensation of the bike's rear wheel leaving the ground.

You just keep trying to die, don't you, Miss Cop? Cero sighs, and forces our body sideways, rolling us off the bike.

I don't know how I don't get run over. I know nothing but radiating pain as my arm snaps between my weight and the ground, the crack loud as a gunshot.

I cannot draw breath. I cannot scream. My rolling body comes to a stop in a small, rocky dip, coated in pine needles and dirt. There's a scream trapped inside me, but I don't know how to find it.

The Aprilia, sans rider, crashes onto its side. Gravity and its momentum wham it against the trees. The ruptured old gas tank whooshes into bright flame.

I can only hope the summer-dried pines don't catch fire and spread.

Breathe, Mags.

I choke in several shaky, wet gasps. My world has narrowed to the break in my right arm, sticky with leaves and twisted beneath my body.

I can't tell without looking at it, but if it's a compound fracture, if the bone has broken skin, I stand the very real risk of bleeding out.

"I can't," I hear myself say, spitting gravel. "It's too much, Cero. I can't do this."

Maybe I'm not a hero, after all. Maybe I never was.

Then I will. Let me in, Miss Cop.

It's easier than ever I thought possible, allowing my wife to pull me beneath the surface of my own mind.

For a moment, it's as though the two of us are submerged in deep water. Her hands cup my cheeks, stroking my temples with her thumbs.

I look into her mismatched eyes and find that I still love this woman. Wrong or right, I can't turn my heart off so easily.

Cero passes cool fingers over my eyelids, closing them, and breeches the surface of our shared consciousness. When my eyes again open, I'm no longer the one looking out.

Chapter Thirty – Tip

...

Vince looks the same as last I'd seen him, which itself is remarkably similar to the *first* time I'd ever done so, back in Principal Kelly's office the first day of Freshman year.

I'd been blowing Gran's landlord for two weeks already. I remember rubbing my sore jaw, looking over my new schedule, when a passing Senior caught my eye.

"Try Carmex," he'd suggested, grinning at my bruised lips. "Plain. Cherry is overrated."

At thirty-nine, he should be showing traces of age. If not the gray hairs Magpie and I occasionally find, then perhaps crow's feet, or a thinning of skin at his hands, his throat.

None is to be found. He's new and bright and ageless as ever. He might've just stepped off the set for a toothpaste commercial.

Enjoying my stupefied stare, he huffs a laugh. He's always had the nicest laugh; rich and bright and warm. It endears him to everyone; invites them to join in.

I attempt to speak, but no words come. All sound and sensation has muted, and I see nothing but him. He is a sharp photo on a blurry background.

He jerks his chin towards the passenger seat. "You gonna get in, or...?"

Saying no to him is not, has never been, an option. I croak the next best thing: "I have to take Zelda home."

"I'll drive you. It's a rental. I don't give a shit if she gets fur in it."

Vince pops the locks. He doesn't turn his head; doesn't watch me open the back door and boost a cowering Zelda inside. Why should he? I won't disobey him. I'd never run.

Zelda only stares at the back of Vince's head, stiff as a plank. An eerie, strangled whine I've never before heard ekes from her throat.

Only she knows what really happened the night of David's murder. I wonder how strong her recollection, her situational awareness is.

You're okay, I think, anxiously rubbing her ears. They're the softest part of her; little velvet points in a sea of coarse and oily. I may as well be petting a bolder, for all the response it garners. I buckle her leash into the seatbelt. *You'll be fine.*

I don't know if I'm directing this towards the dog, or to myself. I just know I'm working on autopilot when I shut her in, and make for the passenger door. I can't look at him as I sit. As I buckle up.

When Vince reaches for me, I don't flinch. Property has no say in such matters. His long index finger traces my cheek. "I missed you. What *happened* to you?"

I must look so old, so haggard next to him. What can I say? *Fire. Grief. Age. Starvation. Poverty. Take your pick.*

Instead I say, "I missed you, too." It's what he wants to hear.

His thumb presses to my lower lip. I know I'm meant to draw it inside my mouth, but the thought sits like a brick in my stomach. Had he pushed those fingers into Magpie, too? I think of all I've heard her cry out during her night terrors. *Please stop. It hurts. God, just let me die.*

Resistance is always a mistake, and now is no exception. His proud eyebrows climb high as he fixes me with a stern look, making my pulse trip. Already, I've disappointed him.

He huffs and releases me, then slinks the BMW onto the street. I sit still with my hands on my knees, staring down at my shoes.

It doesn't surprise me at all when he finds our apartment without instructions. I wonder how long he's been staking it out.

"Make it quick," Vince instructs, but stops me when I get out. "Phone?"

I don't want to give it to him. I do it without hesitation.

Quiet as a mouse, I take Zelda inside and overfill the water and food dishes for her and the cats. Who knows when someone will be home to care for them again?

A nasty thought occurs to me, all but confirming my suspicions on Magpie's whereabouts. Is there any chance Vince would've let me come inside if he thought she was home to protect me? He knows where she is, and it's certainly not here.

I pocket my wallet and glasses, though Vince will probably take those, too. I contemplate the laptop. It's possible to call emergency services from Skype, but by the time I've booted the old dinosaur up, Vince will have grown impatient. If he beheaded a man because I hassled Eva, imagine what he'd do for *that*?

There's David's phone, sitting helpfully on my bedside table. But the only number I know is 911. If I dialed the authorities on *that* phone, and they arrived to find a missing man's dog in my apartment...

I return to Vince's car, having done nothing at all.

He's scrolling through my phone's contacts, reading my messages, when I buckle back in.

"James," he sneers, mood darker than before. "Do you *have* to ride the guy's dick with *every* message? 'What time are we meeting?' 'Want me to bring you a coffee?' I could puke. He's just using your pathetic ass. You know that, right?"

I must have completely lost my mind, because I reply, "James likes me."

This earns me a stare of incredulity, then a laugh. "You?! Babe, you've gotta face reality. *Nobody* likes you, 'cept me."

I tuck the rebellious thought away. "You're right."

He chucks my phone over his shoulder and into the backseat. "I'm *always* right. If you're done being a sadsap, we'd better get moving."

"Where are we going?" I ask, remembering everything Magpie'd told me about her discoveries in the Motel 6. "Is Dorothy with you?"

For a moment, as he backs from the parking lot, I see true happiness in his stunning green eyes. "Hollywood, baby! Don't you worry; she's alive and well. She's excited to see you."

How long do rainbow boas live, anyway? Reptiles aren't my area of expertise, so maybe it's normal for her to hit her late twenties, but hasn't she had trouble shedding since we were kids? That *should* be a death sentence for snakes.

"We got plans for tonight?" I ask, because despite his antisocial tendencies, Vince is even more of an extrovert than Magpie. He sees everyone as lesser than him, yet still craves their attention.

A lanky arm lassos my shoulders. Vince steers with his knees, his free hand spread out before us, drawing me in to imagine our future. "I'm gonna clean you up and show you off. In a few days, we're headed for Scotland. Do you have *any* idea how hard it is to get someone on parole out of the country? Be grateful I think you're worth it."

'Cleaning me up and showing me off' is Vince's shorthand for getting me high and taking me out clubbing. I guess some things never change.

"Scotland is where your dad lives, right?" I ask cautiously. That's something I'm not supposed to know. The cards I found under his bed were a secret.

Vince looks at me, startled, then smiles. I'm glad my question didn't piss him off, though one can never really predict which way his mood will swing. I suspect he's somewhat high, which accounts for the good cheer.

"Smartie-pants. Yep — I've been hanging out with Da. You have no idea, *no idea*, man. The guy is so deep. He's spent the last two years teaching me who I am. *What* I am."

Huh. I wouldn't have guessed Vince was away on a heritage trip. "Does 'Da' know about me?"

"Does he know I'm bringing the love of my life home to stay? Fuck yeah! He's *hyped!*"

I feel that comment like the first rays of sunlight after a long, dark night. It warms me better than any 'good boy,' 'pretty boy,' 'mine; all mine.'

I am *such* an addict.

"You love me?" I ask, voice tiny. I've never heard him *say* it before. It was always implied, but...

I've never seen him look so gentle before, either. "I never stopped, Surfer-Boy. Tip. *Dylan.*"

His hand travels to my leg, prying *my* hand off my knee. His thumb strokes each knuckle, passing burn scars and whole flesh alike, before he laces our fingers together.

When we swerve too far into the adjoining lane, Vince properly steers us back with his free hand. It's funny; he's always been a careless driver, yet I don't think he's ever gotten so much as a speeding ticket.

"So, uh, I know I left things kinda fucky between us, but you know I'm making up for it. Did you like my roses?"

I can't lie to his face. "I loved them. I kept them for as long as I could."

His smile is all teeth. "There's gonna be way more of that from now on. I'm gonna treat you right. Do *all* the sappy shit to make my boy happy."

It's a two-hour drive to Hollywood in good traffic. As it's a Thursday night, it's about as good as it ever gets. Vince plugs his phone into the aux cord and lets a playlist blast, though the fiddles and flutes and other instruments I don't recognize are far from his usual fare.

When he catches my look, he shrugs. "Yeah, I know it's weird. Da got me into some shit from our people. Guess I'm going native."

"That's cool," I say. "That you found him. I'm glad you get along." It sucks that I'll be leaving school and Magpie behind, but if Vince says it's so, then...

"Magpie's gonna worry about me," I point out, because that sounds less confrontational than '*where* is Magpie?'

He laughs again. "That's the best part! She won't be worrying about anyone but herself from now on; I can promise you that. Don't worry about a thing."

My insides chill. He sounds so *confident*. How can I get more information without triggering an outburst? I'm rusty at this game; the game of saying the right things in the right tone to get the right answers. I haven't had to play it in ages, but the muscle memory lingers.

I fall back in my chair, legs parting, inching our conjoined hands higher. I press his knuckles to my inner thigh. "Tell me? Please, baby?"

I can't make it seem like I want answers *too* much, or it'll become another toy to dangle over my head, wherein all the joy comes from the denial. So long as the benefits of talking outweigh the amusement of withholding, I have an edge.

He looks at me, appraising, thumb rubbing my inseam. I resist the urge to duck my head; to hide my ugly face.

I belong to him. Ugly or not, he can look all he likes.

"I will," he promises. "When this is all over. When that little cunt is someone else's problem. Then I'll tell you everything."

...

Nimphidia is an enormous, gaudy hotel with surprisingly little traffic for all its proximity to the Hollywood sign. A place this flashy should be *crawling* with wealthy tourists.

The outside walls appear to be plated with gold, polished to a beetle-wing sheen. I watch my rose-tinted reflection walk alongside Vince's through the seductive aroma of oranges and jasmine.

Under that, I smell something skunky that *might* be pot, but reminds me more of the fug above a hookah lounge.

Vince walks at an easy stroll, all hips and mile-long legs, hands tucked in his pockets. For all that he doesn't touch me, he may as well have me on a leash. I linger at his heels like a well-trained hound.

He attracts glances from passers-by on our way to the lobby. They admire a china-bone face that wouldn't look out of place on a model, or a rockstar; his tall, thin figure; posture that screams he knows exactly what he looks like and how to use it.

He is incapable of fitting in anywhere, so he doesn't try. The tattoos he's spent thousands to acquire stain his arms and throat like black, spider-spun lace. His glossy hair, curly when he lets it grow too long, is cut short to show off piercings and knife-sharp features. He's vain enough to buy only the most expensive, trendy clothing, then has it all altered within an inch of its life. It fits him like a second skin.

Next to him, I feel like dowdy, week-old garbage. I always have. It's just another thing to reacclimate to.

The accordion-doors of the hotel's entrance are ringed with blinking lights. Vince swings an arm out behind himself, offering a grand bow as he opens them for me.

I flinch away from the sudden movement, eyes fixed on his hand. His arched eyebrow is a knife to my throat.

"Sorry," I whisper, throat dry, and allow him to usher me inside.

The lobby is just as dazzling as the hotel's exterior. It glitters; all glass. The tube-like pillars supporting the ceiling are fish tanks, bubbling with neon-blue water, swarming with tropical fish.

I blink, unable to place their genus. They glitter in every shade of the rainbow, but what *are* they? That one there *might* be a tiger barb, but I've never seen one so small. And the creature to the left of it shares *some* similarities to a lionfish, but it can't be; that's *beyond* illegal.

Everywhere I look, I see dull scales; fin rot; creeping parasites. I smell chlorine buildup. I see what I can barely recognize as an Arowana floating belly-up, its fins long since eaten away by predators. It twitches, close to death.

I can almost hear the cries of their abuse. How many rare, exotic fish have died in these walls, just to provide a colorful backdrop for ignorant socialites?

Vince grips the back of my neck, nails pricking, and drags me further into the lobby. "I should've known you'd only have eyes for them," he scoffs; not without affection. "You always were a fish-brain."

"I want to speak to the manager," I reply, meeting his eyes.

I don't *just* want to talk to them. I want to kill them. Slowly. The way these creatures have been, are being, murdered.

Where *is* the manager, anyway? Where is *anybody?* The grand, dome-shaped lobby is large as a football stadium. It's outfitted with immaculate furniture in rich creams and burnished golds. Fine oil artwork and heavy drapery line the walls.

Yet it's empty, save for us and the fish.

"Later, Surfer-Boy!" Vince laughs, the sound carrying far before echoing back to us.

For a second, I resist. I set my heels. I continue to stare him down. *Wrong, wrong. This place is wrong.*

Then I see irritation darken his face, and I remember to be afraid.

I follow him past empty restaurants and shops and bars, all the way to a glass elevator. He waits until I get in, then stands between me and the doors as though half expecting me to run for it.

He needn't have bothered. I remember my place. I watch dully as he punches the button for the thirteenth floor. We rise for what feels like an eternity.

Even the floor of the elevator is glass, allowing glimpses of the mechanics and the levels below while we rise. I wonder if this is how the fish in those pillar-aquariums feel — trapped, surrounded, and struggling to breathe.

When we exit, our footsteps are silenced by plush crimson carpeting down the long, high-ceilinged hallways. It's so quiet I can hear the hum of electricity in the overhead lighting.

The reek of orchids is overpowering. I find its source when we pass a decorative table containing the marble bust of a beautiful child beside a fresh bouquet as wide as I am tall.

With so many rooms, I should see guests and employees, right? This is too creepy. Am I being paranoid?

Finally, we reach Vince's door. From his pocket he draws a long black key. The fob is a single owl feather, curved and gray and, as far as I can tell, real.

He inserts it into the slot below the ovular handle and, with a deep click, unlocks it. The door opens, silent as the grave.

Compared to the sterile, spotless hallway, Vince's room is a relief of normalcy. Sure, the gold-quilted bed is larger than any bed I've ever seen; large enough for an orgy of ten, I'd wager. But it's covered by his rumpled clothes, and the many pillows are in disarray.

Plugged into a socket by the bed is Dorothy's tank. It's rectangular, with a sliding glass cover, and comes up to my sternum when I stand beside it.

I admire her, half-hidden in the coconut substrate. Her mouth is catlike, quirked in the middle and bowing out on either side. She's a comely animal, six feet long, the deep blue rings down her spine iridescent from her heat-lamp.

"Hey, you," I greet. How many times had I worn her muscular body as a scarf while Vince changed her substrate; scrubbed stubborn poop stains off the walls of her tank? I don't have many good childhood memories, but she is one of them.

I want to hold her now, but before I can ask, Vince is crossing the room and throwing open his curtains. Then I'm too busy gasping to speak.

From the wall-sized windows, I see all of SoCal spread below us; a million lights stretching in every direction. I see Mount Lee with its famous sign, glowing in the night. The world is so black, yet illuminated, as though by fireflies. Far beyond, I see a choppy darkness that can only be the sea.

It feels a little like what God might see, should he ever deign to look down from His throne.

"Whoa..."

"Right?!" Vince is all too pleased to share this majesty with me.

What kind of place *is* this?! The view seems off, somehow. It's not just the vertigo talking. I can see faraway things too well, despite my lack of glasses. It's like I've taken on a hawk's gaze. Something about it forces me to avert my gaze, eyes stinging.

I am not meant to see this. It wasn't made for me.

As soon as I look into the beady eyes of Dorothy's chisel-shaped face, I remember that my cousin is in danger. How had I forgotten; even for a second?

"Hey, um. Baby?"

He brightens at the endearment, though he tries to play it off casually. I swallow hard. I'm so hungry for him that when his hand passes over my back, I shiver.

"Yeah?"

"I had some questions."

"Shoot."

He crouches. Rustles under his bed and unearths a large crate, from which he pulls a plastic spray bottle. He slides open Dorothy's tank to touch her substrate, finds it too dry, and sprays to dampen it.

I'm talking gently so that he doesn't see me as confrontational; accusatory. "You really hurt a kid, Vince. Omar is only seventeen."

"Who?" he looks blank until I offer prompts, reminding him of the motel; of the boy he'd taken under the guise of sex.

"Oh, that! I just wanted to grab Mags's attention. Make a splash, you know? Like, 'guess who's back, bitch?!' It was just a little fun."

He says this like it's a reasonable argument; like I'm supposed to agree with his disfigurement of a minor. I instead focus on another instance: "You hurt Magpie, too."

His mind must still be on Omar, because he assumes I'm talking about her scar. "She brought it on herself. Did you see what she did to my ear?! I had to hire a plastic surgeon to fix this shit!"

He folds his ear back, showing me the pink scar that radiates outward from the conch. I envision the way his orbital rings must have ripped a chunk of flesh.

Rather than point out my cousin wouldn't have done this had he not been in her bedroom with a knife, I clarify my statement. "I'm not talking about that. I'm talking about when you... Slept with her. She was too high to know what was going on."

I'm too timid to use the R-word, but he's not. He *laughs*. "Is she going around telling people I raped her?! Fucking liar. We just fooled around some, is all. You should've heard her moan for it."

Oh, I feel sick. Sick, sick, sick. "Did she *tell* you she wanted it?"

"She wasn't saying no."

"Because you roofied the shit out of her."

"Don't get pissy 'cuz you're too chickenshit to admit *you* want her hairy ass, Captain Incest. I did nothing to her that I haven't done with you."

And that's the problem, isn't it? If what he did to Magpie was rape, then that means he also raped me. And that's something I've spent more than half my life trying not to think about.

"Why did you do it?" I ask, stupidly hoping for any answer that will make me understand.

As though there's anything he can say to make this better.

He shrugs. "Does it matter? Why does anyone do anything? I was bored. She was there."

And you weren't, Surfer-Boy.

I don't know how to make someone understand that rape is wrong, but I give it a shot. "What if it happened to someone you care about? What if it was Eva? Don't you see—"

I should have anticipated the slap, but it comes too suddenly. One moment he's spritzing Dorothy's tank; the next, I'm falling to the ground with my face on fire, the crack of impact ringing in my ears.

He stands over me, red-faced, a boot jammed into my gut. "Don't you talk about her!" He snarls through clenched teeth, his hand raised to strike again. This time, it's a fist.

I curl in on myself, holding my throbbing face. I don't make a sound. I've endured worse from him. It's just a matter of going so deep into my mind that I feel nothing.

He doesn't escalate into a proper beating. He only regards me, then smooths his hair back and sits on the edge of the bed, heaving a deep, long-suffering sigh. "I *wish* you'd stop making me do that."

Gradually, I unfurl and sit up. I gather my knees to my chest and rest my chin on top, folding my arms around myself.

He returns to Dorothy's tank. Ever the escape artist, she's slithering from the open door. He slides a hand under her heavy body, deposits her inside, and clicks the glass doors firmly shut.

"Not talking, huh?" He asks, turning to the bed to sort through his clothes for the perfect club outfit. "Real mature."

"Anything I say will make you hit me again," I reply dully, staring at the carpet pattern. "What's the point?"

He sneers. "You're such a pussy. You gonna let me stomp all over you for the rest of your life?"

Again: what's the point? Fighting him doesn't work. I couldn't win before, when I was young and healthy and strong. I certainly can't win *now,* with my body ravaged to hell and back.

"Your cousin is more man than you. At least *she* fought back. Where's *your* fire, huh?"

You ate the last of my fire. I've been a haunted house for years.

That's not true, though, is it? I remember what I did to Navier. I think of the chemicals I'd cultured on a rag and flooded his airways with. If I could do *that* to *him...*

Vince stops his pacing and stands before me, causing me to crane my neck to see him. He regards me with tattooed hands planted on his hips. "What am I going to do with you?" he asks.

"I thought we were going out."

"I think I might've made you sound better than you really are when I was talking to Da. I mean, look at you! You used to be something, but now? Do I even have to *say* it?"

He doesn't. Under his gaze, there is no part of me that isn't hideous. I close my eyes to escape the honesty of that stare. His hand strokes my bruised cheek with such gentleness I want to weep.

"Nobody could ever love you like I do," Vince coos, catching the tear that slips from my eye with his thumb. "I'm the only person who sees past how ugly you are; past every ugly thing you've done.

All I need is for you to say you're sorry, and I'll take you right back. No questions asked."

Back to Vince. Back to the haze of drugs; to the ease of a life without thought or desire. My joys came from making him proud, and my only sorrows were in disappointing him. He always understands, always forgives, and always gives me another chance.

Another tear slides down my face, curving my jaw. This is hopeless. *I* am hopeless.

"What's it gonna be?" He asks, calm and assured. Everything is logical coming from him. He can tell you that black is white, and you'll laugh at yourself for ever thinking otherwise. "I *really* want to be able to take you back, Tip. But it's your choice."

He's a saint in his unparalleled ability to love the unlovable. I hide a sob in his palm, prepared to nod. To succumb.

Then, from the murky depths of my brain, I hear a quiet voice. "I love you, Tip."

How many times has Magpie said such words? She said it before work and after; she said it while she ran, and shouted it when she danced. Sometimes she'd call it from her room, voice high and goofy in the middle of the night. Sometimes she'd giggle it, her cheeks bulging with raw cookie dough. "I wuff you!"

When people say nobody can love you if you don't love yourself, that's a load of bullshit. There is nothing I don't hate about myself. My past, my future, my soul, my goddamn *bones*.

But Mags? She loved me all along; as much and as loudly as she was able. Obnoxiously. Boisterously. She loves me, and that is maybe the one truth Vince can't take away.

I open my eyes and meet his poison stare, holding my ugly, unlovable head high.

"Excuse me," I say to my ex, standing. "I have to go. My kid needs me."

I stride around him and make for the door. I can have a panic attack about this later. I can use every self-destructive coping mechanism in my arsenal *later*. Right now, I have to save Mags.

One moment, Vince is by the bed. The next, he is between me and the door, shoving me so forcefully I stumble halfway across the room just to keep my footing.

In another blur of motion, Vince crosses to the bedside table. From a drawer he levers a small, silver pistol, made twice its size by a matte gray silencer. He takes a wide-legged stance and uses a double-handed grip to point the weapon at me.

"Wrong answer," he purrs, and clicks the gun's safety off. "But that's alright. Unlike you, I *keep* my promises."

Chapter Thirty-one - Tip

bang, bang. my baby shot me down.

...

When he pulls the trigger with nary a muffled hiss of sound, I drop to the ground with no thought as to how I'll land. I feel my pocketed glasses crunch against my hip. My jaw slams the floor so hard I bite my cheek, and blood bursts like wildflowers in my mouth. My ribs weep in protest.

Hearing what must be the world breaking, I roll into the far wall. Only by peeking through the gap in my arms do I see that Vince has shot the floor-to-ceiling window. The glass crumbles to nothing. Countless shards glint on the carpet, but most must be in the street below. The wall is a yawning void.

Vince fiddles with the gun, which appears to have jammed. "Fucking things. Useless." He offers me a grin. "Sorry, babe. I _tried_ to give you an easy out."

He tosses the weapon onto the bed as casually as he'd thrown my phone, and makes his way towards me.

Animal terror has me scrabbling to my feet, searching for an escape. Window? No. Too high up. Door? Vince is between me and the door.

I can fight Vince better than I can fight gravity. Ducking low like Magpie always says to do, I barrel for his legs, ramming him with my shoulder. He's knocked sideways at the impact. His hand seizes my neck and hauls me against his chest. Something sharp pricks my throat.

Something just as sharp strokes my cheek, and by looking down I see it's a curved animal claw, sprouting from the bed of his thumbnail as though it'd been there all along.

All logic takes a vacation. I make a strange, ululating sound in my throat, like the bleating of a lamb.

Vince laughs, running an obscene red tongue over a mouth overflowing with jagged fangs. He looks at me like he's a starving man, and dinner has just been served.

Was this the last thing Navier saw, too?

Vince adjusts his grip around my chest, which kicks me into action. He's much stronger than I am. If his grip solidifies, I'm sunk.

I thrash and flail and, when his hold slips, bash my forehead against his cheek. I hear the pop and grind of a displaced jawbone. His grunt is pained.

"You wretch!" He curses, shaking me.

I spit my mouthful of blood directly into the glowing target of his eye. He *screams*; a throaty, fractured yowl that makes every bone in my body rattle. Though his claws — claws! *Ten* of them! — plunge into my shoulders, once my feet are centered beneath me, I have enough leverage to twist away like I'm fighting free of a thorny bush.

Instinct drives me towards the door, but I see how it's bolted. It will take precious seconds to open, and then what? Do I expect him to let me go if I make it that far, as though once I'm in the hallway, I'm safe? Fat fucking chance. If I don't end this fast, I *will* die.

For the first time in my life, I want to live.

When I turn on Vince and shove his back, he stumbles and nearly takes a knee. Not to be outdone, he catches me shallowly across the chest with his claws.

I shove him again, then grab his arm and whirl, using forward momentum to propel him closer to the window. He doesn't catch on until we're nearly there. I see the moment realization and fury dawn in his unnatural eyes.

"I'm impressed," he hisses, swiping at me. I bite back a moan when his claws pierce my hip, shredding my jeans. I kick his shin, driving him another step as he struggles to stay standing. "I didn't think you had the balls."

I don't know about that, but I have a cousin who needs saving, so I fight to drive him further. We're so tangled that when my high-tops skid on broken glass and I take a spill, so does Vince.

He attempts to climb me, so I rabbit-kick as hard as I'm able, pummeling him relentlessly in every soft place with my heels. His clawed hands, shredded by the glass in the carpet, slick and skid for bloody purchase. When I work my knees against his stomach and buck, he's finally thrown to the window's edge. Another kick and he's tumbling over, claws sinking deep into the meat of my calf.

Like a hooked trout, I'm dragged with him, mutilating my hands on the windowsill as I slide.

For a moment, I am airborne. I feel no pain anywhere; only a weightlessness as I snatch for the curtains.

Perhaps it's my years of surfing that allow me now to surf the air, arcing my body, hands scraping brick. I hear Vince's panicked babbling as though from very far away — "baby; baby, *please!*" — but drive my heel into his face anyway, feeling his nose give way.

Gravity takes care of the rest.

I don't hear Vince hit the alley below. The sound of my own body slamming the side of the hotel drowns him out. There I hang; a hand in the curtains and the other on the windowsill, dangling thirteen stories above the ground with shoulders fit to break. Surely the impact wrenched *something* out of socket.

I sway in the breeze and hear the curtain-rod creak. If I wasn't fit to do a pullup before, I'm surely not *now,* exhausted and bleeding as I am. It's utterly impossible.

I do it anyway.

It's my burn sleeve that saves me — that, and my damaged hand's tendency to lock up. Though my mangled palm is slippery, the stretchy fabric provides enough grip for me to, inch by aching inch, hup my body through the windowsill. Once my chest is on the carpet, it's easy to worm my hips over.

Then I roll, shaking until my teeth clack, unable to release my death-grip on the curtains until the rod gives way and they, too, fall.

I can't bring myself to peer over the edge and look for Vince on the ground; to see if anybody's noticed what happened. If they have, if police come, there's nothing I can do.

"Come on," I cheer myself once my jaw unlocks. *"Come* on, Tip."

I first tackle the challenge of standing, retching as I roll to my hands and knees, jeans protecting me from the worst of the glass. "For Magpie," I add, and use the bed to heave myself into a kneeling position.

I stand bent, forearms braced on the coverlet. The adrenaline high will break soon. Between the pain and terror and exhaustion, who knows if I'll be able to move at all?

I force my protesting bag of bones into the bathroom and under the cold shower spray. Glass tinkles from my hair to puddle in the pink water that spills down the drain. When I shed my clothes, I see that I'm covered in more scratches and cuts than I've ever seen in my life. I look like that nightmare I'd once had, hacking myself to pieces on Tessa's blade.

From the place Vince's thumb penetrated my calf now protrudes the stumpy base of a broken claw, curved and black, half as long as my index finger.

Unfortunately, my ability to feel pain has come back online. I muffle a scream when I pull it out, a thin jet of blood spurting with it.

My hip could use some stitches — I don't like the way the flesh hangs in open strips like that — but my hands are the worst off. The fingers won't move properly, no matter how hard I flex. I pluck out all the glass I can, but see many miniscule shards glittering in the raw meat; the hint of bone.

When I emerge, naked and dripping, and limp to Vince's luggage, I hit the jackpot. He's got basic medical equipment (gauze and surgical tape) to sop up most of my blood; clothes (unwashed and oversized, but whatever); and makeup.

My heart sighs longingly when I unearth the duffle bag that's haunted my dreams for decades: a transportable candy-shop of wonders.

I know I shouldn't do it, but when I reach inside and unearth a rattling bottle of oxy, well, who can blame me? One pill for now to numb the pain, and one for later, when the too-brief high wears off.

I'd take more, but dying after fighting so hard to live would really cramp my style.

Nothing quite pushes the human body past all reasonable levels of endurance than the abuse of surgical-strength prescription drugs.

I feel no guilt in taking his cash, either: a fat stack of bills that will hopefully ease my journey. There are other things inside the duffle. Though not my drugs of choice, the energy from uppers is tempting right now.

Then there are the tiny bags of dirt-colored powder that my veins remember all too fondly. They whisper, singing their siren song — *who will know, Tip? Nobody; that's who!* — but I zip the bag shut and leave it behind.

Junkie or not, Magpie comes first. I can't find her if I'm too far gone to care whether I'm bleeding out.

Once again, it's Dorothy who helps clear my head. Looking her way, I see that there's two bullet holes in the sides of her tank: an entry and an exit. Did Vince's shot ricochet before hitting the window?

She's half-slithered her chunky body through the exit hole. At my gaze, she stops, looking almost comically guilty.

I approach to poke her coils back inside, then do my best to shove the tank against the bed to block it up. If the hotel staff see a large snake on the loose, they might call animal control to kill her. She doesn't deserve that.

I contemplate wrangling the tank onto a dolly and taking her with me, but to do so, I'd have to unplug her lightbulb and heating pad. It's a long drive to Arizona. Without special equipment, I don't think she'd survive the trip. It's kinder to leave her and let the police call a specialist to handle her re-homing.

I dress and steal the keys to Vince's rental car, choosing a neon orange, wide-armed tank top worn beneath an open Hawaiian shirt. The sleeves are long enough to cover the worst of my injuries. Hopefully, I look like I'm leaving a party instead of escaping a crime scene.

A smear of sky-blue lipstick completes the illusion. That's a trick I learned from Gran: no matter how messy one feels, just taking that one extra step makes everything look deliberate and in control.

Peeking at the mess I left in the bathroom, I stop only to grab that claw from atop the toilet tank. I study it for a moment through the sparkly haze of oxy.

Already my logical mind hunts for explanations of what happened, though I might have to sober up before it makes any sense. I pocket the claw for now; out of sight and out of mind.

You're in shock, Tippy-Canoe, my inner Magpie helpfully explains.

I nod. I already knew that. Good to hear her voice, though.

I leave the room and limp along the empty hallway, past the orchids, to the huge glass elevator. As when Vince and I had arrived, there's not a soul to be found. No employees. No guests. Only silence. Perhaps killing Vince also killed the world, and I'm the last creature remaining.

I don't feel any better after leaving the building, stumbling around dazedly until I finally find where Vince parked his BMW; more by clicking the keys' 'lock' button until I hear it honk than through any actual recollection.

I adjust the seat and mirrors, then back it out of its parking space. I haven't driven stick since Gran's car bit the dust, and my focus is shot to shit. I nearly stall the engine twice before I reach an automated tollbooth.

Had there even *been* a tollbooth when Vince first pulled up? I guess I'm glad I stole some of the cash I found in his duffle. I feed smooth bills into the hungry machine until the little stripey arm lifts, freeing me.

Both of my ears actually pop when I drive through the toll and hit an actual road, like I'd just come through a sci-fi pocket dimension. Never have I ever been so glad to see something so mundane as late-night traffic before. So there *are* still people left in the world.

Perhaps it's the shock on top of being mildly high, but when I try to glance in the rearview mirror at the hotel, I skip the curb and smash loudly into a lamppost.

It's not enough to activate the airbags, but it jolts me, and the squeal of metal on cement on *more* metal is horrible. My already battered chest throbs where the seatbelt snagged it.

Before I can curse, or at least acknowledge to myself that yes, *that really just happened,* my cell phone rings.

"Fuck!" I yelp, and hit the four-way flashers when traffic behind me swerves and rubbernecks, honking. The last thing I need is some cop coming to check me out in this sorry state.

My phone rings again. I unbuckle myself and nearly dislocate my shoulder fishing around back for it.

Once it's in my hand, I crawl from the car and wince at the smoky damage — oh, there's no fixing *that* mess — before skittering off to the suburbia beyond said lamp post.

Well, limping, actually. *Fast* limping.

When I see who's calling, all other worries flee my head. I accept the call, though my fucked up hands can scarcely hold the phone. "Mags?!"

"Not quite." Cero's tone is cool. "I'm glad you picked up. Magpie wished to say goodbye to you before it's time for her to go. This is my honoring her final wish."

Christ on a cracker; it's one thing after another! "Where are you?!" I demand.

"Sky Harbor airport," she replies smoothly. "My wife and I are bound for Moscow. Tip, I need to know right now: are you mine, or not?"

I'm inclined to say yes, if only to keep her on my good side, but if the last hour has taught me anything, it's to not make promises I can't keep with scarily powerful, possibly inhuman beings.

"No," I say firmly, and am surprised to hear that I mean it. "I'm mine and mine alone from here on out. Why are you going to Moscow?"

There's a pause. Even as I creep through a ritzy Hollywood neighborhood, I can hear chatter from hundreds of airport travelers on her end of the line. She's actually serious!

"That really is a shame. If you'd agreed, perhaps you'd have been able to find a new body for my wife's soul to inhabit. As it is, we'll both have to make peace with her loss. Goodbye, Tip."

"Don't hang up!" I plead, but it's too late; she's gone. When I hit redial, I get only Magpie's voicemail.

Hell, hell; what can I *do*?! The few cars parked along the street of this fancy-ass neighborhood are all modern vehicles. I couldn't hot-wire them even if I had the proper tools, and they're probably protected by alarms.

The houses are all massive, gated mansions. Breaking and entering is out of the question. I can't reach an airport in Arizona in time to stop a flight by *bus*, can I?

I could call the airport and fake a bomb threat, I guess. Shut the whole place down. That's so deeply illegal that even I, having just committed multiple felonies, balk at the thought.

But if it's for *Magpie*...

Fine. I'll do it. But then I need a backup plan. Stalling the flight isn't enough — I need to capture my cousin's body. I don't give a shit if Cero *is* a gangster ghost snuffing the life out of her; there must be a way to fix this. I refuse to believe otherwise.

Who can I use to battle a ghost? What modern-day army do I have to corral an entity that would defy death itself? Think, foggy brain; think! I need knights. I need warriors. I need—

One Google search later and I've got the number. My thumb slams the call button. It's close to four in the morning, when California bars are required to close, so I can only cross my fingers and hope; *pray*...

Too many rings later, an accented voice comes on the line. "Buenas Ruedas on Fourth; Rosa speaking. How can I help you?"

"Rosa," I gasp, my heart thundering in impossible relief. "This is Tip — Magpie's cousin. Listen: I need every biker you can contact at Sky Harbor airport *immediately*, if not sooner."

Chapter Thirty-two – Magpie

...

I resurface in fragments, catching snippets of the world through underwater blurs.

We're in a... Lobby? A place with evenly-spaced black leather seats and generic carpeting. Strangers of all sizes and ages and ethnicities mill around, talking; reading; waiting. None pay us a lick of attention.

My broken arm is held stable in a cast and sling.

Where are we? I try to ask, and instantly feel Cero surrounding me from every angle, shushing and petting. She soothes me, rocks me, suggests I return to my rest.

I don't want to sleep. I want to know what's going on!

Cero tries to keep our gaze focused down on her — my! — lap, but I catch peripheral glimpses all the same. Luggage. A gift shop. Large windows and, just outside them—

Airplanes! We're in an airport. Why are we...?

As though to answer my question, a pleasant male voice sounds over a nearby speaker: "Flight 741 for Charlotte, North Carolina, will now begin boarding. Passengers should—"

Charlotte? Why *Charlotte?* Charlotte is a hub, positively massive, with flights taking passengers all around the world. Why would that be a desirable destination?

Maybe my wife doesn't intend to share her plan, but we are so entwined now that I hear its echo all the same. **Mother.**

This is the part where I panic.

You can't take me to Moscow! I don't consent to this! This is kidnapping! Cero, you can't do this to me!

She shoves more firmly now, holding me below the murky surface of our shared consciousness. Thrash as I might, she is Everywhere.

My last conscious thought, bitter as any acid, is this: *I thought you loved me.*

...

Flashing lights, red and blue. A siren that does not end.
Police.
Shouting.

Cero is swearing. We are on our knees, police hands on our back, more hands in our pockets, searching, digging... What for? What is — *why...?*

Nothing.

...

Outside air now. Surrounded, headlights circling us, they trap us we've run so far. These are bikers, though not all the same gang — I see different colors different chapters different patches on leather on denim on vests. United with a purpose, and that purpose is us: my wife and I.

Fury and rage, hers and mine. There's no difference anymore. I am we; I am her; I am nothing. I am swallowed whole, a tiny mouse scrabbling inside the fiery stomach of a dragon.

We look for somewhere to run; try to think of slippery words for sneaking and controlling. We hope for weapons but of course, this is an airport. We couldn't have *weapons*—

A biker grabs Cero's arm my arm our broken arm and she we I scream and scream and scream and—

Nothing, again.

...

My head rests on something soft. A hand strokes my hair. I open my eyes to see Ricket's face, focused on a distant point.

There is a sickly sloshing all around me. *Inside* me, too. It's as though we're bobbing in a snow globe full of stars.

My ankles are bound. I cannot move them. My throat burns with salt, as though I've been drinking seawater. I try to speak, but can only rasp.

Ricket looks down at me, his glasses glinting in the lamplight. A boat — we are on a boat, and the moon is high and full. "Magpie? Is that you?"

I am here! I love you!

"What?! No way." I hear the pounding of feet over wood as Tip races across the deck. I struggle to sit up, to look at my cousin, but Ricket pins me down.

Both men are scruffy and sunburnt and unkempt, eyes ringed with deep circles of exhaustion, sporting days upon days of beard growth.

"Look at her eyes," says Ricket.

Tip bends over the bench where we sit, twisting my face this way and that to examine me. His hands are dry and chapped. His cheek shows a fading, greenish bruise.

"It's a trick," Tip says, voice cold with disgust. "Put her under before she tries to jump ship again."

I try to say no, that I'm *here,* that I'm their Magpie, but Tip traps my face between his bandaged palms and Ricket brings something that looks like an oxygen mask down over my mouth.

Cold, canned air fills my lungs, sweet and artificial as diet soda. The more I inhale, the heavier I feel. Down, down, *down* I sink...

•••

I wake kneeling in a dry bathtub. I am not alone.

"Hey," says Cero, her low voice bouncing off the tiled floor.

I look around. She allows it; grants me motion of our head. *My* head.

We're in a perfectly ordinary bathroom, as far as I can tell. There's the shower we're currently trapped inside, our good arm handcuffed to the tap of the tub. My wrist shows raw places, bruises, as though I've been fighting the cuff.

There's a toilet with a fuzzy pink cover to match the rug and shower curtain and towels. A painting of three pink doves on the wall. A standing sink containing makeup and toiletries. On the ceiling, a single strand from a long-abandoned spiderweb dangles.

I'm still wearing the crusty, dirty clothes I'd traveled to Strawberry in. That's good. I don't think I'd've been cool with Ricket or Tip stripping my unconscious body.

When I sway my hip into the side of the tub, I don't hear the expected clack of metal on porcelain. My ring-necklace is no longer in my pocket.

What are we doing in here? I ask, wondering if soon I'll wake someplace completely new.

"Oh, nothing." Even if Cero and I weren't sharing a consciousness, I would've still heard the clipped rage in her light tone. "I've just been trapped in here, listening to my so-called *friend* torture my mother for two days straight. You haven't missed much."

That one takes a while to process. *Wait; we're in Moscow after all?*

"Sure are, Miss Cop. Sorry you had to miss the journey. Boats, trains, a goddamned *helicopter*... If Ricket put in *half* the effort for me that he does for you, we'd rule the world by now."

I'm thirsty.

I scarcely think it before Cero uses my shoulder to nudge the spout of the tub, allowing a thin trickle of water to flow. Feeling foolish, I sip until I've had my fill. Then Cero shuts the tap off again.

Is this how we've been living?

"Your cousin feeds us through a straw. Unlocks us to use the toilet, like we're a stinking pet who can't piss without permission."

From the other side of the bathroom door, I hear a feminine whimper. I stiffen at the sound, but it doesn't come again.

Sick realization spores in my gut. *You weren't exaggerating about Ricket torturing Nina, were you? He's really...*

"He sure is. Knives, pliers, fire... Just be thankful I let you sleep through it."

Oh, God.

What does he want from her?

"What do you *think*, genius? To know how to pull me out of you. Which I've told him he'll never learn from *her*, but I guess stubbornness trumps logic."

Nina doesn't know?

It's a callus thing to ask. I *should* be appalled that my best friend is hurting an old woman for my benefit. Have I always been so cold, to feel indifferent to her plight?

"No, she doesn't *know*. Of course not. I had to coach her through every step of tethering me to you, and it still scarcely worked."

Cero's thoughts are whirling; so snarled it's hard to grasp hold of any one of them. I always knew she was brilliant, but her mind works such leagues beyond my own that keeping up is nigh impossible.

You didn't mean *to give me your cancer,* I realize. *You... Didn't want me to die?*

No, that's not quite it, either.

You wanted to bring me back, like you brought Navier back?

"Not exactly." She tries to push our hair behind one ear; a habitual movement we can't accomplish with our hands bound. "I had to wait for him to die before I captured his soul in Charon's coin. *Then* I sewed it into the wound that killed him. It bound his soul to his corpse. *You,* however, don't *need* to die. Ever."

I don't, huh?

"No! See, once I transfer your soul into an object, I'll be able to sew it into the corpse of your choosing. A new one every day, if you like! A blonde for Monday, a redhead for Friday... I'll keep living in *this* body until you're skilled enough to transfer me into a healthier one. We'll be together again."

Her words tumble from our mouth. I feel her excitement make our heart pound. She's tripping over herself, eager as a kindergartner on the first day of school, determined to show the teacher how smart she is.

This is what Cero got like whenever she didn't have to put up an aloof air of competent mystery. The Cero in love with the world and all its mysteries. This is her life's work, and she's beyond ecstatic to share it with me.

But...

But this is my *body.*

"Oh, don't start that again. Weren't *you* the one to say a body is nothing more than meat animated by electricity? Since when are you the sentimental type?"

She's not wrong. I've always felt adrift from the things that supposedly make up my identity. I'm Indian with no link to my culture. My family are all different blood from me. My gender, my height; do I actually care about *any* of it?

Your cancer came with you, I think, and she sighs regretfully.

"Yeah... There's always something, huh? I'm not looking forward to more chemo, but it's better than being dead. Why didn't you listen to me and get help sooner?!"

She's missing my point. Who's to say the cancer won't come back to haunt the next body, once she's thrown mine aside? And the next, and the next? There's no guarantee it won't follow her for the rest of time.

I can tell she doesn't like this by the rush of heat through our chest. By the way her voice changes again.

"Magpie, you're my *wife*. I never meant to kill you; I only wanted to borrow your strength. The plan, from the beginning, was to bring myself back; *then* you."

I startle us both by replying aloud: "Then why didn't you just *ask* me, first? Don't you think I would have done *anything* to help you? Didn't you trust me at all?"

My eyes are wet, and between my sling and the cuffs, I have no hand to wipe them dry.

We seem to have swapped control of my vocal cords. Her reply is internal: *I trust you more than most. But this was work I had to do myself.*

Nope. Not good enough. "You don't get to make decisions for my body without asking me. Sorry, Cero, but you screwed up."

I'm mad. I'm *furious.* And I have every right to be.

"And I know you don't care, and I was probably just a means to an end for you, but we're so not cool. One way or another, I *will* rip you out of me, even if it kills us both."

It will.

She's so coldly certain. Affronted that I won't do what I'm meant to do, what I *always* do, and blindly follow her schemes.

"You took my choice away from me! How could you expect *me* to accept that?!"

Because we're connected, she knows what I'm thinking: Vince had also silenced my right to say no. What Vince did to me was rape. Now Cero is taking away my right to live, and what that is, is murder.

You would compare me to that *bottom-feeder? His kind are sense-less chaos. Us witches have a vision. We* have *no natural magic*

*giftwrapped to us by birth — everything we achieve is through hard
work and study.*

Wait, what? She may as well be speaking Greek. "All I know is,
you're both selfish thieves."

*What about my right to live, then? My choice? That was stolen
from me — by a father who sold me; by the people who bought me; by
the cancer that killed me.*

I wish I had all the answers. I wish I could have taken her cancer
away. Hell — I wish I could have turned back space and time to prevent her from ever being sold. I am nothing but a cavern of wishes,
and all of it hurts, and none of it is fair.

But there's a difference between life indifferently screwing you
over, and your loved ones *deliberately* using you. One is inevitable.
One is a choice. Considering what her father did, she must know
the difference.

From outside, footsteps approach. The bathroom door slams
open. Tip, a bloody silver knife in hand, looms over me.

"Alright, bitch," he sneers, and strides towards me in a way that
brings Vince to mind.

I flinch. "Tip..."

He stalls, eyes widening, then narrowing again. "Don't use her
voice, Cero; I fucking *hate* that shit."

Inside me, Cero shifts. She's probably used all sorts of tricks to
manipulate Ricket and my cousin. No wonder he's so hostile.

"It's really me, Q-Tip," I promise. "I don't know how to prove
it."

He's wearing latex gloves over bandaged hands. His clothes are
as bloody as the knife. His hair is unkempt; longer than last I saw
it.

In the harsh bathroom lighting, he looks like a gaunt specter
from a bad horror movie.

He sits on the side of the tub, taking my jaw in hand. He tilts my face back and studies my eyes, trying to find my wife in them.

It must be weird, spending an indeterminate amount of time with your deceased in-law using your cousin's body as a meat-puppet.

"Your eyes look normal," he admits, and lets me go. "But I don't trust it. Sorry, Mags, if that *is* you."

I can't fault him for that. I wouldn't trust me, either. "Could you at least put something soft in the tub? My knees are killing me."

He frowns, trying to find the trick in my request, then relents. He pulls a towel off the bar. I shift back as far as my cuffs will allow, and he lays it on the porcelain bottom.

When I put my weight on it, it's an instant relief. "Thank you."

He touches the back of my neck, fingers carding my hair. I lean my head against his leg, thinking, *I love you. I love you always.*

Then I see the glint of his knife through my eyelashes.

"Tip!" I pull away. I am *very* much not a fan of knives near my face. The scar down my cheek tightens in a phantom pain.

But he only lifts a lock of my hair and twists it around his finger, holding it taut. He hacks at it with his blade, and I'm too startled to protest.

After everything that's happened to me, this feels like the least of my worries. Tip wants a chunk of my hair? Fine, I guess. Whatever his reasons may be, I have to trust him.

"I need it," he explains as he cuts. "Antonina said."

In my head, Cero swears foully.

"That pissed Cero off," I tell Tip. "You must be onto something."

It's weird to narc on my wife, but if the choice is to side with Tip, or to side with someone guilty of grand theft body, I'll take the junkie any day. "She's mad, but she isn't saying why."

"She talks to you?" Tip cocks his head, and a hysterical giggle bursts from my throat, echoing off the tile walls. He draws back in alarm.

"Sorry," I tell him, shaking my head. "It's just, she's *been* talking to me for *weeks*. Nonstop. I was afraid I was going crazy, but I guess I'm just possessed! I don't know whether to be relieved or disappointed."

Tip studies me like I'm a sample of water beneath a microscope, and turning the dials just right will show him what I contain. "You didn't tell me that."

"Yeah, *that* would've gone over great. 'Hey, dude, how was work? By the way, my dead wife told me I should kill all my friends because they abandoned our gang!' You'd've booked me a one-way ticket to the loony bin."

His frown deepens. He studies the knife, the hank of my hair, in his hand.

"I need to take these to James," he declares. "I might need to come back for some of your blood."

I nod, though the thought of Tip using a knife on my skin is less than pleasant. Hopefully he washes it first.

"Are you really torturing Nina?" I ask, when he makes for the door. All that blood on his clothes; his knife...

My stomach churns.

Tip meets my gaze, chin high, eyes cold. "There is nothing I wouldn't do for you," he says, and shuts the door between us.

Chapter Thirty-three – Tip

too bad nobody brought marshmallows.

...

My boyfriend sold my cousin to human traffickers.

The ghost possessing her, a victim of trafficking herself, took control of said cousin's body and used it to slaughter every single one of her would-be kidnappers. Then she freed all of their under-age hostages.

The bloodbath and subsequent emancipation *flooded* Reddit with conspiracy theories. It keeps hitting international news sites as the world tries to piece together what *really* happened in Strawberry, Arizona.

Magpie is now more (in)famous than I ever was, and she can't even remember why.

While all that was going down, I went and killed the man who'd sold her.

The fact that he transformed into a fanged, clawed beast and attacked me in an empty hotel that (according to Google) does not exist is still a question mark in my head. I do not have the mental capacity to think about that right now.

If I want Magpie to live as a free woman, I need to rip Cero away from her once and for all.

Cero was — is? — a professional crook. She would've known to hide Magpie's identity in the Strawberry incident. It would be a priority for her, seeing as her goal is to take over Magpie's body and live anew inside of it. Prison would be far too restrictive for her needs.

There's just two little snafus in her schemes. One: Mags is a fighter to the end. And two: the cancer.

I don't think Cero meant to carry her cause of death into the space between, let alone to inject it into her host's healthy body. As

Gran used to quote, "the best-laid plans of mice and men often go awry."

Once upon a time, an apartment like Nina's would have been shared with multiple families. Nina wouldn't have had her own bathroom for us to store Magpie in. Surely her neighbors would've noticed our criminal activity and intervened.

However, as time and housing laws were passed, *khrushchyovka* (tenement-style living) became more and more regulated, ending with many such buildings demolished as fire hazards.

I guess Nina clung stubbornly, illegally, to this one. The other residents are long gone. Now there's nobody to hear her scream.

Go ahead. Call me a monster. I won't argue.

Walking through Nina's tiny home with a fistful of Magpie's hair, I quickly glance around. Aside from evidence of our breaking-and-entering, the place is unremarkable. Sparse. Bare walls. Furniture worn. Wallpaper faded.

The most unusual piece of furniture is a shrine, Japanese in style, to Cero and her deceased father. The whole display is set opposite a rocking chair, as though Nina likes to sit and watch the candles burn in her spare time.

The framed photograph of a solemn-faced baby in its father's arms feels obscene, considering what that man *did* to his daughter a scant few years after the picture was taken.

The photo takes center stage, smack between two tall, half-melted candles, and two urns. I ignore the brown one and instead reach for the red clay urn.

Human remains reduce to about five pounds of gritty ashes, but when I lift Cero's urn, I suspect it's even less than that. I give it a shake, listening to the shifting inside. I'm certain it's emptier than it was when I mailed it to Nina, not long after Cero's funeral.

Makes sense. The stuff is a prime ingredient in tethering Cero's soul to earth.

James and I have gotten a lot of info out of Nina. Most old ladies don't spend their days playing with dead things. Once she's gone, the city won't have to worry about their pets going missing anymore. Or their small children.

I'm not one for witch burning, and I certainly have no room to judge anyone's crimes. That is, until said crimes destroy my cousin's life. She may play the Ingénue, but Nina knew exactly what she was doing. That's something I cannot forgive.

I enter Nina's bedroom, which matches the rest of the place in how worn and homely it is. She's got a table before the window, stacked high with jeweler's things. Lockboxes of valuable stones. Plastic drawers of wires and tools.

It's cluttered, also, with bird skulls and cat vertebra and one human mandible, small and freaky enough to belong to a prepubescent child. All the adult teeth are crammed just beneath the baby ones, ready to burst free.

It's this casual mix of mundane and macabre that reminds me the most of Cero. Like pedicidal mother, like necromantic daughter.

James is slumped in the desk chair with his bad leg stretched before him, elbows on his thighs. His fingers are caked in the unpleasant, pulpy paste of chalk and blood he'd drawn rings on the carpet with.

He's haggard from travel, nights of sleeping on the floor, and days of eating nothing but convenience-store foods. I probably look just as bad, if not worse.

The air is thick with the stink of drying copper. Huddled on the bed is a shaking ball of octogenarian. The quilt she's wrapped in started out pale blue in color. It's now a deep violet shade from her various bodily fluids.

"Are you certain this is correct?" James asks.

From his laptop, sat on the desk, comes a considering voice. "It *looks* right... I've never done this before, so don't quote me on that. Move me so I can see better."

"Hi, Rosa," I greet, closing the door behind myself, kicking one of Antonina's severed fingers aside. "I got the hair."

"Nice."

I lift the laptop and, careful not to direct the webcam towards any carnage (if we get caught, I'd prefer Rosa have plausible deniability), sink to the floor. She can supervise my work.

James's sigil features two overlapping rings, like a Venn diagram. One is the size of a steering wheel. The other is somewhat smaller. Surrounding the rings is ancient Sumerian cuneiform; squiggles and loops and lines written in Nina's blood.

Roughly translated, it reads *Asarualim, grant us a remedy for this error.*

The "error" in question comes in the form of Cero's photograph, pilfered from Antonina's things. I set it down between the hoops.

Cero is a cheerless little girl in the picture, wearing a starched white dress and squinting from the flash of the camera. Said flash makes her blue eye appear red, while the brown one reflects the photographer's hand.

It's not the best photo, but it's the only one we could find of Cero by herself. Rosa rejected the others, featuring family or friends, from fear of muddying the water.

The water is plenty muddy enough. None of us have a clue what we're doing.

I give the urn to James, who opens it. Did I mention my hands don't work? My hands don't fucking work. I'm praying it's just the stitches making things so stiff, but the muscle and nerve damage is severe.

Stretching my shirt over my knees to catch any spillage, I cup my gloved hands and let James pour the urn out into them, trying not to breathe in the dust. I scatter Cero's ashes inside the sigil, half-burying her photograph.

It's not perfect, but Rosa assured us it doesn't need to be. I cover as much of the area as possible, like filling in a coloring book. The pale granules match the dingy carpet.

"Good," Rosa approves. She's at mine and Magpie's apartment, seated at our kitchen table with a dozen occult tomes spread around her. At her side sits loyal Zelda. "Do you have the rings?"

From his pocket, James draws the necklace bearing Magpie and Cero's wedding rings, welded inseparably together by Nina's hand.

"It's hard to read in places, but this here—" he holds the jewelry out to me, but my eyes aren't sharp enough to see such tiny etchings, especially without my glasses "—*repels* Asarualim."

"Yeah?"

"If I'm interpreting this correctly, Cero designed it to muddle Magpie's senses. She *wanted* her to remain ignorant, confused. Compliant."

The lump on the bed gives a wet, hacking cough. A hot knife to the diaphragm will do that to a person.

I mute the call and reach up to give Nina's shoulder a push. My hand comes away red. "You awake? You took a long nap."

She doesn't look at me. She probably doesn't have the energy. "I am not *sleeping,* half-breed merrow bastard. I am *dying.*"

I take her vitriol in stride. "Will destroying these rings break the connection between Mags and your brat?"

She doesn't answer. She probably figures there's nothing more we can do to her; that we're fresh out of threats. Oh, how wrong she is...

I look to James.

He nods, takes up my knife, and stands to face the old woman.

I close the laptop, waiting for a break in her screams to repeat my question.

•••

The melting point of silver is 1,763°F. A well-tended campfire will, in time, reach about 2,012°F.

Considering we're doing this inside a tiny Moscow tenement without so much as a fireplace, we'll be lucky if we don't burn the place down.

My arm itches at the thought. I lost any love for fire after the Jaguar's explosion.

First, I hold the ends of Magpie's stolen hair to a lighter. It catches quickly, shedding curls of ash on my wrist. I hold the flaming bundle and trail its acrid smoke as I circle the room's perimeter.

"This isn't *smudging*," James mutters sourly. "Non-Natives can't smudge. *I* can't even smudge. Do I look like a shaman?"

Okay, so it isn't smudging. As far as I can tell, it isn't *anything* but a way to make the room reek of burning hair. Great idea, Rosa; thanks.

"You know what Vince did to Crown, right?" I ask. "Stabbing him, and all."

James adopts his 'professor' voice. "Crown was stabbed multiple times and left in the trunk of a burning car."

"Not just any car," I correct. *"Cero's* car. Remember her zippy little Jaguar? Magpie inherited it."

He just nods, so I finish my circle and crouch before the sigil. I press the burning hair to the center of Cero's ash-buried photograph, which ripples outward from the point of impact. It's gone in a blazing-blue second.

I drop the hair and cover it with the lid from a cooking pot. The stench goes from awful to unbearable once the ashy carpet starts to melt.

"Vince got to Magpie first," James recalls. "He cut her face and stole her car and left her to bleed out. She called me, so I came to her."

At my feet is a stack of Cero's notes, sketchbooks, art. I start ripping through dress designs and battle plans and feed them to the fire, erasing her from the world one idea at a time.

The flame inside builds, fanned by the movement of the lid. The tenement's disabled smoke alarms lie around me like dead beetles.

"I didn't know that," I admit. Why hadn't she called *me?* "Vince took Crown and drove him to me. He wanted to prove he'd *always* have the upper hand, before making his getaway."

"But you saved Crown," he points out. He's looking at my arm, warped and ugly and disfigured in the light of dancing flames.

The rising heat makes him look distorted, like I'm seeing him in a reflection of water. Fire is a greedy thing, and it hates being contained.

"I did, barely. Vince skipped town. Paramedics asked Crown who'd hurt him, and he said it was me."

James frowns, watching me closely. The lid has grown too hot to touch, so I quickly flip it over and scoot back, making sure the fire extinguisher, the buckets of sand and water, are at the ready.

"Why did he say that?"

"Because it's true, isn't it? It's my fault. I brought Vince into our lives. I put him first, again and again, despite every warning sign. Don't you know, there's nobody an addict won't betray?"

James doesn't seem satisfied with the answer. He keeps looking at me, like he thinks — like he *knows* — there's more to the story.

Then the cooking lid collapses, crunching in on itself like a beer can in a teenager's fist.

We're scientists. When unexpected things happen, we *watch*.

Crumpled balls of burning paper skitter out, rolling across our sigil. When fire hits ash, the whole thing springs to life; dual rings of leaping flames shooting high into the air. It's a good thing James is there to haul me back before I singe some eyelashes.

He stares at me, dark eyes wide behind his glasses. The light has cast an odd shadow over my body, ctenoid like the armored pattern of fish scales. The same pattern does not extend to James; nor to the wall behind us.

James reaches for the extinguisher, but I shake my head. It's odd, isn't it, how none of the carpet is burning? Chalk and bone aren't flammable components. They're almost pure calcium. Why should *that* burn, when the fibrous carpet does not?

"Green," James mutters.

He's right; the fire *is* changing from standard colors to a uniform apple-green.

I wrack my brains for what compound might've caused that reaction. Antimony? Barium? Does Nina use an unusual carpet cleaner? Did Cero's crematorium have a less "natural" approach than its pamphlets bragged?

The flames coalesce into a recognizable shape. A human face. It's not a simple case of pareidolia. The woman made of fire twists and writhes, screaming silent agony into her hands.

She's five feet tall, naked, and solid enough to breathe. Other than being hairless, she's complete: toes on her feet, dimples on her hips, nipples on her breasts. There's even an indent where a navel should be. When she drops her hands, we see a button nose and cleft chin.

Cero steps over the sigil like she's climbing from a bath. On feet that leave sooty prints with every step, she approaches her mother's prone figure on the bed. Touches a palm to Nina's back.

Nina chokes a huge, rattling gasp, and bolts upright through her daughter's fiery form. As she burns, the reek of seared pork filling the room, the old woman speaks directly to us. "Beasts in men's skin. You've killed me, but my daughter will have our revenge."

She laughs, *shrieks* with mirth, even as her clothes catch fire. Her wispy gray hair is a crackling halo of color. She looks fierce; unhinged. She looks like an avenging angel.

When the fire-spirit takes her mother's face in hand, causing the skin there to blacken and split, I get the impression she's trying to do what she always does; trying to steal any crumb of life from her final tether to earth.

Antonina doesn't seem to feel any pain. She wraps her daughter in a tender embrace and closes her eyes, holding Cero with their foreheads touching. Over the snaps and sparks of flame, I hear her humming sweetly. It sounds like a lullaby.

The fire grows so hot that James and I are dripping with sweat. It evaporates before it hits the floor, which crawls with smoke. My throat shrinks from the dry air, right alongside my stinging eyes.

In a sudden burst of energy, James lobs Magpie's necklace at them. It passes through Cero and lands against Nina's body. Hopefully, she's hot enough to melt it into a silvery lump.

The two-person inferno intensifies to a blinding degree. Surely a fire like this could crumble the building! I've seen animated videos of stars collapsing, and those don't hold a candle to these two.

James snatches my hand and hauls me down the hallway, just in time for Nina to fall. The old woman has been eaten down to blackened bones. Without her mother for fuel, the fire — Cero — will soon starve.

"They're getting dimmer," I marvel.

"Look at the sigil," James replies.

I do. It's gone black from soot, but stands out in stark relief to the otherwise untouched carpet. Cero's footprints are still visible, sparks standing out like fireflies where her toes pressed.

Cero herself is nowhere to be seen.

Antonina is only a pile of embers; liquid magma that's already cooling.

Behind the bathroom door, I hear Magpie weep like her heart is breaking.

Chapter Thirty-four – Magpie

...

I've dreamt of Cero every night for the last week. We're slowly making our way back home. There's no reason that tonight, spent in a Parisian suite, should be any different.

There's a fish tank in this hotel's lobby, so big I could've comfortably used it for a coffin. As Ricket checks us in, I nudge Tip and nod to it. "Is that an eel?"

He looks at the tank, at the squiggly ribbon of sand-colored cartilage, and goes still. A minute passes as he stares, then two.

I give him another nudge. "You okay, Tippi Longstocking?"

He's fared surprisingly well after the trauma of the past few weeks. We all have. But sooner or later, it's going to catch up. I hope to be there when it strikes. I'll be whatever he needs me to be.

He looks at me. Tonight, his eyes are the most peculiar shade of green; the sort of green-at-night to make sailors take warning.

"There were fish at the hotel Vince took me to," he says slowly, ponderingly. Like there's something he almost understands, hovering just out of reach. "At Nimphidia. But they weren't *normal* fish. They were—"

Ricket turns to us, card-chip key in hand, and motions we follow him to the elevator.

I roll our luggage as I walk. We only have the one suitcase to share, filled with necessities purchased after leaving Nina's place.

Tip walks oddly. His compulsions are acting up again, likely due to all the stress that catapulted his entire routine into the toilet. Maybe he's counting his steps. Maybe he has to land his feet a specific way against the carpet pattern.

Whatever it is, rushing him would be cruel and unhelpful. We wait until he catches up.

"Remind me to call your parole officer again," Ricket tells him as we fill the elevator and ascend several floors. "I had a hard enough time validating your last-minute 'school trip.' He'd jump on any excuse to arrest you now."

Tip nods.

I flash Ricket a grateful smile. He's gone from "a good friend" to "my hero" in less than a month. The guy might as well be Superman.

When we leave the elevator, I deliberately bump against his cane-free side. I would've taken his hand, but my broken arm is immobilized by its cast and sling. He throws an arm around me, squeezing.

"I couldn't get a room with a view of the Eiffel tower," he apologizes, swiping his key card and ushering us into our room.

"We can see it tomorrow," I offer, though I'm not keen on the idea. Shiny buildings are alright, but they're not the *most* exciting things in the world. "Since we're supposed to take some tourist pictures, and all."

Our official cover story is that Professor Ricket took his star student on a lengthy, suspicious trip across Europe. Something about studying island corrosion in the Atlantic ocean.

Tip's nosy cousin — me — demanded to tag along with the secret lovers. Perhaps I'm a little too invested in Tip's personal life. Maybe I just want a free vacation.

Regardless of my motives, when I realize they're sleeping together, I throw a shit-fit. Tip and I have a knock-down, drag-out fight. By the time we're back in the states, we hate each other so much that Tip moves straight into his professor-boyfriend's house.

I'll have a crying meltdown all over our landlord, miserable that I can no longer afford the rent. I have to go and live with distant family in Texas. (We've already set up a P.O. box in Tyler for mail forwarding.)

Some touristy photos will lend credibility to our tale.

Reaching the AC/Heater unit below the window, Tip cranks off the uncomfortably chill air. France relies on AC less than the states do, but this is a hotel populated by wealthy American businessmen. It makes sense that the rooms have individual units.

"I was hoping we could do something else," Tip starts, glancing at Ricket. "If everyone's cool with it."

We keep deferring to Ricket on this "vacation," though it's not his money we're spending. It's Cero's, which is to say, it's mine. Under torture, Nina gave the boys information on several overseas accounts, each containing more zeros than my poverty-stricken ass knows how to cope with.

I don't know what's stranger: the fact that I'm now, technically, a millionaire... Or that my wife knowingly, unnecessarily left me to drown in poverty for years. Just one more slap in the face, I guess.

Ricket shucks his pants, pulls a chair from the desk, and eases himself into it. He stretches his legs and sets to unbuckling his brace.

I heave our suitcase onto one of the two beds and rifle inside for the essentials: pajamas and an overseas charging adapter.

European power outlets are different than American ones, designed for round prongs. Cero "lost" my phone shortly after calling Tip from the airport, so our only connection to the outside world is through Ricket's laptop.

First, I plug the PC in to charge. Next, I fight my clothes off over my cast, eager for the comfort of my new pajamas. After wrestling with my bra, I fling it halfway across the room.

Tip shoots me the one-finger salute, ducking the airborne fabric. "I was kinda thinking about the, um, Sciences et de l'Industrie?" He suggests, tripping on the foreign name. "I know it's dumb, but..."

Ricket arches a salt-and-pepper eyebrow, a smile gracing his thin lips. "Do you truly believe a biology professor would consider a science museum 'dumb'?"

Tip smiles back.

I decide I like the way he smiles at Ricket, even if it does give me a pang of loneliness. Wriggling into an oversized t-shirt, I ask, "What did you wanna see there?"

He climbs onto the free queen-sized bed and works to unlace his high-tops; a largely unsuccessful endeavor. We're still learning how bad — and how *permanent* — the damage to his hands is.

"There's a STEM educator who works in the oceanic wing," he informs us. "Timothée Bernard. He wrote a thesis on the carotenoid composition of marine red algae. It was *brilliant*. If I could get him to sign my copy..."

"Wait, wait." I hold my hand up to stop him. "You brought some nerd's thesis to a transatlantic *exorcism*? Do you just carry it with you all the time?"

Tip reddens, glowering. "No! Well, kind of. But, I mean—" From his pocket he draws his keyring, the dangling fob of which is a blue USB drive. "—I have the PDF. I could print the cover page, and *then...*"

It's terribly difficult not to laugh. "Never have I loved you, nor wished to push you into a locker, so very much."

His expression softens. His eyes meet mine, the intensity of his earlier green fading. Something about this makes my stomach flip.

Ricket pauses his unbuckling. "I know Timothée. I'll email him and say you want to meet."

You'd've thought he'd told Tip he was a unicorn. His jaw actually drops. "You *what?!*"

"I've run into him at a few academic conferences. He's very ambitious. Hungry for knowledge, and none too gentle in his pursuit of it. He reminds me a little of you, come to that."

Tip makes a sound like a chicken in a trash compactor.

I slip trying to pull my boxers up, stumble sideways onto the bed, and laugh. These two are the world's biggest dorks. Thank God they have each other. They know what they want, and exactly where to find it. Together, they're unstoppable.

I have nothing like that, not anymore. My gang, my heroic fight against child trafficking, is dead. Clay, Rhys, and Crown left me. Navier and Cero died. It's only me and Ricket left. If he says he's done, too…

Like poking a bruise, I scan my brain for Not-Cero, remembering too late that she's not there anymore. That she's not *anywhere* anymore. That I'm all alone.

Surging to my feet, I fix my boxers and tackle Tip, knocking him flat. His mattress springs squeal. A pillow hits the floor with a *fwump*.

Tip snarls, catching me by the neck. "What the *hell*, crazyass?!"

"Love me!" I demand, hiding pathetic vulnerability under ebullient force. *Please*, please *love me*. I chomp his shoulder, just shy of breaking skin.

My cousin swears, ineffectively swatting my back before his hand stills, resting between my shoulders. The irritation leaves him as quickly as it'd arrived.

I release my bite and rest my chin on a too-sharp collarbone, blowing a curl of his dark blond hair out of my eyes. After a moment, he begins to stroke my hair.

"It's weird that it's so short," he mumbles, holding up a lock. I'd had to cut it into a chin-length bob after Tip hacked off such a huge chunk.

"I like it," I lie, pleased he's humoring my affection. "It makes me look mature."

"You? Mature? Ha!"

I blow a wet raspberry into his ear canal, then lick his face. It's a good one; a single long, drippy swipe. Chin to mouth to nose to eyelid. Salty.

He yipes like a spanked hound and throws me off, packing surprising strength behind those twiggy little arms. He curses the way a machine gun fires.

I roll onto my back, grinning at the ceiling. So long as I'm still his annoying little cousin, things between us don't need to change. Don't need to get painful and confusing and weird.

Ricket, sans brace, clears his throat. When we look up at him, he waves a paper room-service menu. "What say you to ordering dinner? I'd murder for some coq au vin."

•••

I'm exhausted, physically and mentally. My belly is full, my blankets are soft, and Tip sleeps soundly with his spine against mine. There's no reason on earth I should still be awake.

I think I just need to grab a drink. I've been dry since leaving California, and it's been chewing on my brain for hours. Days, really.

Our room has a mini-bar. I'll help myself to a little something once Ricket falls asleep and quits looking at me with that mix of Knowing and Disappointment. Every time he does, I feel it boil in my guts. Guilt. Shame.

H sits propped on the other bed, glasses on the end of his nose, illuminated by the blue light from his laptop. He scrolls. Taps.

When he catches me watching, he smiles. "Am I bothering you?"

"No," I lie. "You're fine."

I tug the blanket up to Tip's neck, smoothing his hair behind his ear, and settle back into my pillows. Normally I'd be soothed by his presence, his breathing, but I find I'm growing more irritable by the second.

Ricket resumes typing, his fingers flying over the keys a billion-ty miles per second. *Clack clack clackclackclack...*

The glowy red letters on the digital alarm clock climb closer and closer to midnight.

Why the hell should I have to justify myself? Screw Ricket if he thinks he has any right to judge. Let he who is without sin cast the first motherfucking stone.

I swing my legs out of bed and stalk towards the mini-bar. Ricket's hand catches mine when I pass between our beds.

For a heated second, I feel the urge to clock him in the face. To shatter his glasses and crush his nose with a single swing of my cast.

The rage sets. The horror dawns.

"Oh," I breathe, and see him looking up at me; at my clenched fist.

He tugs my hand. "Come here, dear."

I do, climbing into his bed, shaky with remorse. He sets his laptop aside.

I press into his arms, face in his chest, feeling like there's a bubble at the back of my throat. My eyes sting. "I wouldn't *really* do it," I tell him, muffled.

"I know." He sounds more confident than I feel. His hand settles on the back of my neck. I feel the place my necklace is meant to be, now empty and cold.

That's when the tears come. For David. For Navier. For Rhys and Clay and Crown. For Cero.

For myself.

Ricket slides down and pulls me with him, reaching over my head to switch his bedside lamp off. "It's alright. You can let it out."

Still I fight the sobs as they violently tear from me, twisting my insides in their barbs. I am gasping, heaving, drowning. I am *breaking.*

It doesn't stop until I'm drained dry, my head throbbing, my breath tiny, hitching gasps. My entire face feels swollen. I'm sure by morning, Ricket's shirt will be stiff with snot.

When I finally manage to shut up, Ricket snugs his duvet over us. Stacks his chin on my head. "I'm going to tell you something personal now," he informs me.

I nod, waiting until I hear him set his glasses on the bedside table.

"I met Cero on the night of my first suicide attempt," he says, calm and matter-of-fact. "And I agreed to belong to her the day after my second."

I'm shocked into stillness. He carries on without pause.

"I have a loving family that accepts and supports me. I was closeted, yes, but I was zipping through Navy ranks. I was young and fit and healthy, and the world was my oyster. Yet still I was so miserable that I thought, constantly, of death. It was the song ever looping inside my head: *Die. Die. Die.*"

What is there to say to that?! I reach and take his face in hand, cupping his stubble-roughened cheek. He sighs and leans into me.

"What happened?" I whisper. All my crying has roughened my voice.

Ricket shrugs. "There was no single event that triggered it. Sadness simply clung to me; a tar that grew heavier each day. I thought, often, that I couldn't imagine going the rest of my life feeling this way. One day, I'd had enough. I boxed my belongings, left my keys and wallet, and took a little hike to the overpass above Route 401."

My stomach clenches. If I hear any more, I know I'm going to throw up. I can't carry the weight of his pain. I feel it crushing me already.

Perhaps I'm a terrible friend. Perhaps a stronger person would have heard him out.

Instead, I hug him so tightly that he stops speaking altogether. "Ricket," I cry, my voice warbling out of control. "Ricket, *Ricket...*"

As always, he understands. He knows me to the core.

He kisses the top of my head. "I didn't mean to upset you, dear. Less than three years later, I had a visitor, a stranger, to the mental institution my parents enrolled me in. My leg was destroyed, my Naval career was doomed, and I was addicted to pain medication."

"The visitor was Cero, wasn't it?" Tip asks, making us both jump. We hadn't realized he was awake. "Trust her to come when you were at your lowest."

"Yes," Ricket replies, looking towards Tip's bed, though we can't see each other in the darkness. "She was the one who found me a dealer; a discrete woman who worked for a nursing home. For a fee, she wrote me prescriptions that looked, to pharmacies, perfectly legal."

Cero, acting as the hookup, the plug for a drug addiction? It shouldn't surprise me. She would have *loved* to have someone like Ricket, a tactical genius with Naval connections, on her payroll.

Perhaps she'd heard about Tragic Hero Ricket in the news. Perhaps her witchy connections brought it to her awareness. She was quite the opportunist, my wife.

"She said she'd solve all your problems," Tip intones, voice flat and certain. "That you wouldn't have to think or feel anymore. That she'd do all the thinking for you, and all you had to do was follow her orders."

Ricket is quiet for a long time. He rubs the top of my head the same way he pets Hero when he's feeling unstable. I wonder if we should stop talking about this.

"She did," he admits. "It seemed to me a final attempt to salvage things. A way to stop breaking my family's hearts. And if it didn't work, well. There's *always* still suicide."

"What did she do?" Tip asks. "How did she mark you as hers?" A beat. "It's the tattoo, isn't it?"

This makes me cock my head. *"You* have a tattoo?"

"I do. And yes, Tip, that's exactly it. She waited for me to be released from the institution before taking me in. She weaned me through my addiction. Helped me apply for disability. Found a house I could afford, and got me my teaching position, all by pulling strings and calling favors. Working for her brought purpose back into my life."

I've never noticed a tattoo anywhere on Ricket, and I've seen him stripped to his underwear a dozen times over. If my wife tattooed my best friend's ass...

"It's on my inner thigh," Ricket explains. "Mind out of the gutter, Magpie. If you're terribly curious, I'll show you in the morning."

I *swear* the man is psychic.

"You know what she put in Navier," Tip says. "Presumably she had to go that extra step because he was already dead. I wonder, if someone tried to kill you, whether it would even be possible. If you'd just be... A living meat-puppet, like he was."

"No," I surprise all three of us by arguing. "Ricket, a person, was bound by his own choice. Navier, a corpse — AKA, an *object* — wasn't *given* that choice. He couldn't die, because he wasn't alive. I think by removing the coin from his liver, Cero relinquished ownership of property."

A chilling thought strikes me then. Navier's soul was bound to the Greek coin Cero'd placed inside his liver. Is his soul there still, unable to move on to wherever souls go after death?

Add *that* to the list of impossible problems I need to solve. Navier hurt me terribly, but nobody deserves to be trapped like that forever.

I wonder if Clay or Rhys ever died. What their exact connection with Cero is. I'll have to find them and explain. I doubt they'll believe me, but they deserve a heads-up.

We're all lost in our thoughts for several minutes, before Ricket gives me a nudge. "I apologize for getting so off topic. What I was trying to tell you is that I know what you're feeling, to some extent. I know what drifting without a purpose feels like. And I *certainly* know what chemical dependency feels like."

"You're an alcoholic, Mags," Tip supplies. Ricket huffs at his bluntness.

The truth stings. It does. I want to hide away in shame. I want to curl up under the blankets until everyone stops talking about it. I don't like ripping band aids off, remember?

"I'll... Work on it," I say vaguely, trying to inject a smile into my voice.

Now Tip is the one to snort. "Bull and *shit*. You're talking to fellow addicts, Baby Bird. 'I'll work on it' means anything but."

I feel a lot of stuff then. Anger chief among them. I want to snap at him. I want to hurt him so badly that he lets this subject drop. I want to stomp off and find somewhere else to sleep.

This is what I'd been trying to avoid for so long, and now it's all caught up to me. It's not about the drinking, not really. The drinking is a symptom, not a cause, but that doesn't make it any less dangerous.

"We didn't go through the effort of rescuing you just to lose you again," Ricket interrupts my lowest thoughts. "We're here to help you, Magpie."

Tip grunts his sleepy agreement.

I squirm painfully in their silence, their knowing, their love. Finally, all my breath exits my body in a huge, deflating sigh. I rub my tired, tear-crusted eyes.

"Okay," I whisper, facing the dragon head-on. "Okay, okay. You're right. I need help, guys. Please... *Help me.*"

•••

I've slept mere minutes before Cero appears, sitting on the end of my bed. She gently shakes me until I wake.

"Hey, Miss Cop," she greets.

I open my eyes and see my wife as she'd been the day I married her.

She has a practical bob of white-blonde hair. She'd always been stocky, hefty, so it's a relief to see her with meat on her bones. After cancer attacked, she'd been frighteningly fragile.

She looks sharp in a custom plum tux, her shoes shined to a reflective glow. The square-cut amethyst on her tie pin matches those on her cufflinks. She looks like she could be the CEO of some multimillion-dollar company, rather than a thief, necromancer, and ghost.

"Are you going to hurt me?" I ask.

It'd been pure, blinding agony when she was burned out of me. I thought my skull was going to split from the flames; from all her screaming.

Worse than that, though, was her absence. The silence. The absolute solitude. It'd felt like I was all alone in the world; trapped in an empty, sucking void. It was like she'd died a second time, and took part of me with her.

Cero frowns, disapproving. A teacher correcting a grammatical error. "I never *intended* to hurt you."

"Well, you did! A lot!" I touch my thighs before remembering my trench knives are all the way back in America.

"I know," she admits. "But I promise I only want to talk. Won't you come with me?"

I shake my head, reaching for Ricket, who sleeps by my side. "Why should I trust a word you say?"

My hand sinks *inside* his shoulder with no sensation, no contact. Ricket doesn't react.

Oh. Another dream, then. I pull my hand free and shake it off, disturbed.

"Come because you love me?" Cero tries, a hopeful smile in her voice.

My heart aches at the reminder. She's right, but that's not fair. My love isn't a flaw to be exploited. "No."

Cero sighs resignedly. "Then come out of curiosity. Come because it's your nature to follow snail trails and poke your nose into rabbit holes."

Damn her. I'm a fool, and she knows it.

I climb from bed, my good arm held wide in an exaggerated, '*well, then?*' gesture.

We make an odd pair as we leave the room. Her, in dapper menswear. Me, barefoot, wearing only boxers and a t-shirt.

I don't look back for fear of seeing my abandoned body. Living in a body piloted by another person gave me enough nightmare fuel already.

She opens the door. Instead of an empty hotel hallway, bright sunshine and wafts of citrus pour in.

There's music, too; tinny and familiar. Most humans born under the almighty mouse's reign would've recognized the tune.

"Once Upon a Dream?" I tease. "Bit on-the-nose, isn't it?"

She rolls her eyes, fighting a smirk. The music remains.

When we enter the bright place beyond the door, I realize where we are: Disneyland, right smack in the middle of Fantasyland. To our right is the snow-crested Matterhorn. To the left is Sleeping Beauty's candy-colored castle.

It's a perfect California day; the sun bright, the salty breeze gentle, the air sweet.

We are the only people present. There are no lines, no vendors, no costumed characters, no security guards in civvies, pretending to be guests. The attractions cycle at regular intervals with nobody to man or ride them.

I think back to when we came here on our honeymoon. How excited we were, distracted by every little thing, running ourselves ragged trying to experience it all before closing time.

Cero had seemed less Cero-ey on that trip than usual; less commanding, more lighthearted. I'd gotten the impression she'd truly enjoyed herself without restraint.

The cobblestones are warm under my feet as I choose a path and start walking. Tomorrowland is cooler than kid-friendly, cozy Fantasyland. There are more exciting rides there; roller coasters; a space-themed aesthetic.

Cero stays put, frowning after me. I look over my shoulder and return her frown. Doesn't she want to move along?

"I like it better here," she says.

I guess the whole point of my coming was to talk to her, not to play around in empty theme parks.

I return to her side and follow her to the Dumbo ride. Upon climbing the platform, I fight a grin when I see she's waiting for the purple-hatted elephant to cycle towards us, ignoring the closer options of green and pink and blue.

We squeeze onto Purple Dumbo's back, and then up we rise.

This is a gentle ride intended for small children. We ascend and descend smoothly, the breeze kissing our faces. Once around, twice around; thrice...

Purple Dumbo lowers to the loading platform again, but with no employees to make us climb out, we stay where we are. Again and again. One last ride. Then another.

After a time, I start to wonder how many go-rounds she'll need before she's satisfied; before she's had enough. I glance from the corner of my eye at my wife's face, and see nothing there but grief.

And that's when I understand what she's trying to tell me.

"Oh, *Cero,*" I sigh. "You're never going to be done, are you?"

Cero shakes her head no, looking down at her hands.

"It's not fair," she says quietly. "I lost so much. I never got to be a child. I had to fight to the top just to survive, and then I died young anyway."

Oh, my girl. My wife. My Cero.

I reach for her, taking her hand in mine, lacing our fingers. I rub my thumb along her knuckles as our flying elephant circles, magic feather held aloft. We're together in the happiest place on earth, and I think my heart might break.

"You understand what you did to me was wrong," I say. I've already forgiven her. But I need her to know.

She nods.

"And you know *why* it was wrong?" I press, needing to be certain. She nods again.

Final question: "You know I'm going to leave, don't you? I won't stay here."

She looks at me, and I fear she's going to argue, to say that I have to stay; to keep her eternal company in this happy purgatory. I hold her gaze until she drops it.

This time when Purple Dumbo lowers to the platform, we climb out and continue onwards.

We stop at a popcorn stand, and she scoops a buttery cup for me. I notice that the kernels taken from the machine are replaced, instantly, by more. Always more. I suspect it will never cool or go stale.

I nibble as we walk together, taking the boats through Small World, then choose adjoining horses to ride on King Arthur's carousel.

We saunter through gift shops, perusing, and I fill a large bag with plush cats for her. Figaro and Duchess (and her children) and Oliver and Lucifer and the Cheshire Cat...

Cero rests her chin on my shoulder, offering no commentary as I debate whether Simba and Nala count, then shrug and add them, anyway. Shere Khan and Bagheera, too.

Her fingers brush my back, tracing the outline of the wings she'd tattooed there so long ago.

Without discussing it, we both turn for Sleeping Beauty's castle. I can't hold Cero's hand *and* carry the bag of plushies with my arm in its sling, so she instead links our elbows.

'Once Upon a Dream' is still playing over the park's speakers; tinkling and endless. It'd drive me insane to hear the same song on a constant loop, but maybe such things aren't so bothersome when you're already dead. Cero hums as we walk.

We cross the stone bridge to the arched entrance, and there I stop, facing my wife, looking up into her eyes.

I lean forward, rising on my toes, and touch my lips to her icy forehead.

Cero's arms encircle my waist. She squeezes me close, taking a long, shuddering breath.

"You need to lose this," she says, her words rushed through clenched teeth like it's costing her dear just to utter them. "I don't know if you can get a whole back piece removed... It might be easier just to scar it up. But the design must be destroyed if you wish to be free of me."

For a moment, I don't understand what she's saying. It hits like a boulder to the head just a second later. *What does it mean when Cero tattoos someone?*

I pull sharply from her. "Seriously?!" I bark, some of my previous anger flaring hot and fresh. "You started pulling your shit *that long ago?!*"

Hell; the tattoo came in the earliest stages of our relationship! She *was* scheming against me from the very beginning! I thought she'd given me wings, but really, she'd caged me.

Cero looks away, jaw clenched tight. "You knew what I was when you married me."

"I didn't, actually," I reply coolly. "You kept me in the dark about everything. You caused a whole world of damage."

She doesn't apologize. I didn't really expect her to. Instead she says, flatly, "It is my nature."

This just angers me further. There's *always* a choice, and she chose to hurt. She's no saint, my wife. She's complicated and selfish and can be very cruel.

But I loved her. I love her still, whether or not she deserves it. And after I leave, I know I'm never seeing her again.

I take a deep breath and count to ten, forcing myself to calm. I hand over her bag of cats, and then I take her chin, forcing her to meet my eyes.

"I wish you the best, Cero," I say, and mean it. "I hope you find peace."

We lock gazes for a lengthy moment, and then she nods. Concedes.

I drop my hand and take a step back, then another. I continue this way until Cero turns and enters the castle. Her new home.

Only then do I follow the path I know I must take.

As I travel, I pass enormous topiaries shaped like unicorns and swans and the Loch Ness Monster's slithering coils. I encounter carts full of souvenirs, stands of steaming, fragrant churros, and bubbling fountains of fresh lemonade.

The air near the entryway to Tomorrowland feels different from Fantasyland. Charged, somehow. I feel a temptation to turn back, to join Cero in her castle where I know it's safe; where things will always be happy and warm and the same, always and forever.

After a tense moment of pause, I shake off the needless foreboding. I determinedly frog-march beneath the blinking, flashing archway of stars and space needles...

And wake all at once in a warm bed with Ricket sleeping peacefully at my side. I hear Tip roll onto his side in the next bed over, grumbling at dreams of his own.

Looks like I made it to Tomorrowland, after all.

Chapter Thirty-five - Magpie

poetry kink? sure; why not.

...

"Are you *sure* you want to sell her?" I ask anxiously. "If it's money you need, I'll just *give* it to you."

"Maggie-girl?" Patches' Parkinsons must be giving him grief today. He's sitting rigid in a plastic lawn-chair before his singlewide trailer. "Shut up and take the damn bike. I wouldn't offer if I had doubts."

We're somewhat protected from the late-afternoon sun by the shadow of his turquoise pickup; the very same truck that once shuttled Omar and I to safety.

He watches as I tiptoe 'round the 1978 Harley Electra. The Glide is *stunning;* chrome and navy so sleek it could be a starless night sky.

When I'd heard through the grapevine that he might have a ride for me, I hadn't known he'd meant his *baby!*

Every lever is arrow-straight and, I'm fairly certain, have never been replaced. The tires show no trace of burnout; not a hint of pilling. The hero blobs are in decent condition, and when I dare come close and pop the seat, I find nothing amiss in her wiring.

"I'm hurt, *mija.* You think I would sell you a fairy tale?" Patches scolds my careful examination, folding his shaky arms.

"No!" I look earnestly to him, eyes huge. "Never. I just..."

His lips part, showing off a killer smirk with a few missing teeth. "Thought a rattly old bastard couldn't handle her upkeep, eh?"

I hang my head in shame.

Patches sighs. "You ain't never had a hog, have you?"

"No, sir." I'd ridden Harleys, sure, but they'd always felt wrong underneath me.

Patches nods, considering. "But you love my girl."

This, I can't deny. The Glide looks... Friendly. Never tame, though. Wolves don't make good pets.

She calls to me, wishing me to climb aboard and rev her throttle. It's been too long since she's howled.

"Is she supposed to leak that much oil?" I ask, glancing at the darkened dirt under her wheels.

"You can look it up on your fancy phone, but it ain't unusual. Harleys are dry-sump. It's all in the crankcase to the breather hose."

"I'll take your word for it."

It isn't just trust, either. I don't have a phone anymore; not even a burner. I own nothing but the helmet tucked under my arm and the leathers I wear; some clothes; a few personal items in my backpack.

"Wanna take her for a test-drive?" The retired biker offers.

I drop my bag and rustle inside for my wallet. Patches frowns at the folder of personal information that tumbles free to land in the dirt; revealing 'Georgia Byrd's birth certificate and social security card and passport.

He's seen, and lived, too much of the nomad lifestyle to raise a stink. He keeps quiet as I shove everything back to where it belongs.

"Gonna be honest with you, Patches," I say, straightening, counting out a thick stack of Benjamins and thrusting them his way. "Once I climb on, I'm not gonna want to get off again for a long, long time. I know to my toes I'm in love."

Patches closes his hand over mine, pulling me close alongside all the money. His trembling arms encircle my neck. "That's the right answer. Looks like you're worthy."

I return the old man's embrace with my good arm, the hard plaster of my cast a stony lump between our chests. I bury my nose in his thin white hair and breathe him in — there's that familiar tang of tobacco and pickles under all the oil — and thump his bird-boned back.

I bite back a yelp of pain when he returns the gesture. The 'modifications' to my tattoo are still healing.

He sighs, seeming to collapse in on himself with the action. "You ain't coming back, are you?"

I close my eyes and give the tiniest shake no. I'd promised Ricket I'd keep my true destination a secret, for his family's safety.

"Mm," Patches tucks my newly shorn hair behind my ear with a leathery hand, then holds my cheek, meeting my eyes. "I'm glad I got to know you."

I've been so emotional lately. My family situation is complicated as hell, but I've always had a place in the biker community. His words bring tears to my eyes. "Me, too."

We release each other. He hands me a packet of the Glide's paperwork, as well as a single key dangling from a metal fob. I take both and relinquish his payment.

I don my helmet and backpack and throw a leg over the Glide's back. The leather of her saddle is worn smooth, molded into the shape of Patches.

I'm grateful he's a petite man. This girl will hold me just fine.

"Wanna go on an adventure?" I ask, stroking the sun-warmed metal of her fuel tank. The key slides in without resistance. I give it a twist. She rocks me like a lover, and I laugh in startled glee.

"Maggie-girl?" Patches leans forward, half-shouting to be heard. "If I hear a *peep* about you driving drunk, I'll hunt you down and kick your ass myself."

I nod, lowering my helmet's visor. "That's fair."

Counting the time spent under Cero's control, I'm three weeks dry. I won't get proper help, proper *support,* until I'm with the Ricket family. But I made a promise to my cousin, and I will *not* break it.

"Safe roads," are the old man's parting words.

I would wave to him, but between kicking out the kickstand and figuring out how best to hold the handlebars with my cast-ensconced arm, the best I can manage is a nod.

I release the brake. The Glide is eager to fly. The lightest squeeze of her accelerator has her rocketing, and I laugh again. Oh, *how* I missed this.

Calm down, I chastise, though I'm just as jazzed as she. *Behave yourself until we hit the road. No terrorizing the nice people, okay?*

She grumbles, but obeys. The lowering afternoon sun warms our backs.

We pass a pair of women smoking in their gnome-strewn lawn, and a gaggle of bikini-clad teens enjoying a dip in a truck-bed pool. We pass men chugging lukewarm PBRs, and three kids officiating a wedding between a tortoise and a Basset hound.

At last we're through the park's gates and on a thin ribbon of desert road; dozens of miles of dirt and sky stretching between us and one very special woman.

...

I meet Rosa, as arranged, in a high school parking lot. I only had to circle once before I found her, looking like living summer in a short yellow dress that makes her red lips and nails pop all the brighter.

"Damn," I breathe, raising my visor. "Hey, pretty lady."

She starts, fists clenching, until she recognizes me. Then she rolls her eyes, planting a hand on one generous hip. She uses the other to point sternly. "Keep flirting like that, and I'm gonna start taking you seriously."

"Promise?" I bat my eyelashes, smiling to make my dimples pop.

I edge the Glide into the parking space next to Rosa's Harley and drop my kickstand, still grinning because I know Rosa's checking the bike out... And maybe its rider, too.

Perhaps that last bit is just a dream. And one I shouldn't have, to boot. I am leaving. Rosa is staying. Romeo and Juliet, we ain't.

That thought hurts more than it should. I pretend to forget it. "Where's our boy, Sunshine?" I ask, averting my gaze from her glory.

"'Sunshine'?"

"Roses *and* sunshine. What could be more you?" I dismount and stretch, shaking some feeling back into my limbs so I don't walk onto campus like a bow-legged cowboy.

I peek at her face long enough to see her fighting a smile. *Oh, my heart.*

"Omar is inside the school. I think his homeroom teacher is threatening them within an inch of their lives." She adopts a mean expression and crotchety voice. "No tomfoolery, or else!"

"Aww, shucks. Not even a little tomfoolery?" I shake my head in mock disappointment. "Guess I'll cancel the keg and strippers."

She laughs. Good God above, the sound could light a candle in a hurricane.

I'm still recovering when she throws a heavy arm around my shoulders, pulling me along. "Come on. We want to sit where he can see us."

"Uh-huh." I can scarcely think. She smells, as always, of tequila and lemons, and it makes me stupid.

Just marry me already. Just get on my bike and go. I'll buy you the moon and the sun along the way.

In the last month, I've brought ghosts, gangs, torture, guns, kidnapping, child trafficking, parenthood, and occult rituals to this woman's door. She doesn't deserve my wrecking her peace more than I already have. I keep my fool mouth shut.

We file onto campus with hundreds of other parents and grannies and siblings; a whole herd of proud adults united to celebrate teen achievement.

The ceremony is taking place on the school's football field, which, like most American public schools, sees better upkeep and funding than the rest of the campus combined. The grass is bright green despite the statewide drought.

I'll never understand my country's obsession with this sport.

"Do you want anything?" Rosa asks, when we pass some tables where PTA moms are selling food and drinks.

"Let me treat you. I owe you." *More than I can ever repay.*

We take our snacks to the bleachers and settle, seated on approximately six inches of sun-seared metal. At least we have a perfect view of the field, the stage, and the rows of folding chairs where the kids are meant to be.

The place is tricked out for a show. I watch the school staff run extension cords for a microphone. Across the field, the marching band starts tuning up.

Not for the first time, my eyes are drawn to the tattoo atop Rosa's thigh; the lemons, the thorns, the leaves.

Catching my look, Rosa smiles and points to each of the three fruits. "My older sister," she explains, then points to the second. "My younger sister." Finally she taps the third lemon, front and center of the bunch. "Me."

I knew Rosa was homeless as a teenager. I know she considers parts of her childhood 'tragic'. She'd remained so secretive about any details. Am I allowed to pry? "You love your sisters?"

"I do." Rosa's expression turns wistful. "We talk, sometimes. More so now that Lupita's graduated high school."

"Yeah?" I try to pitch my voice encouragingly, committing the name to memory. Lupita. Little Guadalupe. The smallest of the lemons.

Rosa nods. "They just... Have to keep our contact a secret from our parents, for obvious reasons." She avoids eye-contact and gestures to herself as she says this. Huffs an unhappy little laugh.

In a second, Rosa is all business again. She shakes her curly hair out and gives a devil-may-care grin; all tough; all Rosa.

Taking an enormous bite of her soft pretzel, she suggests a change of subject. "How's your angry Beach Boy doing?"

"Tip's okay."

We'd had an interesting goodbye before I'd left for the room I'm renting. We'd stood close in Ricket's backyard; close enough that I could feel his warmth when he shifted from foot to foot. The sun bouncing off his yellow hair had made it glow like coins.

"Look," I'd told him. At that moment, his eyes were the dullest gray I'd ever seen. "I love you, Sugar Tips. I love you more than anyone in the world. I always will."

"Mags, I... You and I are..." He'd squirmed, looking at everything but me. His Adam's apple bobbed when he gulped. "You know I'd do anything for you."

I knew. I know. I know what it is he still can't say.

"Can I touch you?" I'd asked, waiting for his nod to press against his chest.

His arms had taken an eternity to wrap around me. When they did, I'd found them, us, a perfect fit. Does he even *know* how much he makes my heart ache, sometimes?

His exhale had been long and shaky, stirring my hair. I can still hear his heartbeat; too fast, and then normal, and then slow. Eventually, his breathing soothed.

Rosa watches me curiously. "Is he really sleeping with his teacher? That James guy?"

I've noticed how she likes gossip. I guess bartending is the perfect job for her. "Not anymore. I don't know how much longer Ricket's gonna be his teacher, anyway."

A sweat bee, green as my lost Ninja, makes a literal beeline for my forehead. I yelp and duck, but the poor thing gets stuck in my hair, anyway. It buzzes and thrashes in fury.

Rosa sets her drink aside and gets to work, fingers swiftly untangling the strands of my hair from the insect's tiny body. In seconds, we watch it zip away, reveling in newfound freedom.

Rosa continues to pet my hair, smoothing the rumpled bangs back. She taps my piercings; the orbital rings, the cartilage studs, the industrial bar. "Pretty. That reminds me — I've got something for you."

She turns to fish in her purse while I remain stock-still, ear tingling, face warm. She holds her fist out to me and then flips it over, opening her fingers.

I instantly recognize the silver obol nestled in her palm. It's the same one that animated Navier's body. The coin that trapped his detached soul in his reanimated corpse for over a decade.

"Did you do it?!" I gasp, eyes wide. "Rosa, you're a genius!"

"I know." She waves my praise off. "I had to open it up, see?"

She holds it to her eye, peering into the hole she'd bored through Medusa's head. "It took about a billion moonlit prayers, but Navier is back in the afterlife."

"*Thank* you," I breathe. "I hated the idea of him being stuck in there."

"Hm," Rosa grunts, expression turning sour. She'd disliked the man since first meeting him in the alley behind her bar, fully prepared to beat him bloody for making me scream. Hearing the ways he'd betrayed me had not endeared her to him.

That only made her hard work all the kinder. She hated him, yet she'd helped him anyway. That's the sign of a good person.

I take the coin from her and feel an electric spark fizzling up my arm at the contact, setting my hair on end. "Whoa..."

"It still carries some magical properties," Rosa cautions. "It's mostly benign, but I'm pretty sure it can be used as an adder stone, if you ever need one."

I know what an adder stone is. Stones with holes worn through them by the passage of water are thought to be good for revealing hidden supernatural activity. But I've never heard of it existing, manmade, in the form of an enchanted coin.

Trust Cero to bend the laws of life, nature, and death to create something that shouldn't exist.

It feels strange to tuck such a valuable, unique item into my wallet like any other dime or nickel, but it's as safe a place to store it as any, and there's no chance of my accidentally spending it. It's too thick, too lumpy, to be mistaken for American currency.

As I replace my wallet, my hand brushes something that makes a crackling noise. I quickly seize upon the paper bag, drawing it out.

"I almost forgot!" I exclaim, passing it over. "Your shirt. I washed it."

Rosa peeks inside the bag at the Smashing Pumpkins T she'd loaned me, folded with a dryer sheet to keep its fresh laundry smell.

She hands it back. "Here's the problem: you left *your* shirt in *my* washing machine. If I took this from you now, then the number of shirts between us would be unbalanced."

"So I should... Keep it?"

"Until you're able to get yours. We can't throw the world's shirt ratio off."

"No," I reply faintly. "Who knows what havoc would ensue?"

"Exactly."

I'm not coming back. She knows it. Why is she acting like we'll see each other again?

Even as I think this, Rosa is once more digging around in her purse. She produces a pen, uncaps it, and scrawls quickly across the paper bag I hold in my arms.

It's an email address.

"Mrdr_by_death_grrl?" I ask, cocking my head to read her wide, loopy writing.

Rosa jabs her pen at me. "One, I was fifteen when I made that account. And two, Murder by Death is a kickass band. They have an electric cello."

"I'll have to give them a listen," I say, still dazed. I think I'm smiling. I must look pretty damn stupid, because Rosa just snorts and faces forward once again.

We sit listening to the marching band play the school's anthem. The cheerleaders perform stunts. A redhead with legs that could cave in a man's head shakes her pom-poms as three other girls lift her high above their heads. They give a great heave, and she's airborne; spinning, beaming.

Her friends catch her easily in a basket of strong arms. The crowd screams like her triumph is theirs.

Rosa picks her drink up, stirs it until the ice rattles, and takes a sip. "How is your you-know-what?"

"I haven't been to see a doctor," I reply, though Ricket's been pressuring me to do so. "But I haven't had a single nosebleed since Ricket carved my tattoo up. My blood is clotting normally. My arm is healing. I'm not bruising so easily."

Rosa nods, satisfied. "Good."

It *is* good. Sitting under the tomato-red sunset, watching a flock of purple-gowned teenagers file onto the field, is all excellent. One by one, the grads fill their chairs.

I squint, trying to make out Omar in the crowd, but the constant movement of over-excited kids in matching gowns makes it difficult.

The school mascot, a Ridgway's Rail, arrives to lift the smallest cheerleader in its "wings," spinning and nearly tripping over its enormous foam talons in the process.

It quickly sets her down and begins to walk the bleachers, tossing candies from a fanny pack towards a sea of eager hands.

I behave myself as the principal, a mousy little woman in a lilac pantsuit, clears her throat and addresses the crowd. She greets us, explaining the night's itinerary; expounding on the achievements of a few honored teens.

I keep my smile as the assistant principal warns that nobody should cheer until every kid has received their diploma (yeah, right), and that a professional will photograph every grad. The pictures can be purchased later.

It's only when the names are called that I start to grow antsy. There are hundreds of teens graduating tonight, I have the attention span of a caffeinated hamster, and my ass is starting to argue with the metal bench.

Not only that, but Omar's surname is "Usman." Going by alphabetical order, this is going to take forever.

I ease the pressure on my backside by shifting from cheek to cheek. I count all the men wearing solid red shirts (forty-seven), and then I squirm some more. I don't mean to behave like a naughty child at church, but this kinda stuff has always been hard on me.

Somewhere between "Abelló, Kathryn" and "Akiyama, Koji" walking up to collect their diplomas, shake hands with their principal, and pose for photographs, Rosa tucks her arm around my shoulders.

Her lips brush my ear. "I've got one more present for you. I promised to read you some poetry, didn't I?"

I nod, too aware of my own sweaty palms.

"Stop me if you've heard this one before. It reminds me of you."

I close my eyes, cheeks warming, and lose myself in the flow of her whispered words: "You may write me down in history with your bitter, twisted lies. You may trod me in the very dirt but still, like dust, I'll rise."

She forms every word so carefully, plucking them from the air like ripe fruits. I find myself moving with her words, swaying against her side. Her fingers rub gentle circles into my ribs.

She recites the entire poem from top to bottom, illustrating it in living color with her breaths and pauses as much as the words themselves. The whole thing becomes a type of art, and at last I understand what she'd meant about poems *needing* to be shared aloud.

"Does my sexiness upset you? Does it come as a surprise that I dance like I've got diamonds at the meeting of my thighs?"

My hips rock right there on the uncomfortable metal seat, even as my face flames. I swear, for a single, staticky heartbeat, that Rosa's smirking lips linger on my temple.

"Leaving behind nights of terror and fear, I rise. Into a daybreak that's wondrously clear, I rise."

Holding me tight, Rosa works me down, each subsequent "I rise" softer than the one before.

I reach for her hand long after the poem ends, lacing our fingers, pressing my thumb to the veins of her wrist. Her heart is beating a steady, strong drumbeat that syncs to my own.

"I told you Maya Angelou was a queen," Rosa whispers, smug and fond.

I laugh bashfully, unable to quell the giddy sparks of happiness that light me from the inside.

Calmer now, I resume my focus on the ceremony, grateful when Rosa keeps her hand firmly in mine.

...

The next morning, I pay my bill in cash to Mrs. Jefferson, the owner of the small house I'd been renting a bedroom in.

"Take care, Georgia," she smiles when I make for the door. She stops me long enough to slip a pear, a bottled water, and a baggie of buttered wheat toast into my backpack.

I gratefully return her smile. "You, too, Mrs. J. You have a beautiful home. Thanks for sharing it with me."

"You were a dear guest." She winks, wrinkly old face sweet as can be.

She was kind enough to allow my Glide use of her garage, parked in the sliver of space between crates of food that haven't seen daylight since World War II and her own neat little Honda.

That was a blessing for my peace of mind — even in a nice neighborhood like this, shit happens — and for the Glide. Engines don't take well to California heat.

I don my helmet and mount the beast, giving the woman a wave when she opens her garage door for me. She lowers it again after I ease onto the street.

I'm extra careful as I wind the streets, not wanting to catch a suburban child or cat unawares. Even the Glide, who doesn't much care for 'slow,' understands this necessity.

It's a relief when we hit Interstate 5, which, so early on a summer morning, is largely devoid of traffic. We speed for the HOV lane and floor it down California's snaky spine. Eighty, one hundred...

I temper her after only a minute, though our blood sings for more. As former highway patrol, I know where all the speed traps are.

The Glide's spirit is willing, but I mustn't forget she's close to forty years old, and we haven't been on a long journey together yet. We can take it easy.

I've driven straight into the desert before, but I always had my gang with me. Cero, to scheme. Ricket, for getaway. Clay and Rhys to keep us funded and toeing the legal line. Crown to manage any sudden hiccups in our plans. Navier to follow me, cackling, into the line of fire.

This is my first time flying solo.

What's more, I have no map. No coordinates. Just a vague set of possibly outdated instructions from my best friend. This whole plan is pure chance and madness.

I drive for perhaps an hour, past the urban sprawl to more isolated areas of California, I'm coming up on pure desert very soon, and should pull over to refresh and gas up before it's too late.

A sudden growling at my back makes me jolt. It's an old beast; deep and powerful. And it's not alone.

I find myself flanked by bikes; spindly Choppers and classic Cruisers and one flashy, candy-colored YZF-R6 that makes me drool. And those are just the ones I can *see!* I feel more at my back; in all of my blind-spots.

I am in the eye of a gang, and the snarling, purring, roaring of so many different engines vibrates my blood and bones like I'm kissing a wasps' nest.

When the owner of the YZF signals and pulls ahead of me, I see his Bikers Against Child Abuse cut; that familiar white fist on black. They must've pegged me for a lone wolf and decided to escort me for as long as our paths converge.

I feel surrounded by love; the love a gang shares for one another, and our collective love for the road.

Maybe Patches was right. Maybe I *do* need a flock. I could do worse than this one. My gang has dissolved, but my need to help children has not. Perhaps someday...

There will be time to dwell on that later. For today, my path leads to the desert; to the family of my best friend.

After that... Who knows what my future will hold?

I wave to catch the attention of the biker to my right, jut a fist at the road sign announcing an upcoming rest stop, then hold a thumb to my mouth. *Food?*

He responds with thumb and index finger pinched in an 'okay' sign before surging ahead, finger pricking the sky. *Single file!*

We fall into formation. He swings his arm towards the upcoming exit, and we follow.

I'm thrilled to stop and talk with these people; to hear their stories; to know their adventures before we go our separate ways.

Life is grand. I'm beyond excited to see what comes next.

- fin -

Please remember to support independent authors with your reviews so they can continue to create content you enjoy!

High Tides - Sneak Peek

...

I head straight to bed, pulling the chain of my lamp to bathe the room in darkness. I help Zelda up first and climb in after her, spooning against her back. Her stump-tail waggles as I tuck the duvet around us.

It's when I reach across her to adjust the curtains that I freeze, jaw dropping.

James's large backyard is enclosed by a gray stone wall. The space *between* the wall and the north side of the house — *my* side of the house — is pretty damn narrow. The top of the wall stands just above eye-level.

When I see dozens of shadows and paws moving atop the stone, I crane my neck to look at the army of cats there; milling, wandering, pacing. Their coats range from palest cream to darkest night, bearing every pattern imaginable.

Some are scruffy or scrawny; some are glossy and sleek. Some even wear collars. There must be two dozen animals present. All of them are watching me, silent and knowing.

Zelda whines, cringing away from the window.

I can't help but feel a thrill. In everything that took place last summer, I came to learn of the supernatural. I have firsthand proof that witches are real, ghosts can attach to human hosts, and...

I think to the box I've got tucked in my bottom dresser drawer, containing only a curved claw and a handful of dry Autumn leaves. The former was plucked from my leg after Vince, having gone feral with claws and fangs sprouting from his person, nearly succeeded in dragging me thirteen stories to my death.

The latter started out as a pile of money I stole from his luggage, which later transformed into plant matter before I could spend it.

I'm a scientist. I believe that all things can be explained, no matter how strange. At the first sight of the impossible, I come alive; blessed to know there's more to the world than meets the eye. One more mystery to unravel. One more question to be answered.

I push my window open without stopping to consider the danger, listening to the rustle of fur, the tap of paws.

The cats stare with eyes of blue and green and gold; a synchronicity to their movements that does nothing to alleviate their eeriness.

One cat pushes to the front of the mass. Exceptionally large and fluffy, all the rest seem to defer to him, shifting to give him the spotlight.

The black cat, his white-starred chest bright in the light from my window, looks me directly in the eyes. He opens his mouth to reveal a row of pearly fangs, and speaks with a warm Scottish brogue: "Good evening, Dylan Tippling. Won't you do me the honor of inviting me inside?"

<u>Follow L. Rambit on Goodreads to be notified of new releases![1]</u>

...

About the Author

L. Rambit is a queer Slytherin with a passion for caffeine, animal welfare, fourth-wave feminism, '90s rock, horror movies of dubious quality, and all things oceanic.

In addition to freelance editing, she has worked as a ghost-writer for J.M. Labs Publishing Company, and continues to publish LGBT erotica under various pen-names.

When she's not baking bread, journaling, or making question-able fashion choices, she can be found curled in library stacks, building a loyal army of feral cats, and playing board games with her many niblings.

She is very excited to continue the All My Seas series, and to write more genre-blenders in the future.

www.ingramcontent.com/pod-product-compliance
Lightning Source LLC
Chambersburg PA
CBHW032036050726
47590CB00001B/20